Praise for

DARK DAYS

"An impressive first installment with a remarkable, series-worthy heroine."

—Kirkus Book Reviews

"*Dark Days* plunges readers into the depths of a complex dark fantasy world that begs to be explored."

—Literary Titan

"*Dark Days* by D.W. Saur is young adult fiction on steroids."

—Rabia Tanveer for Readers' Favorite

"An excellent fantasy novel that delivers on so many fronts and is unique to the genre in giving its female protagonist a powerful mission with no romantic subplots or distractions."

—K.C. Finn for Readers' Favorite

"D W Saur's young adult fantasy novel, *Dark Days*, is a thrilling adventure for all ages."

—Emily-Jane Hills Orford for Readers' Favorite

Dark Days

By D.W. Saur

ISBN 978-1-64663-047-9

Published by

köehlerbooks™

3705 Shore Drive
Virginia Beach, VA 23455
800–435–4811
www.koehlerbooks.com

DARK DAYS

D.W. SAUR

VIRGINIA BEACH
CAPE CHARLES

In memory of
Kevin and Chris

Author's Note

*D*ark Days is the first book in the Covenant Saga and does not take place within our confines of history nor the lands which we inhabit. The course of events will, at times, move slower, but also at times faster. The era where you will make your first stop resembles the Middle Ages.

As you read, you may come across words of Gaelic, Swedish, Finnish, Norwegian, and Dutch origin that you are unfamiliar with and may not know how to pronounce. If this happens, I encourage you to refer to the glossary. If this proves to be more of a distraction, then by all means let your imagination flow and pronounce the terms anyway you wish.

Lastly, and without further delay, I welcome you to the land of Sori and my tale of Leigheasan, Veirlintus, Galenvargs, and much more.

CHAPTER 1

A New Chosen One

The greatness and abilities one possessed might never come to fruition, and many believed that Maya Dempsey would squander her potential.

Maya was born into the Leigheasan sect, one of three sects that comprised the Faileas Herimen. They could control minds, were guided by spirits called ascenders, and controlled elements. Powers and abilities varied from Leigheas to Leigheas, but were not obtained until the youth completed the Turas, a multistep challenge culminating in a celebration to grant one official Leigheasan status. First a youth declared themselves an Earcach, a recruit, and began their journey. Most desired the abilities so much that they began their journeys as soon as they were of age, but Maya was different.

Three and a half years past the age of becoming an Earcach, Maya was shunned by the majority of Leigheasan her age; they thought she would abandon their way of life. For the most part, the only members of Maya's sect that spent time with her socially were from the Dempsey Clan. Though the elders of the community did not shun her, they were suspicious of her lackadaisical approach towards officially becoming a Leigheas. However, it was not due to apathy or thoughts of abandoning the traditions of her people, but due to a vision.

From a young age, Maya would venture off into the woods by herself to spend hours meditating. As she grew older, the hours turned into days. During her extended stays in the woods, Maya perfected the skill of surviving off the land. Though all Leigheasan lived off the land, roles tended to be divided between males and females. For instance, men would hunt and skin the carcass, while women cooked and used the hides. This was not always the case for the Leigheasan sect. There was a time in which the women partook in the hunt and the men shared with the household chores. This changed for many of the clans, but there were still a few that shared responsibilities.

Maya, unlike many of her fellow female Leigheasan, desired total independence. She possessed a thirst for knowledge and a desire to outperform not just those her age, but all members of the Leigheasan sect. It was these traits and her connection to the land that had prompted a visit from a strange, almost ghostly figure when she was a child. This figure first appeared just before the age of twelve and once again at the age of fourteen. On both occasions, the messages from the indiscernible figure were similar: *Do not enter the Turas until you're ready. You are close but not ready yet. When you are, I will return.*

Maya assumed it was the spirit of an ancestor, perhaps her grandmother, but she would eventually learn that her assumption was wrong. It was the goddess Nantosuelta making a rare appearance. Though at first Maya was not certain who her visitor was, she understood the message and began an intense training regimen.

To Maya, training was not only about strength, speed, and endurance; it was about knowledge. Most teenagers in the Leigheasan community began learning about general tonics, poisons, medicines, and other remedies, but Maya didn't want a general knowledge. She wanted to know as much as the village dochtúir, who specialized in healing, tonics, poisons and medicine. Maya took it upon herself to become an apprentice to the dochtúir and spent one day a week learning the craft.

Three days a week were divided between weapons and hand-to-hand training, smithing, and conditioning.

Two days a week Maya devoted her time to helping her family.

The last day of the week Maya spent with a group of Galenvargs and Veirlintus whom she befriended, to learn the skill of tracking and hunting. It was during these hunts where Maya witnessed the transformation of her Faileas Herimen brethren. She watched as claws protruded from Galenvarg fingers. Jaws elongated to accommodate a set of fangs as sharp and deadly as the varg of the ancients. Their loose-fitting clothes became tight against now bulging muscles. Hair that once was cut short grew to give a mane-like appearance.

Unlike Galenvargs, Veirlintus had a subtle change. Claws rivalling the sharpest of swords protruded from fingertips, and fangs that tore through flesh as easy as a battleax through armor extend from the gums. However, that was all that changed. In a matter of seconds her friends went from looking as normal as her to becoming some of the deadliest predators known to the realm. Though she couldn't hunt with her bare hands like her brethren, the lessons learned were invaluable. By the time Maya was almost eighteen, she was more knowledgeable and skilled in all aspects of life than her peers. She had achieved her desire to surpass not only those closest to her in age but most of the elders in her sect.

Three days before her eighteenth birthday, Maya went to the mountains to meditate on the cliff known as Diabhal's Fiacail, or Devil's Tooth. Diabhal's Fiacail hung off the first mountain of the Slabhra mountain range, which was located to the northwest portion of Gleann on what was considered, by the Duine population, to be the boundary line between Gleann and Beinn. It was a 2,000-foot hike to the cliff, and once at its top, Maya gazed out on the region. To her right she saw dozens of smoke trails from Leigheasan villages, and in the distance to her left, several stone homes belonging to various Galenvarg clans.

Sitting down, she crossed her legs and reflected on her training and the delay on starting the Turas. Hours passed, and just before the sun set, she was once again visited by Nantosuelta.

"Open your eyes, my child," Nantosuelta whispered in Maya's ear.

"It is good to hear your voice, my lady. It has been too long," Maya said as she opened her eyes to gaze upon a now discernible figure.

"It has, but you have done well since my last visit. I am pleased, though not surprised, to see how dedicated you have been."

"Thank you," Maya replied, trying to contain her excitement. She knew that an appearance by Nantosuelta outside of the Turas was a rare event, so she felt honored that she'd had three visits from her. Feeling as though she could speak freely, Maya replied, "I must admit I was wondering when you were going to return. Due to my age and my failure to attempt the Turas, it hasn't been easy for me amongst my sect. Though I have never doubted, I was getting a bit anxious."

"Imagine how I feel. You have only waited a few years while I had to wait several thousand years for your birth."

Maya knew that it was never wise to question the gods or goddesses, but she could not resist and asked, "Forgive me, as I know one should not question, but I cannot help but ask, why me?"

Nantosuelta circled Maya and answered, "I never reveal one's purpose. I will tell you that you have the potential to do great things if you so choose. You, in turn, also have the potential to do nothing and amount to no more than a ualach." A ualach was a leech on society.

"Do you still want me to delay the Turas?" Maya asked, wanting to get to the root of the visit. "I will do as asked, but I would like to start the next phase of my life."

"I understand your feelings and desires. I also realize that not attempting the Turas when of age has caused social discomfort for you. The advantage is that you know how to live on your own. You, unlike your peers, don't need social conventions to complete your life." She stopped and realized that she was digressing from the point. Nantosuelta regained her thoughts and continued, "Your attempting the Turas will depend on your performance." The goddess moved closer to Maya and saw the young woman's curiosity growing.

"Performance?" Maya asked. "What are you referring to?"

"I want you to enter all the games at the Cluiche," the goddess answered.

"What? That starts tomorrow! And they are for men—" Maya began and stopped midsentence to think. She had never heard nor read a rule stating women were forbidden.

"Not even close to the truth. For centuries women competed in all the games, and almost half of the events' winners were women. There was also a span of a decade that men never held the title of Cluiche champion. It is only in the past few centuries that women have stopped competing," Nantosuelta replied, aggravated.

Maya couldn't comprehend why women would freely stop competing. The Cluiche was one of the great traditions amongst the Leigheasan, and as a child she dreamed of not only competing but also winning the tournament. She always thought this was an unattainable goal.

In confusion Maya blurted out, "Why?"

"It was not due to male dominance or gnéastis, but simply due to laziness. Since the end of the Great War, the fear of being different, primarily from their Duine counterparts, has caused the Faileas Herimen to abandon many of their customs and increasingly adopt aspects of the Duine way of life. This has become evident with the Leigheasan in many ways, but in particular with abandoning the Cluiche. Though Leigheasan women have an active role in their society, most did not want to train, and others prescribed to the Duine way of thought that women should be homemakers. It became unladylike to compete in the games."

"So, you want me to usher in a new era for Leigheasan women?" Maya asked. "Unprepared?"

"There will be trials in the times to come, and the Leigheasan women will need to step out of their comfort zone and aid their brethren when the time arises. To do so, they will need a strong figure to show them what is possible. And you are far from unprepared."

"What are these trying times you speak of?" Maya leaned forward in hopes that the goddess would share a glimpse of the future.

"This is none of your concern for now, but you will know when it comes and be guided on what to do," Nantosuelta replied with a smirk. She appreciated Maya's longing for answers, but as most of the gods and goddesses did, she played with people's desires, providing enough information to intrigue and get someone's hopes up but not enough to leave them satisfied—or lead them where they were unprepared to go.

"By you?" Maya asked eagerly.

"No, by your ascenders. After the Turas, you will not see me again for some time, but know I am watching. Win the Cluiche and complete the Turas." With that, Nantosuelta disappeared as quickly as she had come.

With dusk smeared across the sky, Maya decided to stay in the woods and made camp on level ground away from the cliff. It would take some time for her to fall asleep. Her mind raced with thoughts of competing in the Cluiche and of what adventures could come her way. It seemed like the sun woke her moments after she had fallen asleep. After eating and cleaning her campsite, Maya made her descent down the mountain and journeyed home. Her mother was the first to greet her.

"Where were you this time?" Andrea asked out of curiosity. Both she and Maya's father encouraged Maya to explore Sori and prepared her for extended nights amid the wilderness. Punishment or concerns for her wellbeing were far in the back of their minds.

"Not far—Diabhal's Fiacail to do some thinking." Maya paused, trying to figure out a way to tell her mother that she was going to enter the Cluiche. She stared at her mother in a daze.

"For goodness sake, just spit it out. I can tell when you have something on your mind; there is no reason to stand there looking like a moill," Andrea said, referring to habitual consumers of the hallucinogenic flower of the donnimhe tor, which imparted a glazed, drooling state.

Jumping at the chance at not having to dress up her news Maya announced, "Mother, I am going to enter the Cluiche."

"Excellent news!" her mother exclaimed. "You will do well in the trivia portion. Your wisdom is beyond your years. In fact, I am not sure if there are elders that know as much as you do."

"Not just the trivia portion. All of it," Maya replied. Andrea paused, bewildered. Her encouragement shifted abruptly into a rant.

"The Cluiche matches the best fighters, swordsmen, and archers against one another. Oh, not to mention the capall cuaille! You get hit by a lance and who knows how much damage that can do to you? I will not have it! Women do not enter the tournament games. Do you know who your opponents are for your age group?" Andrea paced the room. "Cedric, Aedan, Fintan, Egan and . . . and those are the only ones I can name. All of them are proper Leigheasan! You could be hurt. I will not have it! I will not!"

Maya had never seen her mother this upset about anything. "Do you forget my training?" Maya asked, hoping to ease her mother's mind.

"You can't use that card on me!" Andrea shouted.

"Mother, you are the best archer there is, and it is hard to find someone better with a sword than Uncle Grady. Dad and Elder Rangvald have taught me the art of hand-to-hand combat, and all my other mentors have me more than prepared. Honestly, the only event I am not prepared for is the capall cuaille, and I am sure my armor will hold up to any blow by a lance."

"Regardless of training, what if they use elements? What do you think a burst of fire to any part of your body or a stone shield against your face will do? Or worst of all, what if a lance does pierce your armor?" Andrea asked.

"Mother, if I have faith that it will be okay, why don't you?" Maya sighed deeply. "Besides, the use of elemental power is forbidden during most of the competitions. Also, my armor is better crafted than a wooden lance. The only way it can pierce my armor is if it's tipped, and if so, then I win the event." Her mother's irrational worries forced her to point out the obvious.

"Assuming that you survive the wound, of course." Andrea stood for a moment to regain her composure and said, "Perhaps when you're a mother you will understand." Andrea walked to Maya and placed her hands on her daughter's shoulders. "I do not wish to see any harm come to you."

"Trust me, I don't want anything to happen to me either. This is not only what I want but what Nantosuelta has tasked me to do." She took a deep breath. "Nantosuelta herself told me that I not only needed to compete, but I must win, and when I win, I will have her blessing to attempt the Turas," Maya replied.

"So that's why you have waited so long? How long have you talked to her?" Andrea was astonished. In over 6,000 years of documented history, there were no more than a dozen accounts of deity visits.

"She first came when I was twelve—"

"Twelve!"

"Relax, Mom. It has only been a couple of times, and prior to yesterday, the visits were only long enough for her to say a sentence or two. Previously, all she told me was to wait for the Turas, but when I was on Diabhal's Fiacail she told me that I must win the Cluiche before I can start the Turas."

"Short visit, long visit, it doesn't matter. Why didn't you say something?" Before Maya could respond, Andrea asked, "Do you know how big of a deal it is to be visited by a goddess?"

"It's not like I had proof. Most who claim to see a god or goddess outside of Turas are lying and tend to be shunned by the community. Not that I haven't been living as an outcast for some time, but at least I wasn't a crazy outcast."

"True, but we could have kept it in the family." Andrea poured a couple mugs of ale. "You should have trusted us enough to come to us."

"Is Dad home?" Maya asked, looking at the two mugs.

"Out in the barn, I think. Why do you ask?" Andrea finished the first mug off.

"Is the other mug for him?" Maya asked.

"Nope, this is all for me. I just found out my daughter has been talking to a goddess, so one of these is for celebration and the other for shock. You decide which one is which," Andrea replied in between gulps of the second mug.

"Okay, just pace yourself. The ale has sat for a while," Maya warned. The longer the ale sat, the more potent it was.

Maya picked up the conversation where she left off before the distraction.

"I understand your point of view, but it wasn't a trust issue. It was more of an *am I sane* issue. After all, the first two times I heard her voice, she was not physically present. It was merely a whisper in my ear, and I assumed it was an ancestor. Now, back to the issue at hand: the Cluiche. I am going to enter with or without your support, but I would really appreciate my family by my side. By appreciate, I mean that I need you by my side."

"Of course you have my support, and the rest of the family's," Andrea said, pulling Maya in for a hug. "Good or bad, we will always be by your side. Just, for the love of the gods and goddesses, don't make us look bad."

"Thanks, Mom. Sign-up for the events are early tomorrow, so we have to leave well before daybreak," Maya said, still in her mother's embrace.

That evening, Maya rested, meditated, prepared her armor, and cleaned her weapons. Tomorrow would be a day of trial, pain, and hopefully reward.

CHAPTER 2

The Cluiche

The Cluiche was held in the Leigheasan arena located in the most central part of Leigheas Gleann. It was the largest structure in the region, constructed to hold most of the Leigheasan community and a select few invited guests from the Galenvarg and Veirlintu sects.

The arena floor was carved ten feet into the ground and was large enough for not only games of sport and competitions, like the Cluiche, but also for theatrical events. The Leigheasan were well known for their acting skills, and their performers were frequently requested to entertain at Cala. The grandstands were built out of stone back when the Leigheasan community was much smaller. It seated just over 20,000. As the population increased, wooden towers called eagle's nests were constructed to add extra seating around the grandstands. The nests tripled the capacity of the arena.

The Cluiche was perhaps the busiest single-day event in Leigheas Gleann. Just a couple of hours before dawn, a deserted arena became host to thousands. Vendors came out en masse to sell, barter, and hand out their specialty drinks, food, clothing, and crafts. Thousands of competitors, ranging from age fifteen to twenty-two, arrived to test their wits, might, and skills. As the sun rose, those attending as spectators arrived to enjoy the greatest of Leigheasan competitions.

The Cluiche was a very structured event but did have some flexibility. As a rule, not all contestants were required to compete in all the events. This allowed contestants to play to their strengths. However, to be considered the champion of the Cluiche, one must compete in all events.

Contestants competed for points in each event that would result in gaining a place point. For example, the winner of the archery event might have an event total of fifty points. For coming in first place they earned five Cluiche points. Second place in an event gained four Cluiche points, third three points, fourth two points, and any position past fifth place earned each of the contestants one point for participating. Those who didn't compete in an event earned zero points.

Maya arrived just as the vendors were setting up their stations, and though she had to sign up, she could not resist the urge to purchase a cup of red cider. Every year the Quinlan Clan sold their famous red cider, a nonalcoholic drink made from several fruits. Without fail, the cider was sold out before the first contest. Bypassing sign-in, visitors, contestants, and other vendors, Maya was the first to arrive at the Quinlans' stand.

"Good morning to you!" Madam Quinlan exclaimed at the sight of their first customer.

"Good morning, Madam Quinlan," Maya anxiously replied as Sir Quinlan brought a barrel to his wife's side. "Good morning, Sir Quinlan."

"And a good morning it is," Sir Quinlan said, setting down the large container. "What can we get you?" he asked as though he had more than one drink to offer.

"A cup of red cider, please."

As Madam Quinlan poured her patron a drink, she asked, "So, who will you be cheering for today?"

"What do you mean?" Maya asked, a befuddled look scurrying across her face. She thought that wearing armor, a bow on her back, and sword by her side was a sure sign that she was a contestant.

"Do you have a young lad you are supporting today, or are you just here to support your clan?" Madam Quinlan inquired.

"No, none of that, ma'am. I am here to represent my clan as a contestant," Maya replied. She patted her sword.

"Oh, how marvelous!" Madam Quinlan exclaimed, turning to her husband. "Aabel, did you hear that? We are serving our first contestant!" Madam Quinlan continued without waiting for her husband's response. "I hope you have brushed up on the books. There will be many bright lads out there today."

"Trust me, I will win trivia. It's the others I am worried about," Maya replied.

"Others?" Aabel asked as he sat a second barrel next to the first.

"I am going to compete in all the events," Maya answered with a grin.

"Well I'll be. This calls for another round, and our first." Aabel pulled out two more cups while his wife, Helen, tried to refill Maya's cup.

"Thank you, but I only have enough coins for one cup," Maya said as she pulled her drink towards her chest.

"Nonsense, these rounds are on the house," Helen stated as she grabbed the cup from Maya's grasp. "You are the first woman to compete in all the events since . . . well, I don't know when, but I know it is worthy of celebrating. So, a free drink or two is the least we can do."

"Besides, we have such a high markup on the drinks that I could give you two barrels and still make a profit," Aabel said before taking his first gulp. "Now, that's finer than any brew on the market."

"Markup?" Maya asked in curiosity, unsure why a vendor needed to make a larger-than-necessary profit. "I thought vendors were only allowed to keep a small percentage for themselves and the rest went to the sect."

"You are right, my dear," Helen said. "Many, many moons ago the elders in the sect noticed how popular our drink had become, so they wanted to make a deal for the good of the sect. They asked us to only sell the cider at the Cluiche and charge a higher rate. In return, we keep fifteen percent of the profits, and the rest goes to the sect. However, this money is set aside in a special account, like a rainy-day account. The thought is that if things go sour for Sori again, then we will have the funding to help our brethren purchase goods or even buy war armaments if necessary. It is a deal that they have with many of the clans, for the greater good."

"I had no clue that the sect did things like that." Maya rolled Helen's words over in her head.

"There are many things that the elders do in secret, but rest assured that anything done in secret is for the greater good. Besides, if everyone knew that the elders had rainy-day funds, then some of the less fortunate might try to take advantage of that. We don't want people to think our elders are corrupt when their heart is in the right place, so mum's the word," Helen said with a wink.

"No need to worry about me. The list of people I associate with contains elders and family. I am sure they probably know about these types of dealings."

"And if they don't?" Helen asked.

"Then they won't find out from me," Maya replied.

"That's a good lass!" Aabel held his mug in the gesture of a toast, and then his attention turned towards the main gates. "Not to cut your visit short, but the line for sign-up is getting long, so you best be getting on."

"You're right, and thank you once again for the drinks." Maya sat her half-full cup on the bar.

"Please take it with you, and show the lads that we women can bring the chrá!" Helen smiled from ear to ear, as if certain Maya could win.

"That's right. Give us all a good show!" Aabel yelled out as Maya climbed off her stool and made her way to the sign-in station.

The sign-in stations were rather simple, just a couple of tables with three taifeadtas, or recorders, taking the names of contestants for each event. Behind each table were flags bearing the symbol for the event: for trivia, a green flag with a golden quill; for archery, a black flag with three arrows in front of a large flame; claíomh troid, a light-blue flag with two swords crossed in front of a shield; capall cuaille, an orange flag with a mounted knight carrying a lance; and lámh go lámh chomhrac, a purple flag with two closed fists that were just about to hit each other.

All contestants waited at the first sign-in station, which was trivia, and moved to the next station to their right after they checked in or respectfully declined participation. After waiting an hour in line, Maya finally got to the first taifeadta, and much to her surprise he was rather off-putting.

"Name?" the taifeadta asked, looking down at his parchment and stuffing his face with ham.

"Maya of the Clan Dempsey. I am going—"

"To shut up so we can move on. Maya from the Clan Dempsey, you are on the list for trivia. All contestants can withdraw without notice, but to enlist in the event you must see the taifeadta at the event. Now off with you," he said, waving his free hand while shoving a biscuit in his mouth with his other.

Maya moved towards the next station but was cut off by the taifeadta she had just visited.

He yelled, "No, no, no! Off with you now, not to the next station!"

"I don't think so," Maya replied with a strong tone. "I am going to compete in all the events."

All the taifeadtas and those nearby in line began to laugh.

"Women don't compete in all the events. It is a rule."

"Show me where it says this in writing," she said.

"Well, we don't have a rule book per se, but it is a tradition that women only compete in the trivia competition. It is for your safety," he stated, chuckling.

"Fret not." Maya drew her sword and swung it so quickly that many didn't see what happened—that is, until the shirt of the taifeadta opened to expose skin. The ham he was holding had been sliced in two, causing a piece to fall to the table, and all of this with not a scratch on his body. "I will be fine."

In a state of shock, the taifeadta muttered, "It appears you will be."

With the taifeadta and contestants staring like moill, Maya moved down the line and signed up for each event. Maya was excited to get the Cluiche started. There was an hour wait till the first event, so she spent the remaining time with her family. They ate, laughed, and shared stories pertaining to the wins and losses of previous Cluiche events. Though the time with her family was welcome, Maya also used the time to quiz herself on possible trivia questions. She drifted in and out of her family's stories until she ran out of questions. Maya then listened to her family and waited.

The time had come for the Cluiche to start.

Due to the age disparities of the contestants, the events with the most contestants were trivia and archery. Though there were some strong twelve-year-old boys, they would be no match for a twenty-two-year-old in lámh go lámh or claíomh troid, so the younger competitors shied away from those events. Since trivia and archery took the longest to complete, they were always the first events of the Cluiche.

Trivia was considered by the more masculine, fighter clans to be an unworthy event for the Cluiche, and most would not attempt it, thereby taking themselves out of the running for first place and an overall victory. Though these clans proclaimed it to be unworthy, really most of their clan participants were far from bright. The odds were they wouldn't be able to answer a single question, so they forwent the humiliation and stuck with their strong suits. Maya, on the other hand, had been preparing for the trivia contest since she was able to speak.

The trivia contest contained three rounds, and in the first two rounds, seven groups of no more than ten contestants competed to send the seven highest scores to the third and final round. Seven questions, worth one point each, were asked in each round. Typically, fewer than ten competitors scored points and moved into the third round. In the rare event of a tie in the third round, additional questions were asked until there was one definite victor.

Each contestant was given a flag. The máistir searmanas, "master of ceremonies," called out the question and then banged a casúr, a small wooden hammer, ten times to give the contestants time to raise their flag. At the tenth strike of the casúr, everyone who raised a flag had a chance to answer. A taifeadta sat near the máistir searmanas in what had been deemed the "tomb"—simply a large enclosed desk—so that no one could see the taifeadta awarding points. The máistir searmanas would not reveal the answer until everyone had answered. This format was not followed in the third round; there, points were only given to the first person to get the answer correct.

Maya anxiously watched the first round from the stands as the seven groups failed miserably. Only two contestants answered more than one question, and though she concealed her delight, Maya was ecstatic knowing that her opponents knew less than she did at the age of five. Time had finally come for Maya to take the stage. She took the quick walk to the center of the arena and sat at the far-right side of the furthest table. Instead of sizing up her opponents, Maya looked straight ahead and waited till the máistir searmanas called out the first question.

"What herb can be found growing under blue mushrooms?" The máistir searmanas paused and began banging his casúr on his table. At the tenth stroke, and with Maya's flag being the only one raised, he called upon her. "Maya."

"Fox weed," Maya confidently replied.

"Correct. Second question: Fox weed is used to cure what illness or symptoms?"

Instantly Maya raised her flag, and when given the nod she called out, "Insomnia, but one must use no more than two spoonfuls due to its potency, which can leave one in a coma-like state for several weeks."

"Correct, which also answers the third question of, 'How much fox weed dosage can one give?' Two more points for Maya. Question four: What is the toxic berry that many confuse with ambrosia?"

Maya was once again the only one with a raised flag and answered, "Golden flax berry."

"Correct. What is the justification for never confusing the golden flax berry with that of ambrosia?"

Instead of raising the flag Maya called out, "Golden flax berry is common throughout Sori and can be grown by anyone. However, ambrosia is only grown by the monks and thus not found in nature, so to speak. Therefore, one should never mistake one for the other."

At this point in the match none of the other contestants had come close to touching their flags to answer, and due to the low number of questions answered in the previous rounds, the master of ceremonies made a judgment call.

"The questions only get more difficult from here, and you gentlemen have not even attempted to answer one thus far, so I am calling Maya of the Clan Dempsey the winner. This is one of the few times in which only one person has answered all the questions in one round, so in light of this, there will only be one contestant from this round moving on to the final round."

The máistir searmanas paused for the crowd's reaction. The applause was thunderous, and when it faded, the máistir searmanas called out, "Bring on the high scorers from the first round!"

From the stands came six contestants. Their walk to the arena's center was slow, and most had their heads hanging low, as if they knew defeat was imminent. Once at the table, they took a seat, and three of the contestants grabbed their flags in hopes they would beat Maya to the draw.

"First question: What age do you have to be to be considered for elder status?"

Ambjörn beat Maya to the draw and was first to raise the flag. "Twenty-two," he answered confidently, knowing that was the youngest anyone had been when declared an elder.

"That is incorrect," the máistir searmanas replied. "Maya, your answer please."

"There is no age requirement. Being an elder is based on experience, knowledge and the vote of the elders, but not age." Maya couldn't hide her growing smile.

"Correct. Ambjörn, the youngest ever to be declared an elder was twenty-two; however, as Maya said, age does not dictate elder status. Elder status is a judgment call by the clans based off the experience and knowledge that one has gained." The máistir searmanas, looking at the next question, smiled in hopes that the earth elementals would beat Maya to the punch. "Next question: What is the strongest metal known to Sori?"

Jagger, from an earth elemental clan, did just as the máistir searmanas hoped and quickly raised his flag. Without waiting to be called on he yelled out, "Dorcha steel!"

"Correct. Perhaps we might see a tight competition after all," the máistir searmanas said excitedly. He glanced down at the next question and quickly withdrew his hopes. "Next question: What deadly herb causes your flesh to fall off, your limbs to deteriorate, and gives the appearance of the living dead just prior to passing?"

Maya jumped at the opportunity to take the lead, raised her flag, and answered, "Gangus ag siúl bás, more commonly known as gangus."

"Correct. What is the odorless and tasteless herb that causes uncontrollable bleeding of bodily orifices resulting in death?"

Wanting to extend her lead, Maya quickly raised her flag to answer. "Dearg abhainn, more commonly known as 'Red River' or 'the Wife's Revenge.'"

"Correct, and this could be the final question of our trivia contest. Dearg abhainn is given its name not due to the river of blood that is produced through its consumption, but due to what?" the máistir searmanas asked Maya, knowing that she would be the only one who knew the answer.

Maya looked left at the other contestants, and with none of them moving she raised her flag as she answered, "Due to how and where it grows. Dearg abhainn is a red, seaweed-like plant that only grows in swamp or marsh lands. The plant grows out of the banks and falls into the water instead of growing vertically like most plants. In doing so, the plant is continually submerged and constantly moving with the flow of the water. When there is a large cluster of dearg abhainn, it looks like a red flowing river."

"That is also correct. Our first contest winner is Maya of Clan Dempsey!" the máistir searmanas called out. The crowd erupted in applause. "Maya, come forth and take your prize."

Maya did as she was told and was awarded a golden quill, the Leigheasan symbol for knowledge. After receiving her reward, Maya turned to give her respect to her opponents; however, they all were halfway to the stands. Shrugging off the poor sportsmanship, Maya made her way back to her family.

"Congratulations!" Felix, Maya's father, shouted. He hugged Maya.

"Thanks, but no time for celebration. I have to check in for the archery contest," Maya said.

"I will take that, and you take this," Andrea said as she grabbed the quill in exchange for Maya's bow.

"Sorry, Mom, but I found out they won't let us use our own bow." Maya turned to head for the field on the outskirts of the village.

"Really? When did that start and more importantly why?" Felix asked as he and Andrea followed.

"This year is the first year. They said contestants who use their own bows have an unfair advantage. Some bows are made from better wood and some have higher tension, giving the bow more power. The elders on the Cluiche council decided that this truly does give contestants an advantage, and to level the playing field contestants will use the same bow."

Andrea shook her head. "Someone must have complained. I'm sure they were tired of seeing the more prominent archer clans winning as frequently as they do, though that shouldn't warrant changing a rule that has been in place for centuries. Sure, the bow helps, but there is much more to archery than just a bow—"

"Let's just say that it makes sense and leave it at that. Shall we?" Felix asked, hoping to silence her. Her clan was born with a bow in hand, and she could go on for hours talking about the finer points of archery. Luckily for Felix, they had arrived at the archery field, so instead of rants, they wished Maya well. Felix turned to Maya and calmly said, "I know you don't need it, but good luck."

A much more pleasant taifeadta assigned Maya to be the opening contestant. Shortly after, the máistir searmanas took his position at the shooting line in front of the growing crowd.

"The first round in the archery competition is simple. Down the range are three targets: one at fifty yards, one at seventy-five yards, and the last one is at one hundred yards," the máistir searmanas said with a severe monotone that would bore anyone to sleep. He had no interest in the competition. "There are two colors on each target," he said, pointing to a sample target beside him. "The yellow is five points and the red is ten points. You will have two shots per target. Maya of the Clan Dempsey is up first. Shoot when you are ready."

Grabbing her bow and six arrows, Maya walked up to the shooting line and drew her first arrow. Taking aim and letting her arrow loose, the shot hit its mark dead center. The second shot was the same as the first, a hit right beside the first. Moving on to the second target, Maya landed both shots inside the red, but both were close to landing on yellow. For the third target, Maya took her time with her aim, breathed deeply, and sent her first arrow into the center of the target. However, her second shot landed just inside of the yellow, giving her a total of fifty-five points.

For the next couple of hours Maya watched her opponents attempt the range. In the end, ten others joined Maya with fifty-five points, and more than a dozen were within ten points of the leaders.

To begin the next round the master of ceremonies stood on a platform and in the same monotone he began his spiel: "Round two is more challenging. The goal is to hit a moving target. The targets will be attached to a cart and carried across the field by a team of horses. The targets are at the same distance, and we will proceed in the same order: fifty yards, seventy-five yards and one hundred yards. You will have one shot per target. Our top ten from the first round will go first. The thirty contestants who do not have fifty points or better will be disqualified after their second missed shot. Those who are twenty points or more down are out of the archery contest and may watch or prepare for your next event."

Maya once again took her place at the line and watched the first team of horses take off. She aimed ahead of the target and sent her arrow to its mark, landing an inch from the center. With the first target across the field, the second horse team took off. Moving at a much faster pace, the second target caused Maya to hesitate. Adjusting her stance and aim, she released the arrow. It hit just inside the yellow. The third set of horses took off just like the second, and without hesitation this time, Maya fired her last arrow. It landed dead center, giving her competitors little room for error.

Taking a seat on the grass, she watched the rest of the top contestants score. They were as good as her except for two. Jagger fell short of hitting his third target. He was now fifteen points from the lead, which was enough to disqualify him from the third round. Ambjörn made up for his lack of knowledge on the trivia contest by hitting all three red marks and taking the lead. Only one of the participants not in the top ten made it to the third and final round.

"The third and final round is the only round in which you will go directly against an opponent. In this round, you will have one minute to hit the target as many times as possible. Your opponent is permitted to distract you and block your shots by using their elements or other creative means. There are two exceptions for this round. The first is that your element cannot harm the shooter, and the second is that you are forbidden from using mind control."

Maya was paired with Ambjörn, and they were the last to go, so she did the one thing she did best, study. The third round was more about strategy than shooting. The wind elementals blew their opponents' arrows so far off course that an arrow never came close to the target. The fire elementals took their vantage point about midway between the target and shooter. They incinerated the arrows shortly after their release, while the rock elements guided the stone arrowhead gently to the ground. The one water elemental used the moisture in the air to create a rainstorm effect on the arrow's path. The rain pounded the arrow to the ground well before hitting the target.

When it was time for Maya and Ambjörn to bout, Ambjörn let Maya go first. Knowing her opponent was a fire elemental, Maya expected him to burn her arrows. Maya gathered thirteen arrows. She broke the tips off six arrows and placed them in two columns of three arrows each. Six more arrows were placed in columns besides the broken ones, and one single arrow was thrust into the ground at her side. The timer would start when she picked up her first arrow, but Maya was in no hurry. She took a deep breath and slowly exhaled.

Maya snatched the arrow by her side out of the ground and let it go. Ambjörn had taken his position halfway down the field, giving him good position to intercept Maya's shots. He focused in on the arrow flying towards the target and shot a long stream of fire at the arrow. This gave Maya time to reach for three of the broken arrows. She quickly placed two between her fingers, drew the third, turned slightly to her left towards Ambjörn, and in rapid succession Maya let them loose in his direction. Ambjörn had destroyed Maya's first arrow but now had to turn his attention to the ones flying at him.

While Ambjörn was taking care of the arrows coming towards him, Maya was able to make two quick shots that landed in the yellow. Maya reloaded three more broken arrows and repeated her process. This time, Ambjörn was prepared and took out all of Maya's arrows. Though she only scored ten points, it was still enough to secure the lead and put pressure on Ambjörn.

"I must say, that was well played," Ambjörn said with the utmost sincerity. "I was not expecting that, but now I am up and you aren't an elemental. What will you do?"

Maya said nothing as Ambjörn stuck six arrows in the ground by his side. Without an element, Maya knew there was only one thing she could do to stop him. As Ambjörn picked up his first arrow, Maya sprinted straight for him. Ambjörn saw her from the corner of his eye, but still he drew his arrow. Just a couple of feet from her target, Maya jumped high in the air and straight towards Ambjörn. She pulled back her arm, thrust it forward, and landed her fist on his jaw.

Ambjörn realized many things during the competition, like his dearth of knowledge when it came to trivia, but his greatest revelation was that he had a glass jaw. He fell to the ground like a sack of potatoes, knocked out. The crowd booed and shouted at Maya until the master of ceremonies intervened.

"The rules specifically say one cannot be harmed by elements and can distract using other creative means. There is nothing against physical contact, and this would fall under creative means. The winner by five points is Maya of Clan Dempsey," the máistir searmanas said very unenthusiastically, but quickly changed his tone as he called out, "Maya, come claim your prize!"

The prize for the archery contest was an elegant handcrafted bow. Both ends of the bow boasted carvings of bear heads to symbolize strength. Above and below the handgrip, wings worked as an arrow rest, while also symbolizing flight. It was capped off with intricate beaded knotwork running along both sides of the bow. Although the bow was an example of the finest Leigheasan craftsmanship, it was never intended to be used, but rather simply displayed as a token of accomplishment.

Just as she did with the golden quill, Maya took the prize to her family and headed towards the next event.

A circular fence was erected in the middle of the main arena for the sword competition. This enclosure was designed to teach people they could not back down or run away from all fights. Maya arrived just in time to hear news that might cost her a high rank in the sword competition.

Pacing around the ring, the máistir searmanas yelled the rules so that all in the grandstands could hear.

"Just as with our other competitions, the rules of claíomh troid are simple: each hit scores a point, and each point is represented with a flag. The first to ten flags wins and moves on to the next round. Contestants cannot use their own weapons and armor, so please report to sign-in stations to receive your armor and sword."

In all of Maya's training, she had never used traditional armor, nor the traditional longsword. Maya had forgotten that tournament rules prevented fighters from using their own weapons due to the threat of injury. Contestants were given a blunt longsword. The longsword was at least twice the weight of Maya's sword, and though she was not weak, the weight would be difficult to adjust to without training. Her personal armor was not only stronger than the armor soldiers used, but also lighter. In addition to the armor, Maya had never trained with a helmet, and she knew this would hinder her performance.

Maya made her way to the sign-in stations set up outside of the ring. Each table had three additional tables behind them for armor, helmets and swords. Maya jumped in a line, and with each step towards the table her anxiety grew. Being nervous was out of character for Maya. If she ever felt anxious, it was due to excitement at taking on a challenge, not fear of a task. With the risk of not being the overall winner, doubt crept in.

"Name?" the taifeadta asked.

She walked up to the table. "Maya."

"Clan?" he asked as his partner, the àita or "placer," began placing Maya in a match.

"Dempsey," Maya proudly stated.

"Versus?" he asked, turning to his assistant.

"Abbán of the Clan Östberg," the àita called out without raising his head.

"Position in first round?" the taifeadta asked his partner.

"Fourth," the àita replied.

"You will go against Abbán in the fourth match of the first round," he said as if Maya could not hear him speak. "Proceed to the first table behind me to be fitted for your armor. Next!" he called out.

Maya tried to contain her emotions as she approached the arming table, but anyone could tell she was upset. Just looking at the armor and swords, Maya knew the armor was too big and the sword would be too heavy. A male Berserker chuckled and moved towards her. Berserkers oversaw what most would call the behind-the-scene actions of the Cluiche. Just before Maya reached the table, he was pushed out of the way by his partner.

"Forgive my husband. He is of the belief that women should not be competing. On behalf of all the women of my clan, we are most pleased with your performance so far."

"Thanks. I am Maya." She quickly became more at ease.

"Zamira, and my oaf of a husband is Rassin. Now, I must say the odds are against you. The armor is going to add close to twenty pounds." Zamira scanned for armor that would be less bulky for Maya's frame.

"I'm not exactly weak, but I don't think I will be strong enough to withstand all that. Part of the reason I have always been so successful in training sessions is due to my speed. This much weight will, without a doubt, hinder my performance," Maya replied as uncertainty grew.

"Don't worry." Zamira paused, and in an attempt to make Maya feel better she continued, "Even if you do poorly in this event, it won't be enough to keep you out of the top five."

Maya looked at the armor and hesitantly asked, "Are you sure?"

"I have been a part of this tournament for many years. In fact, it has been so many that I cannot recall the exact number." Zamira gazed off in the distance, trying to remember. She shook her head. "So the one thing that I do know is how the ranking will pan out. You will be fine, with or without a victory."

"Did you ever compete?" Maya asked as Zamira fitted her with chainmail sleeves to protect her arms.

"Never; the Berserker Clan is forbidden from competition. From the moment of our birth, Berserkers are trained not only in all aspects of combat, but we are also taught to channel our rage into fighting. Even in competition, it is hard to turn it off. I was always told that the elders fear that we will become too violent and turn a friendly competition into a bloodbath."

"Has that ever happened?"

"Not that I know of, but who knows. Maybe the monks have it recorded somewhere. Maybe that's why the elders forbid us from competing, or maybe it was a preventative measure. Nevertheless, I agree with the thought that we would have an unfair advantage and dominate the competition." Zamira did not want to display the same arrogance as her husband, so she immediately turned to Maya and apologized. "I'm sorry. I meant no offense, my dear."

"No need to apologize. It's not a secret that our sect has become a bit soft over the past few centuries. With each generation, it seems like we become a bit more like the Duine. It does make sense to forbid your clan from competition, but it still seems like you should have a chance. If the Berserkers were allowed to compete, then maybe our sect would rise to the challenge and become the more formidable sect that we once were."

Maya winced as Zamira tightened the buckles to the chainmail, securing it to her body.

Looking around her table Zamira said, "It is what it is, my dear. Now, the problem is going to be in the chest plate. You are smaller than most of the competitors, so I don't know how well we can fit you. Ah, here we go," she said, grabbing one at the far-right end of the table. Placing it on Maya, Zamira gave her a once-over. "I believe we have a winner. I think it is just a hair too big, but it could have been worse. Now, we move on to the helmet."

Maya followed Zamira on the short walk to the helmet table, testing her range of motion by moving her arms up and down, across her body, and extended them both vertically and perpendicular. Even with the armor fitting fairly well, Maya did not have the range of motion she was used to. The worst was to come as Zamira placed the helmet on.

"How is that?" Zamira asked.

"One slit for my eyes? How can one fight in battle with this? I can barely see what's in front of me, and I cannot see anything to my sides."

"Okay, how about this one?" Zamira asked, giving Maya a new helmet to try on. "This one is used more for sparring and training, but it will allow for greater vision than the others."

This helmet had an open front with only two bars protecting the face. One bar went horizontally across the helmet around the nose, while the other was in the middle of the opening and went vertically.

"Better. I still can't move that well, and my peripheral vision is less hindered but hindered nonetheless." Maya paused as she moved her head and arms around. "This is going to be more difficult than I had thought."

"It will have to do. Besides, nothing would be worth doing if there wasn't some type of challenge." Zamira walked towards the sword table. "Speaking of challenges, this should be seen as just one more. All the swords are the same length, so there is no choice to be made. I am afraid that they are fairly heavy."

Maya picked up a sword and instantly almost dropped it. The sight of this made several of the contestants and Berserkers chuckle.

"Pay no mind to them, and just remember to do your best. If you lose, then you can still be the Cluiche champion. Good luck." Zamira returned to the first table to help the next contestant.

Maya watched the first three fights. The strongest competitors led the victories, all from the Roark Clan. Abbán stepped into the ring first. He was easily the crowd favorite as their cheers for him continued while Maya entered. With the drop of a red flag, the match was on and Abbán charged.

Maya took several steps back, raised her sword by her side, and waited till she could see how he would attack. Abbán raised his sword overhead and brought it down at Maya's face. Maya raised her sword just slightly above her head and stopped the brunt of the attack. Abbán's powerful swing caused Maya to drop her sword, and his sword continued towards its target, hitting the top of the helmet. Taking advantage of his defenseless opponent, Abbán hit Maya in the chest. Raising his sword high, Abbán brought it down and struck Maya in the head.

Dizzy from the hits, ears ringing, Maya stumbled to the ground. She found herself down by three points, and as she attempted to get up, Abbán hit her on the back to extend his lead to five points. The fight was quickly getting out of hand. Maya needed to score points, but she could barely regain her balance. With her vision blurred, Maya tried to pull off an offensive attack and charged Abbán, drawing her sword to her side. Abbán stepped left, knocked Maya's sword out of her hand, and struck her in the back twice. He then turned Maya around and struck her twice in the chest. Spinning to Maya's back, Abbán connected the final blow—a strike that sent her to the ground and ended the match.

This sent the crowd in an uproar. A new tournament leader meant more excitement throughout the rest of the events. After three rounds, Maya watched her name drop to fifth place—a position that she was more than unhappy with. She either had to win the next two events, or at the very least make sure the leaders didn't place ahead of her.

The rules of the capall cuaille, or jousting, competition were few, but the one rule that would never change was that contestants were allowed to use their own horses. The reason being that horses had a bond with their riders. Under the pressure of the event, the horse needed to feel at ease. Having its owner at the helm meant the horses were less likely to buck or throw the competitor to the ground. The other rule was that the contestants were permitted to wear their own armor.

The armor for the capall cuaille was different from that used in battle— thicker on the upper body, with flaps covering the exposed armpits and a shield attached to the left arm. The helmet had small slots around the eyes to protect against fragments of exploding lances, and the armor on the lower body was thinner to compensate for the added weight on the upper body.

The capall cuaille was the largest competition of the Cluiche because it was a traditional game amongst all clans. The line at the sign-in station was long, but Felix had a surprise for her first.

"Maya, hold on!" Felix called out. Maya had started walking to the arena.

"Sorry, Dad, I'm not in the mood after that horrible display," she responded angrily.

"Maya, stop!" Felix yelled, and as her father rarely raised his voice, she immediately stopped and walked back to her parents. "That's better. Now remember, anger and frustration fog the mind, which leads to mistakes. If there is one thing that is certain, you cannot afford any more mistakes."

"I know. I'm not angry with what happened. I am angry with myself for not being more prepared. I should have known the rules and began training ages ago for the claíomh troid. I can't believe that I made such a colossal oversight." She finally looked Felix in the eye.

"First off, what do I always tell you when something doesn't go the way we expect?"

Maya replied, "Learn from past mistakes so that we may be better prepared for the future."

"What did you learn today?"

"No matter how anxious I am to do something, I must put in the time to prepare for it. In this instance, I should have been training with multiple types of weapons and armors. Also, I should have read up on the rules," Maya admitted.

"Good. Now, you are still young enough to enter the Cluiche again, and if you choose to do so, you will now know how to prepare." Felix guided her towards their favorite capall cuaille horse, Brutus. "Many might consider this cheating, but everyone knows our clan rides the Diana breed, so we are within the rules of the contest."

"Dad, are you saying what I think you are saying?" Maya asked, gazing at Brutus.

Brutus was a rare breed of horse that the Leigheasan called Diana. The Dempsey Clan were breeders and trainers of all animals; however, horse breeding became their calling. The Diana breed took two Dempsey generations to perfect. They sought a very specific size, speed and strength so their horses would stand out not only amongst their sect, but all sects. Each Diana, when fully grown, stood over six feet in height and had a distinct burgundy hue. They could be used as a team to haul loads of lumber, or as individuals to do various jobs on the farm. They were also the fastest land animal, with a keen sense of hearing, and could travel long distances with little food or water. Only those in the Dempsey bloodline were allowed to own or ride a Diana, which meant even those who married into the family, like Maya's mother, were not allowed to own one.

"Well, I haven't said it yet, but yes, today you are going to ride Brutus. Interesting fact, no one has ever lost a capall cuaille match while riding a Diana, which makes it even more surprising that they never banned their use in competition," Felix said, petting Brutus.

"I cannot tell you how much I want to ride Brutus, but I don't know if that is a good idea. It would seem a bit suspicious since no one has ever seen me on a Diana." Maya contemplated the idea.

"True, but most have never seen you on a horse to begin with." Andrea added, "You walk or run everywhere you go." She went to the back of the wagon Brutus was pulling.

"Look at it this way. The Dempsey Clan has never competed in a capall cuaille with a normal horse. The Diana is our clan's choice, so we have tradition to justify your steed."

Maya finally agreed. "Okay. I'll use Brutus."

"Good, and your mother has something else for you." Felix pointed to the back of the wagon.

Maya noticed her mother staring into the wagon with a look of admiration. Curious, Maya quickly joined her and saw an item she had never seen.

"Mom, what is this?" Maya asked, gazing upon a raven-black suit of armor.

"This, my dear, is Elizabeta's armor. She was your fourth great-grandmother on my side of the family. It has been used by every woman in the McGill family when competing in capall cuaille tournaments. Though any woman in the family is able to wear it, it is the oldest who inherits the armor, and since you're the only girl I bore, it is yours."

"How come I have never seen this?" Maya asked, inspecting the armor. There were no designs or distinctive markings. "This is beautiful, but why is it so plain? There isn't a distinguishable mark to signify the McGill Clan or Elizabeta."

"To your first question, I had to stop competing way before you were born. I fell from the top of our barn in my younger days and severely hurt my back. Though medicine has healed my back, I don't want to risk any tweaking or reinjury. Even if that means giving up something I love. Without someone in the competition, it is pointless to have it out.

"To answer your second question, it is plain to strike fear. Many who compete believe they must have the fanciest or most elaborate equipment. Lavish engraving of a clan's crest, golden trim, or polishing with soiléir cóta are all part of an old train of thought that a grand presentation will intimidate. However, Elizabeta believed it's the lack of display that is intimidating."

"It looks brand new. Was it used often?" Maya moved her hands across the armor.

"It was in frequent use, but it has been well cared for over the years and has seen very few hits. Most women were scared to compete against our grandmothers and spent the bouts concentrating on not falling off the horse. The armor has only seen a few broken lances," Andrea explained. "Now, there will be time for admiration later. You need to go sign in."

Maya reluctantly turned and headed to the sign-in station where she found out she was going to be in the second match of the second group. For the current capall cuaille, there were twenty groups of eight contestants that would be narrowed down to the top five contestants. In the first round, a competitor would have to win two matches to proceed to the second round. At most, eighty competitors would face off in the second round, and a total of five contestants would continue to round three. In the event of a tie, an extra round was added to eliminate those not worthy of being in the top five. It was at this point where the competitors' tallied points from the previous rounds determine rankings.

The contest was scored by a hit, broken lance, or unhorsing an opponent. A hit scored one point, a broken lance earned three, and five points were given for knocking the opponent off their horse. The contestants had three lances to score as many points as possible. With the points tallied, the competitors were given a rank numbering one through five. Second place went against fifth, third place against fourth, and first place sat out for a match. The third round consisted of first place going against the lower-ranking of the two remaining contestants. The fourth round, the championship round, consisted of the final two competitors.

Instead of watching the matches, Maya went to suit up and test her range of motion. The armor was light and fit her body just as well as the armor she made for herself. She jumped on Brutus and rode around the grounds to get accustomed to riding with the armor. She felt something she never felt while riding a horse—lack of control. Maya was not in control of Brutus, and this caused her to panic until she heard her father call out.

"Remember, let Brutus do the work. The Dianas aren't like other horses. They know what they need to do." Maya approached her father and his voice softened. "With Brutus's speed and force behind the lance, a hit will almost ensure an unseating. You just have to trust that Brutus will take care of it. Oh, and remember to lean slightly to the left when you are about to strike and to keep your muscles as flexed as possible. This will help you absorb a hit."

"I'll remember," Maya replied. "This is going to take some getting used to."

"The first group is taking a bit longer than I thought," Andrea said as she approached Maya and Brutus. She patted the steed on his neck and fed him a carrot.

"Three lances a match, so it will take some time to finish all the groups." Felix came to Andrea's side. "Who are you facing?"

"Percy of Clan Rafferty."

"The Rafferty Clan is highly skilled in this event, but I know you will do fine." Felix looked over at the line of horses forming near the arena's entrance. "It looks like the first round is almost over. Best if you get going." Both of her parents wished her luck, and Maya was off as her dad smacked Brutus on the hindquarters.

The entrance to the arena floor was through a short tunnel underneath the grandstands. It was nothing elaborate, but wide enough to get a couple wagons through at once. Contestants of the second group, including

Maya, lined up at the entrance gate to wait for their turn to enter the arena once again. Between the shoulders of her competitors, Maya saw the cleanup from the last match. The Berserkers used a liathróid to clear the lance shards, a hollow iron ball mounted to a pusher that allowed it to roll. Inside the ball was a flame fueled by fiailí peet, which produced intense heat for long periods of time. The liathróid was pushed across the arena floor, and any shards of wood were incinerated on contact. Essentially, the liathróid was a hot broom.

As Maya looked on at the last bits of wood burning, the gate suddenly opened, and the horses in front of her moved into the arena. She followed the leader and took her place in line at the end of the arena opposite the gate they entered.

The first match came to a draw after three lances. A fourth lance was brought out, and this time there was a clear winner. Ozzie of Clan Van Berg knocked his challenger off his horse to take the points lead. It was now Maya's turn to compete, and Brutus instinctively knew where to go. He guided Maya to the start line, where she looked down the fencing to see Percy. Wearing polished armor lined in gold trim, Percy looked like a descendant of one of Sori's ancient ruling families. She wondered what he was thinking. Was he laughing at the thought of going against a girl? Was he planning his attack? Thoughts raced through her mind until a lone Berserker, holding a white flag, walked out to the middle of the barrier while another Berserker brought Maya a lance.

Lance in hand, Maya cleared her mind and focused on the task before her. The white flag dropped, the Berserker ran off the field, and Brutus sprinted down the line. Percy was slow to start, and instead of meeting Maya at the center, she met him about a quarter of the way from his start line. Both competitors hit their mark, and both shattered their lances. Percy struck Maya on her shield while Maya hit Percy dead center in the chest. The force of Maya's blow launched Percy from his saddle and onto the dirt.

Maya was victorious in every match of each round, with most of her points coming from unhorsing her competitors. Even though Brutus gave her a slight advantage, she was proving to the crowd that women deserved their place in the Cluiche.

She had entered the final round. Maya's next opponent was Stephan of the Tammi Clan, known to most as the Gach Bua, the undefeated.

Stephan was almost seven feet tall, made of solid muscle. He was easily the most intimidating of foes, but he was the Leigheas who competed the least. Like all members of the Tammi Clan, he only participated in the capall cuaille, and like most in his clan, he had never been defeated in a capall cuaille tournament. The Tammi Clan did not possess elements, but they had what the ancients called seoltóir eyes. Some saw their gift as a blessing, while others saw it as a curse. Seoltóir eyes, also called seer eyes, caused limited eyesight in exchange for the power to have visions. These visions could come at any time, but were most frequent after a touch. The capall cuaille allowed the Tammi Clan to compete because visions and bad eyesight were less likely to hinder performance.

This would not be the case today.

The flag was dropped, Stephan was told to go, and the two forces took off. Almost at once, Stephan was assaulted by visions so strong that he lost focus and fell to the ground before they could attempt to strike each other. The visions poured into his mind like a flood across the Gleann. He saw a land at war, millions of bodies lying on the ground, towns burning, villages in ruins, and the one discernible fighter amongst all the shadows was Maya.

In one scene, chaos surrounded Maya. Fires consumed the distant horizon while soldiers fell to the ground as she cut through the masses. In another scene, Maya led a charge against an unknown foe. Stephan viewed the carnage through the eyes of Maya's opponent, and saw her running uphill towards him. Lastly, he saw Maya standing amongst ruins. All was quiet and very peaceful until the ruins began to shake as the earth opened. Within seconds, the earth swallowed all signs that life had existed, and all that remained was a grass meadow as far as the eye could see.

Fearful that something serious was wrong with Stephan, Maya jumped off her horse and ran to her opponent. A loud voice cried out.

"Stop! Do not touch him!" Stephan's brother Sid commanded those coming to Stephan's side. Sid and Stephan's threorú, a guide and aide who engendered no visions in those with seoltóir eyes, helped him up, and as they did, Sid looked at Maya. "These reactions aren't uncommon for us, but those that render us useless are typically from touch. For this to happen at such a distance means your future is very bright."

"That's good though, right? A bright future is a good thing to have," Maya interjected with concern. She knew that the ways and word choices of the Leigheasan were like those of the gods and goddesses. A word like *bright* may indeed be a positive thing, but it could also have negative implications.

"Yes and no. When we say bright it means things are very clear—there is no question of what happened in the vision. Some visions we get are foggy, so to speak, so we call them dim visions. In these instances, we may see only shadows or have no clue to whom the vision pertains. Bright visions provide a clear view of what happened, whether it is good or bad."

Feeling guilty, Maya pleaded, "Please, let me help."

"The gesture is appreciated, but you cannot touch him," Sid replied, slightly winded from carrying the bulk of his brother's weight. "It can send him back into the vision, and by the looks of him, Stephan does not need to go back there. It is a shame that the match ended this way. We would have loved to see you against Stephan; however, as it is, congratulations are in order. Good luck to you with the rest of Cluiche."

"Wait," Stephan muttered as his brother began assisting him towards the arena's gate. "Maya, come closer, but please do not touch."

She did as she was told. "I am so sorry. I didn't—"

"It's fine. As one in the Tammi Clan, we are used to unexpected visions," he said, cutting her off. "You will be confronted with many difficult choices in the days to come. One day you will wield great power and have to make a choice to use it for the good of your brethren, or to use it for a darker, viler purpose."

With that said, Sid and the threorú carried Stephan out of the arena. Maya stood there in shock and was quickly joined by the máistir searmanas.

"Our winner—" the máistir searmanas started to say, but Maya interrupted.

"I didn't win."

"As you can see, Stephan is taking his leave. Therefore, he is eliminating himself from the competition," the máistir searmanas snapped back at Maya.

Maya tried to think of a way to end the contest fairly. Finally, she yelled, "But I essentially have done the same, so shouldn't there be a draw?"

The máistir searmanas paused, thought about what she said, and hustled over to a group of elders. They seemed to be considering her point of view, and she hoped that they would declare a draw. After a few minutes of deliberation, the máistir searmanas returned to Maya's side.

"After careful consideration, we have decided that there is a tie, and both Maya and Stephan share the honor of capall cuaille champion." He stood there until the applause and cheers of the crowd dissipated. Turning to Maya he continued while handing her the trophy, "We only have one trophy, so you will need to decide who gets it."

Maya looked at the statue of a capall cuaille champion on his horse and responded, "Give it to Stephan, please."

"As you wish," the máistir searmanas replied and rushed to catch up with Stephan.

Walking to Brutus, Maya heard loud cheering outside the arena, which could only mean a changing of ranks. She grabbed the reins and quickly walked outside to the ranking board. She was pleased to see that she was now in third position, which meant she would have to finish no worse than fourth in the lámh go lámh chomhrac to become Cluiche champion.

The lámh go lámh chomhrac consisted of matches, the number of which depended on the number of contestants, and each match was divided into five-minute rounds. There was no limit to the number of rounds; contestants fought until someone yielded or was unable to get up after falling. It was also the only event where the only points awarded were to the victor of a match. For the most part, the matches of the current lámh go lámh chomhrac were nothing to celebrate. Most were over by the third round.

Though Maya took some beatings in the early matches, she utilized her speed, endurance and fighting skills to move into the semi-final match against Angus of the Roark Clan. Angus was a brute of a young man, and the only thing larger than his size was his anger. Both qualities had carried him this far in the competition. Only one contestant lasted more than two rounds with Angus. He was more confident now than in any previous match.

Motioning with his hands to calm the crowd, the master of ceremonies began his pre-round ritual talk.

"It has been a long day, and we have two more matches left before the main event. For the right to fight in the final match we have Angus of Clan Roark and Maya of Clan Dempsey." The crowd erupted in a roar, cheering on their favorite contender. After a moment, the master of ceremonies once again waved his hands to calm the crowd. "Just a reminder: using elemental powers, or any other powers, is forbidden and will result in disqualification. Any one of us can use our power in a fight, but we must be smart enough to know when *not* to use our power. Fighters approach the middle."

"Good luck," Maya said as she approached Angus.

"Silly girl," he said, smirking. "Save yourself some pain and give up now. There is no way you can defeat me."

A lone Berserker was the only person in the arena with the fighters. His task was to start the fight and ensure that once a contestant yielded, or was knocked out, no further blows were inflicted. Looking at Maya and Angus, the Berserker dropped the flag. The two immediately stepped towards each other and began exchanging blows. Maya's speed and endurance carried her into the third round, but Angus's strength and powerful blows were taking their toll on her small frame. They both grew tired, and midway through the third round Maya landed an uppercut that knocked Angus to the ground. As surprised as he was, Maya took several steps back to better defend against an attack. More enraged than ever, Angus reached back, produced a fireball in his hand and launched it towards his opponent.

Maya instinctively did a backflip, missing the flame. As she stood, another fireball approached her. She stepped to the side and extended her arm, catching the flame. Without thinking, Maya began a windup of her own. As she turned and pulled her arm back, the flame changed color. It went from a red and yellow mix to white and blue. She threw the flame back at a much faster velocity. It struck him in the center of his chest. The flame's heat was so intense that his shirt and skin disintegrated just before contact. Cutting through bone, the flame dissipated shortly after leaving Angus's body. Angus collapsed to his knees, and then his lifeless body fell to the ground.

The crowd no longer cheered. Faces were coated in shock. Only the elder fire-yielding elementals mastered the hottest flames of white and blue. This was a skill that took an elder a lifetime to master.

The silence was broken by the máistir searmanas yelling, "Seize her!"

Maya was as shocked as those in the crowd and did not resist the Berserkers when they approached. Her hands bound behind her back with metal clasps, Maya was escorted to the storage room underneath the closest pub. There were no windows and only one entrance, blocked by Berserkers.

There was no way out.

And Maya was trapped.

Maya opened her eyes and gazed into the shadows. She knew she was not the only one in her prison cell.

"Please step into the light, my lady," Maya pleaded.

"How are you, my child?" Nantosuelta asked, stepping forward, becoming fully visible to Maya.

"Confused," Maya replied as dozens of questions raced through her mind. She finally settled on one. "How was I able to do that? I am not a full Leigheas."

"The Turas is a ritual necessary to one being declared a Leigheas, that is true. One cannot obtain ascenders nor receive proper training without it; however, the element portion is strictly ceremonial. The powers of the elements are provided by our world and are with a true Leigheas from birth. Ascenders simply reveal and help guide the Leigheas to use them."

Maya was relieved that she was destined to be a Leigheas but simultaneously worried that this was a sign of something dreadful to come. She was also confused about her ability to use the element.

"I guess it's good to know that I belong in the Leigheasan sect, but how was I able to use it without training? Also, how was I able to change the flame after I caught it?" she asked, seeking clarity. "White and blue are obtained only by some fire elders. How could a tosaithe accomplish such a feat?" A tosaithe was someone new to a trade or craft.

"You are more strongly bonded with the earth than any of your sect. You spend weeks alone in the wilderness, you've mapped all of Sori, you seek the knowledge of elders, and the list goes on. You have tapped into what it means to be a Leigheas, and thus your reactions have become instinctual. You knew that the only flame to harm a fire elemental would be the hottest of fire, and so that's what you produced." Nantosuelta knelt in front of Maya as if she were a friend, not a superior.

"That makes sense, but why isn't it common knowledge that elemental power is with us from birth?"

"Time has eroded many traditions and much knowledge from your minds," Nantosuelta whispered. "Though I have always and will always have a special place in my heart for the Leigheasan, it has been more than disappointing to watch these changes occur."

"I don't follow." Maya was confused at the thought of her community changing or simply not following tradition. The Leigheasan way of life was full of traditions, and its sect taught members to be proud to carry on all traditions. Not following them, or changing them over time, contradicted many beliefs.

"It is very similar to what I told you about women competing in the Cluiche. As the centuries passed, things were forgotten, and traditions have changed to reflect those leading."

Maya was satisfied with the answer, and though she wanted to ask more questions, the current conditions were not right. Instead, Maya asked one final question on the subject. "After this gets sorted out, where can I go to learn about all things forgotten and the origins of our traditions?"

"The monks of Gaeltacht are the keepers of all that is Sori. If your ascenders believe that you are worthy, which by today's display I have no doubt you are, then you will be guided to their dwelling."

"You mean you had doubt before?"

"As I told you before, you have great potential—as I am sure you are aware of, especially after your conversation with Stephan today," Nantosuelta replied with a smirk. "However, I have seen thousands who were destined to lead and instigate change end up choosing another path. A path that led to disappointment, war, and death."

"Can you tell me more about what Stephan saw?" Maya couldn't help but ask.

"Of course not. Stephan knows that his vision has two possible meanings. You could have been doing something great or something vile. He told you nothing that you haven't heard from me, and what he said is true. He knows you wouldn't be the first to disappoint the gods. In addition, he also knows that you wouldn't be the first to live up to their potential. I am sure he is like me and hopes that you will choose the right path."

"Seems like the gods and goddesses like to be repetitive." A grin spread across Maya's face.

"It's the best way to get you to hear."

Changing the subject, Maya asked, "What is going to happen to me?"

"Today was a sad day for all. It is the first time a Leigheas has killed another Leigheas in well over three thousand years. I take that back; a rogue Leigheas has killed a few from the sect, but those were never public. The difference between the rogue Leigheas and your incident is that yours was purely accidental, and provoked. Many think you had divine intervention, some think you stole Bel's wax, and others think you secretly completed the Turas, became a true Leigheas and killed Angus in retaliation for his attack."

"Right, but what is going to happen to me?" Maya asked again.

"How about we listen and find out?" Nantosuelta suggested.

"How?" Maya hoped she would get the chance to become invisible like the gods.

"There is no Leigheas alive that can see us when we don't want to be seen, except for you, of course. The last Leigheas that remotely had the abilities you do passed well over five thousand years ago. She too could see us lurking in the shadows."

"You say this as though you are surprised. Is it not you who gave me my powers?"

"I have bestowed some to you, and others have also given you gifts, which will be made clear to you in time. However, as I said, it was the land that gave you the bulk of your powers. No matter how much we gods and goddesses know or do, the land is a more powerful force than we could ever be. Now, take my hand and follow my lead."

With a wave of her hand, the clasps binding Maya's hands disintegrated, and Maya took hold of Nantosuelta's hand. The two seemingly disappeared.

"This is how goddesses and gods navigate amongst the living without being seen. You and I are completely invisible. No one can see you, but just as important, they cannot hear you, providing that you don't lose touch of my hand."

"Are you sure there is no one that can see us? I can see you, and we are about to go into a room full of elders. I am sure their powers surpass mine."

"There is another with powers such as yours, but he is not here. Now, shall we?"

Nantosuelta tugged at Maya's hand, and the two made their way up the stairs and watched the elders conduct their trial. Over fifty elders, both men and women, representing many of the clans in attendance gathered around the old pub tables.

Clare, the eldest water elemental, stood and opened the proceedings. "Today we embarked into new territory, with our first female Cluiche contestant in modern times, and witnessing our first Leigheas murder. We need not jump to a conclusion, but—"

"Madam Clare!" Tobias interjected. "There are times where formal conversation is necessary, but now is not it. We need to be swift with our justice. We all saw what happened, and we need to address how it happened." Tobias took a seat, and the majority of Leigheas nodded in approval.

"Agreed," Clare stated. "Sir Ulric, can you help shed light on how this was possible?" The crowd turned to Ulric, the eldest fire elemental of Clan Rangvald, who was slumped over in a back corner, caressing his beard.

"Many are assuming the young lass cheated with Bel's wax. Bel's wax does not disappear from one's skin after use. The only way to free yourself from the wax is to use a chisel to break it off. It also gives the skin an orange tint due to prolonged exposure. So, the questions that we need to ask are: did the guards notice an orange tint, a rough texture to her wrist, or did anyone chisel off the wax?"

Clare turned to the Berserkers at the door and asked, "Was any of what Sir Ulric stated witnessed by either one of you?"

The sinsearach Berserker—the Berserker leader—stepped forward and responded, "No, madam. Her hand that held the fire was pale white and soft to the touch. According to Sir Ulric's criteria, there was no evidence of cheating or foul play."

Clare turned her attention back to Sir Ulric. "We all know that Maya has not completed the Turas. She has become a bit of an outcast with those her age, and even members of her own clan are skeptical of her intentions. With this in mind and the lack of evidence, what do you make of the event? How could she have used his power against him?"

"I need anyone who is not a clan elder to leave now," Ulric demanded as he got up and joined Clare at the front of the room.

Without asking why, the Berserkers and three of the pub workers exited. Ulric did not speak until the door closed and the lock latched firmly in place.

"Though we are all elders, it may not be known to many that the Turas does not grant elemental power." Several nodded while a few seemed in awe of this statement. "We are connected to the earth from the moment of our birth, and it is then that elemental powers are bestowed upon a Leigheas."

"Why has this information been kept from us?" Sebastian, a wind elemental elder of Clan Öberg, asked.

"There was a time that this was common information. It was nothing to see children using their elements while playing with each other. In fact, according to my great-grandfather, it was fascinating to see the child fire elementals playing tag at night. Instead of using touch, they would hurl small balls of fire at each other. Many of my great-grandfather's generation felt that it would be best to deny our youth the knowledge of their powers.

"In part, it was due to the fact that the elders would rather not have emotional prepubescent teenagers, whom they were having problems with, wielding such power without knowledge. By the time my generation came along, we were told over and over that the elements were only granted at the Turas, and so we believed our parents and elders, thus causing our minds to block the use of elements. Those of us who know this have kept it a secret, since the Turas is such a large part of our traditions—not to mention that it did help resolve problems with the younger ones," Ulric replied.

Sebastian then asked, "How does Maya know how to use the power?"

Elen, representing Maya's clan, stood up for her. "With this knowledge, it is no surprise she is able to use one of the elements. Maya may be young, and the oldest Earcach to attempt the Turas, but her knowledge about our ways surpasses many in the room. She has spent her years learning about medicine, tonics, geography, history, smithing, archery, fighting, tactics, and so forth. All of this is clear by her performance so far. I think we need to realize what this event truly signifies."

Clare was puzzled. "Which is?"

"Maya may in fact be a new chosen one." Many of the elders laughed at this.

Angered by the response, Ulric slammed his shillelagh, the symbolic walking stick earned during the Turas, against the nearest table, cracking it in half. The room immediately quieted, and the elders turned to Ulric.

"You are elders in a realm where the impossible is possible, where the supernatural lives amongst the natural. So tell me, why is this theory of a new chosen one laughable? We have no evidence it is not the case." Before Ulric could continue Clare came to his side.

"Calm down and remember why we are here," she whispered into his ear.

"Thank you, Sir Ulric," Elen said. "I am not saying it is definite, but one important detail that may influence you is the flame."

Ulric pondered Elen's words and said, "It was blue and white."

"Go on," Elen insisted.

"Blue-and-white flames are the hottest and can only be created by fire elders. I myself only mastered its use within the past twenty years or so." Ulric was once again stroking his beard.

"Sir Ulric, regardless of what type of flame one creates, I think it is too early to say if there is a new chosen one. A chosen one comes in times of darkness, and there are no signs of this."

"I understand, but there was no call for your poor reactions towards Elen. She had a valid point," Ulric said, taking a seat.

"Let's take a vote." Clare was anxious to move the trial forward. "By a show of hands, who thinks this incident was accidental?" Hand after hand rose in the air, and Maya felt a weight lift off her shoulders. "Anyone believe that this was due to malice or ill intent?" Not a hand was raised. "Since this is an unprecedented event and we find no fault on her behalf, what are some suggestions on how we progress from here?"

"I say we deliver an edict stating her innocence and that Angus's actions, which were dishonorable, provoked his death. However, as a punishment she is disqualified from the Cluiche," Ulric proposed.

"I think this is the right decision," Otis stated, rising from his table. He represented the Roark Clan. "However, my clan will not be pleased that she receives no punishment for taking Angus's life."

"Being disqualified from the Cluiche is a punishment. It is the most prestigious competition we have. She is not only a contender for champion but more than likely *would be* our champion," Clare interjected before Otis could continue.

"I agree." Otis moved around the room, scanning the group. "Angus broke the rules and his actions were dishonorable. If he were alive, then we would be conducting his trial and levying severe punishment. However, this is not the case, and the fact at hand is the young lass still took the life of another Leigheas. There needs to be some punishment, and being disqualified from a tournament, no matter how prestigious, is not a punishment. I do believe that if there isn't a more severe punishment, we risk my clan defecting to start their own region."

Everyone looked at each other in disbelief. Several clans had defected before the reign of Tara the Great due to political differences during a time when Sori was not divided into sect-based regions. A clan defecting over a dishonorable act of one of its own members was unheard of and certainly uncalled for.

"Why do you think defecting will be their response?" Clare asked.

"Angus was the eldest son from the oldest family in the Roark Clan. Regardless of the circumstance, his death is a great loss to the clan. There needs to be a physical punishment or imprisonment, not a mere disqualification," Otis demanded.

Breaking the few minutes of silence, Ina of Clan Hansdotter stated, "Twenty lashes before the audience."

"So, you think the same punishment as a thief is appropriate for taking a life?" Otis thought for a moment. "If everyone agrees with twenty lashes, I will support your decision and smooth it over with the clan."

Another vote was cast, and it was agreed that Maya would receive twenty lashes after the games. As the elders disbanded, Ulric pulled Elen to the side.

"Do you honestly believe that she could be a chosen one?" Ulric asked.

"I do. Our fellow elders fail to realize that a chosen one can come not only during dark times, but also on the brink of them. Maya would be a great choice. She is a leader, warrior, and she is wise beyond her years. To be honest, I hope I am wrong. The last time Sori saw the selection of a chosen one was during the Hundred Year War, and I would rather like to be spared another war of its kind."

"I agree, and I do think it is a possibility. However, it concerns me greatly."

"How so?"

"A chosen one this early could mean that a time worse than the Hundred Year War, a time worse than before the signing of the Covenant, a time that could threaten our very existence is coming. If she is a chosen one, then the darkness is gathering—and its storm will soon be upon us." After a moment, Ulric snapped out of his daydream of impending horrors. Elen peered at him in concern.

"Ulric, I shouldn't have brought up the chosen one before the elders; however, I couldn't just sit by and say nothing as the most promising of our clan was being judged. What you just said has me shaking. If thoughts like these spread to feeble minds, we might inadvertently trigger the dark days. Please, not a word of our talk to anyone else," Elen pleaded.

"Of course," Ulric replied and walked to the cellar door with the Berserkers.

Maya and Nantosuelta had already made their way back down, and while Ulric and Elen met privately, Maya and Nantosuelta did the same.

"You look angered, my child," Nantosuelta said, stating the obvious.

"I reacted naturally. If I didn't react the way I did, then I would be the one people are mourning. Well, since I am a fire elemental it wouldn't have harmed me, but he didn't know that." Maya took a breath and continued, "You get my point. I will not sit idly by and take twenty lashes."

"What will you do?" Nantosuelta was fully aware of what Maya would do. Not because she was omniscient, but because she knew Maya. She knew Maya wouldn't let an unjust punishment pass.

"While the event with Angus was unfolding, I felt as though I had more than one element." Maya's pacing increased in speed.

"What did you feel?"

"I felt a small tremble of the ground, a breeze that almost guided my turn, a sense of calm like the one that a wet rag on your forehead brings, and then I caught the flame."

"The earth let you know that trouble was coming, and the breeze made your motions steadier. Water has the ability to calm or to make one panic, but the moisture in the air can help one feel more relaxed, less anxious, and less confused. Catching the flame made it clear you are a fire elemental—"

"This means I have control of all of the elements," Maya blurted.

"Yes, my child, you do. Now back to my question. What will you do?"

"Thousands of years ago, a fight to the death . . . the troid bás! It was used to prove one's innocence, which is ridiculous since it only proved who was a better fighter. But it was a law that has never been repealed. I can call for a troid bás against the Roark champion."

"Are you sure you are ready for trial by death?" Nantosuelta asked out of concern. She believed in Maya, but a trial by death had gone wrong for many great fighters. Though Maya was powerful, just one mistake could bring about an end to a promising life.

"I am. If my people are going to give an unjust punishment, I will make sure they think twice before handing out any more."

Nantosuelta embraced her in a hug and whispered, "The guards are on their way, but I will be close by, watching. When you finish today, you need to complete the Turas as soon as possible."

The Berserkers made their way down the steps, took Maya by the arms, and noticed that her wrists were no longer bound.

"What happened to your clasps?" the sinsearach asked.

"Sorry, I'm new with these fire elemental powers."

Overstating the obvious, he said, "They were metal."

"If a white-and-blue flame can disintegrate bone, then I am pretty sure it can do a number on metal," Maya responded.

"She has a point," the sóisearach aon said, looking at the sinsearach.

"I am still trying to learn how to control it, and the clasps went up in flames. But don't worry; you two should be fine." Maya's smile stretched ear to ear.

The sinsearach placed new clasps on Maya's wrists and led her up the stairs to the pub where the elders awaited.

Clare, still speaking for the elders, delivered Maya her sentence. "Maya, we have concluded that though your actions were provoked, we cannot overlook the death of one of our own. It has been decided that you will be given twenty lashes at the closing of the games. Do you have anything to say?"

"There will be a time for words, but now is not it."

Clare and many of the others were taken aback at Maya's calm.

Clare hesitated. She thought Maya would argue and had prepared a lengthy spiel in defense of their verdict. Instead, Clare nodded, and the Berserkers led Maya out the door to an isolated area outside the tournament stands. The elders followed them out and picked up the games with the final round of the competition. It took close to half an hour for a champion to be declared, and afterwards two posts were drilled into the ground at the center of the arena. The Berserkers led Maya to the post, bound her arms with leather straps, and tore her shirt, exposing her back.

"Today," Clare began, "we witnessed an unfortunate breaking of the rules and the consequences of that action, resulting in one of the few unnatural deaths of a Leigheas in our time. It has been decided that, as punishment for her part in this ordeal, Maya will receive twenty lashes."

The reaction of the crowd was not of approval or disapproval, but more shock. Murmurs and whispers filled the arena as if everyone were talking with a clear tone. It was a day full of firsts; this would be the first public punishment in modern times. Members of Maya's clan did their best to contain their anger while the Roark Clan did their best to contain their satisfaction. With a nod from Clare, the Berserker reared back with his whip.

Maya, who calmly smiled, heard the whip cut through the air. The ground began to rumble at the Berserker's feet, and as his whip flew forward, he looked down to see a crack form. The crack became larger and larger as it advanced towards Maya. It moved quicker than the whip, and the gash in the ground gave way to a rock the size of Maya's upper body. As it burst through the surface, the rock covered her back, preventing the whip from contacting Maya's flesh. Igniting the leather straps in a ball of flames, Maya incinerated her bonds and broke free. Everyone was in awe.

"I will not be your example! I invoke my right to troid bás and challenge the champion of the Roark Clan!" Maya proclaimed for all to hear. Once again, the crowd was torn. Most had never heard of the troid bás, while others were amazed that Maya could wield two of the four elements.

"The troid bás has not been used for ages, and this hardly seems like the offense that warrants such an extreme challenge to its enforcement," Clare replied, trying to calm the crowd.

"If those are your thoughts, then I recommend you take my place. If you aren't willing to take my place, then you leave me no other choice but to invoke the troid bás. Regardless of its dormancy, it was never repealed and still stands as law. As law, once invoked, it cannot be taken back."

Clare looked down at her fellow elders and then to the Roark Clan. "Otis, choose your champion."

Alick, cousin to Angus, stood and proceeded to the arena without discussion. Two Berserkers met the contenders with a cart full of weapons at the center.

"You may take as many weapons as you like, and you may also use your elements during the match. Do you both understand that this is a fight to the death and that you cannot grant mercy?" the Berserker asked.

"Yes," they both replied. Alick grabbed a sword, shield, and spear. Maya took nothing and walked away.

The two walked to their places, about a hundred paces away from each other. Alick was more of a foe than Angus, standing three inches taller than his deceased cousin with a build of solid muscle. Other than build, the only obvious difference between the cousins was Alick's calm and collected nature. Opposite him, Maya sat cross-legged and appeared to be meditating. The Roark Clan's confidence soared, as did their laughter.

As she meditated, Nantosuelta's voice whispered to Maya, "Be conscious of your elements. Your powers do have limits. The elements are at their greatest near a source, and since earth and wind always surround you, they are your most powerful. Water can be powerful depending upon the amount of moisture in the air, but the water element will be far more effective around a water source, which you will always be able to sense. The same is true for fire. The closer you are to a fire source, the more powerful you will be. However, you can use the wind to enhance its potency."

Maya nodded and was seemingly unaware of the start flag dropping. Alick placed his sword in its sheath, threw the shield around his shoulders, grabbed his spear, and jogged towards his opponent.

He threw fireballs at Maya, but he was too far away, and they missed their target. The ground in front of Maya rumbled as five rocks the size of shields burst out and began circling her. Alick threw fireball after fireball on his approach, but all were halted by the earthen shields circling his opponent. Slowly standing, Maya began twirling her finger, and a whirlwind closed around Alick. With the speed of the whirlwind picking up, Alick could no longer advance, and any attempt at an attack failed. Maya sent the earthen shields back into the ground. As she raised her free hand upwards, sheets of rock erupted from the ground like flat spikes, surrounding the whirlwind. The wind ceased, but Alick was now trapped inside the rock formation. In a desperate attempt to get out, Alick tried to climb the walls, but with no grips or traction, he could not reach the top to escape.

Maya produced a ball of fire and threw it so it hovered atop Alick's rocky cage. She focused her efforts on increasing the effectiveness of her flame and used the wind to enhance its size. The flame grew larger and larger until it was close to eight feet wide and four feet tall. With each passing moment, the flame became hotter and hotter. It was burning blue.

It was then that Maya thrust her hands down, launching the flame into Alick's stone prison. His screams were short lived; death was almost instant. Using the moisture in the air, Maya put out the flame inside the cage, and with a flick of her wrist the rocks disappeared into the ground as quickly as they had come. Without saying a word, she turned and walked to the closest arena gate.

The Roark Clan ran to the ashes of their champion while the crowd remained silent. The elders, as well as the crowd, had witnessed the first Leigheas to hold all four elements in thousands of years.

Elen was right.

Maya was a chosen one, and dark days were ahead.

Chapter 3

The Turas

"Morning, everyone." Maya greeted her family with a breakfast of eggs, biscuits and bacon.

"Morning," they replied.

Andrea looked at the spread and asked, "What is the special occasion?"

"Today, I am going to complete the Turas," Maya happily answered. She then poured everyone their morning cup of tea.

"After yesterday's display, do you think it is wise to make the journey? A journey alone may not be the smartest of decisions. Many from the Roark Clan may want revenge."

"I will be fine. The rules of the troid bás protect the victor. Any harmful act committed in revenge will result in a public execution of anyone involved. You both should trust your daughter more. You should know by now all my actions are well calculated."

"Still, let me or one of your brothers accompany you," Felix said, tearing apart a biscuit.

Andrea sighed. "You know the Turas rules. The journey is one of self-discovery, and company, no matter how welcome it would be, is forbidden." She turned back to Maya. "As I know you are aware of, you are permitted to take three items of any kind. So, what are you going to take with you?"

"Besides camping gear and food, I have packed my sword, Grandmother's shillelagh, and Grandfather's shield." Maya was already reaching for her grandmother's shillelagh hanging above the mantel.

Felix was puzzled at the thought of bringing a shield. As an earth elemental, she didn't need one. "Why the shield?"

"Purely sentimental. I want to feel like a part of grandfather is with me."

Satisfied with the answer, Felix asked another. "When are you off?"

"Now. It will take close to a week to reach Meadarloch." She pulled her camping pack onto her back.

"A week?"

"Well, less if I run, but I would rather walk and enjoy the sights."

"I love the trip to Meadarloch as much as the next person, but you have seen those sights a hundred times or more. With something as important as the Turas, you should get there as soon as possible. Why don't you take one of the horses?" Regardless of Maya's logic, he did not put it past anyone to retaliate after the events at the Cluiche. The shorter the journey, the better.

"I don't want to leave you all shorthanded. This is a busy time of the year."

"Nonsense, your mother and I will feel much better with you on a horse. If you take one, we will still have double what we need for the harvest and timbering. Besides, I can always bother one of your uncles for what I need. You will take Scarlett, and I will not accept no for an answer." Felix stood from the table with biscuit crumbs falling from his beard and headed towards the door.

"But Scarlett—"

"I said not a word!" Maya and Andrea gave him a puzzled look. "You know what I mean. You may be the strongest Ligheas in this house, but you are still under my rules." The family began to chuckle. Everyone knew that when it came to his kids, Felix tended to be a pushover, and it was Andrea who laid down the law of the house. "What? I can be strict," he responded with a smile. "Say your goodbyes and meet me at the barn."

Maya gathered the remainder of her things, hugged the rest of the family, and headed to the barn where she found her father placing her saddle on Scarlett. Scarlett was her father's most cherished horse. Since the first Diana, it had been a Dempsey tradition to give those who completed the Turas a Diana to claim as their own, but this was not the reason Scarlett meant so much to Felix. She was the last gift his father ever presented to him, and she served as a daily reminder of the times he shared with his dad.

"While I finish this, will you go into the back stall and get the silver tin out of the storage chest?"

"Sure." Maya went to the stall and retrieved the tin. She noticed a liquid was inside. Upon her return Maya asked, "Dad, what is this?"

"So, have you ever wondered what makes Dianas so special, besides how they were bred?"

"I didn't realize there was more to them besides the breeding."

"Since Sable, the first true Diana, we give those of the Diana breed an annual allotment of ambrosia. The standard dosage is a gallon or so per year; how often the horse travels will determine how many servings it gets. For me, it's not an exact measurement, so there are times when a horse may get more or less. Some breeders simply give them a gallon all at once. Due to its sweetness, I like to give it to them in small amounts so that they get a frequent treat, which probably adds to my inaccuracy."

Ambrosia was a sweet fruit derived from the lotus tree and harvested by Gaeltacht monks. The fruit contained regenerative properties discovered by one of the monks when he noticed the fruit never spoiled. A single ambrosia berry was placed in gallon-sized wooden barrel, often referred to as "the fountain of youth," filled with water, and allowed to ferment for a year. The drink produced was red in color, had a strawberry-like taste, and bore the name of the fruit from which it was derived. Leigheasan consumed ambrosia several times a year to extend their lives.

"Dad, did you truly want me to know this, or are you just stalling?"

"A bit of both," he chuckled.

Maya wanted to know more. "How are you able to get ambrosia? I thought the monks only dispensed it to the pub owners."

"It is true monks only deliver to the pubs; however, there is no rule or law saying the owners cannot distribute ambrosia as they please. I can get a few barrels each year in exchange for a few horses. It may mean fewer horses to sell at Balla, but it is worth it to keep the Dianas around for a bit longer. Plus, it's not like we need the coins."

The Leigheasan sect was community centered instead of profit centered. They did not charge members of the sect for exchange of non-luxury goods. According to the Leigheasan, an item was considered luxurious if it contained materials or ingredients procured from a non-Leigheas. They did require coins from their brethren sects and the Duine for any type of good, as the Leigheasan were charged for purchasing their items in turn.

In addition to their policy of exchanging coins was the rule of disposable funds. A Leigheas could keep ten percent of their profits to procure more materials needed in the making of their goods. The rest of the coins collected were taken to Seomra, or the central bank, which was operated by the Adelsköld Clan. All transactions were closely monitored and recorded by the Adelskölds, but the Leigheasan were free to take as much as they needed to purchase something that would help the clan or fulfill a need that could not be completed by the sect.

"Last question and then I am gone, okay?" Maya asked, even though she knew her father was not going to say no.

"Sure," Felix replied, still brushing Scarlett.

"Does ambrosia work the same on horses as it does on us?" Maya assumed the answer was yes but didn't know for sure.

"It does. It heals and slows the aging process. Scarlett was presented to me on the day I completed the Turas and looks the same now as she did then. Who knows what will be given to you when you finish." He smiled and gave her a hug.

"Love you, Dad. I will be back soon." She hopped on Scarlett and grabbed the reins.

"Once again, I would say good luck, but I know you don't need it." He gave Scarlett a tap on the hindquarters, and Maya took off.

Each Diana had the same stellar characteristics, but Scarlett surpassed all others. With the ability to outrun any other horse, including other Dianas, and to survive excessive spans of time without stopping for food or drink, Scarlett was the most obvious choice for Maya to ride. In doing so, Maya arrived at Meadarloch in half the time she thought she would. It was just after sunset, and instead of getting a late start, Maya made camp and rested easy with Scarlett on the lookout.

Waking before sunrise, Maya fixed a light breakfast and afterwards led Scarlett into the village. Meadarloch was one of the few villages that had managed to avoid modern remodels and keep its quaint aesthetics. Within Maya's lifetime, many of the Leigheasan clans had remodeled their villages to look like those of the Duine. Wooden post-and-beam-framed houses with white exteriors were replaced with frames and exteriors of brick, stones, or a combination of the two. Its quaint look was perhaps one of the reasons that the relatively small village was one of the busiest in the region. Meadarloch saw many visitors passing through—those seeking escape from daily stress in its hot springs or in hiking up the surrounding mountains, and, of course, those entering the Turas.

However, on this day, the village was all but deserted. Shops were closed, horses were boarded in the village stables—not a soul could be seen. An ominous fog had settled in the village the night before and hadn't passed. The inhabitants, fearing what the fog might bring, stayed safely locked in their homes to wait for its passing. Maya knew most of the old sayings, but she was never one to shy away from superstitious signs, and she walked through town as if it were a sunny day.

At the outskirts of Meadarloch, Maya found the path that led to the Naofa Forest. The walk to the forest took longer than she thought. Finally, though, at the path's end Maya met an elder guarding the entrance. Though appearances could be deceiving, the elder in front of Maya looked as though her time on Sori would soon pass, giving some concern as to why this feeble elder was the only one on guard.

"Quite a display you gave the other day," the elder stated as Maya paused feet from her station.

Unsure of how to react, Maya asked, "Is that a good thing or bad thing?"

"Depends on who you ask. But all of us, especially us women, in Meadarloch were pleased with the way you handled things. It was wrong of the elders to punish you for something that was so clearly defensive. I think it was them trying to discourage women in the future."

Maya was grateful for her words. "Speaking of those in Meadarloch, why are you the only one here? And why are you guarding the forest? There isn't a soul moving in town." Maya looked back towards the empty streets.

"Every day, the citizens of Meadarloch take turns guarding the path," she said. "But my fellow clansmen are silly with their belief in the dreaded fog, the flight of the adar, and so on. I have been on this earth longer than most, and I have never seen an omen come true. Where was I?"

"Why you are guarding the entrance," Maya answered.

"Oh, yes. We guard because we wouldn't want just anyone to enter the forest."

"What happens if a non-Leigheas comes? You don't kill them, do you? I mean, please don't take this the wrong way, but you don't seem up to fighting," Maya jokingly remarked, but she also hoped to hear a crazy tale.

"No offense is taken, my dear. I am far too old to get into a scrap." She pointed to the table that contained a couple of pints and a jug. "We require that all non-Leigheasan consume a cup of forget-me-not before entering the forest. Of course, we don't say it's forget-me-not. We say it will give them the energy to get through the forest and back here safely. It is much stronger than the drink we give out in the pubs. By the time they take their second sip, they are knocked out, and then I ring the bell here." She pointed then to an old rusty bell, like a bell one would use at a homestead signaling food was ready, nested on an old wooden pole. "And the visitors are taken to the inn."

Forget-me-not had become a way for Leigheasan to skew the way
Duines remembered their visits if they had seen too much or asked too
many questions about the Leigheasan way of life. No real harm came to
the person. They would be placed next to a dubh codlata, a black candle
made from various herbs and plant leaves known to cause hallucinations.
Comatose, the person who inhaled the smoke from the candle would
dream of the great time they wished they had.

The key to waking a victim of forget-me-not lay in a powder made
from golden roseroot and black peet. This powder was placed under the
dubh codlata, and when the candle burned down, it ignited the black peet,
releasing the golden roseroot into the air for one to breathe. When the
golden roseroot was inhaled, it awakened the one who was unconscious.
This implanting of false memories kept the Leigheasan way of life secret,
and the visitors left happy despite being bedridden.

"I must say that I would love to sit here and listen to your stories and
wisdom, but I must complete my task. Is it okay for me to pass?" Maya
knew she didn't need permission, but she asked out of respect for the elder.

"Of course, my dear. I would say good luck, but I know you will do
fine." She motioned for Maya to pass and continued with a friendly wave.

"Thank you." Maya entered the forest with Scarlett.

Reaching the clearing leading to the paths for each Turas step took
little time. Even though Maya knew her elemental powers, she started
with the elemental step.

"Okay, girl, I will leave you for now." She pulled out a carrot from the
saddlebag. Pointing at some berries Maya said, "There is plenty of food
for you in the woods here. I will be back when it is over. When I whistle,
come pick me up."

Scarlett bowed her head, and Maya began the mile-long walk to
Nantosuelta's dwelling. Unlike others who came to the goddess's home,
Maya was greeted by Nantosuelta herself, who was sitting on a log next
to the pond.

"It is great to see you so soon, my lady." Maya took a seat next to Nantosuelta.

"Likewise, my child. I was pleased with how you carried yourself yesterday." Nantosuelta paused, turned slightly, and stared off into the wood as she tried to find her next words. "Now, I know I have told you before that I would not see you for some time, but this time I mean what I say. After you leave here, I cannot follow. You need to complete the Turas alone and then rely on your ascenders for guidance."

"I understand, and I greatly appreciate all the guidance thus far. Especially for the guidance before the troid bás."

"I am sure that I have provided more vague references than guidance," the goddess replied with a chuckle.

"Shall I?" Maya stood and pulled a token from her pouch.

"Please," Nantosuelta said as she looked to the pond and waved her hand.

After Maya threw the coin into the water and placed her hand on the altar, the pond began to glow. Four orbs broke through the surface of the water, began circling her hand, and one by one all four elements entered Maya's hand. With the last element accepted, the pond stopped glowing, and Maya turned to Nantosuelta.

"Once again, thank you. I know there is a hint of doubt, with good reason, that I will not live up to your expectations. You can rest assured that I will not be like the others who have failed you. I will make you proud."

"You're welcome, and I hope you will. Now finish what you started." Nantosuelta turned and walked into the pond, vanishing beneath the surface.

Maya returned to the clearing, whistling and juggling small balls of each element. She spotted Scarlett contentedly feasting upon nearby berries and turned to the entrance for the Ascension.

Ascension occurred where an Earcach bonded with the spirit of a Leigheas waiting between the realms of the living and the dead. This bonding was a transformative process that resulted in enhanced physical attributes, and through the Oiliúint step, the ascenders provided knowledge to enhance the Earcach's intelligence. The term "ascension" referred to the "rise" to a better form, but extreme changes to one's body and mind weren't guaranteed. The results were only as great as the number and greatness of the ascender or ascenders making the bond. Some became the brightest and strongest in the land while others received only marginal enhancements.

The walk to the top of Sinsear Plateau was far more strenuous than the path of the elements. Standing before the monolith, Maya formed a small mass of each element and launched them forward to activate it. The portal's glow was not as bright as Maya thought it would be, and the figure approaching her was blurry and difficult to see. Finally, a single female figure came through the portal, but a large mass, a mass too large to be a shadow, trailed it.

"Greetings, Maya. We have waited a long time for you," the ascender proclaimed.

"We?"

"My fellow ascenders and myself of course." The woman turned slightly to her left to reveal the identity of the form behind her. Hundreds upon hundreds of followers became visible. "I am Tara, and this is my legion."

"Tara—" Maya paused. "You mean, Tara the Great! You're Tara the Great?" Maya could not contain her excitement.

Tara was known to history as one of the best rulers of Sori in the old days, prior to the division into regions. She was a brilliant tactician, and she cared for her subjects. Tara was so revered that when she decided to ascend with her three brothers, 24,000 of her subjects ascended with her. Even in ascension she was selfless. She felt that future generations would be best served by dividing the subjects equally with her brothers; however, Tara did take her most trusted and skilled advisors, workers, and soldiers.

"The Great, the Conqueror, the Merciful, the Wise, the Tyrant, the Butcher are all titles that I never wanted nor liked. I tried to rule Sori as fairly as possible, and all the positive accolades that came to me from my reign were accomplished by many that you see behind me. Unfortunately, the one who helped me the most was only in my ranks for a short time and disappeared without notice."

"It's an honor to be chosen by you, my lady."

"From this point on, you will drop the formalities. Call me Tara and only Tara. There is also no need for titles or any other pleasantries."

"Understood," Maya replied, trying even harder to contain her elation at being chosen by Tara.

"Are you ready?"

"For what?" Maya asked, almost forgetting the reason she was here.

"Transference. The process is quick and painless."

"Absolutely," Maya anxiously said. Tara and the rest of Maya's ascenders immediately coalesced into a glowing blue mass. A stream of blue light shot into Maya's chest, and after twenty seconds the transference was complete. *"Tara, can you hear me?"*

"Yes. From now on, all you have to do is think my name, and I will be here for you. Our conversations will occur as quickly as a thought. This will allow us to talk without you appearing to be unusual or mad to onlookers. When we cease talking I will lie dormant, letting you live your life until you call on me again."

"This is incredible." Maya was in awe as she looked at her new physique. Though Maya was in shape, she had lacked muscle definition and tone.

"Your new physique will enhance your strength and endurance, which will aid you in the trials ahead. Now, enough gawking at yourself and on to Oiliúint!"

Oiliúint was one of the more critical steps in the Turas; here one received training in a variety of fields from the ascenders. Anything from weapon training to farming could be taught during this time, determined by the knowledge of the ascenders. One could only leave Oiliúint Village with the blessing on their ascender.

With a newfound energy, Maya ran the entire way to the Oiliúint Village, the village that lay both in Sori and the realm of the ascenders. It defied the concept of time or human needs. A day in the village was like an hour in Sori, so neither sleep nor food were needed. The entrance to Oiliúint was one of the most distinct and unique features in all of Sori. The Arch of Oiliúint was a wooden structure that rose twelve feet, gently curved to cross a ten-foot-wide path, and then descended back into the ground to complete the arch. Many believed the arch was a root to a much larger tree. Others believed it was made by a god or goddess since the structure did not have branches, leaves, flowers, or fruit. Regardless of origin, the structure was magnificent to behold.

Maya's training lasted a few months in village time, but less than a couple of weeks in Sori time. Her knowledge of medicine, weaponry, smithing, and fighting were leaps and bounds ahead of other Earcach. Maya learned how to make ambrosia, forget-me-not, the dubh codlata, and other tonics the knowledge of which was traditionally reserved for elders. She learned about battles that Sori's oral history had long forgotten. Within these battles were valuable lessons of warfare and leadership that would serve one well not only in times of war but also in peace. When all the ascenders were pleased with Maya's progress, Tara gave her permission to seek out Gofannon's challenge in the Tástáil step.

During Tástáil, an Earcach finally met Gofannon, god of the forge and giver of the Turas test. Gofannon could look at a pile of ore and immediately envision the weapon he would create; the same was true when he looked at an Earcach. One look, and he knew how to best challenge the Earcach. The tests were designed to play on one's fears and for the purposes of completing something that would benefit Sori as a whole or just Gofannon himself.

For many, the most intimidating sight was the path heading to Cloch Basin.

The dry, dirt path, the absence of life along the plateau's base, the utter silence, and the giant statues of gods and goddesses created a sobering experience. Such a grim environment could cause the mind to drift and lead one to doubt their own abilities.

Nearing the basin, Maya heard the boom of Gofannon's hammer forging another weapon, and though she passed him on the way to the pond, she kept silent. Despite her stealth approach, Gofannon sensed Tara's presence and intercepted Maya before she could take a seat at the water's edge. Though ascenders were seen by all Faileas Herimen—the Leigheasan, Galenvargs, and Veirlintus—as an aura, gods and goddesses not only saw all who accompanied a Leigheas but also could communicate with the ascenders.

"Tara, my lady, I cannot tell you how good it is to see you." Gofannon stopped just a few feet from Maya. Even more intimidating than the walk in was Gofannon's stature. His long red beard and hair and dark, almost black brown eyes complemented his bulky seven-foot frame in a way that would make the bravest of warriors run for the hills.

"*Gofannon, it is a pleasure to see you. It has been far too long,*" Tara replied. "*If only I had the physical presence to greet you with a proper embrace.*"

"I am just glad to see you once again. It has been so long that I was beginning to think you would never come back, but I must admit that I am surprised to see that you have chosen one of your descendants. Regardless of how powerful the ascender, choosing a relative is rarely, if ever, done," Gofannon said as he looked Maya up and down, contemplating her worthiness.

Maya considered herself an expert on her family's lineage, and Tara was never mentioned as an ancestor. Reading Maya's confused expression, Gofannon realized Maya had not been informed. "You didn't tell her?"

"*No, I was not sure when a good time would be,*" Tara replied. Gofannon was instantly mortified that he let the news slip. Tara comforted him by saying, "*Fret not, my dear Gofannon. You broke no trust here but enhanced it by having another source confirm our relation.*"

"Why wasn't this ever mentioned by the family?" Maya asked.

"*Back in my time, rulers faked lineages to protect the lives of present and future generations. No matter how great a leader one may be, their family is always at risk, so we created false records, and families were sworn to secrecy. Speaking of this was a treasonous affair and punishable by death. My granddaughter many generations down the family tree gave birth to your father."*

"Kiley," Gofannon whispered with a hint of desire. "Such beauty, kindness, wisdom and strength. She was one of the few that I invited back, and I was deeply saddened when I learned of her fall in battle." Gofannon was exposing a side that few of the Leigheasan had seen.

Maya loved hearing stories of her family and asked, "Will you please tell me more?"

Gofannon sat for a moment in silence. "I tell you what, I will extend the same open invitation to you that I gave Kiley, which means you can come back as often and whenever you like, and I will answer all your questions—if you complete the most difficult of tests."

Without hesitating Maya cried out, "Deal!"

"Come with me." Gofannon led her to three posts, each topped with a green glass flame. "These are the remnants of the last three who took this test. Their souls and their ascenders are trapped in these glass prisons until Gilroy, the dark Leigheas, is defeated. After each Earcach was defeated, his pet bird dropped off these reminders."

"One of my uncles was named Gilroy."

Gofannon chuckled and said, "Consider this a day of family reunions." He became more serious as he continued, "Your uncle Gilroy became obsessed with all things macabre and condemned by the Leigheasan way of life."

"Macabre and condemned?" Maya was again baffled. "How can there be a gruesome side to our way of life? We are a nature sect and use what the earth has provided us to live a life of relative peace and harmony."

Tara jumped in for Gofannon, *"When one becomes an elder in the community, it is tradition to spend some time with the Gaeltacht monks to learn about the more unspoken side of our way of life. This unspoken side is referred to as the forbidden, and it can be a dark and vile practice that involves what you see before you—imprisonment of souls—and much more devastating things. The forbidden was established several millennia before my time. Many of these things you will learn in time. Your uncle was shunned from your sect due to his use of the forbidden."*

"Why learn about the forbidden if one is to never use it? It seems a bit counterintuitive," Maya inquired.

"Yes, it seems foolish, and it is true that many will fight the temptation to use what they've learned." Though what she was revealing was traditionally told by the monks, Tara decided to expose Maya to one of the more well-kept secrets of the realm. *"What most don't know is that our world has more than just four sects and one continent. There are hundreds, if not thousands, of other sects in the other continents who have the skills to use the forbidden, not to mention those in the other realms. Those sects and realms may not see things as we do, so we must learn about these dark ways as a preventive measure in case the other sects decide to thrust our entire realm into another inter-realm war."*

"What sects? What war? What realms?" Maya was more confused than ever. Where were these other lands located? Were the other sects like those in Sori, or were they different? How could one reach these other realms?

"I, or the monks, will explain all this in time, but now is not it," Tara replied. *"To be honest, I probably said too much. The monks tend to reserve knowledge of what I just shared with just a select few. Even fewer have seen the tomes containing the history of not just what I have said but much more."*

Gofannon took advantage of the lapse in Tara's thought. "Back to the reason that you are here. Your test is to kill Gilroy." He paused to see what Maya's reaction would be, but all she did was stare at him and look ready for more instructions. "I will provide you with the same knowledge that I gave the others. Gilroy will use the powers of illusions and hypnosis to distract you from completing your task. Once you focus on one of the illusions, you cannot escape its vision. As much as you would like to look away, you will not be able to do so, and death is soon to follow."

"Where do I go?" she eagerly asked.

"To a place you know all too well. At the mountain base of Diabhal's Fiacail is the entrance to his lair. If you are successful, you must bring back his head as proof of your accomplishment. If you are unsuccessful, I fear you will join your predecessors. Either way, you will be returning." Gofannon gazed at the imprisoned Leigheasan.

"I will return whole, not in a prison. You have my word." Maya turned from Gofannon and headed back up the dirt path to get Scarlett.

At the clearing, Scarlett was nowhere to be found. Maya whistled, and a couple of minutes later Scarlett approached. Before beginning the journey, Maya reached in the saddlebag, retrieved what was left of the carrots and fed Scarlett.

"Sorry for leaving you for so long," she said. "We are headed to Diabhal's Fiacail."

With the last of the carrots gobbled up, Maya jumped on Scarlett, and they headed for the mountain. Almost a week's ride was ahead of them, and, determined to complete her task, Maya rode well into each night.

Stopping a mile before the entrance to Gilroy's lair so that he would not hear her approach, Maya left Scarlett to rest, feed and drink from a nearby stream. To remain as silent as possible, she only took her sword and grandmother's shillelagh. In less than twenty minutes Maya made her way to the entrance and soon noticed a flaw in her stealth approach. The moon provided enough light for her to travel outside, but in the cave, Maya would not be able to see her hand in front of her face.

The shillelagh had a concave ball top that made a perfect platform for a torch but would also ruin all element of surprise. Choosing to go with the torch instead of waiting till daylight, Maya placed a flame on top of the shillelagh. To avoid ruining the shillelagh, she created a constant stream of wind between the flame and the shillelagh.

She had only taken a few steps into the cave when a voice called out.

"Who enters my home at this late hour?" Gilroy demanded, but Maya did not respond. "Are you scared to talk? A loss for words? I see you're a fire elemental. So were the last three Gofannon sent, and you know what happened to them, don't you?"

Gilroy's voice became louder and more enraged. "Cast out by my own people for wanting to learn. What is wrong with that? And your dear

Gofannon, sending the Leigheasan youth to attempt a task that he is too afraid to take on himself."

Maya now entered a large room and saw Gilroy on the opposite side. From this distance, Maya could not see much beyond a robed figure. The one discernable detail was his hunched stance. Instead of appearing to be her father's age, Gilroy stood like a grandfather or even great-grandfather. As Maya moved close, she saw his hands flail about and then reach for something inside his robe.

"Now you will pay for your people's betrayal and Gofannon's cowardice!"

Maya threw up a three-sided wall of rock to protect herself and keep her eyes from straying, leaving only her front exposed. Gilroy threw four fís crystals, two to each side of the room, that burst upon contact with the cavern walls. Producing bright green, yellow, red and blue lights, the crystals created horrific scenes of Leigheas Gleann being destroyed. Amongst the pictures came the screams and cries of fictitious Leigheasan victims being slaughtered and tortured. Gilroy continued to yell but was indecipherable with all the sounds emanating from the walls. Maya moved toward her target, the rock barrier moving with her.

"It will take more than two elements to stop me!" Seeing that she was exposed from the front, Gilroy cast out streams of fire that took the shape of serpents and motioned for the serpents to attack. Maya sensed water from a stream running through the caverns and used it to create a wave that circled and smothered the serpents.

This evidence of her control over yet another element threw him off balance. Gilroy was trying to come up with his next trick when Maya unsheathed her sword, and then it was too late. Her sword drove through his neck, severing his head from his body.

Maya knelt by the lifeless body of her uncle. The severed hood from Gilroy's robe became a sheath for her uncle's head. Maya pulled the remains out of the cloth and gazed upon him for the first time. The face was that of an elder who had seen a century of strife. His eyes were glossed over with a white film signaling Gilroy had been losing his eyesight. There was no doubt that her father would not have recognized the man Gilroy had become.

Looking at the lifeless eyes, Mays thought, *You were one of the strongest of us but fought as though you didn't know a thing. Why was it so easy to kill you? Did your frail state hinder your abilities? Did you grow tired of living like this?* She could have spent hours trying to answer these questions, but from the corner of her eye, Maya spotted a creature peeping around a corner, and slowly Gilroy's pet bird came into view. The bird came to Gilroy's side and laid sadly by his corpse. Maya knew from its size and behavior it was an adar gwin.

"There is no doubt you are a loyal bird and will dearly miss your master," Maya said as she placed Gilroy's head in a bag. "I am going to need you to deliver a message for me to a place you have been several times. However, once there you will find a new master, one whom, I'm sure, will treat you even better than your previous master. Or maybe he will set you free. Regardless, I need you to take this to Gofannon at Cloch Basin, please."

Maya tied the bag around the bird's neck, and it slowly made its way out of the cave. Instead of heading back to Cloch Basin, Maya set up camp and rested till dawn. At first light, Scarlett nudged Maya awake, and the two made their way back to the basin.

When she arrived days later, Gofannon was waiting at his forge and waved Maya over.

"I must say, when I saw that damn bird I feared the worst but was most pleased to see Gilroy's head and not another flame. By the way, what did you say to it? The damn thing won't leave." He pointed to the water's edge, where the bird was resting.

"I told him that you might be his new master or you might set him free. The purpose of the adar gwin is to serve, and without someone to aid, the bird will wither and die."

"Really? I did not know that. Of course, that is not a surprise. It has been many a year since these hands have held a book." He looked at the bird, and after a moment he said, "Fine, I will keep him, but if I grow tired of the bird, then he will become your responsibility."

"Not a problem," Maya happily replied.

"Come with me. I have something for both you and Tara to see." They walked over to the glass flame prisons, and to Maya's surprise they were still intact. "In conferring with Nantosuelta, we believe it is best for these ascenders to join their lady."

"*What do you mean?*" Tara asked. "*Are these—*" She fell silent.

"The ascenders that are trapped in these vessels are your brothers and their legions. We know you all felt it was best to divide, but in the times ahead we need you all together."

Tara had no idea her brothers were trapped within the flames and was overcome with emotion.

"*I cannot properly express how grateful I am for you reuniting the legions. My dear Gofannon, I wish I could embrace you as we did oh so many years ago,*" Tara exclaimed.

"You are most welcome, my lady," Gofannon replied, and turning his attention towards Maya he said, "Take this." Gofannon handed Maya a small chisel. "All you will need to do is give it a tap and prepare for transference."

Maya did as instructed, and within a few minutes the transference of the legions from all three vessels was complete. For all the ceremony surrounding these trials, the actual process had been quite simple.

"One last stop before you go on to receive your shillelagh."

Maya was led to the back of the forge where Gofannon kept his private arsenal.

"For those who complete my most difficult of tasks, I reward them with a weapon of choice from my personal collection. However, after I saw Gilroy's head I decided to make a couple for you."

"You made a couple of weapons? It takes our finest smiths weeks to forge a sword of dorcha steel. How did you make them so quickly?" Maya asked in hopes he would reveal a smithing secret.

"I am the god of the forge, so I would hope that I could produce something quicker and of better quality than those who send their reverence." Gofannon brought her two swords shaped in the same cuartha style as her own. However, unlike hers, each sword contained two blades parallel to each other, with small spike-like pieces along the blades' interior.

"They are amazing." Maya was at a loss for words as she inspected her swords. "Please tell me about them."

"To make your swords I used, just like you assumed, dorcha steel, and also Gofannon stones. The stones are stronger than anything you will find in Sori, including dorcha steel. You will never need to sharpen the weapons or find a sharper, stronger and lighter sword in this land."

"I am most impressed with your work, but I am curious about a couple things. Mainly, why the two blades and the stones?"

"I thought you would never ask," he said with childlike enthusiasm. "The extra blade and stones between the blades will make you a destroyer of swords. Your opponents' swords will be caught in between the two blades, and as they pull their swords out, the stones will instantly dull the blade. On their next attack, they will essentially be swinging shiny sticks."

"Thank you. This is incredible." Maya was in awe of her new weaponry. "What prevents my sword from being torn from my grasp once one tries to retrieve their blade? I mean, my grip is strong, but against a more powerful foe . . . the threat of this happening is real."

"I made you these," Gofannon said as he reached for a pair of wrist guards. Admiring his handiwork with a newfound zeal, Gofannon slowly handed them to Maya. "Made from dorcha steel and fused with lodestone, these guards will attach to the base of your sword by using this chain." Gofannon pulled the chain from the guard and connected the clasp to the base of one of her swords. "Just connect the clasp here. If your sword pulls from you, the chain will prevent it from leaving your hand and allow you the time to break your opponent's blade."

"How did you just pull the chain off like that? What makes the chain stay on the wrist guard?"

"Lodestone has a magnetic charge. It will allow for a quick connection to your swords and ensure the chain does not get tangled. After you detach the chain from your sword, you simply coil it back onto your wrist guard.

I would advise you to practice attaching the chains as you unsheathe your swords. Also, you might want to wear these at all times. You never know when a battle might present itself. Now, come this way."

Maya was directed to the path leading away from the basin. Gofannon paused, handed Maya her swords, and said, "You did Sori a service by eliminating Gilroy. On your next trip to Balla, see Sir Barker at the leather shop. He will make you a sheath befitting your swords, but those will do for now. Since I am a man of my word, I offer you the same invitation I gave Kiley. You are free to come back whenever and as often as you like."

"I will." With swords in hand, Maya headed up the path and towards the clearing. "*Tara, are you there?*"

"*Yes, and we are most pleased with your accomplishment. Not to mention my personal delight. Though we parted for the good of Sori, it is good to finally be reunited with my brothers.*" Tara had a newfound happiness in her voice.

"*I can only imagine. What happened today would not have occurred if it wasn't for the training provided by you and the rest of the ascenders.*"

"*You don't give yourself enough credit. You would have done fine with any other ascender, but I am glad I waited to be paired with you.*"

"*Likewise. How about we get my shillelagh?*" Maya asked.

"*Sounds good to us.*" Tara spoke on behalf of her followers, and they were off to the final step of the Turas.

The path leading to Ewan's workshop was the longest. He was the caretaker of the crann na beatha trees and crafter of the shillelaghs that came from their wood. Always aware of an incoming Leigheas, he greeted everyone upon their arrival.

"Congratulations!" Ewan yelled out as Maya was in the homestretch of the path. "I am Ewan, and the craftsman of your shillelagh."

"It's nice to meet you, Ewan. I am Maya."

"Hello, Maya. Come over here and take a seat." Ewan guided her to a bench in front of his workshop. "Have some fruit or a cup of cider."

"Thank you." Maya grabbed a cup and some grapes.

"What do you have in mind for your shillelagh, or are you in need of an idea?"

"I have a good idea of what I want. I would like it to be as tall as me, a ball or bowl at the top like my grandmother's here, and just slightly above it I would like a set of wings surrounding the bowl. I want the body of the staff to twist or spiral. Lastly, I would like the base to be a solid knob. Is that possible?"

"I can see that you have put much thought into this," Ewan chuckled. He grabbed a sheet of parchment, doing a quick sketch. "How's this?"

"Perfect. Absolutely perfect," Maya replied with an expression similar to the one she wore when she first saw her swords.

"Good, I'll be right back." Ewan disappeared though a swinging door and then reappeared with a block of wood six feet long and a foot thick.

"Do you need some help?" Maya hopped off her seat and started around the counter.

"Oh no, despite my short stature, I am as strong as an ox. As you may have heard, I am a bit of a talker, so you may ask a question or listen to me rant."

"How about both? Is it true that you have tasted Gofannon's immortal mead?"

"A story I don't usually tell, but due to your accomplishments today I will make an exception. The answer is yes. Gofannon and I have become good friends over the past . . . let's see . . . twenty millennia. It is a funny story." Ewan laughed as he recalled the day he tasted the mead.

"Go on. I would love to hear," Maya pleaded.

"To start, there is something I must share about me that is important to the story. I am what you would call a demigod. My mother, Nantosuelta, had a relationship with my father, who was a dwarf, hence my short stature. She never told me his name, nor do I want to know. It has never turned out well for a demigod to know their mortal parent. The enemies of the immortal parent typically use that information to torment the mortal side of the family.

"Now, on to the main story. You need to keep in mind that the years blur together, so I cannot tell you the exact year. There was a time in which the inhabitants of Sori worshiped a variety of gods and goddess. However, at some point, the only ones praying and giving reverence were the Leigheasan. Over time the gods and goddess became weak and were on the verge of becoming mortal.

"I was taking a stroll one day and ended up walking to Cloch Basin. Thinking it would be nice to take a swim, I headed for the water. I was some distance off, but noticed there was a body lying next to the water's edge. I didn't pay much attention to it at first; after all, many people sunbathe. The closer I got, the more I could tell that the body wasn't moving. Finally, I reached what I had begun to think was a corpse, but much to my surprise it wasn't dead, nor was it an ordinary body.

"It was massive, far too large to be a Duine or anyone from the other sects. It had long red hair and matching beard. The final clue was his clothing—of typical smithing fashion. By this point, I knew it was Gofannon. Back when this happened, seeing a god was not common, nor did they live in Sori. Some lived above, others below, and many more lived in distant lands. Knowing that, imagine my shock when I saw him just lying there next to the basin.

"As a half breed, I have the best of both worlds and none of the drawbacks. I am immortal but can live among any sect without exposure of my identity and have no need of prayers or reverence. Though Nantosuelta is my mother, we are not in frequent contact. We tend to meet once every decade, give or take a decade or two. It was not until I saw Gofannon that I realized the gods and goddesses were in what you would call bás doras. I did the best I could to roll him over, but all I managed to do was get him on his side. However, the movement did wake him, and Gofannon reached for a drinking pouch on his belt. I unbuckled it and gave him sips. In no time, the giant was back on his feet."

Maya leaned back and relaxed into the rhythm of the story. Ewan's words brought it to life in her mind's eye.

"Thank you, my little friend," Gofannon said, sitting up.

"Not a problem. What's in this stuff?" Ewan asked, curious as to what could bring someone close to death back to life so quickly.

"It's an enhanced version of the Leigheasan drink ambrosia. To us, it provides a boost of energy and nothing more. In an hour or two, I will need to take another. Perhaps more than just one drink is needed," he replied. "I am Gofannon, and I am forever in your debt."

"Ewan is the name, and I may recall a favor one day." Ewan immediately considered what he might be able to use Gofannon for.

"Nantosuelta's boy? It is good to finally meet you. She and I are great friends, and she speaks of you often—fondly, I might add."

"I hope you don't mind me asking, but what happened?"

"I was at my forge and started to feel dizzy. At first it felt like I was losing my balance, but it was my home. It was tilting to one side as it began falling out of the sky. I was so dizzy that I couldn't find anything to hold on to, and the next thing I knew, I was falling towards the ground. Although I tried to aim for the water, as you can see, I missed."

"What could cause this? Is it the doing of another god or goddess?"

"No, there is not a god or goddess that would be able to bring down my home. Most don't even know how to contact me. No, this is due to the people losing faith in us. Our power is fading. If enough stop paying respect, then we will become mortal and no different than those we once served," Gofannon grimly said and sat there solemnly. It appeared as though he was pondering what would become of him.

"It's hard to believe that the people have lost so much faith. After all, you and your brethren have spared them from so much."

"Believe it or not, this isn't the first time. The last time brought about the War of the Gods, as we call it, which was the most destructive war that took place in this realm. I must say this does seem worse than the last. At least then we were fighting for the right to be worshiped." With each word his tone grew heavier with sadness.

"You know, my mother told me a story some ages ago about the drink of the gods, the deoch de déithe. It was created as a failsafe in moments like these. If you drink it, you will retain all your powers and remain immortal forever."

"That is just a tale we made up to make those of the land believe that they could never be rid of us. A tactic to ensure praise due to the fear of repercussions."

"Give me more credit than that. I am sure I can decipher which tale is true and which is false, especially when it comes to the topic of the wrath of the gods. If you combine ambrosia with the root of the crann na beatha tree, leaves of the lotus tree, and the feabhas a chur berry, you will have a drink that will produce the same effect as the deoch de déithe."

"How so?" Gofannon asked with a more excited tone.

"The leaves of the lotus tree are much more powerful than its fruit. The lotus leaf will provide the aspect of immortality. The root of the crann na beatha provides strength and the retention of all your powers. The feabhas a chur berry will deliver these to all parts of your body and bind them to your system, thus always making them a part of you."

"Do you think this could really work?"

Ewan could tell he had convinced Gofannon to hope.

"It is worth a try. If it works for you, then it will work for the others."

Ewan stopped working and turned towards Maya.

"It took us several days to get the ingredients needed, and we returned to my home to brew up the drink. I combined all the ingredients, and the immortal drink was born. I named it after the man who inspired its creation, and it has hence been named Gofannon's immortal ale."

"How did you know it worked permanently? And why do you let Gofannon take the credit for your drink?" Maya asked.

"As you know, Gofannon has created his signature stones, the toughest of any kind. You have no idea what power is like until you see him forging those stones. Think about it; it takes time, heat and pressure for rocks to form, and Gofannon can achieve this in a matter of minutes."

"I'm sorry, but I fail to see the connection."

"I'm getting there."

Ewan smiled to such an extent that Maya knew he enjoyed dragging the story out.

"Gofannon has proved his greatness in creating something that nature was not able to do. In turn, a drink that is able to breathe life into the gods must also contain a certain greatness. So, in my opinion, the drink is worthy of the name Gofannon, and I am happy that he gets the credit. All know of Gofannon. Only the Leigheasan know of Ewan, and that is the way I want to keep it. Being relatively unknown allows me to travel and do things that I would not be able to if I were recognized by all the sects. Now you are the only one besides Gofannon and myself who knows the ingredients, so mum's the word."

"Not a word, I promise."

"As for your other question, time has told that the effects do not wear off. I made plenty of the drink and have it stored here just in case another dose or two is required."

Maya largely accepted Ewan's story, but she was curious about one thing.

"One more question."

"Of course."

"I don't want you to think that I am insulting your intelligence, but it seems as though the ingredients for the drink could be fairly common knowledge. How have others never created such a drink before?"

"Good question, and there is no offense taken. I am unlike most in that I have read everything in the monks' archive, so I have a bit more knowledge than most that will ever walk this land. Even the gods do not know where all of the items are located. For example, before the Turas, the members of your sect had never heard of the crann na beatha tree, and none of the gods knew its powers."

"I find it interesting the gods are truly not all knowing."

"Well, to a degree they are like mortals. They specialize in a certain area and focus on that field. All the other things are left up to another god. Simply put, they are oblivious to matters that don't pertain to them. Here you go," Ewan said, handing Maya her shillelagh. "What do you think?"

Maya was overjoyed at the way it turned out. "I don't see how this could be any better. Thank you so much, and thank you for trusting me with your story."

"It was my pleasure, and feel free to stop by anytime. I love company but sadly only see it when someone completes the Tástáil."

"I will, and thank you again." Maya leapt from her seat and headed back down the path to find Scarlett. Scarlett was waiting patiently for Maya's return, and the two journeyed back home to give her family the news not only of her success, but also of the death of Gilroy.

CHAPTER 4

Celebration and Signs of Things to Come

A rriving home, Maya jumped off Scarlett and ran inside yelling, "Mom! Dad!"

"Welcome home!" Andrea cried as she embraced Maya. "We are so proud of you!"

"Thanks, Mom, but I am not sure you will be once I tell you what I had to do." Maya was quick to tone down her happiness.

"Gilroy?" Felix took a seat at the table. Maya gaped at him.

"How did you know?"

"Over the course of the past couple of decades, our sect has seen the disappearance of several Earcachs attempting the Turas, which only happens if there has been a death. Those Earcachs who never returned were amongst the strongest to attempt the Turas, and since Gilroy has been such a menace to our realm, it was rumored that Gofannon sent them to eliminate Gilroy. Assuming that Gofannon only sends the strongest to kill Gilroy, then it was safe to guess that he sent you as well," Felix explained.

"Dad, I killed your brother. Aren't you upset or mad?" Surely he felt some emotion.

"Yes, Gilroy and I were close at one point. Yes, we shared many good times in our childhood and early manhood. But Gilroy lost his way, became consumed with his obsession for all that has been forbidden, and took pleasure in making people suffer. He eluded justice and became the only one to escape the Berserkers. He needed to be punished for his crimes."

Felix gazed out at nothing. Maya and Andrea knew that Felix missed his brother and deep down he desired to see Gilroy one last time—one last visit with the brother that he recalled fondly, not the Gilroy that Sori had come to despise.

Maya's curiosity was growing. "How did he do that?"

"A story for another time, but be assured that I am not angry, disappointed, or anything else. I lost Gilroy long before you came into this world," Felix replied, waking from his daze.

"Dad, I mean no disrespect, but now is the time for me to know. Too often do I hear someone say, 'A story for another time' or 'You're not ready to hear the story.' People dance around and pretend things never happened. I shouldn't have to be an elder to know what he did. It is apparent that we have a dark stain on our family, and I don't even know what happened. Now, it may not look like it, but I am having a hard time dealing with this, so now is the time," Maya pleaded with her father. It was one of the few occasions Maya had asked her family for something.

Felix looked at Andrea as if to ask permission—as if it were Andrea's story and not Felix's. She nodded, placed some bread and meat on the table, and took a seat beside Felix. Clearing his throat, Felix began the tale. "Gilroy became an elder at a young age. Not as young as you, Maya, but young nonetheless."

"I just completed the Turas, so I am pretty sure that I will not obtain elder status for some time," Maya said without thinking.

"Trust me, someone with your gifts will be an elder sooner than you anticipate." Felix turned his attention back to the story. "Now, it was shortly after his elder declaration that he visited the monks and, like all of us elders, learned about the forbidden. Most think that all things forbidden are dark practices, but that is not true.

"There are many things that have been deemed forbidden that are harmless in nature but have great potential for misuse. Things that can bring about great harm not just to others, but also to one's self. For example, shapeshifting can be achieved by almost any Leigheas. During shapeshifting, the ascenders alter the body to give it a new look that can be sustained for lengthy periods. If misused, shapeshifting can be implemented in the most disastrous of ways. One could shift into a general or a ruler and lead a rebellion or declare war for personal gains. Of course, history provides the example, as the power was used to lead a rebellion against Tara the Great."

"*Tara, is that true?*" Maya asked.

"*Very much so. It led to one of the deadliest wars of my day. Unfortunately, I must tell you what you don't like to hear: The story will have to wait for another day, and for now you must pay attention to your father,*" Tara replied.

"Shapeshifting also does a considerable amount of damage to the body," Felix continued. "The skin, muscle, bone structure, joints, they are all twisted, moved, and changed to such a state that it causes irreparable damages. One will age faster and potentially become permanently disfigured if used frequently enough. Many people believed that Gilroy was a shapeshifter. If so, I cannot imagine what he looked like before his death. For these reasons, shapeshifting was forbidden many ages ago.

"What is presented to us by the monks is only a brief overview of the forbidden. An overview that allows us to recognize the use of the forbidden and defend ourselves against the most basic of its attacks. Amongst the methods presented are how to defend against mind control, how to repel lightning strikes, how to save someone from soul taking, and a few others."

"How can one control lightning?" Maya asked, wondering why wielding a force of nature would be forbidden. Leigheasan did so every day.

"To wield the power of lighting, one must ignite the electrical charges in the air, much like how we use our elements. We can defend against this by using our elements to break the charges near us so that the lightning does not harm us. The problem with lightning is that it is uncontrollable. You may only intend to harm one person, but the strike can reach dozens, and so it was forbidden. Gilroy became obsessed with the forbidden. Thirsting for more knowledge, he returned to Gaeltacht several times, and on each occasion, he was misdirected by the monks."

"How so?" Maya followed her question with another. "Aren't the monks supposed to assist with our needs?"

"Yes and no. The monks do assist us in what we want to know but use their discretion to determine what we truly *need* to know. Once the tutelage regarding the forbidden is complete, the monks do not like further probing into the subject."

Though Felix always answered Maya's questions, her interruptions were diverting him from his story. "One of the many things for which I am proud of you is your desire for knowledge and your determination to find answers through asking questions. But if you don't stop asking them, I will never finish this story.

"The monks' archives dive much deeper into the knowledge of the practice. Knowing this, Gilroy spent months digging through massive tomes in vain. It took some time for Gilroy to realize that the monks were showing him useless information, so he began searching through the collection on his own. Finally, after a year of constant searching he came across the Book of Damanta.

"Before Gilroy, the only ones who knew of this book were the monks. Our sect had no desire to know more about the forbidden. Since Gilroy's discovery, the book has become well known, and its myths have spread like wildfire. Gilroy did a brilliant job at spreading many of the rumors, some of them very entertaining."

He almost chuckled at his next thought.

"The greatest of tales is that it is made from the flesh of those that practiced the forbidden, its pages inked in the blood of their victims. The simple fact is that all the books in the archives are written by the monks, who use a parchment made from thin slices of crann na beatha trees.

"Some say that the book isn't truly a book but a diabhoil. The story of the diabhoil is one you need to read, but the short version is as follows." Felix grabbed a chunk of bread, sliced it open, placed a slab of meat in between the two halves, and began eating. "The diabhoil, practitioners of the forbidden, sought a way to be immortal, so many of them took the form of a book so that their deeds and knowledge would carry on forever. Now, keep in mind, several diabhoil books are rumored to exist, but if the monks did happen to own a copy, it would be locked away and guarded. A diabhoil is far more dangerous than the Damanta or any other book containing knowledge of the forbidden.

"What is true is that Gilroy found the Book of Damanta, which contains all the secrets behind the forbidden and only the forbidden. Among the secrets is the one that helped Gilroy escape the Berserkers.

"Gilroy left our village for a new life in the mountains. Several months after leaving, villages in our sect, and those of both the Veirlintus and Galenvargs, reported members vanishing while they were hunting or during the night." As Felix swallowed the last of his snack, sadness rushed over him.

"The disappearances increased dramatically in such a short time span that abduction was the only logical explanation. A meeting of our sect's elders was called. It did not take the Leigheasan elders long to agree it was Gilroy. At the same meeting, the elders agreed to send a group of Berserkers to eliminate the menace. Typically, the moment Gilroy left he would have had the Berserkers on his trail, but no one knew that Gilroy was abandoning our sect. The elders assumed he was simply going off to the woods, much like many of us do."

Felix waved toward Maya as she was a prime example of one spending days in the woods.

"I have my theory as to what happened next, but it is not certain. The Berserkers never returned, and Gilroy thereby accomplished something that no other Leigheas had before: escape the wrath of the Berserkers. Fearful of losing anyone else to Gilroy, the elders did not make any more attempts on his life, and he was left alone to a life of solitude in the mountains."

Maya could tell he missed his brother.

"One last question, if you don't mind."

"Go on."

"Why was my test so easy? Perhaps easy isn't the word, but Gilroy killed so many. Yet our fight, if you even want to call it that, lasted a matter of moments."

"As I mentioned, certain practices of the forbidden take a toll on the body. He might have aged and weakened considerably over the years, though still a formidable foe for the majority in our sect. Your seemingly easy triumph was credit to your training, powers and sheer determination. Whatever tainted our name is now restored by your actions. I will always have fond memories of my brother, but I am forever proud of what my daughter has accomplished, and will. You should not fret over the death of Gilroy. His passing marks the end of a troubled life and the beginning of a promising one."

Felix rose and hugged Maya.

"Now, tell us about your new hardware." He unsheathed her sword.

Maya told her tale, and her parents looked on in amazement at the feat she had accomplished. Never doubting what their daughter was capable of, as parents they never would have imagined Maya taking on such a task. The last thing they wanted was to receive a message relaying her early passing.

"So, what now?" Felix asked.

"I am off to Balla to visit Sir Barker at the leather shop. He will be making me a sheath fitting for the swords."

"Don't forget your robes!" Andrea hollered as she left the room to get more drinks.

Every Leigheas had two robes, one formal and one informal, from the tailor. The informal robe was brown and unmarked to help Leigheasan blend in with the rest of society. The formal robe, black with a sash bearing the element insignia on the left and the wearer's clan crest on the right, was traditionally worn at celebrations, weddings, elder meetings, and other Leigheasan events. Each element symbol was slightly different: fire was $\triangle$, water was ▽, wind was ▽, and earth was ▲. Each sash reflected the color of the elements: red for fire, blue for water, white for wind and brown for earth. If one possessed all four elements, then the sash was purple, though such a circumstance had never occurred in the lifetime of any living Leigheas.

"I won't!" Maya yelled as she left the house. She jumped onto Scarlett and rode off to Balla.

Balla was filled with shops and businesses; all sects were booming. The Leigheasan shops differed greatly from those of the other sects. Their businesses and clan trades were based off their customs and family traditions, whereas the other sects were purely profit-based. The Galenvargs primarily sold the finest furniture and provided some of the best furs for their customers. Though a few Galenvarg families dominated certain trades, no family tradition surrounded the business.

The Veirlintus specialized in high-end clothing and lavish handcrafted jewelry, while the Duine sold anything that would make a coin. A profit motive saw many clans gain riches, but it was the Leigheasan quadrant that saw more coins exchanged for goods than any other.

With a desire to serve and take pride in their work, the Leigheasan sought minimal profits from their patrons, and in doing so they secured repeat business. The Barker, Dane, Elmer, and Forester clans were the first to establish shops in Balla and, for the most part, any Leigheasan village. The Barkers were leather workers, the Danes were tailors, the Elmers owned the pubs, and the Foresters worked with all that was wood. Others owned shops, but these trades were essential in Balla.

Many of the Duines would procure furs from the Galenvargs and then take them to the Danes to tailor an outfit. In the winter the Danes and the Barkers worked in conjunction with each other. The Duines' frequent purchases of Leigheasan goods not only benefited the Leigheasan businesses but also benefited the sect socially. Leigheasan had an easier time blending in with Duines who purchased Leigheasan-styled clothes, drinks, and shillelagh knockoffs.

Maya arrived in the Leigheas quadrant and quickly made her way to Barker's shop.

"Sir Barker, are you in?" Maya asked, coming through the door.

"Just one minute; I am finishing an order!" Sir Barker yelled from his workroom. "Feel free to walk around and take a gander at the products. If you don't see something you need, there is a pen and parchment on the counter. Just write down what you need, and if you're an artist, provide a picture."

"Thank you, will do."

Maya walked around the shop and looked at all the items on display. Saddlebags, sheaths, boots, belts, jackets, and gloves decorated the walls. She continued to kill time by trying on clothing, and though Maya tended to make her own, she knew she would be back to procure a few of the items.

It took Sir Barker half an hour to finish his work, but he came out chipper as ever.

"Sorry for the wait, but I am shorthanded this week while my sons are finishing some business in Frith. I was finishing an order for—" He paused when Maya came into view. "For you, actually. It is nice to finally meet you, Maya."

"Sir Barker, it is a pleasure. You have an incredible shop, and your craftsmanship is second to none," she remarked, taking another glance at the walls.

"Thank you. The craft has served my clan well over the years, and please drop the formalities. Call me Tomas or Barker. I must be honest, I have not had the time that I would like when taking on an order of this significance. It was a bit of a rush order, but I think you will be pleased."

"There was no need for a rush," Maya interjected.

"My apologies for the rudeness. I did not wish to imply your impatience, but Gofannon requested that I work nonstop till I finish. I never wish to disappoint a customer, and this especially holds true when it comes to a god or goddess."

He placed the two sheaths on the counter, and they were as magnificent as her swords. Sir Barker got distracted at his own handiwork and stayed silent while he stared. Finally he spoke.

"Your swords are rather unique and required the use of dorcha steel as the sheaths' interior, which was supplied by Gofannon. Any other material would quickly fall apart against the blades. The dorcha steel will not only withstand the contact of your sword, but will also sharpen your blades each time they are sheathed and unsheathed.

"The design on the leather mirrors that of your shillelagh. Iron wings circling the top and joining to form the belt loop. An iron knob, not very large, at the end, and lastly two columns of knotwork intertwining on the front and back. The final touch is two new belts that match. They have the same intertwining knotwork as your sheaths, and both have wing clasps to lock the belt in place."

"These are amazing. How did you know what my shillelagh looked like?" Maya asked as she held and examined the sheaths.

"Ewan came with Gofannon's message as well as his drawing of your shillelagh. I will trade you for your old sheaths so that you can try on the new," he said, extending his hands.

"What do you think?" Sir Barker asked as Maya buckled the second belt.

"You have done a marvelous job! I cannot tell you enough how thankful I am. Please, let me compensate you somehow. How much can I pay you?" Maya reached for her satchel.

"I appreciate your offer, but even if I were to collect a fee, the bill has already been settled. Gofannon was so pleased with the outcome of your Turas completion that he compensated me for far more than what the bill would have been. Now, don't be a stranger around here, and enjoy the rest of your time in Balla." Sir Barker turned back to his workroom.

"Thank you, but if it isn't too much trouble, can I bother you for another order?"

Sir Barker stopped, turned back to Maya and happily answered, "Of course. What else can I do for you?"

"I have been spending more time on a horse as of late. In fact, I have spent more time this week on a horse than I have spent my entire life and I have found that it takes a toll on the hands, especially when riding a Diana. So, I was wondering if you would make me some gloves, but I need them dyed black to match my armor."

"That is not a problem. Give me your hand." Sir Barker grabbed Maya's hand and jotted down her measurements. "I have some extra help coming in the shop today, so I think we can get you what you need in just a few hours."

"Thank you, and I will see you soon." With her new sheaths by her side, Maya walked out the door.

She suddenly felt dizzy and her head began to ache. Feeling as though she might faint, Maya sat on a nearby bench. Her vision blurred as she gazed out into the street. The people all looked like moving black masses. Her hearing began to compensate for the dimming of her vision, but her lightheadedness only worsened. Horse hooves sounded like thunder, people sounded like they were screaming. Maya heard two voices yelling her name.

"Maya? Are you okay? It's us . . . Carolin and Ele." The voices belonged to Maya's childhood friends, the twins.

"I'm sorry, just give me a minute, and please stop yelling." A sense of relief overcame Maya, knowing it was friendly voices calling out.

"We weren't, but we will tone it down if you need," Carolin replied a bit more softly.

"I don't know what has come over me. I just can't see. I'm dizzy and my hearing is much more sensitive. I have never felt like this before."

"Carolin, go get her some water." Ele pointed to a pitcher on a table outside their family's restaurant. "Maybe it's exhaustion catching up with you. These past few weeks have been more eventful than you are used to."

"Perhaps," Maya said, but she knew this had nothing to do with fatigue.

Just as Carolin arrived with the drink, Maya's vision returned, and she regained her balance. It was a strange sensation that she hoped wouldn't return.

"Here you go." Carolin handed her the glass. "How are you feeling?"

"Much better now, thanks." She took a few sips. "How have you two been? I haven't seen you in a year or so."

"Three, but who's counting. We are the same as ever, but we are settling down soon, so you will have to come to our union ceremony," Carolin answered for Ele.

"Of course, I will, and thanks again for the drink. I have to order my robes. Will you join me?" Maya politely asked but hoped the two would decline her offer. Though at one time the three of them were close, they had grown so far apart in their teenage years that they were practically strangers.

"Sure," they both replied.

On their way to Dane's haberdashery, the twins talked as if the years apart had only been a day. They told tales of Maya serving as their protector against boys, one of whom was going to marry Carolin. Carolin recalled that her fiancé, Quintus of Clan Fisser, once threw mud pies at the twins. Before he could strike Maya, she was on top of him, pummeling him with an alternating series of left and right hooks to the face.

The stories continued as Maya placed her order, and, not wanting to leave Maya, the twins asked her to join them for a quick lunch. Even with a change of venue, the twins carried on their tales of the past. It came to a point where Maya tired of reminiscing, said her goodbyes, and made her way back to Barker's shop to pick up her gloves.

"Sir Barker, it's me again!" Maya called out as she entered.

"No need to wait this time. I have them ready for you." Sir Barker placed the gloves on the counter.

"Thank you," Maya responded while trying them on. "They are still warm. How did you get the dye to dry so quickly?"

"We have a process like the one used with smithing."

"How do you know about smithing techniques?"

"Though we are ages apart, we share the same teacher. Which reminds me that I need to give you this. Consider this and the gloves part of the original order." Sir Barker handed over a jar filled with a black substance.

"What's this?" Maya took hold of the jar.

"Dye for your sheaths. Just place a couple of coats on them before bed. By the morning they will be dry, and will match your armor and gloves. Not that I am in a rush, but is there anything else I can do for you?"

"No, this is plenty, and once again, thank you."

Maya was finally ready to leave Balla and start the trip home. Making good time, the trip was typically just a few days, but Maya wanted to regain her strength and so took her time getting back home. Just over a week after leaving Sir Barker's haberdashery, Maya arrived in Dempsey Village.

Walking through the door of her home, Maya was surprised to find nobody around. She went out to the barn—still not a soul to be found. Maya decided to make the quick trip to the village square. Maya soon discovered the village was a ghost town. She found the streets, shops and homes to be as empty as her family's.

As she turned onto the village square, she was greeted by everyone in the village, tables of baked goods, firepits cooking various meats, and friendly games for all ages.

Maya had been so busy since finishing the Turas that she had forgotten about the Cèilidh celebration that traditionally followed. Her family was joined by everyone in the village, who stopped what they were doing to give their congratulations. After half an hour of hugs and shaking hands, she was finally able to sit, relax, and enjoy a well-earned meal with many of her childhood friends. They laughed, told stories and planned the years to come.

The celebration was short lived, at least for her. Another dizzy spell overcame Maya, and she excused herself from the others, moving to the outskirts of the festivities. She felt as though someone was watching her, and as she scanned her surroundings she spotted a dark figure pass behind the crowd. It kept popping up between the shoulders of the villagers, and everywhere she turned the figure was there. It was just far enough away and just quick enough that Maya could not tell what it was.

Maya called out to Tara. "*Tara, are you there?*"

"*Of course.*"

"*Do you feel this or see that figure?*" Maya inquired while following the figure with her eyes.

"*Yes, but I am not sure what or who it is.*"

"*Can anyone else see what is going on?*" Maya hoped that she wasn't going crazy. No other villager seemed to react to the figure. "*Why isn't anyone else seeing this?*"

"*I believe you are the only one, and I am certain that it doesn't know you can.*"

Maya was still confused about what was happening. "*How is it possible that I can see it?*"

"*I can only speculate, but I am assuming it's either because you survived the encounter with Gilroy or because you have the most powerful ascenders with you. However, there is a distinct possibility that you have been bestowed a host of powers that we don't know about just yet. To know what these figures are, we need to consult with Malaki. He is here with us. He is the most knowledgeable in matters of the forbidden and things from other realms. Please, call on him.*"

"*Malaki, may I speak with you?*"

"*Of course, my lady. What can I do for you?*" he asked, instantly coming to Maya's aid.

"*Do you see this figure off in the distance, behind the crowd?*" She once again motioned with her head and eyes.

"*Oh yes, yes I do. I hate to tell you, but that isn't just one figure,*" he gravely replied.

"*How can you tell?*"

"*By the speed and direction that they are moving. One second the figure is at the back of the crowd to the right; the next, it's at the front to the left,*" *and then it pops up in the middle of the crowd. If one being were that fast, you wouldn't see it at all. There have to be several."* Malaki paused and then muttered, *"I must say, this is not good. Not good at all."*

"What are they, and do they mean harm?" Maya reached for her sword.

"No, they are completely harmless for the time being, but it is a sign that harm will come." Malaki's voice grew a bit more relaxed as he continued, *"What you are seeing are scouts."*

"For the time being?" Maya still had her hand on her sword.

"Yes, as a scout they can do no harm. They can only watch and report; however, their master is a different story."

Maya still did not have the answers she wanted. *"Despite the name being a dead giveaway, what is a scout exactly?"*

"You see, Duine souls can remain earthbound after their body passes. The reasons for this have always been speculative, but it is a popular belief that the person has unfinished business, so they refuse to move on to the afterlife. They can obtain ascension but cannot do so without the guidance of a Leigheas. When a soul is approached by a Leigheas, they become a scout and must do various deeds to prove they are loyal to the Leigheas and worthy of ascension. Once the Leigheas believes they have fulfilled their duty, the Leigheas will guide them to ascension."

"Who else amongst the sect knows about scouts, and what do you think the scouts want?" Tara stepped in and asked.

"There is only one type of Leigheas that will attempt this process, and it is one who practices the forbidden. Gilroy was the only known Leigheas to actively practice the forbidden. Now that he is out of the equation, I think there is another Leigheas who has replaced Gilroy. What do they want? I am not sure. Maya, will you take us to higher ground?" Malaki politely asked.

"The highest here is the watchtower. Will that do?" Maya asked as she headed in that direction.

"Oh yes, that will do just fine. I just need something above the surrounding buildings with a fairly decent line of sight," Malaki replied.

Maya was stopped by her mother. "Maya! Where are you running off to? You shouldn't be leaving your own celebration. The clan has done so much in preparation. It is highly disrespectful, and many of the elders may take offense."

"I will be back, but I need to take care of something really quickly." Maya tried to pull away from her mother.

Andrea was more than concerned that something was wrong. Still holding on to Maya, she asked, "Is everything okay?"

"I am not sure." Maya broke free. "I will explain later!"

The watchtower wasn't the tallest of towers, but it was about a story above the other buildings and provided an excellent view of the surrounding regions. When Maya reached the top, she gazed out onto the countryside and saw what seemed like hundreds of shadowy dots dashing to all Faileas Herimen regions. They also looked to be scampering into Cala, but it was hard to determine at such a low height. She turned to look at areas of the Gleann, and it was the same story. Numerous scouts bounded outward in the direction of other villages.

"*This is not good,*" Malaki whispered. "*With numbers this high, it means they are gathering intelligence.*"

"*What type?*" Tara asked.

"*I would say population numbers, but, to be honest, I am not certain,*" Malaki replied.

"*Malaki, why is it that I can see the scouts and no one else can?*" Maya asked.

"*You are one of Nantosuelta's chosen ones. She has granted you powers that are beyond that of a typical Leigheas. None of us know all of the powers you have, but they will appear when the time arises.*"

"*Wait, I thought Nantosuelta couldn't grant powers? She said the earth grants the elemental power, not her.*"

"*That is true, but she never said that she couldn't grant others. And there is a good chance that you have powers that even she is unaware you possess. Nantosuelta is also modest and arguably the most powerful of the gods. It has always been my understanding that if she wanted to give you elemental powers, she could easily do so.*"

"*There is much that our sect does not teach.*" Maya took a moment to process the information she had just received. With all her thoughts in place, Maya was surprised that her ascenders failed to mention the obvious, so she said, *"If it takes someone with my power to see a scout, then we may not be looking at a Leigheas."*

"What do you mean?" Tara asked.

"Let's assume that only a Leigheas with all four elements, a chosen one, or one who practices the forbidden can see a scout. I am the only known Leigheas to wield all four elements and, apparently, the only chosen one, or at the very least the only known chosen one. The only one known for practicing the forbidden is deceased. However, someone is not only able to see the scouts but can also get them to obey. Based off our assumption, I am the only one who can achieve this."

"Very astute observation, Maya."

Though Tara was wise, she was lost in Maya's train of thought and stated, *"I am missing your connection, Maya."*

"I am the only known person in Sori that should be able to control the scouts, so there must be someone not from here controlling them," Maya clarified.

"That could be right, Maya, but you should not discount someone from the other sects just yet. The forbidden can be practiced by anyone, and I doubt anyone from the other sects will openly practice the dark arts. The Veirlintus have been known to dabble in the forbidden, and I am certain that the Galenvarg have flirted with it as well. Before we jump to someone not of the realm, you need to keep in mind that just because we don't know of something happening doesn't mean that it is not being practiced. With that said, I also need you to be on guard for anything that may seem supernatural," Malaki said.

"More supernatural than Galenvargs and Veirlintus?" Maya asked.

Though Malaki knew she was joking, he answered, *"Just a bit more. I do not have the time to explain the types of things unknown to the land of Sori, but just be on the lookout for things that may seem out of place in our realm."*

There was one thing Maya could not figure out. *"Why does my head spin when I am about to see them?"*

"That is part of using your new powers. The second time wasn't as severe, was it?"

"No, thankfully."

"Once you find a new power, it may bring about the same illness, but each time the power is used, the effects are less and less. By the fourth or fifth time you will be fine, and the power will occur with no side effects." He needed Maya to do one last thing and asked, *"Maya, will you do me a favor?"*

"Anything," Maya quickly responded.

In a deep and foreboding tone, Malaki requested, *"You must call a meeting of the Leigheasan elders and report this. I fear that something vile will soon be unleashed."*

"I agree, Maya," Tara said. *"Based off Malaki's word, this certainly is not good, and all the elders need to be aware of the scouts, even if nothing is currently happening. Inform them, so they can be on the lookout for suspicious activity."*

The Cèilidh continued in Maya's absence. When she returned to the village center she was immediately met by her parents.

"What's wrong?" Felix asked.

"I need to call a meeting of the elders. Everything will be explained in full, but I need all of the Leigheasan elders." She paused and rethought her request. "Not just the clan representatives but anyone who is deemed an elder. They must be here as soon as possible, before dusk."

Her parents had never witnessed this sternness from Maya.

"That's a bit of a problem," Felix replied. "It could take a day or two to get all the elders here. We should get as many as possible, and then they can spread the word."

"You're right," Maya replied, and Felix headed to the fountain in the village center and called for the celebration to cease.

"My fellow Dempseys, I need your ears!" Felix cried out. "My apologies for stopping the festivities, but we are in dire need of your assistance. Due to unforeseen events, Maya has called for a meeting of the elders." The rumbling of the crowd began. "Quiet down. All will be revealed in good time, but for now we need to get as many of the elders from as many clans as possible."

"By when?" someone called out.

"By dusk." The chatter of the crowd picked back up.

Regardless of the clan's feelings on the matter, Felix assigned a Dempsey to each Leigheasan village within riding distances, and by nightfall several thousand elders gathered at Dempsey's village hall. As part of the Leigheasan village charters, each village contained a hall capable of seating at least a thousand people, made from wood or stone, always located at the northernmost point of the village. Each village could customize the building to reflect the families that lived within its boundaries. For example, instead of stone columns, Dempsey Village used wooden columns and carved a Diana horse in each. The exterior bore wooden statues of Dempsey forefathers and foremothers, Diana horses, chandeliers, and other decorative items.

It was common knowledge that elders were requested to gather when something terrible had happened or would happen. With this in mind, the volume of the talk amongst the elders gathered in Dempsey Hall rivaled the cheers at the Cluiche, as they speculated over the reasons for the summons. That is, until Maya stepped onto the platform at the front of the hall. With the crowd silent, Maya began.

"Thank you all for coming on such a short notice, and I apologize for any inconvenience it may have caused, but what I must tell you is of dire importance. I have witnessed scouts. I climbed our watchtower and witnessed hundreds scurrying across our land. There were so many and their paths were so quick that I could not make out what region they originated from, but I do know that they were present in all of the regions."

"Gilroy is to blame!" one elder from the back cried out. Many agreed with him, and the crowd got out of control as elders hurled accusations and yelled at each other across the hall.

"Silence!" Felix cried out. With the crowd quiet he continued, "If there is one thing that I can guarantee, it is that whoever is controlling the scouts is not Gilroy!"

"You are blinded by your family! Your brother is the only one who would dare mess with someone's soul. He is up to something!" Elder Reinhold hollered.

"Mind your tongue, Aidan!" Felix snapped back.

"I assure you, Elder Reinhold, that Gilroy had nothing to do with this," Maya interjected on her father's behalf.

With a grin on his face and a condescending tone Sir Reinhold asked, "How is it that you are so sure?"

"Gofannon tasked me with killing Gilroy as part of my Tástáil." Several of the elder men began to laugh, which only enraged Maya. With a twist of her hand, all five were whisked away from their seats and brought to Maya's side by a sudden gust of wind.

"What do I have to do to prove I am not a feeble little girl? I took out two of our sect's best fighters, and you still doubt me. I take out the one you dared not go after and still you doubt!"

Becoming more angry, Maya closed her fist, tightening the wind circling her captives. Wincing with discomfort, all the prisoners could do was listen.

"Now look at you, rendered useless by a poor little girl and a gust of wind. I did not call for this meeting to be laughed at and mocked. I called this meeting to warn and devise a plan of action. If you want to keep on with your childish comments and laughter, you should leave, join the scouts' leader, and wait for me to end your misery. And I do mean misery. You will suffer in ways you cannot imagine, and it will be through this pain that you realize the errors of not listening to my warnings." Maya slid her sword a few inches out of its sheath.

After a moment, she released the men. Three of the five returned to their seats while the other two stormed out. Clare rose and walked to Maya. Placing a hand on Maya's shoulder, Clare whispered, "I know how you feel, but you must contain your anger and use of your powers. The men in our sect need a gentler approach by a woman. Many of them feel threatened already, and this display did not help your cause."

Maya nodded when Clare finished, but Clare's words fell on deaf ears. Maya knew that she could not take a gentle approach, and she refused to play the role of the lass in distress.

"It appears this year is going to be a year of firsts." Clare turned back to the crowd. "We have read about the scouts, but none of us have had personal encounters. I think it is safe to say that Maya is far more powerful than most recognize and that we need to trust that what she is saying is true. It is obvious that someone is tapping into the forbidden, but *who* is the question. If it were a Leigheas, then there would be no need to scout us. However, if they are throughout Sori scouting our brethren and the Duines, then it is hard to tell which sect is responsible."

"It is impossible for us to guess what they are up to and who the puppet master is," Ulric called from the back of the hall. "I say, for now, we go back to our villages and inform everyone on the matter. We assign elders to inform the clans who were unable to make it tonight. In addition, we will be on the lookout for signs or suspicious acts. This truly is the best we can do for now."

"Agreed," said Clare, and before anyone could interrupt, she continued, "Thank you for coming, and please be safe on your way home."

Maya, disappointed with the way things turned out, joined her parents. They could see the frustration on her face and knew that as a female she would have those who doubted her word.

"It may not have gone the way you wanted, but you got the message across," her father said.

"First off, I must say I enjoyed seeing you handle those gnéastis the way you did. Secondly, you did the right thing and created awareness. There isn't anything else you or the others could have done. Time will reveal the next step we must take." Andrea embraced her daughter, hoping to raise her spirits.

As soon as everyone was dismissed, Otis of the Roark Clan made his way towards Maya and her family. Maya was not too fond of the Roarks, but to her surprise, Otis came in peace.

"Felix. Andrea," Otis stated, nodding in greeting. "Maya, I want you to know that the Roark Clan harbors no malice, and bravo for your performance tonight." He nodded again, turned, and headed towards the exit.

Maya was instantly relieved. The Roark Clan carried a lot of weight amongst the sect, and having their backing was just as good as having the support of a god or goddess. When the time came, Maya might not be able to convince everyone to fight, but Otis would surely be willing.

"Now what?" Maya asked.

"Let's head home and regroup in the morning." Andrea pulled at Maya and Felix.

"Agreed," Felix and Maya said simultaneously.

Thoughts of the day's events kept Maya awake in bed. She decided to take a walk and went to the watchtower. A couple of hours had passed, and all was calm. Suddenly, a dark figure trailing a red aura appeared on the path leading to Beinn. The figure stopped abruptly, like it knew someone had spotted it. It slowly turned towards Maya, and two red dots, like eyes, became visible.

The figure raised an arm, and a black arrow shot into the sky. A few seconds into its ascent, it produced a blinding white light across Sori. Maya covered her eyes, but it wasn't enough. The light rendered her blind for several seconds, and when she regained sight the figure was gone. She knew that this was her first encounter with the scouts' master.

Chapter 5

Planting the Seeds of War

"Father!" Caleb yelled, bursting through the doors of the dining hall.

"Back from Ghabháil so soon? You should still have a few weeks left in this year's posting," Brodde stated calmly as he took a sip of fresh Duine blood from his chalice.

"Father, we are almost out of stock." To soften the fact that they fed on Duines, many of the Veirlintus referred to them as "stock" or "supply."

"Nonsense, my sources say that the crime rate in Cala is higher than ever. By their word, over the past four weeks there should have been at least three drop-offs with well over five dozen Duine prisoners in each caravan." Brodde's tone reflected growing concern.

"Those drop-offs never happened. Since the first missed drop date I have had guards stationed all day and night at the drop-off location and still nothing. No signs of one coming."

"How long do we have until we run out?" Brodde stood and approached his son.

"A week, maybe two." Caleb was being optimistic. In truth, he was uncertain how long they truly had.

"A week? Maybe two weeks left and you didn't bother to let me know! Why didn't you come to me sooner?" Brodde asked with growing frustration at his seemingly incompetent son.

"I sent a formal request for a pass into Cala for you and a Hund representative," Caleb replied.

"Do not call them Hunds!" Brodde shouted at the top of his lungs. "It is as disrespectful as them calling us Fågel. You youths need to learn manners and respect for our given names."

Though Brodde spoke of respect, it had become common practice for elders in Frìth to refer to their offspring or those of younger generations as youths, thereby showing their lack of respect and regard for them as members of their sect.

"Sorry, Father. I hoped to deliver the news with a pass, but the request was denied. I never thought that the pass would be denied. I did not want to worry you or cause panic amongst the council." Caleb produced a parchment from his satchel.

Brodde snatched it from his hands and read the document. Shaking his head and placing the letter on the table, Brodde walked to the window and gazed upon the town of Ar Dtús. He was angry and fearful of the repercussions of the Duines' action. Watching the citizens walk from house to house, shop to shop, and from street to street, he knew that if they could not meet with Cala's council members, then the citizens of Frìth would either grow mortal or seek a blood supply on their own. The latter was more of a concern for Brodde. Snatching Duine citizens would bring about another war, a war that Brodde did not want to see.

"I will go to Cala," Brodde began but was interrupted by Caleb.

"You can't and you know it. The caomhnóir will never let you pass, and no matter how many men you take with you, you will be vastly outnumbered at Cala's gates. The Duine may see it as a hostile act."

"True." This was the first time in decades that he agreed with his son. After a moment, Brodde broke the silence and said, "Send messengers out to Alena, Sasha, Marko, Roderick, and Jürgen. Tell them to meet me at Dragon Lair the instant they get the message."

Caleb did not understand the purpose of seeking only the Ar Dtús elders. "That's it? With a situation this dire, don't you need all of Frìth?"

"There isn't time for that. It will take some of the others more than a week to arrive, but send messengers to them as well. Tell them to get here as soon as possible. They must ride until their horses die." Brodde had high hopes that his son would stop asking questions and do as he commanded.

"Yes, Father. I will see you at the pub." Caleb nodded and started towards the door.

"No, you won't." Brodde marched up to his son and stood inches from him. "This is a meeting of elders, and despite your desires, you are not on the council or an elder for that matter. You are to go back to Ghabháil and figure out the exact time we have left until our supply runs out. Once you know how long, begin thinking of ways to extend it. I will be in touch soon."

"But, Father—" Caleb wanted to explain, but his father grabbed him by his throat and shoved him against the doors.

"But nothing. You are not an elder." Brodde's claws dug into Caleb's neck. "You constantly try to overstep your boundaries. Every time you try to rise above your station, I deny your candidacy for elder status. I simply want you to learn, but you just want titles and status. Your time will come, but it is not now, not as long as you continue to thirst for more than you deserve."

Releasing his son and pushing him out the door, Brodde then put on his long wool coat and made his way from the manor to the Dragon Lair pub. Caleb sent messengers out to those his father indicated and then went to his chambers. Slamming the door shut, he rushed to his desk and flipped it over.

"That prick! I have put in my time and done all he has demanded for decades, yet he still calls me a youth. My service to my brethren has been exceptional, and I possess far more leadership qualities than he has ever obtained. How dare he hold me back!" Caleb furiously paced the floor.

"That you do," a figure called from the shadows.

"Who's there?" Caleb yelled. "Show yourself." Drawing his sword and taking a defensive stance, Caleb prepared for an attack.

"Calm yourself. There is no need for yelling or violence. If I meant you any harm, it would have already been inflicted." The figure stepped forward; one could easily confuse it with a shadow if not for the aura, red eyes, and bony hands that appeared when the figure gestured.

"Who are you?"

"A humble servant. I have watched your kind for some time now and see great potential in you that your father refuses to acknowledge. You did the right thing today, and what did it get you? Accosted by your father. Demeaned, and worst of all, you find out that your father has been denying your elder status for decades." The figure paced back and forth, moving in the opposite direction as Caleb.

"What potential?" Caleb wanted nothing more than to hear of the great things he was destined to achieve. It would be a welcome change from the disappointment expressed by his father.

"For greatness, of course. Sori finds itself on the brink of hardship that has not been experienced since your Great War. This hardship has the potential to elevate not only a leader of Leigheas Gleann, Cala, Beinn, or Frith, but all of Sori. Your people will be out of food in . . ." The figure paused, looked at Caleb and waited for a response.

"Two weeks at the latest and a week at the earliest. Honestly, I am not certain."

"And I bet when your father returns he will say to mix the blood with that of pigs, cows or horses. It will give you a month's supply and time for him to beg the Duine for more prisoners. Then the Duines will have you in their paws. They will cut the supply here and there, make you weak, and then come in for the kill." The figure spoke as though he had seen the future himself.

"That wouldn't happen," Caleb responded, confident that his father's stature amongst the sects would ensure future stock. "Surely there has been some mistake and once we meet with the Duine representatives the supply will be restored. I must admit, my father knows how to get things done, and he will come off looking like the hero of Frìth."

The figure asked, "Or will he? Things do not have to be as you said. Do you want to see what I have seen?"

"You have the power of vision?" Caleb excitedly asked. He had heard tales of this gift but never witnessed it in person.

"I have the power to do many things. For instance, this is not my true form. I can change shape at will but use this one under the cover of darkness." The figure asked once again, "So, how about it? Do you wish to see how you can become the hero? Do you want to see?"

"Please, you must show me what the future holds!"

He was not prepared to witness what he was about to see.

The figure pulled a green fís crystal from his robe and broke it against the chamber floor. A purple smoke rose from the shards, and within in appeared numerous scenes of Sori. Caleb looked on in amazement as the figure narrated.

"The lack of fresh blood will weaken your kind. Duine armies will take advantage of this weakened state and invade Frìth. Unable to fight like you once did, the Veirlintu population will be decimated."

The vision showed Caleb the strength of the Duine army as town after town fell underneath its might. Not a stone was left standing in Ar Dtús.

"Those who manage to escape go to Beinn, only to find the main Duine army is already there. Trapped between the two armies, the last of the Veirlintus will be killed. Your deaths will not be avenged. The Galenvargs, weaker than the Veirlintus, put up less of a fight. With two sects eliminated, the Duine move on to Leigheas Gleann."

The vision now produced images of a second Great War.

"The Leigheasan will put up a grand fight that will last years. The Leigheasan will kill hundreds of thousands of Duine. However, outnumbered a thousand to one, they will meet the same fate. Sori will become a land of the Duine, and the lives and legacy of the Faileas Herimen will be erased from its history."

The vision stopped. Caleb was unable to speak.

"As of now, this instant, this is the future of Sori, but you can change it all. You can lead your fellow Fågel to glory and greatness. The name that history remembers will be Caleb Tjäder, not Brodde Tjäder. Tell me, do you want to face extinction, or do you want to change this?"

At this point, the figure didn't have to ask the question. Caleb was willing to do anything to obtain immortality.

"Of course." Caleb bought into the illusion as true prophecy. "I cannot let this happen. I cannot believe my father is going to let this happen."

"Your father and the rest of the council are blinded by personal gains. Whenever something of this magnitude has occurred in the past, he and the other council members have used diplomacy, resulting in more wealth and land. But this time is different. The time for diplomatic solutions has long passed. The Duine do not intend on resolving the issue, and when he finally realizes this, the Duine will be at his doorstep."

"You make a great argument, and I agree with what you say. My father has made many a coin from preventing disaster in the past. I am sure he will attempt to do the same. The one thing that I am still unsure of is you. So, tell me, why is it that you are not leading the charge? Why use me?"

"In my state, I am unable to fight. Sure, I can kill a few here and there, but I have one leg in your realm and the other leg in a realm for the dead. Me, fighting? I would be more than useless for you or any other commander." The figure turned from Caleb and then proceeded to say the words that Caleb desired. "I came to this realm in hopes to prevent a catastrophe, to find a warrior, and one who can lead but hasn't had the chance. It is you who is destined for greatness, not I."

Caleb quietly thought it over. This was his chance to separate himself from his father, show Frìth he was a born leader, and become the hero for his people.

"What can I do to stop it?"

"Do you have loyal friends? A group that is disgruntled with the tyrannical council, the underhanded deeds of the business elite, the lack of fresh blood? A group that would follow you, even to their deaths?" The figure could easily sway others, like he was doing to Caleb, but he needed

Caleb to lead—not because the figure was weak, but in order to conceal his presence. The fewer who knew about him, the better.

"I do. There are many of us who are bothered by our leadership. If you show them what you showed me, then they will surely join my ranks."

"Good. In fact, *you* will show them what I have shown you." The figure pulled out a pouch filled with fís crystals. "All you have to do is smash the crystals against a hard surface and narrate the story, just as I did with you."

"Since I don't have powers, the men will know these aren't my crystals. Shouldn't you be the one to show them?" Caleb investigated the pouch and was captivated by the crystals. He gazed upon them as though they were the most valuable gems in the realm.

"I cannot show them. It must be you. The troops need to buy into you and your story. I don't need them doubting you in battle. Since I cannot join you on the battlefield, they cannot look to me in a fight, but they will have you for the leadership they need. I need soldiers loyal to Caleb of Clan Tjäder." The figure placed a reassuring hand on Caleb's shoulder.

"Of course. I will get the men we need." Caleb closed the pouch and secured it to his belt.

"One last thing before I go," the figure said, turning before he passed through the door.

Caleb replied anxiously, "Anything."

"Do you know of any among the Galenvarg with the same feelings?" Though the figure knew much about Caleb, he was still unsure of how close he was to the other sect.

"I met several at Ghabháil who are outraged at the current blood situation and a bit disgruntled with the leadership at Beinn. Once I show them the crystals, I know they will bring more followers." In truth he was unaware of whom amongst the Galenvarg he could recruit, but Caleb wanted the figure to have confidence in him.

"Good. For the time being, I will only need a small number. Let's say, when you have twenty-three soldiers I will return." The figure hesitated again before leaving. "You must know that you will be watched at all times. I have many scouts assigned to you, and the moment you stray off course I will be back for a less than pleasant visit."

Caleb seemed to hardly hear the warning. "Before you go, I must ask. If you are but a servant, who do you work for?"

"You, my lord," the figure replied and disappeared through Caleb's chamber door.

Though Caleb had the feeling that he was being used, he could not pass up the opportunity to prove himself, become a Veirlintu elder, and possibly become not only the ruler of Frìth but of Sori itself.

He would no longer live in someone's shadow, but forge a new path for himself. If this figure, this servant, could provide the means to do so, then it was well worth being used.

Chapter 6

Supplies Are Running Low

"Morning, Mom," Maya said, lowering her drink to the table. "Morning. What are you doing up so early? You have had some trying days of late and should rest." Andrea poured a drink of her own.

"I couldn't sleep after the meeting and went for a walk." Maya paused. "Where's Dad? I want to get his opinion on something."

Andrea pointed upstairs. "He is moving a bit slow this morning, so he will be down in a few."

"Morning!" Felix called out, rushing down the stairs. "My ears are burning. Which one of you has been talking about me?"

"Or he will be down now. You weren't trying to get out of cleaning the stalls today, were you?" Andrea poured Felix a cup of tea.

Felix grabbed his cup and asked, "Would I ever do something like that?" With a smile on his face he followed his question with a question. "What is everyone getting into today?"

"Well, I wanted to talk about last night."

"Oh, Maya. Put last night behind you. You did the right thing, and we will come up with a plan of action for our clan today. I'm sure your mother has one already, or at least one in the works."

"No, Dad, it's not that. I mean, I am disappointed with how it turned out, but to be fair, there really is nothing any of us can do now. Something happened after that. I couldn't sleep, so I took a stroll through the village and ended up at the watchtower. I gazed out towards the cosán leading to Beinn and saw this figure."

"Another scout?" Andrea pulled up a seat, eager to hear her daughter's story.

"No, I don't think so. It had the look of a scout, but this one was different. A red aura surrounded it, and what I found to be interesting is that it knew I saw him. The figure stopped, turned to me, and I saw glowing red eyes. Before I could do anything, it shot an arrow that produced a blinding light. When I regained my sight, the figure was gone. It could have easily gone to Beinn, but, to be honest, it could be anywhere."

"It has to be the one controlling the scouts." Felix grabbed his breakfast plate and began piling on the food, but he was clearly focused on what she was saying.

"I think so too. Along with not knowing where it was going, I have no clue where it came from. It could have been Cala, or it could have been here. There is no proof or evidence to say where it started its journey." She paused and then continued. "I find it hard to believe that any Duine would stay in Cala and practice the forbidden, or any aspect of our way of life for that matter. Even in secret, things have a way of getting out in Cala."

"You are correct, my dear." Felix took a large gulp of his tea. "The risk of exposure would be a constant threat in Cala, so much so that it would be impossible to hide. Though the Duine have a history of bravery, I don't think there is a soul in Cala brave enough to take that risk."

Andrea thought for a few moments. "We don't have ties in Cala to know if people have experienced anything out of the ordinary. But we do have contacts all over Beinn and Frith. You should go talk to Jeremias and Willum and see if the other sects have noticed anything."

"You read my mind, Mom. I am going to head out to see them after we finish here. I sent a bird to Jeremias last night asking him to meet me at Willum's office in Dún. Hopefully when I return I will have some more answers. Worst-case scenario is that they will join me in the quest to rid Sori of this figure." Maya grabbed her shillelagh.

Concerned for his daughter's safety, Felix had to say something. Instead of a grand speech the only thing he could say was, "Hold on."

Both Maya and Andrea paused, but when nothing else came out they started out the door.

"Wait, wait, wait! I don't like you going out alone. You are dealing with the forbidden and who knows what else. You need to take one of your cousins or your brother."

"Dad, I really appreciate your concern, but trust me, if I need backup, I am going to the right place. There is nothing Jeremias and Willum won't do for me." Maya had a devious smile. Jeremias and Willum would do anything for Maya because they were afraid of her.

"Too bad breeding between our sects has been outlawed. Otherwise, one of those boys would make a fine husband for you," Andrea added.

"And become the cliché that everyone expects a woman to be," Maya replied. "A woman on the path to become a leader, a warrior, a purveyor of knowledge, halted by love and bodily desires. Too many in our sect would take too much pleasure in my failure, and I refuse to fail."

Maya hugged her parents and spoke sternly.

"Soon we are going to need our women out of the kitchen and in the fight. Promise me that you will gather our clan and begin training those who are out of practice. I fear we are being drawn into another war."

"We will do our best." Felix hugged his daughter, a bit longer than usual this time. "You aren't off on foot, are you?"

"Yes, I will be fine on foot."

"Oh, in that case you need to wait one more minute," Andrea said.

She looked at Felix and gave him a not-so-subtle nod towards the barn. He smiled as if to say, "Messaged received."

"Your father and I were going to give you a gift at your Cèilidh, but the scouts put a damper on the celebration. Come, quickly. This will only take a few moments." Andrea tugged on Maya's arm.

"Okay, okay, but we need to hurry. I am already running late," Maya replied, looking east and wondering how far she would be if she'd left before her parents woke.

Leading Maya to the barn, her father began rambling. "I must say that the past few weeks without Scarlett has had its challenges. I don't think I can stand her being gone for any more trips without me by her side. She knows what needs to be done around here better than I do." Felix pulled the barn doors open. "So, we thought it was about time for you to have a Diana of your own."

Standing in front of Maya was a horse that bore little resemblance to Scarlett, or any of the other Dianas, other than the color. This horse was at least six inches taller than Scarlett, his chest was easily a foot wider, and bulging from his legs were the largest muscle groups ever seen on an animal.

"This here is Saxon, son of Scarlett. He is about to turn twelve. He is not only larger, faster, and stronger than anyone in his family, but he is also the smartest and largest Diana to be bred. A perfect match for you." Felix handed her the reins. "Be safe and return to us soon."

"Words cannot express my gratitude. He is magnificent. Thank you both."

"No need for words. Now, get going," Felix replied.

Jumping on Saxon, Maya took off for Dún.

Since the Great War, Dún had become the hub for the Galenvarg timber industry. Willum's clan oversaw Dún's daily operations, but his calling was in craftsmanship. No one in Sori could match Willum's skill at making custom furniture, and in Cala he was craftsman to the elite. By his side had been and always would be Jeremias, the only Veirlintu to be born on the same day as Willum.

Born into one of the oldest Veirlintu clans, Jeremias worked as a landlord to numerous properties, and served as an advisor to the elders. For the most part, his daily life revolved around a desk. However, he was never one to shy away from a hunt or a night out on the town, so to speak, with Willum.

On Saxon, Maya arrived in Dún a couple days earlier than expected, and it just so happened her arrival was a couple hours after Jeremias's. Both her friends were coincidently waiting at the gates. Upon seeing them, Maya was taken back to their first meeting.

Maya was in the tenth day of tracking an infamous fathach torc, a giant boar nicknamed Maximus. He had wounded several dozen, and killed six hunters. Maya followed Maximus for almost a hundred miles, and finally the beast had stopped in Donn Gleann. After a day in Donn, she found her perfect vantage point not even a hundred yards away. As the sun rose, Maya glimpsed light reflecting from something in the mountains. There she saw two young men taking aim at her prey.

She quickly loaded her crossbow, lined her shot, and pulled the trigger. Maya reloaded and refocused on Maximus, but found that the beast was lying on the ground. Placing the crossbow in its holster on her back, Maya grabbed her longbow and slowly approached the boar.

The two men were also gaining ground on her kill. Maya pulled an arrow from her quiver and let it loose in their direction. She then sent a second one right behind the first. Both arrows landed several yards in front of the two intruders, stopping them in their tracks. Maya was now in clear view of the two young men, her bow was drawn, and she yelled out, "Drop your weapons!"

They did as they were told.

"What are your names?" Maya demanded, drawing nearer.

"I am Willum of the Galenvarg clan MacLeoid, and this is Jeremias of the Veirlintu clan Barraclough."

"Why are you trying to take my kill?" Maya was now within twenty yards.

"We weren't. Well, I mean we were trying to kill it, but we weren't trying to take the remains."

"We have been tracking this beast down for several days now—" Willum started before Jeremias jumped in.

"We saw the beast drop, so we wanted to see it up close."

Maya lowered her bow and introduced herself. "I am Maya of the Leigheasan clan Dempsey. Sorry for the shots earlier, but I didn't want anyone trying to take my kill. I have put more than a few days into this hunt."

"No problem," they both said.

"Do you want to see the shot?"

"Of course." Maya nodded for them to come over. The arrow had hit Maximus in the left eye and traveled into the brain. The accuracy left Willum and Jeremias speechless, and Maya invited the two to dine on Maximus. From that point on the three were the closest of friends, and on the anniversary of that day, the three would gather at the spot of the kill to celebrate their friendship.

"Maya, stop!" Willum was loud enough to wake Maya from her reminiscing, and she quickly pulled back on the reins, slowing Saxon's approach.

"Jeremias! Willum! It is so good to see you both," Maya yelled as she hopped off Saxon. "It's been eight months too long."

"Too long indeed, but it is good to see you," Jeremias said, giving Maya a hug that lifted her off the ground. "I thought you were going to run us over for a second. Your stud here is one giant of a horse. Is he a new breed of Dianas?"

"No, he is just a Diana, and sorry about coming so close." Willum also picked her up and twirled her around. "My mind was miles away thinking about the first time we met."

"Ah, the famous hunt of the infamous Maximus," Willum said, still embracing Maya. After a few twirls, he sat Maya back on the ground. "A young girl took down what hundreds of grown men could not. I still can't believe you killed that massive beast with one shot."

"It would have been a better shot if you two didn't give me cause to rush. After all my tracking, I wasn't about to let you take the first shot, though I am pretty sure you would have missed."

"How much better of a shot could it have been? Wait, don't answer. Not to change the subject, but I hear congratulations are in order. Officially a Leigheas! The word around Beinn is that you possess all of the elements. It has everyone both fascinated and terrified."

"It's not how many you possess, Willum. It's about how one intends on using them." Maya's smirk let them know that she was faking her modesty.

"We were glad to hear from you and are more than happy to see you. However, we are months away from meeting, so your contact does bring about some concern. Not to mention that if you do possess all four elements, some dire times may be ahead. It's not like the gods hand powers out willy-nilly. Is everything okay?" Jeremias asked.

"To be honest, not really. Is there a place we can talk away from prying ears?" Maya looked around at a large number of workers staring at them from their stations.

"My workshop. Let's take—" Willum paused, pointing at Saxon.

"Saxon. His name is Saxon," Maya replied, patting Saxon on his side.

"Let's take Saxon to the stable. We will get him some fresh water and something to snack on while we talk." Willum led them to the stable, and after putting Saxon in a stall they made their way to Willum's shop.

Maya closed the door behind them and began, "While at Balla, and at my Cèilidh, I saw what I've since learned are known as scouts. I climbed the watchtower and saw hundreds of scouts coming and going from all the regions. Then, last night I saw a figure. Like the scouts it was black and had a robe covering all discernible features, but unlike the scouts it knew I was watching it. It stopped dead in its tracks and looked at me with glowing red eyes. Then it produced an arrow and shot it towards the sky, producing a blinding light. I think this figure is the one using the scouts."

Both Jeremias and Willum grew concerned. "Scouts. It has been several millennia since scouts have been seen." Willum rubbed his chin. "I don't think they have been used since before Tara the Great."

"Someone has been studying, I see." Maya always gave Willum a hard time when it came to reading and studying. He often came to Maya for help regarding a project he was hired to do for the sects. They would sit down together to research the problem, but his attention was never that great, and he often never got past the book cover.

"Well, after your first couple hundred years you get bored and decide to pick up a book or two," Willum said with a smirk of his own. Maya continued around the room, examining Willum's handiwork, and called upon Tara.

"*Tara, are you there?*" Maya asked.

"*Of course. How can I help you?*"

"*When was the last time scouts were used?*"

"*To my knowledge they haven't been used since the uprising of Magnus Olesen during the second decade of my reign.*"

"*Who was Magnus Olesen?*"

"*All we knew about him was that he was a shapeshifter and possessed a host of powers. Of course, we didn't know he was a shifter till after his death when he took his true form.*"

"*Was there any connection to the forbidden?*"

"*No, what he had was much like what we Leigheasan have. It appeared that his powers were with him since birth, and they did not have a negative effect on his body, so it couldn't have been the forbidden.*"

"*Do you know what he used the scouts for?*"

"*Scouting, and that's all. He used them to stay one step ahead of his enemies and my troops.*"

"*Will you stay present during my talk with Jeremias and Willum?*" Maya hoped that Tara might be able to fill in gaps or make connections where she couldn't.

"*Of course,*" Tara replied as Maya continued to pace. Turning, Maya now placed her attention back on Willum and Jeremias.

"This is not good news for us, Maya." Willum stopped for a second and then quickly continued, "Do you have any idea of what they are up to?"

"No, but I called a meeting of my elders and made them aware of the situation. Their best advice was to keep an eye out for suspicious activity. It was a rather disappointing end to my first meeting with the elders."

"Not to change the subject, but speaking of meeting with the elders," Jeremias interrupted, "a meeting of the Veirlintu council has been called for today."

"Isn't this the month of the Oráiste Gealach?" Willum asked.

"Yes, what of it?" Jeremias asked.

"I thought your council took the month off."

"They do dismiss daily meetings during Oráiste Gealach, but if the need arises, they will meet."

"Interesting. You learn something new every day, or in my case, every decade or two."

The two of them gazed off as if trying to remember what they were discussing.

"Hey, we need to get back on point." Maya snapped her fingers to call their attention. "Do you know what the meeting is about?"

"Food supply—"

Maya cut Jeremias off before he could explain. "Food supply?"

"Our supply of blood. I cannot recall when it started, but we began referring to Duine prisoners as food supply, stock, and some of the younger generation make up new names more frequently than they bathe."

"Of course, sorry. What about it?"

"We are running low. Duines have missed a couple of drop-offs, and it is rumored that we have about a month left."

"Less than that, is what I've heard," Willum added. "All of Beinn is in an uproar about it. From what I have been hearing, the longest we have is two weeks, and the shortest is a week."

For such a dire situation, the two seemed to be unfazed by the news. "You two are rather calm about it."

"That's because my family has prepared for this. We always knew there would be a point where the supply would run low. Before I was born, my father had a hidden door installed in our cellar that leads about twenty feet further into the ground. The temperature remains cool, like a winter's day, all year long. This allows us to keep a supply of blood, a six-month supply to be exact."

"That is a brilliant idea," Jeremias said. "I wish we had thought of that."

Ignoring Jeremias, Willum looked at Maya. "My voice may conceal my concern, but rest assured, I am worried."

"Are you?"

"I am, and you know it!" Willum's voice rose in anger. "My sect cannot control themselves like the Veirlintus. A week without blood is hard but doable. Two weeks, we become hungry. A deep desire for blood creeps into our thoughts, but still we manage. By the end of the third week the desire takes control, and we will ravage the countryside killing all the game we find. This is not enough. Finally, in the fourth week we will move on from the woods and on to Cala. I am pretty sure that I don't need to state the obvious of what will happen when we move to Cala.

"Though we may be brethren, the Leigheasan will be in trouble as well. Those close to Galenvarg villages will be in danger, and there is the chance they could spread inwards once done with the villages on the outskirts of the Gleann. The Veirlintus will survive much longer with no blood. They can do that deep sleep thing, slow their heart rate down, and survive on a fraction of the blood that Galenvargs need. Times like these, I wish we Vargs were more like bears. Hibernation would help solve this problem."

"Calm down, Willum. She is just testing us, and for good reasons. Maya needs to see if this figure has gotten to us." Jeremias poured Willum a cup of mead. "Despite Willum's poor reaction, he is right, Maya. The situation is going to be far more taxing on the Galenvargs than on my sect. The way Willum described a Galenvarg's hunger was far more pleasant than the way it really is."

"Sounds like there is a story. I know we don't have time for it, but we are not leaving until I hear it."

Jeremias looked at Willum, who muttered, "Go ahead and tell her."

"A few hundred years ago, the more elite members of our sects began a betting circuit involving Galenvarg prisoners. My father was among the participants, and he brought me along to several of the fights. They would starve the Vargs for several weeks and then have them fight against one another till death. Granted, you are strong with . . . let's call it supernatural power, but a starving Varg has brute strength that you have never seen before. Not only can they snap limbs like twigs, but they can bite through bone as if it were a slice of bread. If the prize wasn't awarded right after the kill, the Vargs ate everything in sight, including the bones."

By Jeremias's tone, Maya knew that he had witnessed the horrors up close.

"What was the prize?"

"A supply of blood that would level off the cravings." Jeremias stared at the floor as he answered.

"Wait, back up a minute!" Willum interrupted. "What do you mean 'if this figure has gotten to us'?"

"I agree with Maya. This figure is more than likely in control of the scouts. Its appearance so shortly after the scouts is not a coincidence. Scouts are on the lookout for something, and my guess is it's some*one*. All objects worth taking are with the monks, and only the Leigheasan elders know how to reach them, which means they wouldn't bother scouting all the regions. If they wanted some*thing*, then they would only scout the Gleann."

Willum said, "That makes sense. Going under the assumption that he is looking for someone, there isn't anything we can do right now. There are close to a million of us Faileas Herimen—"

"There's more than a million."

"Really? Okay, there are more than a million of us, and who knows how many Duine there are, so until more is revealed, we are dead in the water. It literally would be worse than looking for a needle in a haystack. At least then we would know what we are looking for."

"Unfortunately, I think you are right, Willum. There is a big part of me that wants to attack this head-on, but right now, there is so much that we don't know," Maya said and took a seat at Willum's workbench. There was a moment of silence until Maya asked, "Back to your sects for a minute—is there any plan of action for the blood supply?"

"Well, I should find out when I return, but I do know we have not been able to reach Cala's council," Jeremias replied. "I was told that one of the guards at Ghabháil had requested a day pass but was denied. I still don't know who it was or why the pass was denied."

"*Maya,*" Tara said. "*I might have a temporary solution.*"

"*Please, go on.*" Maya was willing to hear anything that might help keep the peace.

"*Propose to the Leigheasan elders a blood feast. It was something that I used before, and it was highly successful. At the very least, it will delay things long enough for their sects to meet with Cala's officials.*"

"*I don't follow. What is a blood feast?*"

"*One week invite the Galenvarg clans to partake in a community lunch. They bring sustenance for you, and the Leigheasan will provide blood for the Galenvargs. Then the next week you do the same for the Veirlintus.*"

Maya jumped in before Tara could finish. "*Our village dochtúirs will be able to draw blood from each of us. Enough at least to satisfy the hunger of both sects and perhaps enough for them to take a small supply home.*"

"*Yes, but you also need to ask Willum and Jeremias to ask their elders to start Willum's family practice of storing blood, and leeching of the prisoners.*"

"*Leeching of the prisoners?*" Another concept Maya was unfamiliar with.

"*They need to draw blood from the prisoners without killing them. Let the prisoner regain their supply and then redraw. It will take three times the number of prisoners and cost more food consumption, but it will provide a greater food supply for both sects in the long term.*"

"*Thank you,*" Maya gratefully replied. Tara's advice might not only prevent a war but also provide a solution for low supply runs in future days.

"*My pleasure.*"

Maya told Willum and Jeremias of her plan, and both agreed to take it to their elders. This effort, if successful, would delay the draining of the blood supply, but it would not prevent depletion if leeching was not implemented. If the Duines continued to not fulfill their quota, then in a month's time, even with leeching, there would not be enough prisoners to satisfy the hunger of the two sects. The Faileas Herimen would either have to continue the blood feast or use the threat of war to reestablish the prisoner supply.

Jeremias cautioned, "Maya, you need to be careful. The odds are that this figure is looking for someone powerful, and you are perhaps the most powerful in Sori. Send a messenger if you have any encounters with this figure, and if at all possible, don't fight it alone. We may not be the strongest in our sects, but three versus one is a lot better than one-on-one."

"You will be amongst the first to know," Maya replied and was then led by Willum to the stables to get Saxon. Once reunited with her steed, Maya headed home.

Chapter 7
Crisis Averted

Once again, the Leigheasan elders were gathered at Dempsey Hall, and this time most were unhappy about being called away from their homes so shortly after the previous meeting. Despite the grumbling amongst the elders, Maya walked to the front of the hall and began, "I know you are unhappy about being here, but once again—"

Maya was cut off by Elder Tobias.

"So far, your last meeting was for nothing. You are not an elder, and yet you are calling meetings of the elders. You are breaking the way things are done. I don't care how great your powers are; we have a protocol!" Tobias exclaimed with anger in his voice. Many nodded in agreement.

"If you are concerned with formalities, Tobias," Otis said, rising to stand alongside Maya, "I say we put Maya's elder status to a vote. After all, it is not age that determines an elder but experience and knowledge. She has experienced more than most, knows more than most, and sees more than most, so she deserves a vote."

"Otis, how is it that you come to the side of the one that killed two of your clan's most promising young ones? After all, weren't you the one that demanded punishment with the threat of your clan defecting?" Tobias hoped to convince Otis that there was no good reason to support Maya.

Otis did not feel the need to validate his actions, but he indulged Tobias and replied, "Yes, I did desire punishment, and yes, my clan was outraged with the death of Angus. It was after our grieving period, for both Angus and Alick, when the clan came together and expressed their feelings regarding this young lass. As you all know, the Roark Clan holds a warrior in the highest regard."

Tobias laughed and interjected, "You aren't really going to hide behind the Onóir code, are you? We have had over two thousand years of peace, so an ancient philosophy regarding a warring society does not apply to our way of life."

"Tobias, one of the many foundations of our sect's beliefs is the respect for all ways and philosophies of life, even if we do not agree with them. You are starting to show signs that you need to join the Duine. Now, I suggest you take your leave or shut your mouth while I conclude."

Tobias didn't know how to respond, so he stood quietly and let Otis finish.

"As I was saying, above all other things, our clan holds the warrior in the highest regard, and she has proven herself to be a fine warrior. For that, she has the support of my clan." Just as Tobias thought Otis was finished, Otis turned the attention back to Tobias. "Let me ask you, Tobias, why are you so willing to object to a sect member in need of an ear? Why are you so willing to discredit her? What is it about this young lass that makes you feel threatened?"

Instead of responding, Tobias took a seat and hoped the attention would soon be drawn away from him.

Clare now came to their side and called out, "A majority vote is needed, so all that oppose to Maya's elder status, please raise your hand." Clare gazed out and saw it was an obvious minority. Instead of counting, she said, "All those in favor." She looked out at well over a thousand hands raised. "I don't think it is necessary to count when it is more than obvious those in favor greatly outnumber those against. Congratulations, Maya, you are officially an elder."

"Thank you," Maya said, nodding. "Now that we have that over with, I bring about concerns regarding our brethren to the east. For reasons unknown at the moment, the supply of Duine prisoners has stopped, and they are running low on blood. Within two weeks they will be out, perhaps four if they ration. If the Duines fail at bringing more shipments, then the need to feed will take over. It will either thrust us into another war with the Duine or cause us to be put in the feeding paths of both the Galenvargs and the Veirlintus."

"Why haven't they gone to Cala to see what is going on?" an elder shouted.

"I am not sure on all the details, but a request for a pass was denied. The Veirlintus are meeting soon, so within the next day or so I will find out what their plan of action is going to be."

"I mean no disrespect," Deven of Clan Simola said as he stood up. "But instead of assuming things or having us wait for further information, you should know all the facts before you call a meeting. We can't just stop our lives. There are fields that need to be plowed, timber to be cut, traps for fish and game to be set, and a host of other duties that need to be fulfilled."

"I agree that I should know all the details before coming to you, but you know a pass can take a couple weeks or more to be granted. If I came to you in a couple of weeks or perhaps in a month with this information, we would be too late, especially if the request for another pass is denied."

Clare interjected on Maya's behalf. "You make some valid points, Sir Simola, but so does Maya. All of our time is valuable, and waiting for another pass to come is not acceptable. The lack of blood is perhaps a more serious threat than that of war."

"Until we hear about the diplomatic solutions, do you have a plan to help our brethren?" Otis asked.

"A blood feast," Maya replied and continued with the details. "We have our village dochtúirs draw blood to feed the sects, and in return they will feed us with their game. The extra blood can be taken with them so they can ration it out later. By doing this we give ourselves a few more weeks to get in touch will Cala, and, by then, if they keep rejecting our requests, then let the war come."

As soon as Maya finished, the elders began talking amongst themselves, and some concerns arose.

"If they drink our blood, will they become part Leigheas?" Cecilia of Clan Jansson asked. "I am more worried about them gaining elemental powers. I care for my brethren deeply, but the last thing we need is a Veirlintu or Galenvarg with the power of the elements."

"Tara, do you know the answer?" Maya asked.

"They will not. The Galenvarg and Veirlintu genes are dominant and repress the traits in foreign blood. The process literally works by eating impurities and using the good to heal and revitalize the body. All that makes us a Leigheas is considered an impurity. On the opposite side, if you ever get bitten by a Galenvarg or Veirlintu, it acts as a recessive trait. You get all the benefits of being either one but none of the craving for blood. You may get some side effects like the animal rage.

"Duine blood, on the other hand, does not contain any strength to fight off the venom, so to speak, of a Galenvarg and Veirlintu, so they are converted. Well, that is, if they survive, which most don't. If the elders are still worried, mention that we had to do this back in my time and nothing bad came from it."

"What about the Duine who convert to the Leigheasan life?" Maya asked out of curiosity.

"Once accepting the Leigheasan way of life, the Duine becomes a Leigheas. By taking part in ambrosia and other tonics of ours, their blood gains strength to become dominant over the blood of the other sects. However, their blood will still be seen as an impurity to the Veirlintus and Galenvargs."

"Thank you." Maya turned her attention back to the elders. "No, this was a common practice ages ago and nothing came from it."

"How do you know this?" Tobias asked.

"My ascender told me. She explained to me in full detail how they conducted their blood feasts. Nothing came of it beside a full stomach, so to speak," Maya confidently replied.

Tobias huffed. "How do we know your ascender is credible? For all we know, your ascenders could be off their rocker and purposely leading you, as well as us, astray."

Before Maya could even ask, Tara spoke up. *"Maya, you have my permission to tell him."*

"Are you sure?" Maya asked. *"I thought it was an unspoken rule to not speak of our ascenders to prevent the clash of egos, jealousy, and fear. The last thing we need is the sect agreeing with me out of fear. As much as I need their help, I need to know they are working with me because of the greater good."*

"Yes, it is true that we are not supposed to tell who guides us, but we also aren't supposed to discredit one's ascenders. You need to put an end to the doubts, so you have my blessing."

Turning her attention back to the audience, Maya reluctantly replied, "I must say that it is one of my ancestors, one of my great-grandmothers."

"See! I knew it!" Tobias yelled as he jumped out of his seat. "We are being led by a family who has only brought grief to our sect. What if your grandmother is as vile and destructive as Gilroy?" Many of the elders were now nodding in agreement with Tobias.

"You have no right!" Felix called out.

"Father, please calm down. I will handle this," Maya whispered to her father. Felix took a step back. "You see, Sir Tobias, the one you are doubting is one you should never discredit. The records are skewed, but, nevertheless, I am a descendent of Tara the Great, and it is she who chose to be my ascender."

Once Tobias heard the name, he took a seat and sat there with a grim look on his face. He knew that doubting the one that Tara has chosen would not end well for him.

"Before I go on, I must say that my family has been shamed by the deeds of Gilroy, but it was the Dempsey Clan that brought Sori justice for his vile exploits. If you, Sir Tobias, or any other member of this sect tries to use this dark stain on my clan against me or any other Dempsey, then I will demand iomlán bás against their entire clan. With that said, is there anyone else who doubts me or my intentions?" Maya scanned the room.

The mention of an iomlán bás split the elders between alarmed murmuring and utter silence. Iomlán bás was another ancient weapon in her intellectual arsenal that called for the entire clan to battle in a fight to the death. Maya's use of the troid bás and the threat of iomlán bás showed an increasingly violent side that made many elders worry she had been affected by the forbidden. Maya was not only flexing her muscles but also her knowledge of Sori's history. In skipping peaceful diplomacy and moving directly to what the Leigheasan called bhagairt, a political philosophy used by leaders with military backgrounds who used the threat of extreme force to get their way, it seemed as though she wanted to become sect ruler.

"I do not wish to lead with fear, but if I am to be continuously questioned and mocked, then you leave me no choice. If a young man stood before you, would you give him the same skepticism as you have me? I would never have thought members of my sect would treat another like this."

Elder Kjellbjörn Ludowicus hesitantly stood and said, "Maya, I am not a doubter and am in favor of the blood feast, but I have an idea that might expedite things on the diplomacy end. I have a pass to Cala to discuss using one of their ports to bring my fish to Balla. The pass was written for four guests, which I intended to be my family. However, you and two of your trusted from our brethren sects can join."

"When is your pass good for?"

"Since it's a business pass, it was valid starting today and good for two weeks from now. I was going to leave this morning, but with word of this meeting, I stayed."

"With approval tonight, I will happily join you. Thank you, Elder Ludowicus, for your kind offering."

Maya looked out across the crowd.

"So, let's call a vote. All in favor of a blood feast raise your hand." Everyone in attendance raised their hand. "Dempsey Village will host the event, and I request that those living to our south come at the end of this week and those to our north come next week. Furthermore, I need our thirteen Balla representatives to come to Balla the day I am off to Cala. I will be calling for a meeting of all sects with the caomhnóir if things don't go well."

Before Maya left the hall, she wanted to send messages to Willum and Jeremias to join her trip to Cala. She made her way to the foyer and found three birds resting on a perch. Grabbing some parchment, Maya quickly wrote the two messages and placed them in the holder on each bird's leg. She sent them on their way and went home to rest.

Unlike the Leigheasan, the Galenvargs had an elder council of thirteen. The council also represented Beinn at meetings with the caomhnóir. Most of the council lived in the capital city of Keltoi, which was also the site for the council's chambers located in Ceann Hall. With this being the case, it was far easier for Willum to request a meeting. Though Willum's intent was to divulge the facts and Maya's proposal, he hoped to find more information about their current situation.

"Council members, I greatly appreciate your time and your hasty response to such short notice. As we are aware, the food supply is running low, and, for reasons unknown, we have not received a drop-off in some time." The council members all nodded in agreement and Willum continued, "I do not wish to overstep my station, but I also do not want to waste time, so before I continue, I must ask one thing."

"Go on, Willum," Leemas urged. He was Willum's grandfather.

"Does our sect have a plan for extending the current blood supply or a plan that will secure a Duine drop-off?"

"Council, if I may?" Leemas asked, and with another nod from the council he was granted permission to speak on their behalf. "We have a poor plan, a poor plan indeed. We are seeking a pass to speak with Cala's officials, but other than that, we don't have an answer. Any action we take could be seen as a declaration of war, so we must seek out diplomatic solutions."

"Grandfather and council elders, I mean no disrespect, but the plan is more than a poor one."

He paused to see how the elders responded, and to his surprise they nodded or waved him to carry on.

Willum continued, "If we wait for diplomacy, we may be out of time. I do agree that we must seek a pass, seek answers for the missing shipments, and more importantly, restore the shipment. I believe that I may have a solution that will hold us over until diplomacy prevails. My good friend, Maya of the Leigheasan, has proposed a blood feast. Their dochtúirs will draw blood for us to drink, and in return we will provide some large game for them to eat. This will extend our supply for at least a month and provide enough time for us to sort things out with Cala."

"This is a great plan. I also believe that we need to think long term for other supply shortages," a member spoke out.

"Agreed," Willum replied. "We suggest that during times of surplus, families start storing a supply in a cellar and cycle out every couple of months before it expires. In the short term, we need to change tactics at Ghabháil to leeching the prisoners so that the supply of blood will last longer. Instead of a prisoner feeding us once, that same prisoner can feed up to a few dozen times, maybe more, over the course of a few years."

"This process will cost us more in food and crops," Oleg of Clan Ivarsson interjected. "I am not sure if our treasury can support this type of effort for the long term. The only way to do so for continual decades would be to raise taxes, and we know how poorly our people respond to new taxes."

"This is true, but for the moment, and the foreseeable future, we have plenty of game and crops. What we don't have is blood, so we must begin the leeching process immediately to ensure our survival and prevent a war. If we start leeching, then a week's supply can be doubled in just a few days, and the blood feast will allow us to create either a stock at Ghabháil, or personal stocks."

Leemas replied, "This is a good idea, Willum. I understand your concerns about the finances, Oleg. However, if we are low on crops, we have enough coins in our treasury to purchase food from the Leigheasan without raising taxes. Oleg, if the council agrees, I will join you in creating a committee for studying ways to raise revenue and secure Leigheasan farms to assist us."

"What if we are proactive, and instead of forming a committee or waiting for the crops to run low, we go ahead and hire the Leigheasan to grow the crops for Ghabháil? If we run out of coins to support the food efforts, then I am sure we can barter with the Leigheasan. We all know that they could care less about coins, so I am sure they will accept game or other goods for crops," Elina of Clan Ludin suggested.

"Let's vote on it. All those in favor of hiring the Leigheasan to grow crops?" Leemas asked and scanned the room. "All present are in favor, so I will send word to Clare of the Leigheasan to see who we can make these arrangements with. Willum, we are in your debt for your assistance today."

"There is one more thing," Willum said before the council was dismissed.

Leemas moved his hand forward and replied, "Continue."

"Maya has witnessed scouts in our region and the one that is assumed to be in control of them. We both believe that something vile is coming and need everyone on the lookout for things out of the ordinary. Maya, Jeremias Barraclough of the Veirlintus and myself will be looking further into this dark one. I will report once we have more information."

"Agreed. There have only been a few recorded events of scouts, but what follows those sightings did not bode well for Sori. Once again, I am going to speak for the council, with your permission."

Leemas paused to seek the approval of his peers. All the elders indicated compliance.

"It goes without saying that the blood feast is accepted and appreciated. In addition to the food, I want each of our clans to bring a grand gift for the Leigheasan. Since Willum has a friendship with Maya, I would like him to become an ambassador to Cala and work with Maya on getting the Ghabháil situation resolved. As Willum said, be on the lookout for suspicious activity as well as informing your clans on what is happening."

All of the council agreed with Leemas and they parted ways. With the council gone and the chambers empty, Leemas turned to Willum.

"Going after this dark one may prove to be a difficult task that could cost you your life. I know you are strong, but these dark things tend to be associated with the Leigheasan forbidden. Believe me when I say *dark*; it is very dark and very strong. It has the power to become us, control us, and annihilate all of us. The instant you three cannot handle things, come to us, and you will have all the soldiers you need," Leemas said, grabbing his grandson's shoulder. "I cannot say it enough. We are forever in your debt for working with the other sects. I am more than proud with how you have turned out. Let us know when the feast will take place."

"Thank you, Grandfather. I will be in touch soon." Willum embraced his grandfather and left.

The thirteen Veirlintu council members and each of their advisors gathered in the council room of Brodde's manor. Due to Caleb's actions, all the members were aware of the problems at Ghabháil. The discussion of the issue became heated as the council was split between resolutions. Blinded by the thought of no fresh blood, some of the council members were irrational in their ideas.

Allsing of the Clan Kroon yelled out over his fellow council members, "I believe our best course of action is to go to Balla and demand the caomhnóir call a meeting! If the Duine and caomhnóir refuse to meet, then we send a declaration of war!"

"There is no need for talks of war!" Brodde barked back. "Many of you are becoming as foolhardy as my son. One request was denied, and for reasons we are not sure of. There is no need to lose your senses. Besides, it does us no good to go to war and kill off our food supply. I want rational solutions!"

"We will still have a food supply with the Duine gone. We can use the Leigheasan as our supply. All we have to do is make the same arrangement with them as we had with the Duine." Allsing's plan came so quickly that it seemed as though he had thought about it before.

"You are serious?" Brodde asked. "The Leigheasan don't have criminals, and if they did, they wouldn't be living for long. They have many laws pertaining to death penalties, most of which are public events. The only way to achieve a blood supply from the Leigheasan, at the level we currently have, is through enslavement and war. We are a strong sect, but by no means are we capable of taking on the Leigheasan in battle. Their powers are beyond our strength and numbers. We are no match for them. If you ever bring up that idea again, I will have you strung up in the center of Ar Dtús square."

"Permission to speak, council," Jeremias pleaded.

"Granted," Brodde replied.

"I have been in contact—a friendship is more like it—with a Leigheas for many years now, and I recently spoke to her about our supply being low."

"Traitor!" Hybbert of the Clan Clibburn cried out. "You discuss matters of the council with someone outside our sect? You know this is outlawed until all deeds become public, and until then it's a vow of silence!"

"For the love of the gods and goddesses, shut your mouth, Hybbert," Sasha of the Clan Elo interjected. "The rumor of the blood shortage had spread through Frìth and beyond well before we began this meeting. He broke no rules nor anyone's trust."

"Sasha is right, Hybbert. You need to sit there with your mouth shut and wait until we directly speak to you. Jeremias, please continue," Brodde said.

"Thank you," Jeremias said and continued where he left off. "She proposed a blood feast. We bring some of our large game in exchange for Leigheasan blood. This will buy us a week or two and allow us to start something new with our stock. If we then begin a leeching process at Ghabháil, we may extend our supply for over a month. In the long term, this process will allow us to use one prisoner for a couple dozen blood withdrawals, perhaps more. Between the feast and the leeching of prisoners, it will give us time to meet with Cala and come to a resolution, whether it's peace or war."

"A blood feast," Brodde said with a laugh. "Such a simple solution that your panic blinded you from seeing. Many of your actions today make me wonder if we need a new council."

Watching the reactions of everyone in the room, Jeremias realized that he could not disclose the information about the scouts and the forbidden. He knew that if he told the council, the feast would be canceled, and the Veirlintus might see it as a conspiracy between the Duine and the Leigheasan against the Veirlintus, thus giving Allsing's plan for war more validity than it deserved.

Brodde wrote on a parchment and brought it over to Jeremias. "I want you to take this pass request to Balla and see what you can find out about the missing shipments."

"Do you think it is wise to send him, Father?" Caleb asked.

"You dare question me, here, of all places." Brodde's words squeezed through his clenched teeth.

"I believe—" Caleb began.

"Leave! I told you to watch your step, boy! From this point forward, you will not enter with the council!" Brodde yelled, motioning for his private guards to escort Caleb out of the room.

Instead of throwing a tantrum or being forced out of the chambers, Caleb calmly walked out on his own accord and smiled as he closed the door. He would use his father's actions today to prove that Brodde was acting as more of a dictator than a council member. Caleb was deviously overjoyed that this simple act would only further his conversion of loyal Fågels to Frìth revolutionists.

With the doors closed, Brodde turned his attention back to Jeremias. "I do not trust my son, so leave when you feel it is best, and watch your back." Brodde handed Jeremias the parchment.

For now, the peace was still intact, but the true test of Sori politics was soon to come.

Chapter 8
The Failed Deliveries

"How long till we are ready to leave?" Captain Acker asked.

Reviewing the list Sergeant Major Brasher replied, "Just a few minutes, Captain. The last of the prisoners are being loaded now."

"How many this time, Sergeant Major?" Acker inquired with a yawn.

Finishing the tally, Brasher stated, "Forty-two prisoners, fifteen escorts, and three wagons, Captain."

"I will ride with the lead wagon, and you will take the second or third. It doesn't really matter—not like they are going to escape. The only thing that matters is making camp before nightfall." Captain Acker pulled his hat over his eyes and leaned back against the back brace of the wagon's seat. Instead of staying alert on these trips, Acker used them to catch up on sleep, typically to nurse his hangover.

"Yes, sir," Brasher replied, walking off to the second wagon. Turning to the private at his side, he mockingly repeated the captain. "'I want to make camp before nightfall.' We have twelve hours to reach a site that is seven hours away. How does it feel to belong to a unit whose captain can't even read a map?"

"When you put it that way, not good, sir." Private Fields looked thoughtful. "If the captain can't read a map, how did he get promoted to such a high rank? You would think that is one of the first things one should know. After all, it is about the easiest thing to do."

The sergeant major began laughing uncontrollably as they climbed into the steering seat of the wagon. "Get comfortable, Private," he said. "I am going to enlighten you on how things are done in Cala. For starters, our military is as corrupt as our government. Money can buy you anything in Cala. Titles, positions, ranks, and the list goes on and on. Captain Acker purchased his rank last month, and if you don't have money, the highest rank you will receive is sergeant major."

Over the next several hours Sergeant Major Brasher shared many of the dirty dealings in Cala. The journey to the prisoner drop-off was a day-and-a-half ride, but the Duines built an outpost to break up the journey. The outpost was nothing special as it only contained a single-room bunk for the captain and a place to tie up the horses. Upon their arrival Fields was once again shocked.

"Let me guess, Private, you expected a bunkhouse for all of us?" Brasher asked, trying not to laugh.

"Well . . . yes," he said rather disappointedly.

"So much to learn." Brasher handed Fields a crate. "You and the other privates distribute the bread rations to the prisoners. Then you all can start on dinner for everyone."

Dinner was simple, meat and beans, and took the soldiers little time to consume. With the sunlight fading, it was time to distribute night guard duties and rest before another long day's ride. All was going well until a few hours after midnight when Brasher noticed something moving in the distance.

"Fields," Brasher quietly called for the private. "Fields." Again, no response. "Fields!" he shouted, as quietly as possible, hoping he did not raise alarm. Finally, the private appeared at the sergeant major's side.

"Yes, sir," Fields replied, short of breath.

"Where were you?" In an angry but quiet tone, he proceeded to tell the young private how to properly make rounds. "You are never supposed to leave shouting distance without letting your partner know, especially your commanding officer. I must always know where you are."

"Sorry, I heard something around the prisoner wagons, so I walked the perimeter to see if anything was there. Did you hear something too?" Fields asked in concern.

"Was anything near the wagons?" Brasher asked instead of answering Fields's question.

"Not a thing. There were no signs of prints, animal or person, and nothing stirring in the distance. You may not know me well, but I know there was something there."

"To be honest, Fields, usually when a soldier tells me a tale like that, I tend not to believe them. However, this time I believe you. I haven't heard anything, but I keep seeing this dark figure over there. About fifty yards out. It has this strange red glow."

"I don't see it." Fields scanned the area but could not see a thing. "Nothing, sir, but that doesn't mean a thing. There isn't a person or animal in Sori that can make sounds and leave no trace of being there. A red glowing anything is not native to Sori, but it's a sure sign that something is out there. If I heard something and you saw something, then I will bet coins that someone or something is tracking us."

"You're right. I think we need to go check it out. Go wake a couple of the others to take watch until we return," Brasher ordered.

Fields did as he was commanded and returned to Brasher's side to make a quick patrol. At first there was nothing, no signs of anyone in the clearing. When Fields turned to his left, towards the trees, he spotted the red glow.

"Brasher, over here. Next to the trees. Do you see it?" Fields asked.

"Yes," Brasher said. "Slowly, try not to make a sound as we go."

Brasher draw his sword, so Fields did the same. The closer to the glow they got, the more discernible the ghostly figure became.

"You there. What is your business here?" Brasher asked.

"Well, good sir, I need some help," the figure replied and turned around.

The sight of the red-eyed, faceless, seemingly limbless figure immediately filled the soldiers with fear. Brasher nervously inquired, "What are you?"

"A traveler in need of help." It rose higher off the ground.

"Are you a Leigheas?" Fields asked as his heart began to race.

"I take offense to being called a Leigheas, or any of the sects for that matter. I am far greater than any one of you," the figure angrily replied.

"If we help you, will you be on your way?" Brasher was able to contain his fright, but a glimmer of hope entered his voice at the thought that this figure might leave them in peace.

"Of course," the figure replied.

"What is it that you need?" Fields asked.

"Well . . . I need you." The figure launched itself at the soldiers. They were unable to react quickly, and the figure's hands moved through their armor, ribs, and latched onto their hearts. Tightening its grasp, it pulled the two soldiers closer and released its poison into them as it squeezed.

"You see, a Leigheas can only twist your mind to do something small, like relinquish a treasured trinket or make you accept a lower price for a good. They can do this as much as they like as long as they do it to one person at a time. I, on the other hand, can reach inside you, turn you into my servant, and control as many as I want. My power knows no limits."

Fields and Brasher helplessly watched the veins in their arms turn to black. The darkness ran through them quickly, painfully, and only finished when their eyes turned as black as the night. To test his control, the figure treated the two as if they were marionettes. First the figure raised their right arms, then their left, and then both at the same time. Lastly, he made the soldiers turn around while waving their arms in the air. The figure was satisfied and had his fill of fun, so he sent his newly turned soldiers towards the Duine camp. Upon their return, Brasher and Fields were greeted by their watch replacements.

"Find anything?" Private Blackman asked.

Private Hendrikx scanned their faces and asked, "What's going on with your eyes?"

Without a word, Brasher thrust his sword into Private Blackman. Fields took out Hendrikx, and then the two killed the remaining sleeping soldiers. Many of the prisoners woke when Brasher and Fields began killing their comrades. Hoping to be released, the prisoners kept silent so their cries wouldn't wake the sleeping soldiers. When all the soldiers were slain, the prisoners became vocal, begging for their freedom. Fields and Brasher turned their attention towards the captain's quarters. Fields broke down the door to Acker's cabin, and Brasher pulled him from his slumber.

"Unhand me, Brasher!" the captain screamed. Acker's lack of military training and general weakness showed; he was powerless against his intruders. Brasher dragged him out of the small quarters by his legs. "Brasher! Release me! Fields, kill the sergeant major! Fields, stop standing there and help!"

Fields did not respond, and Brasher threw Acker next to a couple of dead privates. Fields handed Brasher a spear, and, placing a foot on Acker's chest, he thrust the spear into his throat. They watched as the life drained from Acker's body and then stood waiting for further instructions from their new master. Moments after the life escaped the captain's body, the figure once again appeared.

"Bravo, men. Bravo." The figure emerged from the trees. "You did well, very well, indeed. Now, place the dead bodies with the last prisoner wagon and gather all your supplies." Brasher and Fields did as they were told. Once finished, they regrouped with the figure. "Brasher, follow me in the second wagon and Fields in the third."

Without hesitation, Brasher and Fields went to their respective wagons and followed the figure as he directed them towards the forest. With a wave of his hand thousands of trees vanished as if they were never there, creating a path wide enough for the wagons towards the Aiten Díog. The prisoners, wrought with fear, pleaded to be released. The closer the wagons got to the ravine, the louder they screamed. Just before reaching the edge, the figure flew off his wagon and watched it fall into the ravine.

Upon Brasher's approach the figure called out, "Thank you for your service." The other wagons followed the first off the cliff, into the depths of the chasm.

Once back at camp, the figure waved his hand, and the trees reappeared as if they had never moved.

Standing in the middle of the camp, the figure looked around at the imprints left by the wagons, bodies and the blood that stained the ground. With another wave of his hand, all traces of the soldiers' presence were erased, leaving no evidence to suggest the prisoner transport made camp. His hand straight up in the air, the figure launched an arrow, producing a bright-green light across Sori that lasted for just a few seconds. Within moments the figure was surrounded by his dark servants.

"Your first task in your path towards ascension starts with finding me someone from each sect who is disgruntled. One who wants to step out of the shadows, who will do whatever is necessary to achieve their goals, and most importantly, one whose mind is weak. I need someone who is easily manipulated. While you search, be on the lookout for those who are strong. Look for the strengths beyond that of physical power. Be watchful for those who wield multiple powers known to the land and ones who are strong with the skills of leadership. Now, be gone!"

With that, the scouts took off to scour the lands of Sori. While he waited for the scouts' reports, the figure would stop several more of the transports—the first step in implementing his plan, a plan he hoped would bring Sori inhabitants to their knees.

CHAPTER 9

Business and Pleasure

Jeremias and Willum knocked on Maya's door and waited for someone to answer. No one came to greet them, so the two decided to check the barn. After riding through the night, the short walk to the barn was welcome. They passed many of Maya's relatives conducting morning chores—children feeding the pigs and hanging laundry to dry, teenage boys chopping firewood, and many wives tending to their gardens. The barn was as deserted as the house, but before they turned back, they heard that all too familiar sound of banging and clanging steel coming from behind the barn.

Instead of walking around, Jeremias and Willum walked through the barn and couldn't help but stop and look at the Dianas. After half a decade of visits to Dempsey Village, they still were amazed at the size and beauty of the horses, but also envious that they would never be able to own one.

"Willum, do you think that she would ever let us ride one? By one, I mean Saxon. He is by far the largest animal I have ever seen, and I can't help but wonder what it must be like to ride him. Could you imagine riding him into battle? The sheer sight of him would send most running, and those left would be trampled under these mighty hooves. Just look at the size of them. Truly amazing."

"You know that old saying, 'There are no stupid questions'?"

"Of course, I hear it all the time."

"Well, that was a stupid question, and if you hear that all the time, then you might want to rethink your questions before you ask. We may be like brothers to her, but if you mess with her family's traditions, then may the deities have mercy on your soul." Willum grinned and finished with, "You know Maya won't have any."

"Let's move on, shall we?" Jeremias asked quickly so that he wouldn't think about the wrath of Maya.

Walking out back, Willum and Jeremias saw Maya hammering away, her father stoking the fire, and her mother sitting on the fence watching the two while eating an apple.

"Good morning, Madam Dempsey!" Willum loudly called so he would be heard.

"Willum, Jeremias! Welcome!" Andrea cried out, running over to greet them.

"Good morning, Madam Dempsey," Jeremias said. Andrea squeezed the breath out of him.

"We weren't expecting you two to come here."

Willum had a befuddled look. "What do you mean?"

"Maya sent a message to see if you would meet her in Balla for a meeting in Cala. She knew it would be pushing it timewise, but thought you two would like to be there."

"Well, we never got a message. We left for here not long after Maya left Beinn. I got a delivery, and Jeremias has to clear up an order."

"Oh, well, it all worked out then. Will you two be able to make the journey?"

"If Felix agrees to take my delivery, then I am good to go."

"If you deliver a message and note what they need, then I am good as well," Jeremias added.

"It's settled then. You shall join her on the trip."

Willum peered over the fence to see Maya's handiwork. "What is she making this time?"

Andrea walked them over to the forge where Maya was placing her work in the water barrel to cool off. "Maya, the boys are here!"

"Come on over!" Maya hollered over her hammering. "I am finishing some armor for Saxon!"

When the banging ceased, a grin crossed Jeremias's face and he asked, "You think he will need some armor, do you?"

"It is better to have it and not need it than to need it and not have it. You know me. I like to be prepared for any occasion, so I must have my horse prepared as well. Besides, if you had a horse like Saxon, wouldn't you do everything you could to keep him around as long as possible?"

Looking at the plates of steel, Willum couldn't figure out what was going on, so he asked, "How come you are using plates instead of chainmail? Doesn't chainmail provide more protection?"

"That is a good question. Why are there so many pieces instead of one?" Jeremias was holding Saxon's chest plate.

"As you know, for the past few years"—Maya pulled a sheet of steel out of the water—"I have been practicing many trades, and in the trade of smithing and forging Elder Haldan Rangvald has taught me some great lessons. Among the lessons was a way to get rid of the impurities in the ore to create a stronger and much lighter product. Works for swords as well as armor."

"Still doesn't answer the question," Willum said, walking around the shop, only to discover a faceplate for Saxon. It resembled a mix between a bull and a boar, equipped with horns and tusks. It was so detailed that the only way one could tell it wasn't real was by the color.

Moving over to Jeremias, Felix jumped in and explained their rationale behind the armor. "To keep the weight down we have chosen to protect the most vulnerable spots of a horse. Of course, mail covers all major parts of a horse, but it also covers extraneous parts as well, adding unnecessary weight."

"The armor I have made is lighter, stronger, and once connected using a leather harness it will protect the same areas as chainmail." Noticing Willum's discovery Maya called out, "Of course, the faceplate will protect some, but it is mostly for show. The rest of Saxon's armor is on the bench over there." Maya pointed to the far side of the shop.

Jeremias walked over to the bench and inspected her work. Picking up the pieces, he was amazed at how light they were, but he doubted their durability.

"Are you really serious that something this light will protect better than mail? It just seems that a sword or ax could go right through it, or at least cause some major damage."

"Try it out. You have your sword, don't you?" Felix asked.

"Are you serious?" Jeremias asked again.

"Of course, go on. Strike it as much as you like. If you can damage the armor to such an extent that it will need to be reforged, then I will let you ride any Diana of your choice," Felix replied.

"Are you serious? Any Diana for just a hole in the armor?"

"I am a man of my word. If you prove that an ordinary Sori blade can damage her armor, then you deserve the chance to do something to which no one outside our clan has been afforded the opportunity."

Jeremias unsheathed his sword and struck the armor as hard as he could. Not a scratch on it, and the only sign that it has been struck was a slight smudge. Setting his hopes on riding a Diana, Jeremias struck the armor several more times. His efforts were in vain as the blows only added several more smudges.

"More durable than mail and lighter. This will save Saxon from carrying hundreds of extra pounds," Felix said, patting the speechless Jeremias on the back.

"I want some. When we get back, you must make me some. I'll pay if need be, but I must have some," Jeremias begged.

"When we sort out this thing with the figure, it will be one of the first things on my list."

"Hold on! I want some too!" Willum exclaimed with childlike jealousy.

"I will make you some as well, Willum." Maya chuckled at the two.

"Thank you," Willum happily replied.

"Honestly, it's the least I can do for you both, especially since I am risking your lives." Maya walked over to some unfinished leatherwork. Paying no mind to their expressions, she held up a satchel-like leather bag and explained how the armor was going to work.

In getting caught up in explaining the process, Maya had forgotten to show them one of the more interesting aspects of the armor. "Oh, and one last thing. Willum, can you put the faceplate down?" Willum did as he was asked and took a few steps back.

With a flick of her wrist, flames shot out from the horns and tusks of the mask. "Could you see this coming at you for an attack?"

Jeremias's jaw dropped. "That is one of the greatest things I have seen."

"Let's go get some food!" Felix announced, placing a finger under Jeremias's chin to close his mouth.

At the table, Jeremias and Willum pulled out a steel drinking container called a lager, and poured some of the contents into their mugs. The lager preserved the taste of the blood, and unlike leather containers it did not absorb large quantities of its contents.

"Sorry, but after a long night's ride we need a bit of replenishing," Willum stated.

"No need for apologies. Though we haven't been on this world as long as the two of you, we have seen a cup or two of blood being consumed," Andrea replied.

"Since we are somewhat on the subject, I would like to ask you a question about the blood supply." A touchy subject at times, Maya knew they wouldn't say no considering the current circumstances.

"Sure, feel free to ask anything. I actually don't mind helping others understand the consumption, and I'm sure Willum won't mind."

"Currently, there is no leeching process at Ghabháil, which means that a Duine will give you a one-time supply of about eight pints of blood. Is this correct?" Maya asked.

"Correct," Jeremias replied.

"So, how is it that a stock of no more than a few hundred Duine can supply hundreds of thousands of Veirlintus and Galenvargs?"

"That is perhaps the best question that I have ever been asked, but it also one that requires the utmost secrecy. If I tell you, you must swear the answer will remain with us and us alone. No one outside these walls can know."

Jeremias waited for their agreement.

"For centuries before the creation of Ghabháil, our sects had a very similar process of obtaining blood. There was a facility where our eolaís drew blood from the homeless, hikers or prisoners. They processed it and then delivered it to a few pubs throughout Sori, aiming to reach all those in need quicker than having a central location. In order to get a ration of blood, a Galenvarg or Veirlintu went to said pubs, ordered a drink that shall remain nameless, and they would receive a ration to tide them over.

"This process worked well until about ten thousand years ago when our sects had a sudden increase in birth rates. As the population rapidly grew, our eolaís realized that they would need an unobtainable amount of Duines to satisfy the hunger of the sects. They spent a couple of decades researching and experimenting until they found two solutions to their problems. The eolaís discovered that our sects can still thrive on two ounces of Duine blood per week. At the same time, they found that the coinín's blood is very close to Duine blood and it has properties much like our Galenvarg and Veirlintu blood."

The coinín was a small, carnivorous rabbit-like creature.

"It has the same mutation that allows for it to live longer by using the blood of others—in their case, the blood of other animals. Our body is not able to tell the difference between the blood of the coinín and that of the Duine. They also have frequent mating habits and tend to get overpopulated. Our eolaís established a farm, which is now at Ghabháil, to breed the animal in large numbers. Once they are a certain size, their blood is harvested, mixed in with that of the Duine, placed in wine bottles, and ready for distribution.

"This process has kept our sects from starving in times when the stock of prisoners has fallen to record lows. We must also have a steady supply of Duine. If the coinín were the only source of blood, then they would be hunted to extinction in a matter of years. Since this discovery the elders have kept it a secret, but as the years passed they have encouraged all members of our sects to raise the coinín ourselves. This way, if a member of the sects needs an extra boost of substance, they obtain what they need without exhausting Ghabháil's supply. It is also the reason why rare coinín has become one of the signature dishes at every restaurant and pub in our regions."

"That is most fascinating." The tale captivated Felix. "I had no idea that there was an animal whose blood was so close to any of the sects. It is truly remarkable."

"Wait, if it is such a secret, how is it that you came to know of it?" Maya asked.

"The secret has been part of my family for several generations. My grandfather, six generations or so back, was one of the eolaís who made the discovery, and he was one of the first ones to operate a coinín farm. In fact, it operated until the opening of Ghabháil."

"First off, fear not, my dear Jeremias. Your secret is safe with us. Secondly, do the soldiers stationed at Ghabháil know this secret?" Andrea asked.

"To my knowledge, they do not. The processing is conducted by a group of eolaís, and from what I have been told the guards are not allowed to be in the same room as an eolaí. However, this could be a tale, and the guards may indeed know," Jeremias replied.

"How come more coinín couldn't be used to help delay the lack of blood?" Maya asked.

"As I said, if we increased the consumption of coinín without monitoring the birth rates, then we would be worse off than before. If we kill all those eligible and used them now, it would extend our blood supply a few months, but then we won't have coinín old enough to reproduce for quite some time, and thus the strain on our sects would return. I am sure the eolaís have done all that they can to stretch out the stock."

The group talked about less serious matters while Andrea whipped up a quick breakfast. She cooked extra food so they could take some for the road. While Andrea cooked, Felix hitched Saxon and two other horses to a four-seat carriage.

Not long after the wagon was packed and the plates were empty, Elder Ludowicus arrived, and the group headed to Cala. The trip was pleasant, and the group was entertained by Elder Ludowicus's stories of his childhood. Before entering Cala, they stopped at the Leigheasan quadrant of Balla to stable their horses.

"Here you go." Kjellbjörn handed the three of them their passes. "They are unnamed, but we might expect a little hostility since I did not specifically state that I would be accompanied by a Galenvarg and Veirlintu. However, that's their clerical error and not mine. Shall we go?"

With a nod, they walked towards the path leading to the gate of Cala. During the day, the caomhnóir was always visible at the top, pacing around, looking down, and ensuring the peace was kept. It became the custom of the Faileas Herimen to hold their passes high as they walked past the tune, or tower, as an added precaution to keep the peace. As the group walked by the tune, they kept to tradition and held their passes above their heads so that the caomhnóir could see.

The Duine region was similar in size to those held by the other sects, but was much more developed and populated. The Duines could have placed their sect's council hall in numerous places, but they placed it near the gate to Balla, perhaps to limit the Faileas Herimen's time in Cala. The guards at the gates checked their passes, stamped them with a green bear, and let the group pass. It was a short walk to the council hall, and upon showing the guards their stamped passes, the group was permitted to enter.

The council hall was a modest one-floor structure with a four-tiered seating platform at the end opposite the doorway. The platform was behind a bar, a four-foot-tall, spiked, metal picket fence that stretched from wall to wall. Two dozen soldiers were stationed on both sides of the gates. They served as protection for the council members. On both ends of the platform's highest tier, a set of double doors led to a meeting room for the council. The council members, one from each of the Cala districts, were aligned ten per row and wore bright-red robes with a bear insignia, reflecting the flag of Cala.

"Welcome, Sir Ludowicus and guests," Councilman Swindlehurst stated, opening the proceedings. "I know we typically open with your request, but since this is not your first trip here and you always ask for the same thing, we want to expedite the matter at hand. We are aware of your need for a port as well as your typical proposal, but we want to offer a different contract due to our growing need for food. Instead of taking your supply to Balla's market, you can unload them at Titan port, and we will give you five coins more per fish than your asking price. In addition, we will pay you the same rate for as many deliveries as possible in a month's time. This contract will never expire by our hand but only by yours."

Swindlehurst handed a contract to a soldier, who handed it to Ludowicus.

"Agreed," Kjellbjörn stated as he signed the contract and then handed the document to the record-keeper, who scurried up the platform and out through the door leading to the council's private chambers.

"Are there any other matters you need to address?" Swindlehurst asked.

"There is," Maya said, taking a step forward. "My name is Maya of the Leigheasan clan Dempsey. This is Willum MacLeoid of the Galenvargs, and Jeremias Barraclough of the Veirlintus. We are representing our sects regarding the concerns with the absent prisoner shipments to Ghabháil."

"We have concerns as well. We have sent . . ." Swindlehurst had forgotten and was reminded by the councilman next to him. "Three transfers over the past month with a total of almost two hundred prisoners and fifty soldiers. Not a single soldier, wagon, or horse has returned from these trips, so we stopped all transfers. Though we have a rather large army, we cannot afford to lose any more quality soldiers. Not to mention the panic it would cause if the word of missing people were to spread. We covered up the deaths with a false story of training accidents and gave the families fair compensation."

Jeremias, Willum and Maya looked at each other in confusion and shock. If the Duines were telling the truth, then someone was intercepting the shipments.

"Council members," Jeremias began, "we have had guards stationed night and day since the first missing shipment, thinking that it could have been delayed. However, not a single shipment has come across our path, much less three shipments."

"So, the Faileas Herimen swear they had nothing to do with this? Nor have any knowledge of what happened?" Swindlehurst asked.

"To our knowledge this was not due to the action of any member of the sects. If it was, they were not acting on behalf of our councils. It would be an act of treason to murder another member of the sects, and if we had a term more severe than treason, then its punishment would apply to the one who interfered with the stock. Though I know many of low character, I cannot imagine someone stupid enough to interfere with incoming stock," Willum answered.

In the moment of silence that followed, Maya took the opportunity to speak. "Council, I have some news that may upset you, and I need your word you will not act in haste or anger upon hearing it."

"Well, when you put it that way, we of course want to hear, and I promise we will try our best to contain ourselves." Swindlehurst looked at his fellow councilmen. When he saw nods from his associates, he motioned with his arm for Maya to continue.

"We believe someone is using the forbidden and this person could be responsible for the disappearance of the shipments—"

"Seize them!" a council member in the back row yelled out. The guards drew their weapons, gates to the fence opened, and they advanced towards the group.

Maya smiled at Swindlehurst, and he knew by her smile that if the soldiers attacked the Faileas Herimen, then nothing but death would come to the council and the rest of Cala.

"Stay where you are!" Swindlehurst yelled. "Councilman Edwards, mind your tongue!"

At this point, Maya wielded a ball of the four elements combined, and the council members looked on in horror. Maya's ability to control all the elements had surprised many amongst the Faileas Herimen. However, the Duines rarely saw an element in use and had never seen anyone able to wield that much power. Swindlehurst knew that Maya had the potential to be more dangerous and destructive than an army ever could be.

"Councilman Edwards, is it? Any sect sending a lone representative is going to send the one who can do the most damage if threatened. I assure you, I am that Leigheas, but luckily for you I come in peace."

Maya paused as the elements grew from the size of an apple to that of a melon.

"However, if you break the peace we have here once more, rest assured that these guards will not save you from the pain I will bring you, your family, and your sect. Cala will lay in a field of rubble and ash." The elements disappeared, and Maya turned her attention towards Councilman Swindlehurst.

"Councilman Edwards, you are excused!" Swindlehurst commanded as he stood and pointed to the chamber door. "Your actions are most disrespectful! If you knew your history, you would realize that the Leigheasan do not acknowledge those who practice the forbidden as part of their sect. In other words, we are all on the same side! Now go to the chambers and wait!"

Edwards obeyed. Swindlehurst turned his attention back towards Maya and said, "My apologies, but you also have to understand that some of us older Duine, like Councilman Edwards, fear the forbidden more than anything else in the land. They know one who practices such things will not abide by any treaty or law."

"Apology accepted, and his fear is understandable, just not his reaction," Maya replied. "Willum, Jeremias and I are investigating the forbidden matter, but we need to find a solution for the supply shipments. We are requesting a meeting of the sect representatives with the caomhnóir to see if he has any knowledge of the forbidden being used, but also if he has a peaceful solution to the problem. Perhaps he could provide his protection on the next shipment, and if something does go wrong, we can trust his neutral testimony on the responsible party."

"I think that is a great idea and one that will help clear up this matter. Keep in mind that he may not be willing to join the transport. He is tasked with the watch over Balla, not Sori. When do you want this meeting?" Swindlehurst asked.

"I would have liked for it to be today, but I realize that it would be impossible to get all sect representatives at Balla so quickly. How about a month from now at midday?"

"I will make the arrangements with the caomhnóir." Though Swindlehurst was helpful, he was in a rush to be rid of Maya and her friends. "If there is nothing else, we thank you for the warnings, the visit, and once again I apologize for the actions displayed today."

"One last thing, councilmen," Willum said before taking his leave. "We are posting our most trusted guards on night duty to see if they spot anything related to the forbidden. Specifically, we are looking for a dark figure, wearing a robe, surrounded by a red glow. If anything of this sort is spotted, we will send a message to the other sects detailing what we saw immediately. It is a way to keep everyone in the loop. We ask that you join us in this effort."

"Consider it done." Swindlehurst nodded and left for the council chambers.

The group walked out of Cala and into the Leigheasan quadrant of Balla. There they parted ways with Ludowicus, and Maya guided Jeremias and Willum to the pub. Maya spotted many of the elders whom she had asked to join them at Balla and informed them that they were not needed after all, but provided details of the next meeting. Maya turned her attention towards Sir Elmer and walked over to the bar. Knowing the Elmer Clan very well, Maya asked to use the office upstairs for a bit more privacy. Willum and Jeremias joined her after they got their drinks, never ones to miss the opportunity to partake of Elmer's blue ale.

"Do you think Swindlehurst was telling the truth?" Maya asked, pacing the room.

All Veirlintus and Galenvargs had a keen sense of hearing and could recognize a person lying by their increased heart rate. Jeremias replied, "He was, and if he wasn't, he is perhaps the best liar in Sori. Heartbeat was consistent the entire time—well, except for the part when he was yelling at Edwards."

"William, what do you think?" Maya asked in hopes that his Varg hearing might confirm Jeremias's conclusion.

"For now, we have no reason to think he is lying. There is one thing that bothers me, and that is their lack of action for the men they have lost. If that had happened to one of our sects, there would be immediate meetings with Cala or possibly a declaration of war. If he told the truth and they did lose that many men, we are lucky Cala hasn't taken action."

"I think they haven't due to lack of food," Jeremias added. "If they are willing to pay more for Ludowicus's fish than his asking price, then that can only mean they are desperate. So, if a few dozen soldiers go missing, that means food and money for others. It shouldn't have taken the disappearance of three hauls to make them cease transactions. After the first never came back, there should have been an investigation. Their reaction makes me doubt they would have ever brought this to our attention, or whether they even care. I find the entire situation to be a bit puzzling."

Maya nodded in agreement and replied, "Good point. It also makes sense considering the high number of prisoners they have sent. What was it he said? Over two hundred prisoners, right?"

"I think he said it was almost two hundred, but what of it? That is great news for us." Willum took a large drink of his ale. "If we had over two hundred in our cells from just one shipment, then it probably would be the best month Ghabháil has seen in . . . well, in ages."

"The lack of food leads me to believe they are becoming overpopulated. When food is scarce and there are more people than can be provided for, then the crime rates soar. Just like how it did prior to the Great War," Maya said, taking a seat. "We may be seeing a new twist on past events."

"My grandfather constantly says, 'If you don't learn from the past, then the past will repeat.' That may not be exactly what he says, but it is something to that effect. Nevertheless, you get the point." Willum turned his attention to the last drop of ale in his cup.

"So, is he the reason you started reading?" Maya jokingly asked.

"Actually, he is. One day he walked into my house and found me passed out of the floor. He found the biggest book in the house, dropped it on my head and told me to start reading. Every month he had a new book for me to read."

Maya and Jeremias burst out laughing.

"You have got to be kidding me." Jeremias tried to contain his laughter. "How come I have never heard this story, and more importantly why do you still read them?"

"You've met my grandfather. I love him to death, but he scares the crap out of me. If I disobey him, it might be an axe thrown at my head the next time." Willum glumly sat his empty cup down. "Maya, have you seen any more scouts or the figure?"

"No, which also brings some concern. Scouts gather information, and their absence could mean the figure has found what he is looking for, for the time being at least. I must say, I am rather happy with their absence. It is a rather creepy and strange sensation to suddenly see a ghostly figure appear."

"That or the figure knows you're able to see him, so they are working around you or under the cover of darkness," Jeremias replied.

Maya nodded and added, "True. I guess this leaves us waiting until he begins the next step in his plan. Switching topics, do either of you know how the leeching is going?"

Jeremias shook his head, but William spoke up. "I hear it is going well. I think it will be the trick that saves the sects."

"Good to hear."

"Okay, well, we have a long trip ahead of us, so we must be off." Jeremias stood to take his leave.

"Willum, tomorrow is your blood feast, and, Jeremias, next week is yours. If anything happens before I see you again, send a message and

I will be by your side in no time." Maya paused and thought about the distance Willum would have to travel; he would never make it to the feast. "Willum, why don't you come back with me? With the Dianas pulling the wagon, we can travel through the night and make it sometime before noon."

"That sounds good, but I have to meet my family at the Halvvägs Sten tomorrow. From there we will join in on the feast. Now give me a hug before you leave." Willum held his arms open and embraced Maya. "We really do appreciate what you are doing to help us."

"I know you do."

"Okay, that's enough, you two. He's a taken man after all," Jeremias said, laughing.

Maya turned to Jeremias and gave him a hug as well. "Be safe on your travel back."

As the three headed downstairs, Maya was the only one who headed for the door. Noticing that she was by herself Maya asked, "Where are you two going?"

"We are going to . . ." Willum trailed off.

"Really? Couldn't think of one excuse? Got to see a man about a horse or settle our debt with Sir Elmer. Nothing?" Jeremias asked and then continued, "Well, since quick tongue here didn't think of anything, might as well fess up. The blue ale calls us for another round or two. Honestly, it's just so good, and we don't make many trips to Balla."

"It is, Maya. It really is and we don't. We really don't." Willum reverted back to an almost childlike state.

"Just don't drink too much. You never know when I might need you two. When I do, I will need both of you with all your faculties. Willum, don't linger too long. You need to hit the road as soon as possible if you intend to meet your family."

Maya started to laugh as she walked out. Jumping up on the wagon, Maya took off for home. She would have to ride at full speed the rest of the day and night to get home in time to help the rest of the Dempsey Clan prepare for the welcoming of thousands of Galenvargs.

Prior to the break of dawn, all the clans south of Dempsey Village arrived to begin the blood-donating process with the dochtúirs. By dawn, the Galenvargs began to show up. Maya was late to arrive but was still able to help the dochtúirs and distribute the food brought by the Galenvargs. It was close to midday when Maya heard someone yelling her name.

"Maya!" Willum called out as he approached her. "Due to the numbers, our council arranged times to come. Others are for coming for lunch and dinner. Is that okay?"

"Of course it is. I was wondering why there wasn't more already here when I arrived, but that plan actually helps us out." Maya gave Willum a hug. "I am surprised to see you here so soon. I figured you wouldn't have been here till later or not at all. How's your head?"

"It's fine, for the most part. A little bit of a headache, but I will survive. I only had one drink after you left and made great time. One more thing before you're off." Willum presented a gift from behind his back. "It's nothing big, but I wanted to say thank you. This may very well be the thing that prevents a war, so it called for something a bit more personal."

"You shouldn't have." She opened the box and discovered the treasure inside. "Do you know what this is? It's a violet edelweiss! Do you know how rare this is? How did you get this? I've never even seen one." The violet edelweiss was the only known flower that would never die, even when cut from its stem.

"Yes and yes. My clan's tradition upon reaching manhood is to climb Galenvarg's Peak and retrieve a violet edelweiss. This is the one I plucked upon reaching the peak."

"I can't." Maya tried to hand the flower back. "I can't accept something that means so much to you and that is so much a part of your family's heritage."

"Yes you can because if it wasn't for you, then who knows what shape we would be in. By the way, not a word to anyone on its growing location. There are only a few clans who know where it grows, and we like to keep it that way. Now come; I want you to meet the wife-to-be." He pulled her along.

Willum introduced Maya to his soon-to-be other half, and the day-long feast went off without a hitch. Dempsey Hall was filled with gifts of thanks, and the Galenvargs took a supply of blood to last them a month.

The following week was just as pleasant with the Veirlintus—until shortly after the start of dinner. Not long into the feast Maya went back to her home so she could replenish the bread supply, and to her surprise, a visitor greeted her.

"I did not expect your feast," the figure said, stepping out of the shadows with its glowing eyes. "This was a brilliant idea that I did not anticipate. It has put a delay into my plans."

Maya's arms prickled with goose bumps and her gut sank. A horrible feeling took over. "You are not welcomed here." Maya drew her sword.

"Sheath your sword. I come in peace . . . for now." The figure paced around the kitchen. "My scouts spent days searching for a Leigheas that I could use. They reported that you are the strongest of your sect and seem to believe you are the brightest. I was very surprised to discover your ability to see me. Only a select few see me when I don't want to be seen. Based on this, I am sure you have a host of other powers that may not have come to fruition yet."

"What do you want?" Maya impatiently asked with her hand still on her sword.

"Isn't it obvious? I want you to join me, of course." The figure stepped closer to Maya.

"What's your endgame? What is the point to all of this?" Maya wanted answers.

He calmly said, "If you join me, I will reveal my plan as needed. Now, what is your answer? Will it be yes or no?"

"If you ask today, tomorrow, or the next, my answer will be the same. No."

"I have many gifts, and among them is the gift of sight. I trap my vision in these crystals, and when they break, my visions can be seen. Let me share with you what is to become of Sori."

The figure broke the crystal, and Maya saw the same scenes that Caleb saw. He narrated the visions just as he had done with Caleb, but the visions did not have the same effect. When it was over, Maya immediately began laughing.

"You do know this is the same pile of crap Gilroy tried to shovel— visions of Sori being destroyed, the death of my loved ones, and the end of the Faileas Herimen. Let me ask you this, where am I in these visions, or any of the Leigheasan, for that matter? Your vision of the future is missing essential details. Believe me when I say that if someone threatens my clan, I will be the first to defend it. Your crystals and vision are a smoke-and-mirror display, nothing more."

"Gilroy had no real gifts. His powers were, as you call them, a smoke-and-mirrors show. Your 'forbidden' is a joke, and you know nothing of real power. What you saw is the truth. The only things that matter are the events, not individuals. You and your sect will be eliminated if you don't join me in my quest."

"*Tara, do you feel that? It feels like he is squeezing my head.*"

"*Yes, he is dragging this spiel out in efforts to control your mind, but your body isn't letting him in.*" Tara's tone grew angry. Ascenders did not take kindly to those trying to harm their Leigheas.

With this newfound information Maya replied, "You say you come in peace, but you try to invade my thoughts."

"Interesting." The figure immediately stopped trying to control Maya. "Never have I come across one who could resist my mind control, let alone feel my attempt to do so. You truly are one of a kind."

"You should hope that you never find out how unique I truly am. Now, since you violated your act of peace, you must return to the hole you came from, or we can settle this in a more unpleasant way." Maya once again unsheathed her swords.

"You may be strong, but you are a fool. Regardless of your powers, your days are numbered." With that, the figure turned and passed right through the door. By the time Maya opened it and stepped outside, the figure was gone. Maya rushed off to find Jeremias.

"Jeremias!" Maya cried. "The figure was here. At my house!"

"What did he want?"

"He tried to get me to join his side and enter my mind, but somehow he couldn't. I can't say what is to come next or when, but I am sure we don't have long."

"Well, the first thing we need to do is tell the sects. We promised we would get a message to them, so let's ready the birds for Beinn and Cala. We will speak with the council members who are here, and I will let the others know when I return to Frìth."

"Sounds good. Are you ready?"

Jeremias was confused. "For what?"

"Glory," Maya replied with a smirk.

"You do know we could die, right?" Jeremias asked as she hustled to the birds.

"Glory doesn't come just from winning. Even a martyr can achieve greatness," she yelled from a distance.

Jeremias stood and mumbled, "Yeah, but I would rather not die."

"What did you say?" Maya shouted back.

"Nothing!" Jeremias picked up the pace and caught up.

With the messages sent, council members informed, and the day's feast over, there was nothing anyone could do but wait for the meeting at Balla and continue to be on the lookout. Maya rested uneasily with the remembrance of the figure's visit and the thought of what lay ahead.

Chapter 18

The Building of an Army

"Some display by your father. How's your neck?" Arnolf handed his longtime friend a drink.

"It's fine, you can't even tell where his claws were now. People joke about their parents not liking their children, but I am certain that my father has hated me since birth," Caleb replied, bringing the ale to his lips.

"That is probably true. After all, he did give you a Duine name. Your father was, and still is, angered by your decision to run Ghabháil. He has no clue about how well you run things. He's too blinded by his frustrations to see the truth of the matter.

"You stopped the bribing of guards in return for extra rations, you streamlined deliveries, and eliminated the wasteful spending on luxury item for guards, thus saving the sect hundreds of thousands of coins in taxes. Your day will come, don't worry," Arnolf tried to reassure his friend, but he knew that, in life or in death, Brodde would find a way to crush the hopes of his son.

"As long as my father is alive, I will never have a chance to be an elder, achieve high rank in our army, or anything else I desire beyond what I already have. He finally openly admitted that he is holding me back from being voted on as an elder. So I have been thinking and wondering." Caleb lowered his voice, leaned closer to Arnolf, and asked, "What if my time is now?"

"You have got to be joking. You ask something like that after your spiel. If your father is keeping you from advancing, then the only way to rise is to get him to resign from council." Arnolf took another gulp of his drink and then began laughing. "You have a better chance taking him out."

"What if that is possible?" Caleb lowered his body to the table and drew closer to his friend.

"Wait, you're serious?" Arnolf also drew nearer. "If you kill someone on the council, even your father, it's death for you. There will be no trial, no escape, just death. Or they might make an example of you in public. The things they will do to you then are far more unpleasant than anything you can imagine."

"Do you trust me?" Caleb quietly asked.

"I did until you asked. Now I am wondering if I should. I have half a mind to drink myself into a stupor so that I can forget this conversation took place."

"Give me five minutes of your time and I promise you that I will have proven that now is my time," Caleb pleaded. Arnolf was his first stop in seeking a recruit. If he could not convince his best friend and most trusted colleague, then he would not be able to recruit anyone else.

Arnolf was curious. "I will hear you out, but I do not promise anything. If I say no and this plot gets exposed, you better not drag me down with you."

"After I show you this, there is no way you will say no. I need a room away from people." Caleb looked around.

"How about the cellar?" Arnolf suggested. "You get to be all secretive, and I get to sneak in a free round, or twelve, if this conversation goes sideways."

"That will work." Caleb led the way to the cellar, and once down, he pulled a crystal from the pouch the figure had given him. "Watch and listen."

Caleb smashed the fís crystal and began to narrate the scene, just as the figure had done with him. Arnolf was astonished at the sights.

"This isn't some sort of Leigheasan mind trick, is it?" Arnolf asked. "I mean, if this is true, we have to start mobilizing soldiers. At the very least, we need to build up armaments. There is no way we can let the Duine invade."

"This is no trick. The one who brought this to me doesn't have ties to the Leigheasan. He is something else, something I have never seen, but I am sure he is on our side and ours alone." Caleb paused to see if Arnolf would say anything else. When he didn't Caleb continued. "You said it yourself, something has to be done and soon. The longer we wait, the more time the Duine will have to prepare."

"Have you taken this to the council?" Arnolf asked. "This can sway them more than your father's words. Seeing is far more powerful than just words."

"Why? My father rules the council and would banish me from Frith. He would then lead the charge himself and only enhance his legacy. This needs to be done by us, the next generation of leaders."

Taking a drink, Arnolf paced around in a large circle. "How do we really know if this is real? What if our revolt is stomped out before we even begin? What if we revolt, start a war, and are crushed by the might of the Duine army? You know they easily outnumber the Faileas Herimen a hundred, possibly one thousand to one."

"Your concerns are justified. But if we do nothing, we will die, either from starvation or war. And if it is going to be war, why not give ourselves the advantage? Why not live or die by *our* choice, and not by decisions that have been handed to us?"

Arnolf nodded. "You're right. It is a matter of time before we begin to starve. Why not lead the charge while we are still willing and able to fight?" Arnolf asked, reiterating Caleb's point. "Who else do you have on board?"

"With you on board, the total comes to—" He paused, and when he saw Arnolf's spirits lift Caleb finished, "One."

"You have got to be kidding me! Just me?" Arnolf started to pace again.

"Okay, that was a poor attempt to lighten the mood. You are the first I came to because I want you to be my second in command. I know of a few others, and I also must go talk to a couple of the Hunds. The one that came to me told me I have to get twenty-three others, a total of twelve Fågels including myself and twelve Hunds, to join our ranks, and then he will meet with me again."

"Getting other Fågels on board won't be a problem. We can easily get several hundred by the end of tonight. The difficulty is going to be in finding Galenvargs to join the cause. For now, let's focus on getting the Veirlintus we need, and perhaps they know of some Hunds who'd be willing to join." Arnolf paused to consider anything he'd missed. "What do we call this contact of yours?"

"He never gave a name, and until he does we will just call him my contact. Where or who do you think we should start with?" Caleb eagerly asked.

"Well, the Pilkvist Clan is the most pissed-off clan in general. And they despise your father and the council. They have a set of twins, Ebbot and Eger, who I am close with. They will be the best ones to start with. They live down in Bouden."

The ride to Bouden took three days, and they arrived close to midnight. The twins were at the pub. Much to Arnolf's surprise, the twins weren't drinking but simply people watching. Ebbot was the larger of the two, with a more unkempt look: shaggy hair, long beard, and a sleeveless shirt exposing tattoos from his shoulder to wrist. Eger was clean shaven, hair slicked back, and he always wore formal attire: black pants, white dress shirt and a vest. They conducted all types of business with people from both the upper and lower classes, so their appearances were designed to ensure that they would not alienate customers. Eger dealt with upper-class patrons and Ebbot dealt with the middle to lower classes, a simple strategy that served them both well.

"Arnolf, it is good to see you, but your friend . . . not so much," Ebbot said, sitting up in his chair. "You should have given me notice of your plans to bring someone here. Who is this that you bring to our humble home away from home?"

"This is Caleb, son of—" Arnolf began.

"You dare bring a council lackey here!" Eger yelled, shoving the table forward and erupting to his feet.

"Yes, but wait till you hear what he is offering." Arnolf motioned for Eger to calm down. Upon his host resentfully taking a seat, Arnolf pulled up a chair. "For years now, your clan has plotted an overthrow of the council. Plotted, but never acted. Caleb is bringing you a chance to act."

Arnolf paused and looked around to see a room full of patrons watching their conversation unfold.

"Can we go to your office to discuss this further?" Arnolf asked.

"Ebbot, go get a drink," Eger commanded, and Ebbot did as instructed. "You have until Ebbot finishes his drink." Eger led them towards the office with Ebbot bringing up the rear.

With the door closed, Caleb pulled out a crystal, broke it, and began the spiel. Ebbot and Eger had never witnessed the forbidden, and this was all the proof they needed to join sides with Caleb and Arnolf.

"You two have yourselves an army." Ebbot sealed the deal with a handshake.

"An army?" Caleb was under the impression he was getting a few recruits, not an army.

"You two may think we have only plotted, but we have prepared. One cannot lead a takeover, build an army, or supply that army without preparation. Come, let's take a ride," Ebbot sternly demanded.

The twins took Caleb and Arnolf to an area called Aon Fear Talamh, commonly referred to as No Man's Land, about thirty miles outside their village. The location was riddled with hills containing underground tunnels and caverns from which no explorer had ever returned. The moonlight guided their path, and Caleb recognized the location. He grew concerned that perhaps the Pilkvists had led them to an execution.

"Is No Man's Land really the base of your operations, or have you brought us here for something else?"

Ebbot ignored his question. "We have over five hundred in our organization, enough weapons for three times that many men, forges for the making of weapons, and a supply of blood to feed every member for a month. All this with not a single soul outside of our organization knowing what is going on here. No Man's Land is the perfect place."

"Clever, very clever," Arnolf replied. "I've heard it is a labyrinth of tunnels and impossible to find your way back. How did you do it?"

"Every tunnel, path, and cavern has been marked with paint and signs. Specific areas are marked 'No Entry.' These areas dive into depths to which not even we dare follow. Every person who joins us is given a map of routes with brief explanations on the quickest way out," Eger explained. "Natural holes lead to the surface all throughout the system, keeping a steady flow of air, and we placed a few miles of piping vents leading to Marbh Talamh Lochán, so the smoke from our forges will vent outside."

"Can we go in?" Caleb anxiously asked.

"The tour stops here. We brought you here to show good faith, so to speak. We want a sign of commitment from you. Nothing difficult, just answer a question and answer it honestly."

"I think I can manage that."

"The crystals and visions were not of your doing. Are you in charge, or are you just the puppet?" Eger asked.

"I am in charge, but a contact provided me with the visions."

"Is this contact a Leigheas?" Ebbot joined the conversation.

"No. However, it knows the ways of the Leigheasan. To be honest, I don't know what or where my contact comes from, but I do know we will have an edge in our overthrow of Frìth."

"And the conquering of Cala, right?" Eger was eager to build an empire for his sect, but more so for the chance at ruling. He'd gathered this army to benefit himself, and no one else.

"Of course."

"Okay," Ebbot said. "What is our next course of action?"

"I have to talk to a few Hunds—twelve, to be exact—and once I am done, my contact will meet with us," Caleb replied.

"Just twelve?" Ebbot laughed. "Consider it done. We have about two hundred Hunds in our ranks. I will pick the most loyal and we can meet tomorrow."

Caleb replied, "You made my job easy. It is greatly appreciated. Now, I have a question for you."

"Go on."

"You have just a few hundred in your organization. How many more can you get to join?"

"The five hundred can easily be tripled with my clan alone. And that number will triple with the right persuasion. Now, where do we meet?" Ebbot asked.

"Oak Manor in upper Frìth, but it will take four or five days to get there."

"Fine. We will be there in six days with Hunds and Fågels." The plotters shook hands. It was a simple gesture, but as good as signing a name to a contract.

Well into their journey home, and far away from the twins, Caleb and Arnolf began to talk openly about their newfound partnership.

"Do you think we can trust them?" Caleb asked.

"You cannot trust anyone in what we are attempting to do, and, more than likely, we will not be able to trust anyone after we have done it. The rebalance of power always depends on greed, so you never know what to expect once things have changed. It is best to look at them this way: they are hired hands that we don't have to pay."

"Truer words have never been spoken. You know, I am rather surprised at how easy this has been," Caleb said, reflecting on his efforts. "We are talking about a takeover of Frìth, a war on Cala, and no one has objected to either one."

"The fact of the matter is that I have been unhappy for many decades. The Duine have no regard for our lives, so what's it to them if they don't send us our supply? Meanwhile, we look like simpletons waiting for our next handout. Cala treats their homeless better than they treat us. At least their homeless can rely on the arán lines to fill their bellies. We have to hope that each drop-off will have more than two dozen prisoners just so we can pass out rations.

"And your father is ruling the council like a tyrant. He never allows them to speak, conducts all the negotiations for work contracts, and none of them will stand up to him—worse than scared little children. Do you know he refused to renew my shipping contract? It costs me close to a thousand coins a month. And if I feel this way, there are bound to be thousands of others."

Caleb sorrowfully replied, "My father is taking out his hatred for me on those I am close to. He is more than abusing his power, and even if we didn't plan our revolt, I think we would still have to eliminate him."

Arnolf wanted to put the past behind him and plan for the next step. "How do you get ahold of your contact?"

"I don't have a way to make contact, but he said he would return when I had the number of soldiers he desired."

"How will he know when you have the numbers?" Arnolf asked, looking around as they rode.

"He told me that I am being watched."

"Well, he better show up, or we won't have to wait for your father to put our heads on a platter. The twins will beat him to it."

Nestled in northeastern Frìth, Oak Manor was home to Björn Tjäder, Caleb's grandfather, and upon his death it passed to Caleb. The ride to the estate took Caleb and Arnolf several days. When the sixth day arrived, the two began to prepare for the evening feast, killing and cooking a deer, as well as a hog. They baked bread, prepared side dishes, and retrieved enough wine to serve a pub an entire weekend.

"You're lucky to have a place like this." Arnolf lit the candles in the dining hall. "The only thing my grandfather gave me was the hide of the first bear he killed."

"My grandfather and I were close. I spent much of my childhood up here with him working on the estate. Though I was fond of my time with him, it was the time away from my father that I cherished the most."

"I didn't realize you were so handy around the kitchen either." While most men would mock Caleb, Arnolf was genuinely impressed by his culinary skills.

"Once again a benefit of living up here most of my life. My grandfather was possibly the wealthiest man in Frìth and could have easily hired more servants than he needed. Instead, he insisted on doing things himself and would always tell me that doing it this way built character."

"Well, he wasn't wrong," Arnolf snickered.

Time passed rather quickly, and soon a loud knock came from the front door. Arnolf went to receive the guests, and just as the twins had promised there were eight additional Fågels and twelve Hunds.

"I hope you have food ready. That ride is brutal," Ebbot complained, pushing through the door.

"To your right and down the hall," Arnolf replied.

Ebbot skipped the introductions and piled his plate high with meat, potatoes and bread. The others followed, and it was half an hour before anyone said a word beyond "pass the so-and-so." Caleb was alone in the kitchen when he saw the figure.

"I am surprised at how little you had to work in completing your task." The figure emerged from a dark corner.

"I hope you don't take it as a sign that I am not committed to the cause."

"Not at all. Some of the greatest generals have won wars without having to speak a word. People just need a figure to unite behind, and you will be that figure. It is they who will do the dirty work."

"I have to ask, how did you know when I had enough recruits?"

"Good question and let me show you." The figure lifted his arm and touched the air beside him. Instantly, another black figure appeared. "This is what your monks call a caillte anam, but most refer to them as scouts. They are Duine souls that do a master's bidding in hopes to attain what the Leigheasan call ascension. I use them to keep an eye on you and many others across the land."

"That is incredible." Caleb was in awe. He had always believed in spirits, and now he was finally witnessing one.

"They are but one of the many things I have to show you. However, that is enough for now. Our guests have feasted, so let's strengthen the cause."

"Wait, I cannot introduce you as my contact. What can I call you?"

"Call me Dullahan," the figure said.

Emerging from the kitchen Caleb announced, "My esteemed guests, I am pleased you have come, and I know many of you may be skeptical of my intentions. As proof that I plan to do as I say, I want to introduce you to the architect behind our plan, Sir Dullahan." He gestured towards the kitchen entrance.

Dullahan glided into the room, and the guests viewed an immortal being for the first time. Though they remained calm, no one moved, touched their food, or spoke.

"A bit of a dramatic introduction. Nevertheless, we do not intend to take over just Frìth and Beinn. We will control all of Sori. I can see that you all have many questions, but I am sure one of the first is why should you or anyone else believe me? I have many gifts, and one of these is sight. I will show you what is to come of your sects. For those who have seen the show, just sit back and relax." Just as he had done before, Dullahan pulled out the crystals, smashed one against the wall and narrated the scenes.

As the vision had faded, and before Dullahan could speak, Zander of the Veirlintu clan Bartholomew asked, "If this affects all of the Faileas Herimen, why aren't any Leigheasan present with us?"

"My scouts did an excellent job at finding those who would contribute to the cause. The Leigheasan see my gifts as the forbidden and will cast me out without hearing my words."

"Are they forbidden?" Zander asked.

"By Leigheasan standards, yes, my powers are considered forbidden. Do you know why they are forbidden?"

"Well, no," Zander replied.

"To limit the powers and capabilities of the Faileas Herimen. You all are capable of more than logging, tailoring, and serving drinks. You are capable of more than just showing your fangs and growing claws. I will show you how to make a blood supply last forever, how to control the elements just as the Leigheasan do, and how to have the gift of sight. I will show you this and more upon our victory."

"How do we know you have powers beyond this smokescreen?" Edof of the Galenvarg clan Göransson asked.

Growing tired of the doubt and questions, Dullahan slowly approached Edof and whispered in his ear. "Do you want a display of my power?"

"I think it will help us all." Edof laughed and looked around the table.

"Would you indulge me and please stand up?" Dullahan humbly asked.

Edof looked a bit puzzled at the request, so Caleb interjected, "If you want a display, then you need to stand up." Edof rose and stood a few paces away from the table.

Dullahan then touched Edof, who froze in place. Unable to speak, move, or blink, Edof was helpless. Dullahan then moved to Edof's back, reached into him with both hands, and pulled. As Dullahan stepped back, a blue figure bearing the likeness of Edof became visible. When the connection between Edof and the blue figure was completely severed, Edof's body fell to the ground. Dullahan closed his fist, and the blue figure was absorbed into his hand.

"What did you do?" several guests cried.

"He said he wanted a display of my power, so I showed him. I took his soul. I am growing tired of your questions. You have two choices in this matter: you will stand by our side, or you will lay at our feet."

"We are in," Ebbot replied without hesitation. The rest around the table nodded.

"Good." Dullahan then asked, "Are any of you good with metal?"

Dullahan revealed the next step in his plan. A step that would secure a foothold in their rising rebellion.

CHAPTER 11

A Shift of Power

Maya, Willum and Jeremias were invited to the meeting between the caomhnóir and the sect councils; however, Maya missed the first hour. Upon her arrival to Balla, she felt a strange energy in the air, and it intensified the closer she got to the tune.

"Tara, do you feel this?"

"Yes, this is most unusual."

"Do you know what it is?"

"No. I will confer with the others and get back to you."

"The sooner the better. I don't like where this is going."

Maya climbed the spiral staircase and opened the doors to the meeting room. When she entered, the debate was still going, so she quietly took a seat behind Willum and Jeremias, who were already seated near the back. Maya's arrival went unnoticed by everyone, including Willum and Jeremias.

Maya leaned forward. "Guys, what did I miss?"

Willum shushed her without turning around.

"Rude." Maya tapped Jeremias on the shoulder and asked the same question. Jeremias gave the same response.

Though unusual, she didn't dwell on their reactions and gazed around the room. There were more than just council members at the meeting. There were also personal guards. Maya quickly became bored as the meeting dragged out. The sects and the caomhnóir went around and around with the evidence presented, regarding the shipments, but no progress was being made.

"So far I have heard from all sects, and the only thing we have to go by is each other's word. No one knows what happened. In turn, you are just accusing each other of fault and not finding out what actually happened," the caomhnóir stated.

"Sir Caomhnóir, we know you have been alive since the creation of the Covenant, and it is the guidelines of the Covenant that we are following. Its guidelines state that 'any violation of said covenant will be appealed to the caomhnóir for investigation, thus to ensure peace among the sects.' A missing blood supply is a violation and must be addressed by a neutral party," Clare stated on behalf of the sects.

"I understand that, but the simple fact is that no one has proof of foul play. There were no traces of the shipments entering Faileas Herimen territory. However, we do have records showing the documentation of the soldiers and prisoners leaving Cala. In addition, to this date, none of the soldiers have returned. There are no signs of their wagons, horses, or if they made camp.

"So, I ask you, where is the proof that the Duines failed to deliver the shipment? To the Duines I ask, where is the proof to show the Faileas Herimen took the shipment and killed the Duine soldiers? Quite simply, it appears that multiple shipments have disappeared into thin air, and no one here can really prove or disprove anything." The caomhnóir showed more frustration as the conversation waged on.

Maya suddenly felt a surge of energy, and her head started to ache. She had a sense of déjà vu when she heard,

"So far I have heard from all sects and the only thing we have to go by is each other's word that no one knows what happened . . ."

Maya lifted her head, and as the caomhnóir continued, she called upon Tara.

"*Tara, can you hear them?*"

"*Yes, the speakers are repeating what has already been stated. We were late getting here, so I wonder how long this has been going on.*"

"*How is this possible?*" Maya scanned the room as Clare spoke.

"Sir Caomhnóir, we know you have been alive since the creation of the Covenant and it is the guidelines of the Covenant that we are following . . ."

"*The energy that we feel has to be connected to the repetition. It must be coming from the figure,*" Tara suggested. "*I would have never imagined it to be this powerful. It is able to control everyone in the room at once.*"

"*How can I stop this? Is there a way to break the cycle without harming everyone in the room?*"

"*I am not sure. Once again you need to call on Malaki. I am sure he will have the answer,*" Tara replied as the caomhnóir responded to Clare.

"I understand that, but the simple fact is that no one has proof of foul play. There were no traces of the shipments entering Faileas Herimen territory . . ."

"*Malaki, do you have any suggestions on what I can do?*" Maya rose and began walking around the hall.

"*The figure is using mind control just as we do, but on a much larger scale. To achieve this, he must concentrate without interference. If we want this to end, we have to find the figure and break his concentration.*"

"*How is it that I am unable to see him? Is it possible that he isn't in the room?*"

"*Yes, it is possible, but unlikely when controlling this many people. Perhaps he is using something to mask himself. He knows your power is great enough to see through his, so it is very possible that he is using something like a rinn, like the Rinn of Laufeyjarson. Cloaking devices are common in many realms.*"

Maya inspected the shadows, using her shillelagh to poke the dark areas in hopes of hitting the figure. She continued to do this as she moved closer to the caomhnóir. The closer she got to the caomhnóir, the more Maya noticed something was different. He was missing the glow of his ascenders.

"*Does anyone else see the caomhnóir?*"

It took Tara a minute, but she responded with, "*He doesn't have ascenders with him.*"

"*How is this possible? He was supposed to be part of all the sects.*"

"*When we leave here, we need to visit the monks and get answers,*" Malaki suggested.

Tara was quick to interject, "*But for now we have to focus on breaking this effect the figure has on the elders.*"

Maya's search was futile. She could easily be chasing the figure in a circle or be nowhere close to him. Recalling Malaki's words, without consulting Tara or Malaki, she walked to the center of the room. Her presence continued to go unnoticed, and once there she turned her shillelagh into stone. It now had the look of a Berserker war hammer.

Maya jumped into the air, reared the hammer back, and slammed it onto the stone floor on her descent, producing a shock wave that shook the entire tune. As the wave radiated out, it not only broke Dullahan's concentration but also the cloak pin holding the rinn to his body. The rinn flew from him, revealing his location in the room. Everyone else was knocked unconscious.

Dullahan launched towards Maya, reaching out in hopes of turning her into his puppet, just as he did with the Duines Brasher and Fields. Before he could make contact, Maya shoved the hammer against his chest, stopping him.

"How?" Dullahan demanded. "No one in this realm should be this strong! No one!"

Without responding, Maya swung the war hammer again, this time aiming for Dullahan's head. A sword extended from his hand and stopped the hammer in its tracks; the stone disintegrated to reveal her shillelagh. Maya threw her shillelagh down and unsheathed her swords, but as she did, Dullahan took off through the nearest window. Following him, she jumped and used the wind to guide her to the ground safely.

Dullahan waited for her to land. Instead of trying to match sword skills or powers, he decided to use brute strength. Maya swung her swords, but missed as Dullahan ducked to her side and connected two punches to her ribs. Dullahan's touch caused the cloth of Maya's shirt to disintegrate, and her skin burned, turning grey. It was like the touch of death itself, draining the life from Maya.

Maya dropped her ineffective swords, and the two exchanged blows. However, Maya's efforts were in vain. With each punch, the skin on her hand burned and peeled away. With each of Dullahan's blows, she became more battered, bloodied and bruised. The final hit that laid her low was a punch to her cheek that radiated through her face. Blood spewed from Maya's mouth, and her eye swelled shut, an outline of Dullahan's knuckles imprinted on her cheek. Maya fell to the ground and was fighting to stay conscious when she heard her name.

"Maya!" Jeremias yelled, running to her.

Willum joined Jeremias, and their beast-like nature came out as they transformed on the run. Willum's yell rolled into a growl. His jaws unleashed a set of fangs dripping with drool. His shirt tore at the seams as his muscles were freed. His fists unclutched to allow claws to grow freely out instead of into the palm of his hand. Jeremias was the less intimidating of the two; his dagger-like fangs were nothing compared to the set of teeth snarling from Willum's mouth, and the growth of his claws was minimal. The display would leave any onlooker believing that the Galenvargs were the fiercest of the sects. Dullahan fled before he could finish Maya off. Willum started to pursue Dullahan, but there was no trace of the figure.

Jeremias yelled, "Willum! Stop! I need your help!" Willum put away his hunger for vengeance and rushed back. "We need to get her to a healer."

"The closest Leigheasan village is a good twenty-minute ride from here, and I'm not sure if she will survive that, even in a cart. Her wounds are like nothing that I have seen, and they seem to be getting worse," Willum replied.

"The pub in the Leigheasan quadrant is not that far, and the Elmer Clan is fond of Maya. They will want to help."

Willum spotted a hand cart nearby and rushed it to Maya's side. They carefully picked her up and placed her on the cart.

"Grab her swords," Willum commanded before they left. Jeremias retrieved the rarest weapons in Sori and placed them at Maya's side.

Barging into the pub and clearing off a table, they gently laid Maya down. With no patrons in the pub, Sir Elmer and his sons rushed over to offer their assistance. Elmer closely examined Maya's wounds and was dumbfounded.

"What could have caused such wounds? Did you boys see who did this?" Sir Elmer asked.

"It was a fight between Maya and this—" Willum paused. "We really don't know what it was. We are just calling it the figure until we find out its name."

"A fight? An exchange of blows shouldn't have been able to do this to someone. This is most strange," Sir Elmer said.

"Sir Elmer, is there anything you can do?" Jeremias feared the worst. If Maya didn't survive, what would become of Sori?

"A couple things, but my skill set is making and pouring drinks, not healing. You must get a dochtúir. The closest is in Dunmanway," Elmer replied.

"Willum, will you go?" Jeremias asked. Elmer interjected.

"It would be best if you both went." Jeremias and Willum didn't question him and immediately left for Dunmanway. Though the Faileas Herimen shared their knowledge and many crafts, there were still several things that the Leigheasan kept private.

Taking a closer look at Maya's wounds, Elmer thought that she must have been infected with a poison. Dullahan's marks on her were now black with a halo of grey veins radiating from the center.

Sir Elmer cried out, "Gunnar!" His eldest son quickly appeared from the back storeroom. "Run to the cellar and get a barrel of ambrosia."

Gunnar returned quickly with a barrel, and then his father ordered, "Hand me a rag." As Gunnar ran behind the bar to get a rag, Sir Elmer opened the barrel.

"Here you go, Father." Gunnar handed him the rag. "What are you going to do?"

"Ambrosia is best while ingested, but it can be absorbed through our skin. It will help in the healing of her wounds. It won't be a complete healing, but it will be enough to stabilize her and to keep her from crossing over. I want you to use a spoon and give her a little bit at a time so she won't choke."

The two began doctoring to the best of their abilities, and to Gunnar's surprise, it was helping. Small portions of Maya's flesh began regenerating, while the burns on her face, arms and ribs lessened in severity. The ambrosia was healing her from the inside and out. Luckily for Maya, it wasn't long before Jeremias and Willum returned with Dunmanway's dochtúir.

"Sir Elmer, we brought Sir Adema from Dunmanway," Jeremias said as he opened the door.

"Please, call me Vilken," Sir Adema said, shaking Sir Elmer's hand.

"Vilken, I'm Wolfgang Elmer and this is my son Gunnar."

Vilken nodded at Gunnar and noticed the barrel of ambrosia on the table. He panicked and tried to shield it from Willum and Jeremias.

"Vilken, I too sought to hide our secrets from them, but time is of the essence, and they did save her life. I trust that they are confidants of Maya," Sir Elmer stated. "The doses of ambrosia have helped, but not to the extent we hoped it would."

"What's ambrosia?" Willum asked as Vilken examined Maya.

"It is a drink that we use to rejuvenate the body. It works on us much like blood works on you," Gunnar explained. Both Willum and Jeremias were shocked. "Haven't you ever noticed that we Leigheasan tend to live much longer than the Duine?"

"When you live as long as we do, you tend not to pay attention to age," Jeremias replied.

After examining Maya's face, hands, exposed ribs, stomach and back, Sir Adema was uncertain of how to treat the wounds. "These wounds are unlike anything that I have ever seen. What caused this?"

"None of us witnessed what happened, but we are certain it was due to a fight with one who practices the forbidden," Willum answered. "This figure is more like a ghost than a person. It lacks discernible features, wears a black robe, hovers above the ground, and it can appear and disappear at will. Judging from Maya's wounds, it is able to make contact. Until now we thought that this figure was truly more of a ghost than a person."

"I can only treat this like any other burn wound. I have some herbs that I will wrap in a leaf and then tie to her ribs, stomach, and back. I won't tie it to her face but place it there with some láibduille. It will help prevent it from falling off, plus assist with the healing."

He quickly did as he said and then spoke with both Willum and Jeremias. "These wounds are beyond what we dochtúirs can treat and beyond the use of the forbidden. I may not know everything in this world, but I do know that this figure, as you call him, is not from our realm. Her village dochtúir will be able to continue the treatment. I will send word on what I have done. You also need to recount the events to her family and dochtúir. Beyond this, I do not know how to help her."

Sir Adema turned to the Elmers, shook their hands, and left for his home.

"Sir Elmer, we cannot thank you enough." Jeremias pulled the remaining coins from his money sack. "Will this be enough to cover the cost of her care?"

"No payment needed. Our way is to take care of our own and those in need; we don't profit from misfortunes such as this," Elmer replied.

"Thank you, but I insist." Jeremias placed the coins in his hand.

"Next time you come in, the drinks are on me." Elmer took the coins to his cash box.

"Deal." Jeremias helped Willum pick Maya up.

"Actually, can we get a pint of blue ale for the road?" Willum asked.

"There's no time for that, Willum. Go get Saxon and hitch the cart to him so we can take her home," Jeremias ordered.

Willum brought Saxon as close to the pub door as possible, and the two loaded Maya into the cart so she could rest on the journey home. Though the distance wasn't great, the trip seemed like weeks to Willum and Jeremias as they watched their friend lay unconscious at death's door.

After the events at Balla, all the representatives agreed to adjourn for another day. Despite this agreement, the Veirlintus were not only upset that Balla was no longer a haven for the sects but also by the fact that their blood supply would continue to be delayed. The Veirlintu council met at Brodde's manor immediately after departing Balla, to discuss measures to be taken.

"Are there any thoughts on how to get our supply?" Brodde asked, taking his place.

"I think we need to march to Cala with some of our best guards and demand that we escort the troops," Marko suggested.

"Do you think they will consider this an act of war?" Sasha asked.

"Does it matter?" Caleb asked, stepping out of the shadows and walking to the center of the room.

"Who let you in here?" Brodde asked, looking around for someone to admit to their mistake. "Where are my guards?" Brodde yelled, but no one came to his side.

"Council, I ask you to hear me out. As you know, my father is not one to listen to others, so I ask you to listen to my plan," Caleb pleaded, and to Brodde's surprise, all the council members nodded.

"Thank you." Caleb continued, "If you go to Cala with troops, they might see it as an act of war and retaliate by killing our men. After all, our men would be vastly outnumbered. As a result, we would be thrust into war and be free to obtain our supply by force. If they don't see our troops as an act of war and willingly give us the supply, we simply march back with the stock we so desperately need. It's a victory either way."

Caleb's intentions were not to persuade the council but rather to be a distraction. Dullahan concealed himself and twenty-two of Caleb's revolutionaries in the shadows just behind the guards and advisors to the council.

Quickly tired of the talking, Dullahan waved his hand, and his plan was set in motion.

Dullahan's Galenvargs had made metal detainment clasps. Before the meeting, the Galenvargs snuck into the council room and attached them inconspicuously to the council's chairs, positioning them to close around the ankles, wrists, and throat. Small blades along the interior of the clasps ensured that when sealed upon the victim, the clasps would maim enough to deter movement. Any excessive movement had the potential to clip an essential vein and cause bleeding out within moments, though had the council members known what would immediately follow, they might have struggled regardless.

With the wave of his hand, Dullahan locked the clasps in place around the council members' appendages, while the rest of Caleb's crew killed the guards and advisors. The massacre would appear to be an attack by the Duine. In Cala anything could be bought, so Duine spears and swords were easily procured. Spears were thrust into backs, as close to the heart as possible. Caleb's crew then slit their throats. The precise execution left the victims propped up by the spears and looking on at their dying comrades as the life drained out of their bodies.

"You pathetic excuse—" Brodde began, but Caleb quickly approached and grabbed his father by his hair, sliding his blade across his father's throat, and pulling Brodde's head over the blade to deepen the cut. He then pulled his father's head back, severing his vocal cords and finally silencing him for the first time since he'd joined the council.

"Most of you are wondering why this is happening. Frith needs new leadership, and since you never stood up to my father, you will fall by his side."

Dullahan interrupted.

"Words, words, and more words. What is it with you all and talking? Monologues and explanations just kill time and give someone a chance to ruin the moment. Just kill them all."

Within seconds the remaining council members joined Brodde in the afterlife.

Gazing around, Dullahan was pleased with their work. "On to Beinn!" he cried.

Eliminating the council members of Beinn required a more distant approach by Dullahan and the Veirlintus. Galenvargs had a keen sense of smell that was so powerful it would detect the Veirlintus, even with Dullahan's abilities to hide their presence. This task was for the Galenvargs.

The assassination also relied on the rogue group's ability to procure an item that could not be bought. Manach cochall, or monkshood, was a rare flower whose poison was scentless and known to only be held by the Gaeltacht monks. It was nigh impossible for a non-Leigheas to obtain. Even the Leigheasan were forbidden to procure the poison from the monks. Large doses of monkshood would kill anyone almost instantly, while smaller doses could take up to six hours. Dullahan, a keeper of many rare and forbidden items, gave Ebbot and Eger enough monkshood poison to kill each council member twice.

Dullahan ordered Ebbot and Eger to plant spies as servants in the homes of the council members and deliver the poison with their evening dinner. Each home was assigned three of their spies so that there would be plenty of help to eliminate witnesses. The plan went off without a hitch. The poisoning was followed up with Duine spears and Duine swords. The same fate met anyone near the scene of the crime. When their deed was done, the spies met with Dullahan at the northernmost bridge between Frìth and Beinn.

"All have returned I see," Dullahan said with a pleasant tone. "Any problems?"

"It was surprisingly easy, and there were few witnesses to be dealt with," Berk of the Galenvarg clan Bergfalk said.

"Good. For the rest of the night, go home and rest up. Tomorrow we start a war!" Dullahan cried out. He turned from the group as they shouted praises and meaningless words. With Caleb by his side he said, "Create an uproar about the deaths of the council members. Use your name to fill the open seats with those loyal to us. I will visit the pubs and markets to plant the seed for war in their ears."

Chapter 12

The Monks and Transformation

Waking up, Maya knew she had been unconscious for some time. Upon seeing her mother, she asked, "How long has it been?"

"Just over a week. How do you feel?" Andrea moved to her daughter's bedside.

"Despite getting my ass kicked, I am fine." Maya sat up, pulled her body towards the top of the bed, and rested against the headboard. "His punches burned like nothing I have ever felt. It wasn't warm but cold, almost like jumping into a frozen lake in the winter." Maya started to get up but Andrea stopped her.

"Just lay there and relax until you have regained your mind." Andrea tried to push Maya back onto the bed.

"I'm fine," Maya said, pushing her mother's arms aside. Standing, Maya examined her arms and touched her face. Not a scar or trace of a wound. "What did you all do? You can't even tell that I have been in a fight." She walked to her wardrobe.

"Sir Elmer fed you ambrosia. The dochtúirs wrapped your wounds with herbs, and I filled a barrel with ambrosia and let you soak in it for hours. I am not going to lie; you gave us all a fright. We weren't sure if you were going to pull through."

"Thanks, Mom, but where did you get a barrel full of ambrosia?"

"Let's just say your father has his ways and leave it at that." Andrea looked through her daughter's armoire.

"I guess my body is a bit too stubborn to let one fight take me down." Maya put on her tights, a sign she was putting on her armor.

"Oh no! No you don't!" Andrea cried out. "You just woke up and now you want to get back in the fight! You need time to rest! You will put down those tights and put this on!" Andrea barked and handed Maya a pair of lounging pants and shirt.

"Relax, Mom, I am just going to the archives. A fight is the last thing on my mind. There will still be time for me to rest and heal before anything else happens. The armor is just a precaution. If I had it at Balla, then it might have saved me from being so close to death's door." Maya reached for her leg padding and began the laborious process.

Finally she settled her chest plate into place. It bore the Dempsey family crest along with the image of two bucking Dianas on the sides, front hooves touching as if they were protecting the crest. All pieces of her armor were dyed black and allowed for a unique combination of protection and flexibility of movement.

"Fine, but I want you to take Jeremias and Willum with you," Andrea replied.

"You know they can't go. Can you buckle this please?" Maya had difficulty buckling the last couple of straps to her chest plate.

"Why do I bother speaking to you?" Andrea asked rhetorically, coming to Maya's side.

"Don't be like that. If I don't do what I have to do, then who will? And how many lives will it cost?"

"Times like these make the mother come out in me. You cannot imagine the things that were running through my mind when I saw you on that cart. I hope to never see the sight again."

Andrea stopped what she was doing and gave Maya a hug. The embrace only lasted a moment. Andrea perked up, buckled the last strap and asked, "Will you at least join us for breakfast?"

"Can you place it in a satchel so I can eat it on the road? I need to get there as soon as possible. I still don't know how far I have to travel." Maya put on her sheaths. It was then that she noticed something was different. They were no longer the light brown of unstained leather but black, like her armor. "How—"

"Your father dyed them while you were asleep. Come, let's get you some food for the road." The two walked downstairs to the kitchen and were greeted by Felix.

"I am happy to see you moving about." Felix handed Maya a satchel full of food. "We were worried that you would be out for another week, or possibly even longer."

"Me too, and you read my mind." Maya grabbed the satchel.

"Well, when I heard the news this morning and you moving about upstairs, I knew it wouldn't be long before you would need to go."

"What news?" Andrea and Maya simultaneously asked.

"Both the Veirlintu and Galenvargs council members were killed a few nights ago. All of Gleann is just hearing about it this morning."

"All of them?" Maya asked.

"Along with advisors, guards, and some family members. They were all stabbed in the heart with spears, throats cut on most, and others were decapitated. All done with Duine weapons."

"Jeremias, what about Jeremias?" Maya asked desperately.

"He and Willum visited here a couple of days after dropping you off to make sure that you were going to make it. I think it is safe to say that they are still traveling," Andrea answered for Felix.

"But I am sure things are not okay in Frìth," Felix continued. "Nor Beinn, for that matter. Even with a replacement council to fill the void, the sects must be in uproar and wanting vengeance." With a mouthful of carrot, Felix said, "Saxon is ready, and I must say your armor is incredible on him. I will have the armor for Willum's and Jeremias's horses done by the time you return, give or take a day or two."

"It was to be my task to complete, but thank you. I don't think I would have it done by the time we need it." Maya headed out the door, and her parents followed.

For the first time since she'd seen the scouts, Maya felt at peace. Most would consider it a strange sensation at such a dire time; however, Maya was one step closer to fulfilling her destiny. Although self-driven to learn and train, the path that Maya had been placed on was in part due to the guidance and training provided by her family. Instead of immediately jumping on Saxon, she gave her parents a hug.

"Just one last thing," Felix said, pulling a helmet from behind his back. "I know our sect typically doesn't wear helmets in battle, but I made one for you." It was a full helmet that mirrored Saxon's faceplate. "The faceplate moves up, and these two knobs here on the back lock it in place. Even with the faceplate up, you will be an intimidating sight with your demon-like horns. When you need to take a break from the helmet, just run the strap through the ring on the back and lock it in place on the saddle."

"Thank you. This is amazing. I cannot thank you enough, and I promise I will return soon." Maya placed the helmet on her head, and after jumping on Saxon, they rode to the edge of town.

Maya reined him in and called out to Tara, "*Tara, where do we go?*"

"*To Meadarloch. I will let you know where to go from there, but for the moment Meadarloch is our destination. How are you feeling?*"

Saxon took off at full speed.

"*Much better now. I am just a bit sore. I don't know how I am going to defeat this figure. Nothing I tried came close to affecting it. It appears his power is far greater than what I possess.*"

"*First off, doubt is the path to failure, and failure is the door to defeat. In times like these you cannot afford to doubt yourself or your actions. If you make the wrong decision, you must learn from it and move on. Secondly, there are a couple of things that you need to know regarding the monks. The first: the monks tend to remain neutral in these matters, so their advice may be vague enough to help but not specific enough to tell you what to do. The second: it is important to not get discouraged if they aren't of any help. Though the monks are friendly, you just never know what, if anything, they will divulge."*

The rest of the journey was silent, and for the first time in a long time, Maya enjoyed the view of the countryside. Just prior to arriving at Meadarloch, Maya once again stopped Saxon and aimlessly studied her surroundings.

"Where do we go now?" Maya asked Tara.

"Just to the west, around the mountains and to the coast."

The area of coastline Tara directed her to was no more than twenty feet above sea level. Maya guided Saxon over to the edge.

"Gaeltacht is beneath your feet, and the entrance is just off the cliff. Walk to the edge, jump off into the water, and enter the cavern below," Tara instructed.

The monks received their name from the caverns they resided in, the vast caverns of Gaeltacht. The Gaeltacht caverns extended up underneath the Naofa Forest and to depths so far beneath Sori that not even the monks had visited. All sects in Sori knew of the monks' existence, but their location was only disclosed to Leigheasan, and only when the ascenders of a Leigheas believed they were ready to visit the sacred hollows, typically shortly after achieving elder status. Even then, many ascenders did not know where the monks were located, so many Leigheasan had never visited the monks.

Maya did as she was told and jumped into the water below, but when she bobbed to the surface there wasn't a cavern to be found.

"Look up towards the cliff wall and see if you see the root system."

"Okay, I see them," Maya replied. She couldn't not notice it. The roots ran as far as the eye could see.

"Do you notice anything about the roots?" Tara asked, hoping Maya would see the clue.

Maya examined the roots and quickly found something unique. *"There is a single spiral in the middle."*

"And the single spiral is our symbol for what?"

"*Knowledge.*" Maya thought for a second and cried, "*Wait, that's it! That's the entrance!*"

"*Indeed; now go ahead.*"

"*It's an earthen wall. Do I swim under to an entrance or use my element to part the earth?*"

"*No, just swim straight ahead.*"

Though Maya did not fully trust her instructions, she started for the wall. Once at it, she passed through as though it wasn't even there. About forty feet past the cavern entrance, Maya's feet touched the rock bed below. She reached dry ground, where she was greeted by two giants and a gatekeeper. The giants didn't speak a word. Instead, they shoved their weapons, a sword and an axe, at Maya, and though they did not make contact, it was enough to let her know to stop.

Maya had never seen any living creature larger than Saxon and was amazed at the sight of the giants. They were at least three times her height and over one and a half times her width. Armor covered their legs, chests, and non-striking arms. Their heads lacked protective covering, exposing their unkempt hair and beards. It was hard for her to imagine anyone trying to enter without permission, or daring to try.

"Greetings, Maya, we have been waiting for you," the gatekeeper said. "The guardians of Gaeltacht that you see here are Ole and Ola. They have kept Gaeltacht trespass free for more years than we can count. They and their brother Olav, whom you will meet later, are the last giants left on Sori. You may call me Brother Keeper."

Maya was still in awe, but to keep from just staring she replied, "Hello, Ole, Ola, and Brother Keeper. The entrance you have is pretty remarkable. How are you able to produce such a grand illusion?"

"We monks, just like you Leigheasan, have gifts, and one of our brothers is skilled with the power of illusions, as you call them. He provides the false wall so that no one will discover our location."

"Interesting. You said that Ole and Ola are the last giants left on Sori. Where else would they be?" Maya also immediately followed up with, "Why do they call you Brother Keeper?"

"You will learn more of them later, but in short, our world has two more continents, one for the more supernatural, like the giants, and one for the distant descendants of the Duine. To answer your next question, we monks don't have names. To help visitors call on the brother needed, we introduce ourselves by the job we are tasked to do. I am Brother Keeper because I am the gatekeeper into our humble home. Now, come and dry off." Brother Keeper stretched out his arm with a towel for Maya to dry off.

With a wave of Brother Keeper's hands, Ole and Ola withdrew their weapons and allowed Maya to pass. Maya toweled off and was introduced to another monk.

"Thank you, Brother, for welcoming Maya."

Brother Keeper bowed and went back to his post.

"Maya, you may call me Brother Guide. I am the eldest brother here, and as such I am tasked with escorting our visitors and answering general questions. If I cannot provide a sufficient answer, then I will take you to a brother who can provide the answer you seek."

"Sounds good to me."

"Where would you like to start?" Brother Guide asked, looking out into the caverns.

"This is probably the easiest for me to answer. I would like to see all that you can show me, so a tour would be great," Maya said excitedly.

"Not a problem." Brother Guide proceeded to take Maya to the closest room.

The room closest to the entrance was considered by the monks to be the most important room, and regardless of the proximity, the archives would always be the first stop on a tour. Gaeltacht was a vast and magnificent place that held many wonders, but the monks were, first and foremost, purveyors of knowledge.

"The single largest chamber in these caverns is our archives. It is several levels, but please don't ask how many. It is an answer we will never divulge." Walking through a large opening, Maya witnessed rows upon rows of marble shelves holding a magnificent collection of leather-bound tomes.

Brother Guide pointed to the two brothers in the room. "Brother Seer records all the events that take place in Sori. He knows all that is happening and all that will happen. Working at his side is Brother Archivist. When Brother Seer finishes a new volume, he stores it, preserves the collection, and grants access to volumes that our visitors need. We all have a telepathic link to Brother Seer, and once a week we meditate to receive his updates. Before you ask, the answer is no, we cannot communicate with everyone telepathically. We only have that gift with Brother Seer."

"So much history." Maya touched a shelf with a reverence that few of any age displayed, much less those in her age group. She wanted to dive into the collection and learn everything about Sori, but she knew she didn't have time. Instead she asked, "How does one person record all of the events in Sori?"

"Good question, and the answer is one doesn't. We have many brothers who are seers, as well as archivists, and they take turns at the helm. There are several working in the back of the archives, and others who are sleeping or tending to other chores." Brother Guide motioned for Maya to follow him. She didn't want to leave but was led out of the archives and down the corridor, where she met the third giant.

"Olav, this is Maya," Brother Guide said, bowing to Olav, a sign of respect for him and his duty.

"Hello, Olav," Maya greeted him. He smiled and nodded in return.

"Olav, would you please open the door?"

Olav did as requested, and Brother Guide led Maya into a room with three glowing portals. "These portals are gateways. The green to my left takes us through time, the purple ahead will take you to the other continents, and the red to my right takes us to other realms. No matter which portal you pass through, you will always end up in the home of monks like us."

"You have mastered time and intercontinental travel? Wait. You said realms. What realms?"

"The portals predate us monks, but we have harnessed them. They are only used in dire situations under the direction of one of the brothers.

On your next visit, I will explain these further, especially the realms, but for now, just know that we are not alone. Now, on to our last stop before we get to your real questions."

Brother Guide continued down the corridor to a room with three chambers. A U-shaped stream ran through all three chambers.

"This section is reserved for the botanical gardens. To the right, herbs, ahead are plants used for tonics, and to the left are forbidden plants." A messenger bird flew by.

"I didn't know you had messenger birds here."

"We have bred these birds for thousands of years. It was we who presented them as gifts to the sects upon the signing of the Covenant." A bird alighted on his shoulder. Caressing the bird's wing, Brother Guide continued, "I bet you didn't know these birds are highly intelligent, did you?"

"No, not at all. I have never thought about it. I just assumed they are trained."

"They are indeed, both smart and trained. The fact of the matter is that they are smarter than most who walk on two legs. With the aid of some of our herbs, the birds have the ability to learn."

"How do they learn?" Maya pondered the implications for applying this practice to other animals.

"Every six months the birds are cycled out with new ones. They then fly to their sanctuary here amongst the plants where several of our brothers inform them of new births, new homes, and changes to Sori. They do this in a process similar to ascender transference. Each bird has the ability to learn on its own, but the monk's update of information is crucial." The monk paused, pondering whether he'd answered all of Maya's questions.

Maya interjected, "What about the possibility of people tracking the birds to this location?"

"Our birds fly a high, distinct path when coming here from any point in Sori. The path is so unique, lengthy, and arduous that they cannot be followed. Even you with your clan's Diana horses would lose sight of the bird and tire the horse out well before reaching our location. Now, time is of the essence, so please ask your questions."

"There are so many to choose from, but first I need to know: what am I fighting? The figure is the most powerful being I have ever seen, and it's not mentioned in any text I have studied."

"This figure, as you call it, or Dullahan, as he is calling himself, is a fomoire. A fomoire is the vilest of creatures that one can summon."

"What do you mean summon?" She doubted he meant it in the sense of summoning a neighbor to come visit.

"Summoning is a forbidden practice that allows one to create portals to other realms, primarily to the dark realms. It is much like the ascension process, but what comes through is pure evil. Just like our ascenders, the fomoires vary in strength and power. There are three types of fomoires. Dullahan is of what you might call a medium strength."

"Medium strength? You have got to be kidding." Maya was alarmed. "Honestly, I would hate to see one that is stronger. Fighting this Dullahan was futile, and the only thing that came close to affecting him was the shock wave. How am I going to defeat him?"

"The fomoire has a bond with its master, and if you kill the master, you send the fomoire back to its dark realm. However, you can also send a fomoire back to its realm by using a scythe."

"The harvesting tool?" Maya couldn't imagine a scythe bringing down such a powerful enemy.

"Same name but different object. In this instance, a scythe is a small handheld weapon crafted from the bones and blood of one who practiced the forbidden."

"How does the scythe actually work?"

"To explain this, I must backtrack, so please bear with me. When a fomoire leaves its realm, it is breaking all inter-realm laws. To escape its realm, it must be summoned, and to avoid punishment for breaking the laws, the fomoire takes on a cloaking form.

"This is the form in which you see him, and if he breaks this form, then his presence will alert the Rudianos, essentially bounty hunters who are tasked with retrieving those who violate inter-realm laws. Due to the summoning process, the fomoire establishes a connection with its summoner, or master, a forbidden. The scythe is made from the bones and blood of a forbidden, and thus simulates the master of any fomoire. Once stabbed with the scythe, the bond with its master is broken, the fomoire breaks his cloaking form, and becomes paralyzed."

"How does it paralyze the fomoire?"

"Perhaps paralysis is not the right term. For the fomoire to be in our realm, it must take orders from a master, and the scythe creates a new master bond with the fomoire. Since the weapon does not have the power to order a fomoire about, the fomoire simply stands still. One of the more interesting things about our cosmos is that there are natural laws, perhaps *supernatural* laws is a more fitting term, that cannot be violated no matter how strong the being or deity."

Maya sat in silence for a moment, taking in the information. "Two questions. The first: how do the Rudianos know where the fomoire is located? The second: who created these natural and supernatural laws?"

"Both are good questions, but the answers are uncertain. We monks are part of a brotherhood located in every realm and thus are sent information regarding all the realms and its sects. However, there is information that is intentionally left out so that no one realm is all-knowing. For instance, if we knew how a Rudianos could find a lawbreaker, then surely someone would try to create a way to go permanently undetected. As for a creator of the laws, we have no idea, and we have never been told about what can or can't be done. It is something that we discover as we go."

"Interesting." Maya silently absorbed all that she had just learned. "I don't know who the master is yet, and I am not sure if I will survive another fight with the fomoire. I have to find a scythe. Do you know how I can get one?"

"The only one known to exist in Sori is buried with the only Leigheas to send a fomoire back, which is in the middle of the Croí." The Croí of Beinn was a heart-shaped lake; its shape could not be detected from the ground, but from the mountains the form was easily seen. "The Leigheas took on the fomoire in what many of us monks consider one of the greatest one-on-one fights that ever took place. Would you like to hear about it?" Brother Guide asked.

"Of course, I never miss the opportunity to hear a tale of battle. I would like to hear anything you are willing to share," Maya excitedly replied.

"The Leigheas and the fomoire fought for hours. They exchanged punch for punch, matched sword for sword, and power against power. The Leigheas fought bravely and had backed the fomoire against the Croí, but the fomoire parted the water and lured the Leigheas to the middle of the lake. The fomoire knew that if he perished, then so would the Leigheas. They fought and fought, until the Leigheas landed a punch that caused the fomoire to stumble and lose sight of the Leigheas's attack. The fomoire never saw the scythe coming, and the weapon struck him in his side. The fomoire's connection with its master broken, a portal opened, and the fomoire was pulled back into its realm. The water collapsed atop the Leigheas, and in his weakened state, the swim up was too much. Not halfway to the surface, he drowned, and his lifeless body, along with the scythe, floated to the lakebed."

The monk looked contemplative as he finished his story. "You know, our tactic is to answer rather than direct. However, when the Covenant, or any other essential binding document, is broken, we tend to assist more than usual. With that said, you will not only need to find the scythe, but also break one of the Faileas Herimen laws. The interbreeding law forbids the union and the creation of hybrid sects; however, for you to survive another fight with Dullahan, you need the properties of the Galenvarg and Veirlintu."

"Wait, you want me to become part Galenvarg and Veirlintu?" Maya perked up. She always wondered what it would be like to live like a Galenvarg and Veirlintu.

"Yes, you need their regenerative properties. Galenvargs are fast healers, and animals also tend to be more immune to toxins and poisons. The latter will be handy in the years to come. Veirlintus are faster still at healing, so you will need their added abilities. Your healing will become very rapid, much quicker than that of either a Veirlintu or Galenvarg. As an added benefit, you will become stronger, faster, and your senses will be heightened. Now, you may not like what comes next. You will need to use your friends Willum and Jeremias to complete this task."

"I am not sure how I can convince them to willingly turn me." Maya's enthusiasm at the thought of becoming both faded as she realized the problems it would cause with her closest friends.

"You will find a way," Brother Guide replied with a smile.

"Is there a way I can do it without being bitten?" she asked.

"Now you're thinking. You can simply drink their blood. A bite contains the venom that helps one turn, but it runs through their entire body, so a bloodletting procedure will work just as well." Brother Guide clapped his hands, and another brother quickly appeared with a drink. "There is one thing I must ask of you." He grabbed the drink and handed it to Maya. "We call this tonic saol fada. It contains the leaves of the lotus tree, root of the crann na beatha tree, and the juice from a grape to give it some flavor and color."

Maya was hesitant to drink. "What does it do?"

"It will enhance the healing properties of the Galenvarg and Veirlintu. Ambrosia, as you know, is derived from the lotus tree. What you may not know is that the leaves of the tree are far more powerful than the fruit it bears. Unlike ambrosia, the leaves will never leave your system and are essentially the gateway to immortality. The root of the crann na beatha tree will help strengthen your body so you can withstand the mightiest of foes. With this drink and the blood of your brethren, you may just outlive the gods."

"It sounds a lot like Gofannon's immortal mead," Maya said as she looked at the cup's contents.

"Where do you think we got the idea from?" Brother Guide replied with a smile. "Ewan is very, very clever, like his mother."

Maya finally brought the cup to her lips and drank until it was empty. She instantly felt her remaining wounds healing. "This is amazing. I can already feel it working."

"This tonic is designed to work on its own, but it will work faster mixed with the blood of your brethren. Now, is there anything else you would like to know?" Brother Guide asked.

"Actually, there is. When I was at Balla, I noticed that the caomhnóir lacked ascenders. Since he is supposed to be all of us, how come he doesn't have ascenders?"

"Our creation of a guardian was not well received by Nantosuelta. She refused to take part in the process and blocked the caomhnóir from gaining elemental power and the assistance of the ascenders. Though he is not a full Leigheas, we still raised the caomhnóir with knowledge of all the other aspects of the Leigheasan way of life—though, in fear of retaliation from Nantosuelta, we also kept him from partaking of drinks and tonics used to enhance our lives or provide powers, allowing him only that which would prolong his life."

Curious, Maya asked, "Why did she object? It seems like she would welcome someone who could keep the peace and settle disputes without bias."

"Gods and goddesses tend to intervene, just as we monks do, with the lives of the sects, but their interaction is limited. A caomhnóir interferes too much. The point of your life is to live by free will and choose what paths you take. It doesn't matter if the path you choose is peace or war as long as it is your choice. The caomhnóir would substitute free will with fear. A life of fear is not what the gods and goddesses want for you."

"But with war comes fear."

"But with war also comes choice. You may choose to fight or choose to assimilate. However, when someone greatly shifts the balance of power, let's say with the forbidden, the deities pick a chosen one to help balance the power back to its previous state." The monk gestured towards Maya. "The caomhnóir is essentially a symbol of the sects trying to act as a god. I'm sure if we consulted the other deities, they would have similar objections to those of Nantosuelta. No one, especially the gods, wants to feel as though they are being replaced."

"If you knew the caomhnóir was not accepted, then why did you carry on with its creation?"

"The caomhnóir would exist with or without our help, but it is important to note that the Duine came up with the idea of the monks raising the caomhnóir. We agreed because we thought it would be best to provide a more educational and unbiased upbringing. Out of all the sects, the Leigheasan could have provided this, but it would have caused jealousy amongst the other sects, so they decided that we should raise the guardian. Now, I am afraid your time is drawing near, and you must get on your way."

"Can you do one last thing for me?" Maya asked with high hopes that it would not be a burden on Brother Guide.

"It is not often that I enjoy talking with those other than my brothers and the giants, but I have truly enjoyed our chat. It has been a long time since we have encountered a Leigheas who desires knowledge. I am happy to do something for you. What do you need?"

"Can you send a bird to Willum of Clan MacLeoid and Jeremias of Clan Barraclough telling them to meet me at the Croí?" Maya asked.

"That can be arranged. Good luck on your travels." Brother Guide bowed and walked Maya to the cavern entrance.

Once at the entrance, Maya used the wind to guide her to the cliff outside instead of swimming. Closing her fist and pulling her arm out, a series of steps extended from the cliff's side, disappearing once she'd climbed past. On her ascent, she was passed by the messenger birds dispatched to Beinn and Frìth. Saxon greeted her at the top. Maya jumped on her steed and made her way into Meadarloch.

"Hello, is anyone here?" Maya asked, entering the office of the village dochtúir. Not hearing a response, Maya once again called out, "Hello, is anyone here?"

"Yes, yes. Calm down. I am here. How can I help you?" A rather short hunchbacked man stood from behind the counter.

"Are you the dochtúir?" Maya asked in confusion. She had never seen a dochtúir in such seemingly poor health.

"Yes, yes," he impatiently replied. Placing a box that was resting on top of the counter underneath, he continued, "Now, how can I help you? I have lots to do and little time to waste, and right now, you are wasting my time."

"Do you have anything for drawing blood?"

"Of course, but not for you." He began walking off. "Those types of tools are reserved for the clan dochtúirs." Before heading to the back room he turned his back to Maya to pick up a vial he left.

His task was interrupted as Maya unsheathed her sword and split his counter in half.

"I am pressed for time, so I can either take what I need, or you can be hospitable and bring me what I need."

"Fine, fine. I will bring you what you need," the dochtúir replied, looking at his destroyed counter and stock. He slowly walked to his medicine room but then suddenly darted towards the back door. Maya waved her hand, and a gust of wind closed the partially open door. A flick of her index finger moved the latch in place, locking the door, and a rock cage burst through the floor, trapping the dochtúir.

"Poor choice, my little friend." Maya now turned her attention to Tara. "*Tara, who do I need to speak with to get the right tools for the letting process?*"

"*Call on Agatha. She is my most experienced dochtúir.*"

"*Agatha, are you there?*"

"*Yes, my lady. How can I help?*"

"*I need to conduct a bloodletting to become part Galenvarg and Veirlintu. What are the tools I need?*"

"*Look on the bottom shelf and grab the black bag,*" Agatha instructed, and Maya did as she was told. "*Open it up and see if you find a velvet pouch or similar.*"

"*Got it.*" Maya pulled out the velvet cloth. She unfolded it and found a bronze tube with a needle point on one end and a large open end shaped like a horn on the opposite side.

"*This is a letting horn. You will place the needle end in the vein, and the blood will flow down the tube into a vial. Grab two small vials on the shelf in front of you. What else do you need?*"

"I can make the forget-me-not and a dubh codlata, but it would be easier if he had one here," Maya said as she began looking around the shelves.

"Look beside the door and push on the wall. Every dochtúir keeps those items in a hidden room so the more valuable items aren't stolen or discovered by the other sects."

Maya did as she was told. She pushed the wall back and then slid it to the left, behind the rest of the shelving. The room contained more than she needed and much more than she knew of.

"Agatha, it seems like you have been here before. How do you know so much about this place?"

"All dochtúirs agree to set up our offices the same in case we ever find ourselves forced to use another's office. Then we will be able to find what we need, instead of wasting time searching for it. It is a very practical and efficient system."

"Makes sense." Before leaving, Maya turned her attention towards the dochtúir. Through the rock slabs, she grabbed him by the collar of his shirt.

"I am not sure what your problem is, but you aren't fit to be a dochtúir. Our dochtúirs are supposed to be compassionate and aid another Leigheas whenever called upon. Fix your demeanor or move on from your trade. Do you understand?"

"Yes, will you please let me go?" he begged.

"When I am far enough away, the cage will collapse, freeing you from all but a miserable life. If you go to the others in the village, tell them Maya Dempsey stole your items. I am sure they will be more understanding than you."

Placing all the items in a saddle pouch, Maya took off for Beinn. The trip took days, which caused Maya some anxiety. Willum and Jeremias were waiting on the dock when Maya showed up at the Croí.

"How are you two doing?" Maya asked, jumping off Saxon.

"Stressed. A lot has changed since we last met," Willum sadly replied.

"Maya, there is a lot to fill you in on, but we are a step closer to war. Frith is split between those who want war and those who don't. Those who do are mobilizing under Caleb, the son of the late Councilman Brodde."

"Beinn is no different," Willum added.

"Willum, was your grandfather among those killed?"

"He was, along with my grandmother, and a couple of my uncles who were in the house as well."

"I am so sorry. You should be with your family, not here." Maya embraced her friend.

"I cannot tell you how great a loss it is to me, but my grandfather would not want me sitting around at home; he would want me here to help you and assist in ending this rebellion before it begins. Helping you is the best way to honor him."

"Understandable, and to get to the point, I brought you here for your help and to share what I found out. After a visit with the monks, I learned that the figure is called a fomoire, and it is going by the name Dullahan. It can be stopped by a dagger called a scythe. The scythe will break the connection with the one who is controlling it, and it will then be sucked through a portal back to where it came from."

"Let me guess; it's somewhere in the lake," Willum suggested as he gazed out on the Heart of Beinn.

"Yes." Maya was already stepping into the rowboat. "Are you coming?"

Getting into the boat, Willum and Jeremias each grabbed an oar to start rowing.

"You're kidding me, right?"

"What?" they both asked.

"Do you forget who you are riding with? You don't need oars." Maya chuckled and waved her hand, and the boat took off towards the middle of the lake.

When they neared the middle, Maya put her hands together and then moved them apart. As she did, the water laboriously parted until Maya could see all the way to the lakebed. She used the wind to descend and help her land safely on the ground. Moving her hand ever so slightly to the right and left, the muddy earth was whisked away layer by layer until the bony remains of a Leigheas were unearthed. Careful not to disturb the

Leigheas, Maya grabbed the scythe, recovered the remains with the earth that had become its tomb, and made her ascent to the boat.

"What did you need us for?" Willum asked as she got into the boat.

"I thought you two could fill me in when we get back to shore, and then we can make a plan of attack."

"Makes sense," Jeremias added.

Back on land Maya broke out her breakfast and began to eat. She also pulled out the pint of forget-me-not and offered it to Willum and Jeremias. It would take some time for the drink to take effect, so Maya asked about the situation in Beinn and Frìth.

"How are Beinn and Frìth holding up since the attack?" Maya asked.

"I am not really sure. I've been with my family since we found out about the murders. After I got your message, I came straight here. All I know is what we said earlier: some want war and others don't."

"Same here," Jeremias said. "As bad as this sounds, you getting your ass kicked saved my life. I would have been in the council chambers and among the dead, but I am not sure what is going to happen. Your bird spotted me before I even made it back home. I only know what I do because of passing travelers."

"Oh, I have to take back what I said," Willum interjected and then added, "On the way through the villages coming here, I did hear a lot of blame pointing to the Duine. My father said they found Duine-style weapons, but Duine would have never gotten the drop on my grandfather."

"It's not like the Duine couldn't have a hand in it, but we know that this is part of Dullahan's plan. Dullahan is strong, very strong."

Maya stopped as she realized Dullahan's power might be irrelevant.

"Regardless of his power, I would think that in order to kill the council members in the council chambers, Dullahan would need help from those who know the area the best. At the very least, he would have to know how to go undetected by a Galenvarg or a Veirlintu. Even with his power, killing all the council members and many others in one night is a heck of a feat. Covering the distance alone is impressive."

Maya tried to think of ways to expose Dullahan and show the people the Duine weren't to blame; however, getting him to step out of the shadows willingly would be more than a difficult task.

"It wasn't just at the council chambers. Well, at least for the Galenvargs it wasn't. My grandfather was killed at home."

"This gives our argument more validity. There is no way a Duine would be able to freely walk about our regions without being noticed."

All three sat in silence until Willum said, "This is great," referring to the cup in his hand. "How come you have never offered this to us before?"

"Because it's not a drink you share with your closest friends." Maya stood and worriedly looked at them.

"What do you mean?" Jeremias pulled the pint from his lips and looked at the contents. He neither saw nor smelled anything out of the ordinary.

"I needed you two here so that I can get you to turn me. The monks told me that to defeat Dullahan I need to become both Galenvarg and Veirlintu. I knew the best shot I had at doing so was by asking you two to help, but I was pretty sure you both would say no."

"Damn right we would!" Willum yelled as he stood and then immediately fell down.

"Maya, did you give us forget-me-not?" Jeremias asked, fighting to keep his eyes open.

"I'm sorry, but I had no other choice. I must face Dullahan alone, and I need your strength to defeat him." By the time Maya finished her sentence, both Willum and Jeremias were asleep. She cut the dubh codlata to length, placed it on top of the roseroot and peet powder, and lit the green wick. All went according to plan with one small exception; Maya failed to realize that this candle was a slow burner, as denoted by the green wick. White-wick dubh codlata would burn for hours, but a green wick lasted days. She thought she had cut the candle length for an hour, but the candle would burn for a day. Unaware of her mistake, Maya began the blood-letting process.

"Agatha, are you still there? I am not really sure what I am doing, so I would appreciate if you could guide me through this."

"*Of course.*" Agatha talked her through finding a vein, inserting the needle, and draining the blood. "*You need to thoroughly rinse out the letting horn before you repeat the process with Jeremias. If you don't, you risk Jeremias's exposure to Willum's blood.*"

"*How do I do that?*"

"*Typically we use a solution called glannigh, but we will need to improvise. Rinse off the letting horn, then use your fire element to shoot a constant flame for ten seconds. That should eliminate any pathogens and venom there may be.*"

Maya cleaned the horn and then proceeded to take blood from Jeremias. Once finished with the letting, Maya stared at the blood-filled vials. She had never desired to drink blood, nor did she think she would ever have to do so. After a few moments of hesitation, Maya decided to get it over with as quickly as possible and chugged both vials.

"*Is that it?*" Maya asked Agatha.

"*You may feel a little dizzy and pass out, but that is all.*"

"*I feel fine,*" Maya replied, but as she said this, the world started spinning and faded to black.

While Maya slept, the changes from the two diseases began to affect her body. Her hair went from brown to black, and her eyes darkened as the traits of a Veirlintu were exposed. The Galenvarg side of her was exposed as claws and fangs extended and retracted while she slept. Though Maya had the assurance that these attributes would enhance her potential and not dominate her life, she would have to learn how to control the more primal animal instincts.

Maya was still sleeping when the dubh codlatas ignited the peet and released the herbs to awaken Willum and Jeremias. Fully awake, the two spotted Maya passed out just feet away. Willum grabbed a bucket of water, threw its contents on Maya's face and jolted her awake.

"How stupid could you be?" Willum yelled. "You could have died by mixing our blood!"

"The monks . . ." She paused. "The monks gave me the task, so I knew I would be fine. Plus, my ascenders told me before the blood feast there would be no real negative consequences. My trust in them is second only to my family, which is the area that the two of you fall into."

"Regardless of how many sources you had, the taking of our blood was wrong, and you really shouldn't have. No one from the sects has ever mixed our blood together; no one really knows what could happen," Jeremias said.

"Why are you so calm?" Willum demanded. "You should be outraged!"

"There is nothing we can do now, Willum, except be there for her in case the hunger strikes. Speaking of which, from this moment until we say otherwise, you are to remain at one of our sides. If the hunger does come, you will need one of us there to help you. The first time is always the hardest for a newly transformed, so we'll be there to help."

"I'm not saying that everything is okay, because it's not, but what do we do now?" Willum asked.

"We wait to see what Dullahan does next. I'm sure his next move will come soon." Maya embraced her friends as a way of an apology.

CHAPTER 13

The New Councils

All of Beinn was in an uproar with accusations and cries for war, but their thirst for vengeance would be delayed as the council was reassembled.

In the event of assassination or untimely death, advisors were in place to assume council members' responsibilities. Each advisor shadowed the councilman until the time of their passing, their resignation, or removal from the position. The advisors could be heirs of their family or a trusted friend. To allow new perspectives on situations, the council did not place regulations on who could be a council member.

The exigencies of Caleb's plot had left the Galenvarg council's successors unscathed. Once the advisors were informed of the events, they rushed off to the council's chambers in Keltoi, the Beinn capital.

"Greetings, everyone," Noak of Clan Eklof stated as the thirteenth new councilman arrived.

"Greetings," they all replied in unison.

Noak continued, "We all knew there would be a day where we took position in this chamber as an official council member. I think I speak for everyone when I say we wish it did not happen this way."

He paused and looked around the room to find many nodding in agreement, some tears being shed, mourning the loss of a mentor, friend, and relative.

"I know this may be hard to hear, but I am going to explain the findings of last night's events. Duine weapons were found at the murder sites, and the kills were consistent with Duine training. The murder of the council is considered the second act of war, the first being the cutting of our food supply. We have also been warned that there is a dark figure practicing the forbidden. I think it is safe to say, the Duine are the only ones foolish enough to use the forbidden."

"What about a rogue Leigheas? That is not unheard. Remember the problems that Gilroy caused?" Reinar of Clan Granlund interjected. "How many of our brothers were taken in the night by that piece of carnlem?" Reinar, being of upper class, seldom used foul language. Instead, he used technical terms—*carnlem* referred to feces.

"Gilroy never bothered a Faileas Herimen," Arie of Clan Langbroek called out.

"That's not true at all," Noak corrected. "He was responsible for the disappearance of dozens of vagrants and many of the poorer hunters. Who knows what types of experiments he conducted on their poor souls. Despite that, if there is one thing I can guarantee, it is that these acts were not committed by a Leigheas."

"You do realize how difficult it would be to achieve such as task without some type of power, don't you?" Reinar asked.

"Okay, perhaps guarantee is a poor choice of words, but I do not think it is the Leigheasan. There is no reason the Leigheasan would interfere with the supply shipments, only to offer a blood feast to make up for the loss of supply. They also wouldn't have warned us about the use of the forbidden."

"These are good points." Arie rubbed the hair on his chin, thinking the situation through.

Wanting to move on, Noak asked, "Now comes the question of how we retaliate."

"Meet with the caomhnóir and the other sects at Balla to find out who is responsible," Annamette of the Clan Winstrom suggested.

"That will not do. Following political protocol has only gotten our most revered savagely murdered," Noak replied.

"What does following political protocol have to do with their murders?" Annamette asked.

"If we had acted instead of trying to be diplomatic, then our council members and the others would still be alive," Noak replied.

Bernhard of Clan Ramecker couldn't take any more of the hypotheticals. He cut off his fellow councilmen and yelled out, "We are off topic! There is no point in discussing what we should have or could have done! So, let's get to the point of why we are here."

"You're right, Bernhard. What about the other Faileas Herimen?" Reinar asked. "Have they had any attacks like these?"

"We have not gotten word, but if it has happened here, I am sure it has happened in Frìth. I am not so sure it would happen in Leigheas Gleann," Noak answered.

Annamette asked, "Why Frìth and not Leigheas Gleann?"

"We have heard many rumors coming from the Gleann, and they are all consistent with little to no variation. It appears that the Gleann has discovered a new chosen one. A young lass named Maya of the Clan Dempsey, who controls all the elements and a host of other powers. It is also rumored that she hasn't reached her full potential. I don't think any sect in Sori is foolish enough to mess with Leigheas Gleann," Reinar answered for Noak.

As they spoke, a messenger bird arrived at the window. Reinar accepted the message and read: *Frìth council murdered. Duine weapons at scene. War?- Caleb.* Reinar had a grim look on his face as he turned to the council.

"Some of our questions have been answered. This is a message from Caleb, son of Brodde, stating Frìth's council has been killed as well, and it appears to be a Duine attack."

There was a moment of silence so the council could think. War was now at Sori's door, with the potential to be more destructive than the Great War. Some of the council feared that it could mark the end of the Faileas Herimen, regardless of victory or defeat. A victory could devastate the food supply, while a defeat would cause every last Galenvarg to be hunted and killed. Hoping to break the silence and get rid of the unpleasant thoughts, Annamette spoke.

"I know many of you are thinking about war, but we cannot wage a war against Cala alone. My suggestion is to mobilize and prepare an army. We should have blacksmiths forge weapons, shields, and armor day and night. Order our engineers to build siege weapons and have patrols running at all hours. Prepare for a battle, but do not declare one." This would at least buy them some time to seek out other alternatives to war.

"That is a great plan, Annamette. You are right. We aren't equipped to fight a war just yet," Noak responded.

"What is going to be that last straw that causes us to make a declaration?" Arie asked. "We surely can't allow another attack to happen without retaliation. We need to draw a line at some point."

Reinar suggested, "If the Veirlintus go to war, we must support them. Though they have greater numbers than we do, they are still outnumbered at least ten to one. With us on their side, we can slightly balance out the odds."

"In addition, if we have any more attacks we will retaliate," Noak added. "Is that agreed?"

"Agreed," the council replied.

"Send word to Frìth of this past night's events and inform them of our plan of action."

Word of the council's deaths spread across Frìth faster than wildfire through the Taran Forest. By breakfast time, all the residents of Frìth were aware of the slaughter of their leaders. To quickly provide leadership, the residents looked to tradition. Customarily, council seats were inherited, but four of the council members did not have heirs to take their place. Considering this, Caleb called an emergency meeting of the new council members to discuss replacing these vacancies with his men.

"Forgive me for not meeting in the council room. The events of last night are still fresh on the floor, and I wish to spare us all from its sight," Caleb remarked as he opened the first session of the new council.

He closed the doors to the dining hall, and as he walked to his seat, he began his prepared speech.

"We embark on new territory with the murder of our council members. We have four seats open, and to expedite things I have names for your consideration. Arnolf of Clan Olofsdotter, Ebbot and Eger of the Pilkvist Clan, and Addie of Clan Vinter."

"I agree with Arnolf and Addie, but having a Pilkvist on the council is not a good idea, much less two of them. They are too unpredictable, too angry, and a bit on the psychotic side. Though our council's decisions were dominated by Brodde, the decisions were still well thought out. For the most part, Brodde acted for the greater good of the sect. If a Pilkvist is voted to the council, then their impulsiveness could affect Frìth in the most devastating of ways," Councilwoman Karri of Clan Ulfsson stated.

Caleb was unhappy to meet any type of resistance but kept his calm as he addressed Karri's concerns.

"Madam Ulfsson, I understand your reservations about Ebbot and Eger, and you are just in having them, but Ar Dtús and all of Frìth are in an uproar. Its residents are seeking either leadership, vengeance, or refuge from harm's way. Ebbot and Eger have a great rapport with numerous clans, have loyal Duine friends whom we can use as spies, and will lay their lives on the line for our sect. They can lead, fight, and provide a safe haven for members of our sect in ways of which you are incapable. We are on the cusp of war, and when that time comes, you will beg to have a Pilkvist by your side."

"I agree with Caleb," Councilman Odolf of Clan Bréhal spoke up. "I am not saying war, but we need to prepare as though war is coming. My grandfather used to tell stories of the Pilkvist Clan's bravery during the Great War." He paused and chuckled to himself as he recalled the stories. "Come to think of it, bravery may not be the word. Perhaps it's their madness. Nevertheless, we need their kind in times of war, and they do deserve our consideration. I am not saying yes or no, but just to put our personal feelings aside and think of what will be best for Frìth. Just consider instead of reacting."

When he finished, he looked over to Karri, and she nodded in agreement.

"I am not so sure a war is needed. This assassination is too perfect," Councilman Timo of Clan Hallman added, looking around the room.

Caleb struggled to keep composure. Karri asked, "What do you mean too perfect?"

"Perhaps perfect is not the word; maybe staged is a better fit," Timo clarified. "If the Duine were going to kill off our council, why would they leave their weapons behind? Why weren't the kills more graphic to throw us on the trail of someone else? This seems, to me, to be the work of someone who wants us to think the Duine are responsible."

"The Duine have set the stage for this by cutting off our food supply. I think it is safe to assume that the Duine believe that the lack of food had weakened us. In this weakened state, they kill off the council to provoke a war against a handicapped enemy." Caleb tried to win over the council with an equally logical argument.

"You both bring up some valid points," Karri said. "I think we should wait until we reconvene at Balla with the sects before we jump to more conclusions or into a declaration of war. After all, the Duine have lost men in the missing shipments as well."

"I think we need to meet with the Duine council instead of all the sects at Balla, to see if they claim responsibility for the actions," Timo suggested.

"Sir Hallman, I yield to your logic. Would you feel comfortable with me riding to Cala tomorrow to speak on our behalf? I would like the rest of the day to mourn and bury my father." Caleb realized that the new council would be more of a problem than he estimated.

"Of course. We all need time to grieve," Timo replied.

"Before we dismiss, I suggest that we leave here with a functioning council to present to our clans a unified sect." Odolf was concerned that they missed the purpose of the gathering. "I say we approve Caleb's suggested members on a temporary basis with the understanding of possible long-term service. I am sure they will be valuable members of the council, but they need to prove they deserve to be on it."

The rest of the council unanimously agreed.

"We shall meet when I return from Cala."

Caleb watched the council leave the manor.

Creeping out of the shadows, Dullahan asked, "What do you think we should do now, my lord?"

"Sir Hallman, Madam Ulfsson, and their families need to be taken out." Caleb looked at Dullahan. "But we need one more so that we don't continue to raise suspicions it was an inside job. Someone who didn't speak today."

Caleb turned in a circle, trying to visualize everyone in the room. With a smile, he figured out the third target.

"Adler Leino. He has two other brothers in line for the council and was quiet as a mouse today. Their deaths will give us the push we need to convince everyone in Frith that it is time for war. Of course, we will replace them with members loyal to our cause, and war will come no matter what. If the citizens don't want war, then the council will vote and force them to go."

"Now that your father is out of the way, you are starting to live up to your potential. I will meet you at sunup, and I expect a declaration of war this time." Dullahan quietly made his exit.

"Arnolf!" Caleb yelled. Arnolf opened the dining hall doors and quickly came to Caleb's side. "Tell Ebbot and Eger to meet us at dusk with more Duine weapons. Oh, and congratulations on your acceptance to the council."

"Thanks. I will have them here before dusk," Arnolf replied and proceeded out of the dining hall.

Dusk came, and the twins arrived with ten Fågels, thirteen Vargs, as well as enough Duine weapons to kill triple their targets.

"Do not take this the wrong way, Ebbot, but Hunds cannot go with us tonight. Suspicions are out that the acts may not have been committed by a Duine, so we need to make sure no Galenvargs are spotted." Caleb turned his attention back to the map of Sori laying on the table.

"Don't worry, they won't be going. I just wanted to introduce you to Noak Eklof. He is one of the new councilmen of Beinn, and these are his most trusted troops," Ebbot said with a grin.

"All committed to our cause?"

"All of us," Noak replied. "My family has been friends with the Pilkvist Clan for centuries and members of their cause for decades. We are all tired of the Duine politics and begging for their scraps. You think your father had control of contracts? It is nothing like the Duine control. In my life, I have lost three businesses to them revoking my contracts just so their friends could gain another business. I only survived due to my advisory position on the council."

"What is the situation in Beinn?" Caleb asked.

"Did you not get our message?" Noak asked.

"We did, but I wanted an update since this morning."

"We are preparing for war. Our smiths and engineers are working nonstop on armaments. We sent word to all clans and villages of our intentions, and, thanks to your ruse, the majority are willing to fight. Thousands have signed up and are working on the war effort. There are still many that are undecided, but they are not willing to speak up against the majority. We can have at least ten thousand soldiers ready tomorrow and a number of siege weapons."

"How many siege weapons?" Arnolf asked, hoping to hear a large number.

"With what we have and at our rate of build, we will have over twelve siege towers and twenty trebuchets."

"Why couldn't things have been this easy with our people?" Caleb asked Arnolf.

"Wouldn't be much fun if there weren't any challenges, I suppose."
Arnolf turned his attention back to Noak. "We need more than that, but
we cannot build here and transport them across the Díog. Can you double
that if we provide the manpower?"

"Of course, especially if they bring tools, nails, and some ore."

"Consider it done. Once we take care of things here, we will send as
many men as possible," Arnolf happily replied.

"Noak, I want to thank you for your assistance in this matter. Your
friendship is most welcome. We will send word before the night is over
with our plan for tomorrow and, as Arnolf said, plenty of men and supplies
to assist you." Caleb shook his hand and they parted ways.

Under the cover of darkness, they marched to the home of Adler
Leino. With no pets, kids, or a wife, Adler would be the easiest kill of
the night. He was a poor excuse for a Veirlintu since he lacked tracking,
hunting, and survival or awareness skills. Adler lived off his mother's name
and her money. The sad sap never woke from his slumber when Caleb
entered his home, and he continued to sleep as a spear was thrust into his
chest. Though he was dead, Caleb still slit Adler's throat to simulate the
council kills. They moved on to the rest of the Leino heirs, who, unlike
Adler, put up a fight, but with strength in numbers, Caleb prevailed.

Caleb moved on to Madam Ulfsson's residency. As the third largest
in Frìth, the Ulfsson manor allowed for easy entry. Despite the ease of
access, Karri would not go down as easily as her home. Hearing doors
creaking that shouldn't be, she grabbed as many knives as she could from
her kitchen and headed to the library.

"No need to sit in the dark, Caleb," Karri called out, standing next
to the library door. "Be a dear and light the fire and candles, so we can
see your deceit in action."

"Very clever. How did you know it was me?" Caleb asked, flames
flaring around the room. Karri walked into the room with her knives
behind her back. Counting the numbers, she knew that she did not stand
a chance at surviving the night.

"With your father ruling the council all these years, treating you like a dog, and you being so quick to blame the Duine, it was easy to see what happened. Tell me, why do you want war so badly? Isn't it bad enough that we have the blood of thousands on our hands just so we can live? Or is it that you have grown tired of the regions and want an empire of your own?"

She flung the knives at her assailants. Caleb shielded himself with a book on the table next to him, the blade embedding itself in the pages. Of the five knives thrown, only one hit a target, causing a minor wound. Karri turned to run and four crossbow bolts struck her, two through her calves and two through her back. She fell to the floor.

"With such fire, I wish you had been trustworthy enough to join our cause." Caleb now walked to her, spear in hand. He bent over her and whispered in her ear, "You're right. Soon I will be emperor of Sori." Caleb then grabbed her head and slammed it on the floor, breaking Karri's nose.

"I wish I could have gotten the chance to watch you die," she said through the blood. "If only your father had the foresight to put his boot to you when you were born."

"Madam Ulfsson, the council thanks you for your service and your sacrifice." Caleb twisted the spear through her back and into the floor on the other side. Bending over, he grabbed her head and cut her throat to ensure life escaped her body. "How's . . . what's his name?" Caleb asked, turning.

"Dietmar, sir. His name is Dietmar, and he will be fine. A bit more than a flesh wound but not too deep," Ossi of the Clan Dəlilər answered as he wrapped Dietmar's wound.

"Good. Sir Hallman will be at the pub till closing, so we have plenty of time to set up at his house."

They chose a more direct method with Hallman. They were welcomed in by his wife. Within minutes, Hallman's wife and children were killed. Stumbling into his home several hours later, Sir Hallman was taken off guard when he laid his eyes upon Caleb, Arnolf, Ebbot and Eger, as well as others he didn't know.

He quickly put two and two together and slurred, "So, it was you and not the Duine."

"Are you surprised?" Caleb asked.

"No, not really. You have always been a sneaky little boy who was up to no good. So, are we going to do this?" Timo had difficulty standing upright.

"Well, you could fight."

"Fight? I can barely stand," he replied as leaned on a counter to prop himself up.

"Makes our job easier." Arnolf approached Sir Hallman.

"Just promise me that you will not harm my family," Hallman pleaded as Arnolf raised the knife to his throat.

"They are already awaiting you in the afterlife," Arnolf said, and before Timo could react, Arnolf's blade cut deep into his throat. After a few seconds, he stumbled to the ground, and Arnolf finished the drunkard off by putting a spear into his heart.

"I want every siege weapon we have on their way to the Amháin tree by dawn. Have Beinn send as many soldiers as possible to escort the weapons and make a camp to hold our armies. I will rally Frìth after dawn and lead them to meet the Hunds. In a week's time, we will march to Balla. Ebbot, send all the men you have to Beinn with as many supplies as they can carry as soon as possible."

The group disbanded, and once again Dullahan crept from the shadows.

"Well done," Dullahan stated, floating to Caleb's side.

"Thank you. I must say, I am not sure how effective we will be. Our army isn't trained, lacks proper military leadership, and is poorly supplied and running on emotions. Will the emotions carry us through next week, next month, or even next year? I fear what could happen if our takeover isn't quick." He looked at Dullahan and asked, "How will we get by the caomhnóir?"

"The caomhnóir is vulnerable to mind control, just like anyone else. I will distract him while you march on Cala's gate. It would be wise to set your trebuchets as close to Balla as possible and then attack."

"Agreed." Caleb turned from Dullahan and left for his home.

The morning came, and bells all over Frìth chimed to let the clans know of a meeting at Ar Dtús. Those who could reach the meeting in time joined thousands of Veirlintus in armor alongside thousands of others who had no clue what was happening. Caleb emerged onto the balcony of the watchtower overlooking the crowd.

"Thank you to all of those who came on short notice. Last night, more families of our new council were assassinated, and once again, weapons of the Duine were left behind. We have tried diplomacy to settle our differences with the Duine, but that failed when the sanctity of the tune was breached and the minds of our council were invaded. To prevent more assassinations, to restore our blood supply, and to establish Faileas Herimen dominance over Sori, we must attack Cala!"

The soldiers yelled and beat their chests, while many who had just learned of the second attack joined in. No one in attendance was against the war, and thousands of men were already lined up, eagerly waiting to join the Veirlintu army.

"Those of you who are willing to fight, join your brothers and report to our armory to receive your armor, weapons, and unit assignments. We will march to meet our Galenvarg brethren within the hour. To war!" Caleb yelled, and the crowd began to chant.

"Chun cogadh! Chun cogadh! Chun cogadh!" *To war! To war! To war!* This Veirlintu chant had been used as a rallying cry since the ancient days of the sect.

As his fellow Veirlintus chanted, Caleb looked down upon the mass of soon-to-be soldiers. Arnolf joined him. Every street was filled with men ready and willing to fight, and thousands of soldiers were departing for the Amháin.

"What do you think our chances are?" Arnolf asked.

"If you asked me this a few hours ago, I would have said poor at best."

"And now?"

"Now, I believe you are talking to the future emperor of Sori."

Chapter 14
The Final Phase

"It looks as though things have progressed nicely," Dullahan's master said, staring out at Amháin.

"They have, and, much to my surprise, with ease," Dullahan replied.

"Are they aware they are pawns?"

"I think Caleb had his suspicions at first, but I am certain that he now believes he is in control. Out of all the realms I have been to, this one has been the easiest to manipulate," Dullahan answered, creeping closer to the window.

"The Covenant was a much-needed temporary solution to end the war. The caomhnóir and a trade center was a good short-term idea; however, despite what most think, it was never designed to last this long. After the Great War, the population was decimated to such an extent that a trade center and individual regions made sense. In just a few decades after the war, Sori's population boomed, and its trade became too large for one small center."

Dullahan's master moved away from window. With a sigh, as if bored by his own story, he continued, "As the years passed, Cala became more and more corrupt, and its leaders wanted more coins than they could ever use. This greed caused them to turn their backs on the Faileas Herimen, and it is the Galenvargs and Veirlintus that suffered the most. The elite in Beinn and Frìth have had a taste of Cala's lavish lifestyle and have placed a strain on their sects' small businesses by underbidding their contracts. Those businesses that survived did not last long. While the little guy goes under, Cala's elite expand operation so that they can build bigger and more elaborate homes.

"The only sect that has remained true to its self-sustaining and community roots is the Leigheasan. This is why your attempts in Leigheas Gleann were futile. Frìth had many to choose from, and Beinn's alpha-Varg mentality was begging for someone to step up and make the first move.

"War is a necessary evil in all realms. Take this realm, for instance. The continent to the east has a war every one hundred years, and on the continent to our west, numerous clans battle on a regular basis for fun. It just so happens we are using this war for our purposes. It would have happened sooner or later. The caomhnóir was designed to be a guard, not a politician, and is useless in situations such as these."

"What is our next step?" Dullahan asked.

"This depends on the outcome of this war. I may need you to fight, but my goal is to let the sects kill off hundreds of thousands before we swoop in with our terms for peace."

"I will happily fight, if there is a need. Are you ready for transference?"

"Yes. How many scouts do you have ready?" the master anxiously asked.

"Several thousand. They will increase your traits like strength, speed, combat skills, but . . ." Dullahan paused, as if afraid to continue. "I will not be able to give you elemental powers yet."

"That was not our agreement!" the master yelled, grabbing Dullahan. The skin of his hand deepened to a dark grey. Dullahan's touch burned, just as it had Maya, but unlike with Maya, the master's skin healed as quickly as it burned. "You promised they would bring elemental powers, and not just one. I need all of the elements!"

"I am not strong enough for that yet. Please let me explain," Dullahan pleaded. The master eased up on his death grip, and Dullahan continued, "I need the essence of Faileas Herimen in order to gain the power I need to provide you with the elements. With this war I will be able to take their essence as they die and then transfer them into you. I promise you, master, I will not fail. You will be more powerful than anyone in Sori, including the Leigheas Maya."

Dullahan was released, and the master relaxed for transference.

"You better not fail me, Dullahan. Get on with it."

Dullahan raised his arm, shooting a black arrow into the sky. A red light shot in all directions, spreading to all edges of Sori. Dullahan's scouts recognized the signal, and within minutes they had gathered before their master. There were so many that a sea of black flowed from Dullahan's location at the Ceit Trinse to the Amháin. Dullahan touched the first scout, and in unison the scouts touched each other's shoulders.

With the scouts locked together, Dullahan pointed to his master with his free hand, and a blue light was expelled from his palm, into his master's chest. The scouts, who were absorbed into Dullahan, were released through the blue light and into the master. Within a few seconds, all the scouts achieved ascension, but Dullahan's master was not pleased with the results.

"I don't feel any different. I thought I was supposed to get bigger and stronger!" the master yelled. His frustration erupted quickly, and he stalked towards Dullahan.

"The size and strength increase are dependent on one's physique. You are already well built, so the process may only slightly increase strength. Regardless of how little or how much the gain, the results will take time to show," Dullahan replied as he stepped away from his approaching master.

"Why is this, and why didn't you explain this prior to the gathering of the scouts?" his master demanded, halting.

"The ascension process is primarily for the former Leigheasan, and those who do ascend spend months training themselves for the process. In addition, they already have a host of powers, so their contributions are instantaneous and great. Your Duine ascenders have to get used to this new bond, but it will come."

Despite the bond shared between a fomoire and its summoner, Dullahan was lying to his master. Ascension could be achieved by anyone, but only those who were former Leigheasan contributed to the enhancement as ascenders.

"I grow weary of your continual delays. If I don't see results soon, I will send you back to your realm." The master turned his back and left to find a better vantage point for the events Dullahan promised were coming.

Leaving the Croí, Maya, Jeremias and Willum made their way towards Willum's home in Keltoi. They passed many villages that were either completely or largely deserted.

"Where has everyone gone?" Maya asked.

"Usually when places are this deserted, it means a call for a sect meeting has been announced. When that happens every village bell goes off. Did either of you hear bells?" Willum asked.

"No," they replied in unison.

"To be fair, we haven't been up that long, so they could have gone off prior to us waking. After all, the forget-me-not did give me one of the best naps that I have ever had," Jeremias added.

Maya was unfamiliar with the way the other sects conducted many of their affairs and asked, "Where would they go for a meeting?"

"Same place we are going, Keltoi. It is one of the more central locations and has a very large square. We should be there within the hour."

Jeremias asked, "What do you think it's about?"

"No clue. My guess is that a new council is being declared, but with the way things have gone lately, I wouldn't be surprised if it was something else."

"Speaking of council, you served as an advisor to your grandfather, didn't you?" Maya asked Willum.

"Only from time to time, and it was mainly to provide insight on the economic side of things. I like to leave the politics for Jeremias. Why do you ask?"

"Just wondering. I thought that since you helped, you would be a shoo-in for a position."

"Oh, well, grandfather and I had talked about that, but I decided not to take him up on his offer. I don't want to be bogged down with meetings that discuss nothing at all. I will help the council whenever it needs me, but I am not one to waste my time like they tend to do," Willum explained.

"Interesting." Maya was used to the efficiency of the Leigheasan elders. She didn't realize that her brethren sects were so unproductive.

"He's got a good point, Maya. Our councils do waste a lot of time. We are both lucky to be able to come and go as we please. In light of recent events, this may be a poor choice of words, but serving on the council is a death sentence. They spend a minimum of ten hours a day plotting about how to gain land, expand their businesses, or how to take over even more businesses. Such a waste. Let's face it, our council members are far removed from the people they represent."

After a few minutes of silence, the group finally came across a villager.

"Excuse me, madam," Maya said. "Can you tell me where everyone is off to and the reason?"

"Keltoi. Our council was murdered several nights ago, and the Fågels had another attack on their new council last night. Most of the men have armored up, and rumors of war are going around," the lady replied.

"Thank you." The villager hurried away. Maya turned her attention to Willum and Jeremias. "It makes sense since all we have seen are women and young children."

"Wait, did she say the Veirlintu had another attack?" Willum asked.

"I think so, but maybe she is mistaken," Jeremias speculated.

"Maya, how long were we knocked out?" Willum growled.

"Just an hour. Why?"

"Because if it was just an hour, there was no time for another attack. There was no additional attack prior to Maya drugging us."

Maya looked through her satchel to pull out the remains of the candle she had cut. Looking it over she finally realized her mistake: the wick was a green. "Okay, so I made a mistake and used a multi-day candle. It is true. We did lose a lot of time."

"What the Ifreann, Maya!" Willum yelled. "This could have been a disaster! Jeremias, I swear if you don't start reacting more, I will . . . I will . . ." For the first time in a long time, Willum was at a loss for words.

"Why do I need to overreact when you are doing such a good job for the both of us?" Jeremias replied. "Look at it this way: If war has begun, then Maya kept us out of harm's way for at least one more day. Instead of getting the best nap ever, I got the best night's sleep I have had in easily over two hundred years. Really, it's a win-win."

"Once, just once, I would like you to take my side."

"I'm sorry," Maya cut in. "I made a rare mistake, but we need to focus on the task at hand. Willum, how long will it take to get to your home?"

"If we ride without stopping, we can make it there by midmorning. Why?"

"I need to find out if there has been a declaration of war, and if so, I need to get word to my fellow elders. I have a plan that may prevent a massive loss of lives."

"Well, it will take us some time to get to Willum's home, the battle will be near Cala, and it could take some time to get all the Leigheasan you need for your plan." Jeremias scratched his head in thought. "If you send a message to them now, they should arrive by the time you need them."

"That's a good point. Willum, where can I get a bird?"

They went to the closest messenger center, and Maya wrote her note: *All elemental elders, meet me a mile from Amháin. I will meet you as soon as possible. Do not leave, no matter how long I take. - Maya.*

Maya rolled up the message and placed it on the bird's foot. Her clan was the only one she trusted to get the word out to their sect. She leaned over the bird and whispered, "Please take the note to my father and mother, Felix and Andrea of the Leigheasan clan Dempsey."

The bird flew off, and Maya and her friends continued towards Keltoi. They arrived to find dozens of lines with hundreds, possibly thousands, of men waiting to be seen. Seen for what would be the first question Maya asked. Thousands of others were already dressed in armor, chatting, and banging their swords against their shields.

"This does not look good, Willum." Maya scanned the crowd, her head on a swivel.

"No, no it doesn't," Willum said, searching for any familiar faces.

"Excuse me, sir?" Maya asked the closest man. He turned and gave her a stern look. "What is going on here?"

"What does it look like?" he responded with a sour attitude.

"Where I come from, we politely answer questions from strangers."

He snapped back, "Then go home."

"Not good," Jeremias said, covering his face with his hand.

The newfound animal side of Maya took over as she jumped off Saxon, grabbed the man by his throat, and threw him up against the wall. Her claws dug into the skin, her fangs protruded from her mouth, and her blackened eyes showed the man his own fear.

"What are you?" the man asked.

"A traveler seeking answers to simple questions," Maya answered. She was starting to draw the attention of others in line.

Willum looked at Jeremias, who waved him on. With Jeremias's refusal to act, Willum jumped into action. "Nothing to see. He owes my friend some coins, that's all." Willum turned to Maya and tried to shield the event with his body. "Maya, just take it easy. This isn't you; it's just a bit of our rage is all. You're not used to it yet. Just relax, and he will tell you everything he knows. Right, friend?"

"Yes!" he screeched. Maya released him. "Our council was murdered, and so the new one has ordered the creation of an army and the building of supplies. All men and women who can contribute to the effort have been asked to come and sign up. We are waiting to see what unit we are assigned to."

"Has war been declared?" Willum asked.

"No, not yet, but they are sending troops as we speak to Amháin. We are waiting to see if the Fågels declare war. If they declare, we will go to war to aid them. We will go to war even without the Fågels if there are more Duine attacks on our sect. There is also a rumor that the Fågels were attacked last night." As he finished, a bright-red light lit up the sky. Everyone covered their eyes.

The mention of a potential attack on Frìth caused Jeremias's heart to race. "Maya, I need to get a message home to see if all is well." Jeremias turned his horse around. "I will meet you at Willum's house."

Jeremias headed away. Quickly Maya refocused. "Willum, I need to get to a watchtower! Now!" Maya cried, fearing the worst.

"This way!" Willum yelled and ran for the nearest alley.

Willum led Maya several blocks to the east to Keltoi's bell tower, where on a clear day one could see almost all the way to the Amháin.

They arrived at the tower and found Saxon already there.

"How did he know?" Willum asked, busting through the door.

"I have stopped asking how when it comes to the Diana breed. They always seem to know where to go and what to do," Maya explained as they ascended the tower.

Having climbed twenty flights of stairs, the two peered out across Sori, but only Maya saw what was happening. Thousands of scouts from all corners of Sori were heading to the same location. The land was black with them.

"*Tara, are you seeing this?*" Maya asked. "*Is he attempting to transfer these scouts?*"

"*Yes, but there is some good news,*" Tara replied.

"*How so?*" Maya asked.

"*These scouts, though high in number, may not be as effective as Dullahan thinks. These are regular Duine souls. They offer no power to someone like*

Dullahan. They only can help mentally. Of course, that all depends on how intelligent the souls are."

"*That is good. We don't need Dullahan any stronger than he already is.*"

"Maya, what do you see?" Willum asked.

"Dullahan is gathering his scouts for transference."

"I take it that's not good."

"Actually, it isn't as bad as you think. He won't be gaining any power."

"That is good news," he said.

Looking to her left, Maya saw the next sign of things to come. "*Tara!*" Maya pointed so Willum could also see Caleb's army.

"War has come to Sori," Willum grimly said, as row after row of soldiers came into view. "There will be no talking the sects out of it now."

"How long do you think we have?" Maya asked, hoping for some good news.

"Assuming that his army either matches or surpasses Beinn's, I would say we have several days. A few days just to get them out of Frìth, and then a couple more to gather and march to the Amháin. Now, let's get a much-needed drink." Willum abruptly headed down the steps. "We need some type of lift, instead of all these steps."

Maya and Willum made their way back to Willum's house and found Jeremias waiting at the kitchen table.

"Did you get a message home?" Maya asked, taking a seat.

Jeremias poured them drinks. "I did. I told them to send word to both here and your home just to make sure I can get an answer." Willum grabbed his drink and began pacing around the kitchen. "What's the plan?"

"By now Dullahan has completed the ascension. Frìth and Beinn are moving soldiers into position, and I'm sure that Cala is organizing." Maya avoided the question as she took a drink and began thinking.

"Is there any chance that diplomacy will work?" Jeremias asked.

"No, both our sects are moving soldiers and siege weapons into position. Soon all of Beinn will be armed for war, and I assume Frìth is just as prepared. War is what they want, and nothing is going to stop them now," Willum added.

"Jeremias, how much does Caleb know about warfare?"

"Only what he's read. He is a descendant of great warriors, but no one living has seen battle."

"What do you think his first move will be?"

Jeremias and Willum pondered that for a moment and then Willum posed, "The siege weapons. He can begin the siege with just a minimal number of soldiers. All he would need is enough to protect them from being attacked."

"That wall is built well, more than well, and it would take a while to create an opening. So a siege would be his best option," Jeremias added.

"There is nothing that can be done regarding the siege attack. There isn't time to stop that, but I should be able to prevent troops from entering Cala. However, for my plan to work I have to wait on the Leigheasan elders."

"Speaking of which, don't you think we should go to meet them?" Willum asked.

"Let's go, and you can fill us in on your plan along the way," Jeremias said, taking the last gulp of his drink.

The three ran back outside, jumped onto their horses, and rode for the rendezvous point. Maya informed them of her plan as they went.

"There is one last thing, and I need you both to keep calm." Maya readied her request as Willum's and Jeremias's horses struggled to keep up with Saxon.

"Why does everyone say 'I need you to keep calm,' when they are about to say something that will cause panic?" Willum replied. He noticed Jeremias shaking his head and asked, "What?"

"She needs our support, not your drama. Carry on, Maya."

"I am going to wage this battle by myself," she said as she nudged Saxon forward to avoid seeing her friends' reactions.

"Like Ifreann you will!" Jeremias yelled out.

"It's about time," Willum added, relieved to finally see Jeremias show some emotion.

Maya pulled Saxon to a halt and looked at her friends. "I have no choice. I need to show the Duine that the Leigheasan had nothing to do with this revolt, and my plan will ensure the least number on both sides are killed. I cannot focus on any of that if I put you in harm's way."

"Maya, we have lived long lives, much longer than we probably should have, and if we are to fall in battle, by your side, then so be it, but we will not idly sit by and watch you risk your life," Jeremias said.

"You won't be just sitting on the side. Command the Leigheasan if the battle does not go our way."

"We might," Willum replied.

"Felix! Felix!" Andrea exclaimed, running to the barn. "Felix!"

"Coming!" He climbed down from the barn loft.

"We just got a message from Maya." Andrea was out of breath as she handed the letter to Felix. "She needs all the elders."

"I take it that it is safe to assume that Beinn and Frìth are going to attack Cala." Felix looked at the parchment. "The elders to our west won't make it in the time she needs them. I am not sure how many she needs, but I do not think enough will come."

Andrea suggested, "We can use the Dianas. Hitch the wagons to a team and have each wagon stop at three villages. Even with the extra stops, the Dianas will be able to get hundreds, if not thousands, of elders to Maya."

"Brilliant idea. Our clan has at least a dozen wagons that can reach . . ." Felix paused while he did the math. ". . . close to thirty-six of the forty-five eastern villages, which should be enough to get us through until the others arrive. The other families can send their wagon teams west. I will hitch our teams and wagons, if you go tell the rest of the clan." Felix headed for the horse pen but quickly turned back to Andrea. "How many birds do we have in the village?"

"I think ten, but it may be less. Why?"

"Send them with messages to the clans furthest away," Felix added.

"Will do." Andrea ran off to rally the Dempsey Clan.

Gathering the clan in the village center, Andrea informed everyone of Maya's message and their plan for getting the elders to the battlefield. Though Maya requested only elders, Andrea also instructed her clan to have any other elemental Leigheasan come as quickly as possible. She assigned heads of households and eldest sons to gather the elders from the villages farthest away. The second and third eldest would relay the messages to those closer in. The children ranging from eight to ten years of age were assigned the villages within running distance, while everyone else left to meet Maya. By the time Maya arrived, thousands of Leigheasan were awaiting, and with each passing moment, more and more arrived.

The movement of troops took time, days longer than Caleb wanted, but the rebellious army finally reached their destination. Nothing progressed until Caleb made it to the battlefield. Balla's location made a direct assault on Cala's main gate difficult, so Caleb adjusted his battle plans.

"Move the trebuchets up into range and offset to the west of Balla," Caleb ordered, and the soldiers began moving the weapons closer to the wall.

Just over a dozen siege towers accompanied the trebuchets. At least six towers were placed on each side of the siege weapons so that they would not be harmed while making the advance to the wall.

As the siege weapons advanced, Caleb ordered his commanding officers to form columns: two battalions deep by two battalions wide. Once the wall came down, these 4,000 soldiers would be the first to attack, so they were instructed to move into position in front of the trebuchets. In case things took a turn for the worse, Caleb kept four brigades in reserve at the Amháin and several divisions back in Dún. Caleb hoped to conquer Sori with the fewest number of soldiers in recorded history.

In war, it wasn't the commander of the army who enjoyed the fame or was remembered for the victory; it was the generals leading the fight who become immortal. Caleb knew this, and instead of staying safely back at the tree, letting his generals take his glory, he made a surprising move. Caleb dug his heels into his horse and joined his soldiers in front of the trebuchets.

"Are we ready?" Caleb asked Arnolf.

"In a moment," Arnolf replied. "The last of the trebuchets are getting ready now." Arnolf pointed behind him. "I felt it best to have a grand assault at once instead of having a few fires here and there."

"Good. Make sure you avoid the tune. Dullahan is in there keeping the caomhnóir occupied, and he must not be disturbed. Any disruptions to the tune will break Dullahan's concentration, and with the caomhnóir awake, the repercussions will be severe. His powers surpass, or at least rival, those of the Leigheas lass, so I would like to keep him out of the fight."

"We have lined our sights to ensure we will not directly hit the tune. After a few dozen hits, we should have Cala's main gate and much of the wall around it destroyed. It may take three to five volleys from each trebuchet, but I don't expect much more than that," Arnolf informed Caleb.

"Good. I want cré coimeádán fired as well," Caleb ordered. Cré coimeádán were oil-filled clay canisters often used as munitions for trebuchets. "This will help soften any defense they have prepared or gathered."

"What if there are none?" Arnolf jokingly asked.

"Then I get what I want with greater ease," Caleb said. "I want Cala burned to the ground."

Arnolf switched back to talking of strategy. "I was told that we have four wagons with cré coimeádán on their way from Beinn. There will also be more coming after those arrive."

"What do you mean you were told? Aren't you sure? I need to know they are on the way!"

"This is a new side from you." Arnolf was a bit taken aback by Caleb's sternness. "It was a poor choice of words is all. There are four wagons on the way. There will be more arriving once we have the wagons free."

"Fine. Next time, just tell me what you know instead of telling me what you hear," Caleb said, and with Arnolf's nod of affirmation he continued, "Let the assault begin on your command." Caleb led his horse a few paces behind the trebuchets to get a better vantage point on the damage.

Hundreds of stones weighing between 100 and 200 pounds bombarded Cala's wall and gate. With heavy damage inflicted, Arnolf decided to use the cré coimeádán, but the first few volleys failed to pass over the wall. The fuel burned out on the ground, and Arnolf moved the trebuchets forward.

After repositioning, the trebuchets sent one volley to test the distance, and this time the canisters sailed over the wall. It only took a few canisters from each trebuchet to set most of Cala around the wall ablaze. Pleased with the results, and with the gate still intact, Caleb ordered a halt to the cré coimeádán and they resumed launching the stones. For hours, stones pummeled Cala.

"Maya," Jeremias said, tapping her arm. "Caleb has begun the siege." He pointed south where he could see the movement of the trebuchets on the horizon.

"We are almost there." Maya nudged Saxon, and he took off towards the mass of Leigheasan in the distance, leaving Willum and Jeremias behind.

"I am so glad the gods and goddesses chose her," Willum sarcastically said.

Jeremias started to laugh and nudged his horse to a sprint in a futile attempt to catch up with Saxon.

"Now you leave me and I am sitting here talking to my horse wondering why I chose you as my friends." Willum gently tapped Etty with his heels, trying not to fall too far behind the others.

Maya had reached her rendezvous with the Leigheasan, and she wasted no time in addressing them. "My fellow Leigheasan, the war you see unfolding in front of you was not provoked by a Duine. It is the result of a powerful entity using the forbidden. It is not our war, and if you choose, we can stay out of it—for now. But war will come to our doorsteps one way or another. We can put an end to this revolt today and prevent the loss of many lives. I need you to trust and follow me."

Otis stepped up and yelled, "You have our shields, swords and elements! Command as you wish and we will follow!" The rest of the Roark Clan banged their weapons on their shields.

"I need the strongest earth elementals to follow me. I need the rest of the earth elementals to circle the battalions behind Amháin. Those who are non-earth elementals need to stand in front of those at the Amháin, so that you can protect them from a Galenvarg or Veirlintu attack. If you are on a horse and not one of the ones I immediately need, please give your horse to someone who is making the charge with me. We are about a mile out and cannot afford the time it will take everyone to run onto the field.

"On my signal, which will be a bright-blue flame flying in the air, I want you to raise a rock wall surrounding the trebuchets and the battalions getting ready to charge. I, and I alone, will climb over the wall and eliminate those inside. If I stop Caleb, then I may halt the advance of the other Galenvargs and Veirlintus. You can lower the walls when you see a second blue flame across the sky."

The Leigheasan quickly divided into the groups Maya needed, and Otis once again stepped forward. "Ready on your command."

Maya nodded at Otis, and, unsheathing her sword, she turned Saxon towards the battlefield and charged. Hundreds of earth elementals followed. Even with their horses in full sprint, they fell a few hundred yards behind Saxon's pace. Once in position, Maya jumped off Saxon, sent him to safer ground, and waited for the other Leigheasan to arrive. Finally, everyone was in place.

"*Tara, are you ready?*" Maya asked, producing a flame in her hand that quickly turned blue.

"*The important question is, are you?*" Tara replied.

CHAPTER 15

War and Deception Revealed

S tones and cré coimeádáns flew overhead. Maya placed the flame in the
air between her hands. The flame expanded as she separated them, until
it was the size of Maya's torso. Maya threw the flame high, and with the aid
of the wind she carried the flame higher and higher. With the signal burning
bright in the sky, the earth elementals lifted their hands, and a rock wall
erupted from the earth, encircling Caleb, his troops, and his siege weapons.

As Maya quickly advanced, she noticed a cloud developing high above
the rock wall. Assuming this was one of Dullahan's tricks, she paid it no
mind and refocused on her task. When she was about fifty yards out
from Caleb's trapped army, Maya lifted her hand, and an earthen staircase
leading to the top of the wall was expelled from the ground. Climbing the
stairs at a full run, Maya jumped high into the air at the top. Now entering
the confinement of the rock wall, she used the wind to guide her descent,
and, airborne, she divided the battalions with two walls of fire, splitting
them into four quadrants.

Landing in the quadrant at the bottom left, commanded by Arnolf, Maya unsheathed her swords and waited for Arnolf to give a command, but he was frozen with fear and didn't utter a word.

"Command?" an officer asked Arnolf. He repeated, "What is your command, sir?"

Once Maya saw that she wouldn't have to go on the defensive, she took the offensive and rushed their front line. Even upon seeing Maya's charge, Arnolf offered his troops no direction.

"Lock shields!" an officer yelled, and in unison his front line locked their rectangular shields. Their second line stood with spears between the shoulders of the front line and awaited Maya's charge.

Stopping feet from the line, Maya sheathed one of her swords and smiled at the second line. With a wink, a gust of wind blew them back into the lines behind them. The front line stood agog as Maya bent forward to touch a shield. The soldiers behind them could not see what Maya was doing, but they felt their shields warming. The shields heated rapidly to the point that they began to melt, and in an instant the steel shields went from hardened protector to molten incinerator of flesh and bone. The molten steel sliced through wrists, knees, and feet. Over a hundred soldiers were incapacitated in the blink of an eye, and screams filled the air.

Horrified, Arnolf stumbled to the back of the troops, yelling, "Attack! Attack! Attack!"

The second line of soldiers stepped forward with their spears, launching their weapons at Maya. Putting her hand up in a stop motion, the spears halted midair, and with an upward flick of her hand, the wind carried the spears into the sky. When she closed her fist, the spears rained back down on the soldiers, who desperately raised their shields overhead.

Unsheathing her second sword, Maya ran forward, slicing through the Galenvargs and Veirlintus with little resistance. Hundreds of soldiers had fallen, either to Maya's sword or their own spears. As they died, a bolt of lightning descended from the cloud above and struck their corpses. Seeing no immediate danger to herself, Maya ignored the lightning and focused on the nearly 200 soldiers crowding the fire wall at the back of the quadrant.

"*Tara, are you there?*" Maya asked.

"*Yes, but you seem to be doing well enough without my help,*" Tara replied.

"*Leigheasan are typically only able to control one mind, right?*" Maya asked.

"*Yes, but . . .*" Tara paused to think. "*It is not uncommon for someone of your power to be able to control more than one. I do recall one Leigheas who was able to control eight men at once.*"

"*How many do you think I can control?*" Maya asked hopefully.

"*I am not sure. The only way to be sure is to simply try.*"

Maya took several steps back to give herself distance from her enemy. Focusing on a small group of six, she clumsily entered their minds. She raised their swords, turned them around, and had them attack their fellow troops. A dozen fell before the Galenvargs began to fight their own. Maya took over a couple more soldiers each time one fell, and soon she was effortlessly controlling twenty people at once.

It was a sight to behold as Maya stood without breaking a sweat, letting the enemy do her light work, until Arnolf was not only the last one standing, but also the only one who Maya was not controlling. Wanting to fight Arnolf herself, Maya rewarded the remaining twenty soldiers for their service by having them thrust their own swords through their hearts for a quick death.

"Maya, please, let's talk," Arnolf begged. "Just let me go, and I will convince Caleb to end this for you. He will listen to me. You'll see. Just give me a chance to talk it over."

The closer she came, the more he knew his pleas were useless. Arnolf whipped his sword from his side, hoping to catch Maya off guard. Maya caught his sword between her blades. She aimed for the base of Arnolf's sword with her other weapon, and broke his sword in two.

Arnolf once again pleaded for his life. "Please don't do this. We can end this together." Without a word, Maya sliced an X into his torso with both swords. Arnolf fell to his knees, holding his wound and attempting to keep his innards from falling out. Arnolf was still pleading as blood spurted from his mouth. Holding her crossed blades to his throat like shears, she removed his head. As his body thudded to the ground, a bolt of lightning struck him. Maya picked up his head and threw it over the flames.

A soldier ran to Caleb with Arnolf's head. "Sir, this came flying over the fire. I don't think this bodes well for us."

"Throw it back over. I will give my friend a proper burial when this is over," Caleb replied, trying to contain his emotions. Caleb knew the words of his soldier were true: it was a sign of what was to come.

Maya now turned her attention to the unnatural lightning. "*Tara, what is this lightning?*"

"*You need to call on Malaki.*"

"*Malaki, you are needed once more.*"

"*How can I be of service?*"

"*As each soldier died, their corpses were struck by a bolt of lightning. The cloud has since gone from white to a dark grey. What is this?*"

"*This is Dullahan's work. He is gathering Faileas Herimen souls to increase his powers. As he collects more and more, the cloud grows darker.*"

"*What powers, and how much can it increase?*"

"*It is hard to say, but I assume it will be elemental and mind. It could be just physical strength. Provided he uses the souls for his own means, even with the scythe this increase in power may make it far more difficult to defeat him.*"

"*What do you mean, 'Provided he uses the souls for his own means'?*" Maya asked.

"*Remember, Dullahan was summoned by a master, and Dullahan has his own powers, and little need of these souls. I bet he is transferring them into his master, not himself.*"

"*I can't believe I missed that! I have been so focused on defeating Dullahan that I forgot about the person who brought him here.*" Maya paused. "*I think I know who Dullahan's master is! It must be Swindlehurst. He is one of the most influential Duine and has the most to gain.*"

Before Maya could continue, Tara interrupted, *"Maya, you need to refocus on the task at hand. Worry about Dullahan and his master later."*

"You're right. Thank you, Malaki," Maya said. She turned her attention to the next quadrant.

Maya sheathed her swords. She wanted to end this battle as quickly as possible, so she turned to her elements. As she raised a finger, the flames shot up several feet. She used her right hand to guide the perpendicular walls of flames, closing them in on the quadrant and widening the flames as she did.

The mass of soldiers scrambled away from the encroaching wall. Several attempted to hurl their comrades up and over the earthen wall to their backs, but even the strongest soldiers could not boost their friends high enough to reach the top. The soldiers panicked as the heat from the walls closed in. In their panic, they began to attack one another. At first the soldiers shoved each other directly into the flames, but they shifted tactics to hacking at one another to get a position farther back. A pyramid of bodies piled up, and a fight to the top ensued.

The last man standing had a magnificent view of Maya's carnage, but his efforts to escape and live another day were in vain. The fire was now over twenty feet wide in both directions, the rock wall was another fifteen feet higher than he could jump, and the flames were beginning to incinerate the base of the pile of bodies. A scream that could wake the dead erupted as the last soldier of the quadrant was engulfed. Maya waved her hand, and the fire was extinguished. The upper-right quadrant was now free, but the lower right was still behind the walls of fire.

"Ebbot, give the command," Eger said.

"She killed two thousand men with the effort that it takes to kill one," Ebbot replied. "What can we do against that?"

"Snap out of it!" Eger yelled, punching his brother in the face. "You're a Pilkvist! Now, start acting like it! Command the men, or you won't have to deal with that little girl taking you out. You will have to deal with me!"

"Sorry, brother. Attack!" Ebbot yelled at his troops and continued to yell, "Attack! Attack! Attack!"

As the soldiers charged, Maya smashed her fist on the ground, and thousands of stalagmites burst through the earth's surface. Bodies were impaled through the chest, back, stomach. Once again, almost an entire battalion was killed in an instant. Maya lifted her hand, stood, and raised her hand over her head. The stalagmites rose higher, ensuring that anyone left alive was dead or incapable of fighting. As she lowered her hand, the stalagmites receded back into the earth.

Maya marched towards the few hundred that hadn't joined the charge. At her come-hither gesture, thousands of spikes protruded from the wall behind the soldiers. A shooing motion from her left hand produced a gust of wind that picked all but the twins up and launched them into the spikes. Despite their horror, the twins charged Maya with swords held high.

As they swung their weapons, Maya dropped to her knees, bent backwards, and watched the swords miss their target. Maya jumped up behind the twins and shoved her hands in their backs, breaking through the skin, muscles, and ribs like slicing through bread. She found her way to their hearts and in one motion pulled back, tearing the twins' most vital of organs from their bodies. Ebbot and Eger fell to the ground, and Maya threw their hearts back into the cavities from which they came.

Looking out at a sea of dead bodies and ash, Maya turned to the lower-right quadrant, which contained the ringleader. The walls of fire lowered, and Caleb and his troops turned to see Maya standing alone. As Caleb inspected the battlefield and saw the thousands of corpses covering the ground, his hopes of conquering Cala began to dwindle. Maya raised her hand, and once again rocks rose with it; these were no larger than a coin and round like a ball. Hundreds of thousands of them floated before her like locusts. With the force of a shock wave, she hurled them forward. Their velocity drove them through shields, armor, and bodies as if the soldiers weren't even there. Those who didn't react in time to drop to the ground were riddled with holes from their waists to their skulls.

Caleb and a few dozen soldiers were the only ones left. Maya raised both hands, creating a whirlwind around the remaining soldiers, sparing only Caleb. The wind carried these last soldiers hundreds of feet into the air. They begged her to stop. Maya eventually closed her fists, and the wind dissipated. The soldiers met their deaths on impact.

"You're Maya, right? I have heard a lot about you," Caleb said, struggling to sound calm. "Look what you've done here. Join your brethren, and the Faileas Herimen can rule Sori without the fear of war, strife, or Duine conquest. We will establish a new order. We will never again lack a food supply, and will be free to travel across the land without threat of persecution. Together, we can make Sori great once again."

Maya walked to Caleb with her hand extended, as if to shake, and a smile on her face. So unexpected was this gesture that Caleb sheathed his sword and extended his hand before he thought to question her intentions.

"I am glad you have come to your senses. Together, we will make great rulers of this land," Caleb said.

Maya missed his hand and thrust her hand through his stomach, producing a flame inside Caleb that boiled his innards. When the flame turned blue, she expelled a continuous stream of blue flame through his mouth and into the sky, signaling the rock elementals to disband the wall. As the wall came down, Maya extinguished the flame and removed her hand from Caleb's gut. His lifeless body dropped to the ground, and the rebellion of Caleb Tjäder became the shortest-lived war in Sori's history.

Barging through the door, Dullahan's master bellowed, "I demanded the best soldiers and you brought me sheep for the slaughter! One battle against one Leigheas! One! Four thousand soldiers lost in a matter of minutes. Not to mention, your reserves are surrounded by hundreds of the Leigheasan."

"This is no ordinary Leigheas," Dullahan replied and pleaded, "Please calm down, master. I am trying to concentrate." He pointed to a body wearing the robe of the caomhnóir, lying facedown on the floor.

"You think! She is part Veirlintu and Galenvarg now!" the master screeched.

"What? How do you know this?" Dullahan grew worried.

Dullahan's victim began to stir. "What happened?"

"See what you made me do. I lost control." Dullahan shoved his arm down, and a gust of wind slammed the man's head into the floor with enough force to knock him unconscious.

"You lost control? Did you not see the battle?"

"No, you needed a decoy to blame everything on and demanded that I take care of it. I am trying to take care of it by erasing his memory and imprinting false ones, but you barged in here and interrupted me from doing just that."

Dullahan's master was furious with this disrespect. He ran up to the ghostly figure, grabbed his robe and threw him through the chamber doors.

"Finished?" Dullahan asked as he reentered the chambers, none the worse for wear. "Now, how do you know she is both Galenvarg and Veirlintu?"

"Besides being able to sense the difference in her compared to anyone on the battlefield? Since when could a Leigheas rip out someone's insides without blinking an eye? That passion for a kill comes from a Galenvarg or a Veirlintu. Not to mention her hair is as black as the night. She is now everything that I am and more! Stop what you are doing and end her life!" the master commanded, looking down at the unconscious man on the floor. "I don't know why you didn't have this one walk off the tune. I have never liked him."

"As you wish, but first, let me transfer the elements to you," Dullahan replied.

"I better have them all, or you better not return from your fight with the Leigheas."

"With the power of four thousand Faileas Herimen souls, I will be able to impart all of the elements unto you," Dullahan said, raising his hand.

"Wait!" the master yelled. "I want to be able to control minds as well. I will need to do that soon, very soon."

"As you wish," replied Dullahan.

The cloud over the battlefield was now black, and it began to make its way to the tune. It only took a moment for the cloud to position itself directly overhead. A blue beam of light shot from the cloud to the top of Dullahan's hand. The souls began transferring into him, and as they did, the cloud shrank, until all were transferred and the cloud ceased to exist. Dullahan placed his hand on his master's chest; a blue glow emerged from his hand and surrounded his master's entire body. When Dullahan removed his hand, the glow continued for several seconds, and then the light retreated into the master's chest.

"You now have the power of all the elements," Dullahan said, stepping back from his master.

"How do I use them?" the master asked.

"Think of what you want to do and it will be done. Most, including myself, use hand gestures to help them focus, but it is not necessary."

"Good, now get going! I want that Leigheas's head on a spike!" the master yelled as he produced a ball of fire. Dullahan took off towards the battlefield as his master tested his new elemental powers.

Trebuchets were still firing on the city. Remembering what she had once done to her shillelagh, Maya covered her sword with stone. Producing a much larger war hammer, she approached the siege weapons, and within striking distance she reared back with the stone hammer and slammed it on the ground, expelling a shock wave that tore apart the weapons, and sent the operators back several feet.

Suddenly feeling as though she was being watched, she turned to find Dullahan a few feet away. She charged him and punched him in what she assumed was his face. Her fist burned and turned grey but quickly healed.

"I see you have had an upgrade or two?" Dullahan said. "You do realize that fighting me is futile, right? You have a better chance of getting rid of me by killing my master than defeating me with any form of combat."

"Why is it that the first thing people want to do in a fight is talk?" Maya asked as she prepared for Dullahan's attack.

She dodged a punch, then another, and suddenly embraced Dullahan like a Veirlintu embraced their victims. Maya lodged her fangs into the shoulder region. As her fangs dug deeper into him, Dullahan began to laugh. Her face entered a constant battle between burning and healing from the fomoire's touch of death. The further she dug her fangs into his body, the louder he laughed.

"A bite? You think you can kill me with a bite?" Dullahan cackled.

Maya knew this attack wouldn't harm Dullahan, but she had succeeded in distracting him from her true weapon. As their embrace continued, Maya pulled out the scythe and swiftly stabbed Dullahan in the back. The creature squealed and spasmed. She removed it from his back, and stabbed him in the chest. Pulling the scythe out of his chest, Maya waited. The shadow that cloaked the fomoire began to peel away from his body, exposing a feeble old man wearing a loose-fitting tunic.

"Tara, isn't he supposed to be pulled back into his realm?" Maya asked.

"Yes, but I have not had encounters with a fomoire, so I am not sure—" Tara broke off as a portal opened behind Dullahan.

A figure twice Maya's size in gold armor stepped through the portal and stabbed Dullahan with a spear. Once through Dullahan's body, the spear transformed and expanded on both sides until it formed a coffin-like cage around him. The figure removed its helmet to reveal, much to Maya's surprise, a face no different than any on Sori.

"Greetings. My name is Brandow of the Clan Rudianos. We are what you might consider Berserkers for all the realms, tasked with returning those who break inter-realm laws to face justice. We are forever in your debt. Take this pendant as a token of my thanks and as an apology from my people for the trouble this one has caused."

Brandow handed Maya a necklace with a thin ring the size of her palm, marked with a symbol like the triskelion used by her clan, and at the center was a red stone.

"This is one among many pendants used as keys for safe travels across the realms. You will need it soon." He bowed, grabbed Dullahan, and stepped back through the portal.

"I wasn't expecting that. I kind of thought he was going to get sucked back in," Maya said to Tara.

"As did I, but it seems that you are destined for greater things."

"Maybe," Maya said. She headed towards Amháin and Caleb's reserve battalions.

The reserves were between Maya and her fellow Leigheasan. As she neared them, Maya called out, "Leave now and all is forgiven. Stay and you will meet the same fate as thousands of your brethren. Mercy will not be given for those who stay."

It was an easy decision for the reserves. They dropped their weapons and took off for the quickest path home. Maya looked around at her friends and family as Willum and Jeremias rode up. The Leigheasan erupted in cheers, but she motioned for them to be quiet.

"We are not done. There is still a matter of Dullahan's master." Maya turned back towards Cala to signal the rock elders to come to the Amháin.

As Maya waved, she noticed a figure at the top of the tune also waving. The caomhnóir. She smiled but suddenly noticed a sea of arrows coming from above the wall. His wave wasn't one of appreciation or congratulations; it was a signal for attack. The rock elders were oblivious to what was happening above their heads, and suddenly it was over. Hundreds of the Leigheasan lay dead from thousands of arrows. It suddenly became very clear to Maya who Dullahan's master was. The very one tasked with protecting Sori was the only person that wouldn't be suspected of such treachery and deceit.

A flood of images poured through Maya. The one that stood out was seeing the caomhnóir without ascenders. Without Nantosuelta's blessing, the caomhnóir could not become a Leigheas and ultimately a supreme being. He had used Dullahan to emerge not as a mere peacekeeper but as a ruler.

As she pieced the puzzle together, Maya suddenly became dizzy and dropped to her knees, blind. She knew now that this was not an attack but rather a sign of a new ability, and this time, instead of spotting a scout, she began to have visions. Visions of events that she had never witnessed. These sights made it clear why diplomacy had never prevailed.

Maya saw the caomhnóir summoning Dullahan, and their first interaction. An exchange of pleasantries was followed by Dullahan's first act of war. She saw Dullahan's treachery in manipulating the Duine soldiers into killing their own and then erasing all signs of a struggle.

In the Veirlintu council chambers she saw Caleb's treasonous slaughter of his father and the Veirlintu council. She then saw the murders at Beinn, and, finally, the murders of the three newly elected members of the Veirlintu council. Her final vision took place inside Cala's council chambers. A hooded figure spoke with Councilman Swindlehurst of the upcoming attack, instructing Swindlehurst not to retaliate when the Faileas Herimen attacked Cala's gate—to only respond when soldiers entered Cala's boundaries. Finally, Maya's visions ceased, and she quickly regained her sight.

"*Tara*," Maya said as she tried to regain her balance, standing.

"*I am here,*" Tara replied. "*Are you okay? Visions can take a lot out of a person.*"

"*I am fine, but that was incredible. I saw everything as though I were there. Does this mean I can see the future as well? That would have been handy a few weeks ago, but still would be pretty awesome to have in the days to come.*"

"*Perhaps, but we will not know until it happens. Are you sure you are fine? You shouldn't try to confront the caomhnóir if you are not 100 percent.*"

"*I am fine. I feel much better now than when I first saw the scouts. I think the mix of blood and the monk's concoction help to counteract the side effect of new powers. I am aggravated that our efforts in preventing this war were all for naught. Trying to find a peaceful solution would have never worked.*"

"*No, no it wouldn't have, but you cannot dwell on things that have already happened. How something starts is far less important than how things finish. So, my question to you is: are you ready to finish this?*"

"*Of course,*" Maya said and started running.

"*Tara, what powers do you think the caomhnóir has?*" Maya asked as she made her advance.

"*I think it is safe to say that he has the ability to control minds. I also suspect that he has elemental powers now.*"

"*Why do you think that?*" Maya inquired.

"*The rock elementals surely would have shielded themselves if they were in control of their own minds. And I cannot be certain, but I believe the sheer number of souls stolen by Dullahan could made him strong enough to grant elemental powers as well.*"

"*How can I defeat him?*"

"*That is a good question. Both of you now have the blood of the Galenvarg and Veirlintu, so your wounds heal at an accelerated rate. A battle of elements would merely tire you both with no clear outcome. I believe the only way to defeat him is to inflict major wounds. Sword combat is your best bet for now.*"

"*Sounds good to me,*" Maya replied.

Maya's advance was halted when the caomhnóir signaled for a second volley of arrows. She paused, created a dome-like stone shield to protect her, and waited for the arrows to miss their target. Before the archers could get off a third volley, Maya pulled off her most taxing elemental feat to date.

It was difficult to say if the Duines were being controlled by the caomhnóir or acting on their own accord; however, Maya wanted revenge for the deaths of her fellow Leigheasan. Though the archers stood safely behind Cala's wall, which stood fifteen feet high and ten feet deep, Maya knew she could take them all out in one swoop. Maya ran behind the tune and focused on the wall. She could not move it in one piece, but she could certainly break it to pieces. She vibrated the stones until they broke free from the mortar that held them together.

Sensing when all the stones were free, she made a punching motion that sent thousands of stones flying, trampling over the archers and obliterating homes and buildings for several blocks. Thousands of lives were lost, and the land of Sori had no wall for the first time in centuries. The only benefit to Cala was that the stones suffocated the flames that had been spreading through the city. Unfazed by the magnitude of what she had done, Maya used the wind to lift herself to the top of the tune, and when she landed, the caomhnóir was waiting.

"Your performance has surprised me. I never would have thought the sects would produce someone with your abilities," the caomhnóir said. "You did do me a favor by eliminating Dullahan. His incompetence was staggering and delayed my plans too many times, giving you the time to become a hybrid."

Maya just wanted to attack, but couldn't help asking, "Why did you do this? You are supposed to protect our sects, not destroy them."

"I have spent thousands of years watching. Sure, I judge a case once or twice a year, but I mainly just watch. Watching the sects move from whining and complaining to extorting one another and then back to whining and complaining. The Duine, Galenvargs, and Veirlintus have become so corrupt that they have distorted the purpose of a caomhnóir and Balla. All I did was add a crack into a large rift, then sit back waiting to swoop in and end the war myself."

"So, instead of using diplomacy, you wanted to start a war just so you would look like a hero when you ended it? And then what?" Maya asked.

"Become ruler of Sori. Sori needs a caomhnóir to guard it in its entirety, not in a lone city. I expedited things to avoid another Great War."

"You avoided nothing. Our actions—right or wrong, good or bad—are irrelevant. They are ours to take. You were to be neutral. If our decisions led to war, you should have let us go to war. If our actions called for meetings upon meetings, then you should have let it be. We are meant to have free will, not be forced into actions. All you did was take advantage of your unearned position for personal gain."

"Perhaps, but we have talked enough. How about we end this and see who will inherit Sori's fate?" the caomhnóir said with a smile.

The caomhnóir drew his swords, and Maya did the same. They charged, and the clash of weapons sounded like Gofannon's hammer at his forge. The two failed to wound each other, and caomhnóir's blades dulled and weakened under the might of the dorcha steel. To rid Maya of her swords, the caomhnóir launched a ball of fire at Maya's face. He then used a gust of wind to knock the weapons out of her hands; however, Maya's wrist guards negated his efforts.

Maya quickly sheathed her swords, charged the caomhnóir, knocked him over, and sent his swords to the edge of the tune. For a moment, Maya was on top of the caomhnóir, connecting several punches, but overall she did little damage. Pushing Maya to the side, the caomhnóir stood and regained his balance. Smiling, he moved his hand forward and expelled a stream of fire at her. Maya instantly raised a stone wall from the floor to shield her. The heat of the flame became so intense that the rock was melting. Knowing she only had a matter of seconds, Maya raised her hands. Two additional stone walls rose to the right and left of the caomhnóir, and Maya began to push the walls together. The caomhnóir was forced to cease his attack to avoid being crushed by the walls.

Maya needed a moment to figure out her next move. She heated the moisture in the air, shielding her location with steam.

"*Tara, I am running low on ideas. Got any advice?*" Maya asked.

It was Malaki that replied, "*I have an idea that will end this.*"

"*I am all ears,*" Maya said as she quietly moved around the tune's roof.

"*I need you to take a seat, clear your mind, breathe slowly, and think of what you would like us to do. You have the power to allow us to come back to your realm and do as you bid. We can achieve what you wish without being harmed or failing. But you have to surrender your desire to physically fight and focus on mentally fighting.*"

"*Okay,*" Maya said, sitting and crossing her legs.

With her attention no longer on the elements, she would soon become visible. Ignoring this, Maya cleared her thoughts, relaxed her body, and envisioned the torment her ascenders would bring the caomhnóir. A bright-blue light and shock wave burst from Maya, lifting the fog. The caomhnóir found himself gazing upon Tara, who stood behind Maya. Tara slowly walked to the caomhnóir, reached through his chest, and began separating him from his elements. A white shadow was being ripped from his body, and the caomhnóir dropped to his knees. The elements were as integral as bones, and with the separation came intense pain. Yelling in agony, the caomhnóir was powerless to stop Tara, and finally she achieved full separation. She tossed the white shadow to the wind, and the souls of 4,000 Faileas Herimen were free to travel to the afterlife.

The caomhnóir staggered to his feet and towards Maya. Tara quickly blocked his path. Attempting to fight, the caomhnóir threw punches that passed right through Tara. She then stepped directly into the caomhnóir's body. This separation process was more graphic. The snout of a Varg crept out of his stomach. It emerged slowly with its front legs, moments later its hind legs, and finally Tara completely separated the Galenvarg essence from the guardian. Next, a pair of wings extended from his back. Beating faster and faster, the wings assisted the Veirlintu in its escape. The Galenvarg and the Veirlintu circled the guardian and then bounded off the tune, never to be seen again.

Once Tara and the ascenders had taken all the Galenvarg and Veirlintu away from the caomhnóir, all that remained was a Duine. A Duine who was now unprotected by regenerative properties and subject to a mortal life. Tara exited the body and walked back to Maya.

"*Maya, you need to wake now,*" Tara said, and Maya did as she was told.

Maya awoke to see the caomhnóir change. His body was swiftly catching up with his age, and with each passing second the guardian got older and older. Muscles began to disappear as the flesh wrinkled and drooped from his body. Hair fell from his scalp, teeth poured out of his mouth, bones deteriorated, and finally all that was left of the caomhnóir was a pile of dust.

Maya was tired, weak, and grateful that it was finally over. She walked to the edge of the tune to gaze upon Sori. She saw her friends and family awaiting her at the Amháin to the north. To the south, Maya gazed upon an ominous sight. Stretching across the landscape of Cala were nothing but buildings, multi-floor structures as far as the eye could see.

"*Tara, I can't believe we missed this.*"

"*To be fair, you didn't have this type of vantage point when you previously came. There isn't another place in Sori that will give you a view of Cala such as this,*" Tara replied and then noticed the mass of soldiers just blocks away. "*Look, the Duine army is gathered.*"

"*They must be still waiting for the Galenvargs and Veirlintus to breach. Should I say something?*"

"*Maybe a gesture of goodwill to inform them the battle is over. This may help prevent any retaliation from the Duine.*"

"*Okay, here goes.*"

She gathered her thoughts, then called to the Duine, amplified by the wind.

"Put down your weapons and bury your dead. The threat is over, and for the moment, peace is restored. In a week's time, the council will reconvene to see how we progress from here, but for the moment you need to mourn, rebuild, and rest. No further harm will come to the Duine."

The Duine soldiers looked to their commanding officers, who were busy thinking of their best course of action. Though the officers had not seen the events unfold, they knew that Maya had defeated an army on her own. As the moments passed, Maya readied for an attack that never came. The order was given to put down their arms, and Maya immediately relaxed.

"*Tara, I have some serious concerns. I think by preventing a war in Sori, I forced one upon the other continents.*"

"*How so?*"

"*A war in Sori would have dramatically reduced the Duine population, which they are in desperate need of. Now there is only one thing that the Duine can do.*"

"*And that is?*"

Maya didn't want to face the thought of the repercussions, but she finally said, "*Colonize.*"

Chapter 16

Looking to Tomorrow

The house began to shake, and books tumbled off the shelves, Swindlehurst grabbed hold of his chair, and a sound louder than a thunderstorm filled the room.

When it stopped, Swindlehurst asked, "What was that?"

"I'll go check." The man sitting across from the councilman was his brother, Cromwell. He quickly got up and left the room.

Swindlehurst rose and examined the map on his desk. Figures were strategically positioned to reflect the distribution of Caleb's rebellion. Swindlehurst moved his hand from Cala, across the sea, and over to lands in the south. Several moments passed before the councilman was joined once more.

"Maya has squashed the rebellion and destroyed much of the boundary wall," Cromwell announced upon his return.

"How many Leigheasan are coming?"

"It's just her." Swindlehurst looked up. Cromwell's eyes told a tale of horror. "But she is battling the caomhnóir. Should we send the army? I have thousands ready to reinforce those already there."

"No. I was instructed to only fight if there is an invasion into Cala. If Maya is battling the caomhnóir, then she knows he was behind all of this, not us. I was paid to not interfere, and that is all."

"But we needed this war. You know we can't afford to keep supporting the population."

Swindlehurst nodded and headed towards a small table in the far corner of his office. He waved for his guest to follow.

"The war would have certainly helped solve our problem, but we are not prepared to start a fight with Maya, especially this close to home. I certainly don't want to become a casualty, do you?"

"Of course not, but our coins are being drained, and you know what our people are like when they get desperate."

Swindlehurst knew his brother was referring to the events that caused the Great War. Lying on the table were stacks of papers with two of interest for the topic on hand. One was a map of the continent to the west, and the other was a design for a ship.

"What do you think?" Swindlehurst asked.

"Looks like a map I've never seen and a drawing for a massive ship. Are you suggesting—"

"We are going to begin Plan B. Work has begun on ships that will carry thousands across the sea." Swindlehurst pointed from the drawing of the ship to the map. "The only problem is that I need someone I can trust to oversee the colony."

"Do you want me to oversee the operations?"

Swindlehurst moved over to a serving tray and poured two glasses of wine. "Who better than my brother? How does Governor Cromwell sound?"

Cromwell grabbed the glass, held it up, and his brother did the same.

"Sounds like an offer I can't refuse." They gently touched the two glasses together. After a sip, Cromwell asked, "What are you going to do about Maya? She poses a real threat."

"That she does." Swindlehurst took a drink. "But soon she will have a tough decision to make."

Maya made her way to the ground and whistled for Saxon. She saw the surviving Faileas Herimen well on their way home. Maya looked down at her hands and forearms. Trails of dried blood looked like a map of Sori's river system. Maya's thoughts went to what she had done to Eger and Ebbot. She saw splatters of blood on her armor.

"*I wish I could say seeing it gets easier,*" Tara said.

"*I wish I didn't have to spill anymore blood.*" Maya breathed deeply and looked back to Cala. "*But I know this is just the beginning.*"

As Saxon came into view, Maya was overcome with joy, as if she were gazing upon him for the first time. For a moment she was able to forget all that had occurred. Saxon came to an abrupt stop, flinging dirt yards past Maya. Maya wrapped her arms around his neck the best she could, and Saxon laid his muzzle on her shoulder.

"Let's go home, boy," Maya said as she swung up on the saddle.

Maya did not get far before being met by her parents, Willum, and Jeremias. Andrea jumped from the wagon before it came to a halt and ran towards Maya, who halted Saxon and dismounted.

"Maya!" Andrea cried.

"Mom," Maya choked out, and she caught her mother in her arms.

"I was so worried." Andrea pulled back, tears forming.

"For them or me?" Maya asked, grinning.

Andrea gave Maya a light smack on the shoulder. "You have too much of your father in you."

Felix hopped off the wagon and rushed to Maya's side. "Thank the gods and goddesses you're alive."

"Of course, they were on her side, but we had a little to do with it too," Willum said, pulling his horse to a stop.

"It was more me than him," Jeremias boasted.

"I'm glad you boys were there." Felix shook their hands.

Maya backed away from her mom and jumped back on Saxon. "I think we should head home. I'm sure Willum and Jeremias could use a good meal."

"And a good drink," Willum added.

"We will have plenty of both," Andrea said. "Along the way you tell us everything." Andrea gestured at Maya in amazement, suggesting she noticed Maya's changes.

They started their journey back to the Gleann, and Willum and Jeremias wasted no time in recounting Maya's journey. Maya stayed quiet and enjoyed their rendition.

"Are you going to tell them about Cala?" Tara asked.

"No, not today. There is going to be plenty of time for that, but for now we will enjoy our time together."

Glossary of Terms

Adar (*a-dar*) - a giant species of bird that most consider to be one of the first species of bird in the realm. It spawned many breeds that served most of the sects as either messengers, fighters, or as a means of transportation.

Adar Gwin (*a-dar win*) - a breed of the adar bird and peaceful cousins to the adar hindlefar. The adar gwin can learn and communicate with people through telepathy.

Adar Hindlefar (*a-dar hindle-far*) - a breed of the adar bird. Though smaller than the original adar bird, the adar hindlefar is not only the largest of its spawn, but also the most violent. This breed of bird was never known to exist in Sori but existed in other parts of the realm, particularly Austrfold. Like all adar birds, it can learn and communicate with people telepathically. The adar hindlefar is responsible for the adar omen. This omen states that if the sun is blocked out, but no clouds are around, then death from an adar is near.

Àita (*a-ta*) - placer. Àita is the term used for those who place contestants into events.

Aiten Díog (*a-ten di-ag*) - largest ravine in Sori. The Taran Forest borders it to the west and Frìth to the east.

Amháin (*a-wan*) - a lone willow tree located in Ionad Ghleann.

Aon Fear Talamh (*an far tal-ma*) - area of Frìth commonly referred to as *No Man's Land*. The name for the location is due to the numerous underground tunnels and caverns into which every explorer of its depths has vanished, never to return. The area is riddled with hills that contain entrances of varying sizes to the caverns at their bases.

Ar Dtús (*a duce*) - one of the largest cities in Frìth, a lone road connects it to Ghabháil.

Arán lines (*are-ran*) - arán line refers to Cala's bread lines or what most would call a soup kitchen. Due to the growing homeless population in Cala, the council set up the arán lines to feed those who cannot take care of themselves—not out of generosity but to keep the homeless from stealing or becoming more violent. The arán lines typically pass out rations of bread, soup, wine, and some type of meat.

Ascender(s) (*as-sen-der*) - the spirit of a Leigheas that exists between the living and the dead. The spirit comes back to the land of the living by attaching to a host during the Ascension step in the Turas, and serves as guides to the host.

Ascension (*as-sen-shen*) - step in Turas where an Earcach gains the accompaniment of Ascender(s).

Babhla *(bab-la)* - a bowl of meat stew. Babhla is a famous dish during Sori winters that is made from multiple types of meats.

Balla (*bal-la*) - originally a Duine fort and later a trade capital.

Barra Village (*bar-ra*) - a village known for its pub, where those who do not pass the Tástáil go to ease the burden of defeat.

Bás doras (*boss door*) - a dire situation, one in which death is almost certain.

Beacha céir (*bee-ka ker*) - a substance that is used as a clear coating that protects clothing or other goods from decay or the elements. It is made from péine tree sap and coincréite powder.

Beinn (*bane*) - northern region of Sori, home to the Galenvargs. Beinn is a mountain region and home to the Bennachie Mountains, the largest mountain rage in Sori.

Bennachie (*benn-a-chie*) - mountain range in Northeastern Sori.

Bel (*bell*) - ancient fire god, created a wax that when melted and applied to the skin allows anyone to hold/touch fire.

Berserkers (*ba-zerk-ers*) - clan of Leigheasan that work as the sect's mercenaries. Berserkers are a more primitive clan that do not wear the traditional robes or dress of the Leigheasan. They are easily spotted in villages due to typically wearing clothing made of animal skins and being general unkempt. One of the more unique aspects of the clan is that they wear the hide of bear, made in such a way that it fits like a suit of armor, while hunting those who have broken Leigheasan law. Those in the Berserker Clan have first and last names, but amongst fellow Leigheasan and the other sects, they use their appropriate sinsearach and sóisearach titles.

Bhagairt (*bag-air*) - a political philosophy used by leaders with military backgrounds, who use the threat of extreme force to get their way.

Breitheamh (*brit-ham*) - a judge.

Bouden (*boo-den*) - village home to Ebbot and Eger.

Caillte Forest (*kat-tle*) - forest located directly to the south of Ghabháil. Although the trees in the forest are not dense, Caillte Forest is home to the liús eite shrub. The liús eite is a plant full of poisonous thorns that causes death within minutes. There are more of these plants in the Caillte than there are trees in the Taran Forest.

Caillte anam (*kat-tle a-nam*) - a lost soul, also commonly referred to as a scout. The caillte anam are Duine souls that have remained earthbound once their body expires.

Cainteoir(s) (*kon-tur*) - emissary.

Cala (*ka-la*) - southern region of Sori, home to the Duine.

Caomhnóir (*keev-nor*) - guardian.

Capall cuaille (*ka-pal ka-ill*) - jousting competition held at every Cluiche. Capall cuaille is also a common game amongst most Leigheasan clans.

Carnlem (*car-lam*) - the technical term for feces. Carnlem is one of the many terms used by the upper-class Faileas Herimen instead of profane language. It is used by most as a means of insult.

Casúr (*ka-sur*) - a small wooden hammer that is used typically by a máistir searmanas or a breitheamh presiding over trials.

Cath of Fuil (*ka of full*) - the Battle of Blood.

Ceann Hall (*can*) - Beinn's council chambers located in the capital city of Keltoi.

Cèilidh (*kal-lee*) - Leigheasan festival of celebration on completing the Turas. Typically conducted by the entire clan, but in some cases, it is celebrated with just the immediate household family.

Ceit Trinse (*kit trench*) - a trench spanning the width of Sori, a natural division between the north and south.

Chomhrac (*kom-rack*) - combat.

Chrá (*kri*) - torment or pain. A common rallying cry at tournaments that involve a physical contest, where the crowd shouts, "Bring the chrá!" It is used to not only wish someone good luck, but also to encourage the contestant to inflict as much of a punishment on his opponents as possible.

Chun cogadh (*kun kad*) - a Veirlintu chant that means "To war" and has been used as a rallying cry since the ancient days of the sect.

Ciorcal Lána (*kar-cal la-na*) - Circle Lane, road that circles the tune of Balla.

Claíomh troid (*ka-leev tred*) - sword-fighting contest of the Cluiche.

Cloch Basin (*kla*) - basin located on the leeward side of Sinsear Plateau, home to Gofannon, and site of the Tástáil step of the Turas.

Cluiche (*clif-fe*) - yearly Leigheasan competition in which representatives from all clans, ranging from twelve to twenty-two years of age, meet to battle in a contest of jousting, hand-to-hand combat, sword fighting, archery, and knowledge. The highest honor one can receive is the Cluiche champion. However, winning a single event is just as important as it raises one's personal status amongst the clans.

Coincréite powder (*kon-krit*) - a powder made from crushed stones and other agents that is used as a bonding agent in beacha céir.

Coinín (*kon-in*) - a small rabbit-like creature. Unlike the rabbit, the coinín is a carnivore and lives off small rodents. Its blood is very similar to that of the Duine and contains the same type of mutation as the blood of a Veirlintu and Galenvarg.

Comhaontú(s) (*come-han-too*) - a legal binding agreement. Comhaontús are typically used in peace agreements, political resolution, contracts, and any other matter in which legal actions could be taken for breaking of terms.

Crann na beatha (*crown nu ba-ha*) - tree of life, strongest wood known to Sori. The trees are used for making shillelaghs for the Leigheasan.

Cré coimeádán (*cre co-mo-dan*) - oil-filled clay canisters that range in size and are used as munitions for trebuchets.

Croí of Beinn (*cry of bane*) - a heart-shaped lake whose shape cannot be noticed from the ground, but only from the mountains. In casual conversation, it is often referred to as either the Croí or the Heart of Beinn.

Cuaille (*ka-ill*) - a pole. When used in reference to the capall cuaille, a cuaille means a lance.

Cuartha (*car-th*) - curved. Cuartha pertains to anything that is curved, but in the case of swords it is a style. These swords are similar in length to a longsword, but they have a curved blade, like a crescent moon. They are lighter in weight, and depending on the maker the cuartha sword tends to be more durable.

Damanta (*da-man-ta*) - a rare book within the Gaeltacht archives that contains all the known details about the forbidden.

Dearg abhainn (*dag ab-hann*) - odorless and tasteless herb that causes uncontrollable bleeding of bodily orifices, resulting in death.

Deoch de déithe (*dock de death*) - drink of the gods. A mythological drink that is said to give its drinker immortality.

Diabhal's Fiacail (*dia-vail fia-cal*) - Devil's Tooth, cliff in the Slabhra mountain range. A diabhal was a creature in many fairy tales used to keep children from misbehaving. It was characterized by its serpent-like appearance and one giant fang sprouting from the front of the mouth. It is said that the fang digs into the brain and sucks out all ambitions, desires, and curiosity, leaving behind an obedient child.

Diabhoil (*di-a-bol*) - a person, who once practiced the forbidden, who sought to be immortal by taking on the form of a book to ensure its knowledge would be used for all eternity. Diabhoils are rare, but there are several known to exist in the realm.

Dochtúir (*doc-tor*) - a Leigheas doctor who specializes in healing, tonics, poisons, and medicine.

Donnimhe tor (*don-knee tore*) - a shrub that bears a brown flower that when consumed has hallucinogenic properties.

Donn Gleann (*don glen*) - the valley surrounding the Croí of Beinn. It is widely known as the Brown Valley due to the brown grass that grows in the area. The grass is full of nutrients that attract a variety of wildlife.

Dorcha steel (*dor-ca*) - hardest known steel in Sori. Dorcha steel is the personal choice of steel for Gofannon, who creates the deadliest of weapons. Only a few in Sori possess the skill to forge a weapon out of dorcha steel, but they are not near the quality of those made by Gofannon.

Dubh codlata (*duh kod-a-ta*) - a black candle made from various herbs and plant leaves that are known to cause hallucinations. However, in a comatose state the person who inhales the smoke from the candle will dream of the great time they wish they had. There are two types of dubh codlata: white wick and green wick. White-wick candles are meant to burn for hours while a green-wick candle is meant for a multi-day burn. The candle is placed on top of a powder made from golden roseroot and peet that will ignite when the flame touches the powder. The golden roseroot is then inhaled, and the unconscious victim will awake.

Duine (*du-ne*) - one of the four sects that inhabit Sori, a human sect without powers or supernatural capabilities. The term Duine can refer to the sect or to an individual person. Duines (du-nies) is often used when one is referring to large numbers of Duine but also refers to the entire sect.

Dullahan (*dull-a-han*) - the name given to a shadow-like figure. Dullahan is also a specific type of fomoire. Dullahan is both singular and plural. The fomoire have a hierarchy that revolves around power and abilities. Three are three types: measahan (*mes-a-han*), dullahan, and láidirhan (lar-han). The measahan are considered the weakest, with their predominant power being mind control. The dullahan are strong and capable of mind control, soul taking, element wielding, and much more. The láidirhan are the most powerful and are the rarest type of fomoire, with their might rivaling that of the gods and goddess. The láidirhan have no limitations on what they can and cannot do.

Dún (*doon*) - Faileas Herimen fort.

Earcach (*ear-a-cash*) - recruit of the Leigheasan.

Éire (*e-ah*) - prior to Cath of Fuil, Éire was the northernmost region in Sori.

Elemental (*el-e-men-tal*) - term applying to at least one of the earth's elements: earth, wind, water, and fire. Elemental is a blanket statement in casual conversation to define the powers of a Leigheasan.

Eolaís (*elas*) - doctor/scientist of the Veirlintu sect.

Ewan (*e-van*) - a demi-god, son of Nantosuelta; master craftsman, maker of shillelaghs and caretaker to the crann na beatha.

Fågels (*fog-el*) - slang term to refer to Veirlintu. Fågels are a close relative to a bird of the night that survives off drinking the blood of the larger animals.

Faileas Herimen (*fay-las air-men*) - term used when referring to Leigheasan, Galenvargs, and Veirlintus as one group. Loosely translated as "Shadow Creatures," Faileas Herimen became the common term because the sects' fear of exposure lead them to commit their deeds and practices under the cover of darkness.

Fathach torc (*fa-hoch toss*) - giant boar that is the size of most bulls. It is a tradition in many Faileas Herimen clans to kill a fathach torc as a rite of passage, a rite that often results in death. The most sought-after fathach torc was named Maximus and was killed by Maya of the Clan Dempsey.

Feabhas a chur berry (*fea-bus a cure*) - a berry whose juice allows tonics and herbs to bind to one's body. For example, herbs that aid in healing bones when taken with the feabhas a chur berry will be carried to the bone, providing instant and permanent results, a practice only conducted by the monks.

Fhealltóir (*fea-all-tor*) - traitor.

Fiailí peet (*fi-ali peat*) - a type of fuel that is made from the fiailí weed and peet. The fiailí weed is a plant that burns at high temperatures and for long periods of time. It also is very difficult to get to burn, so peet is added to ignite the weed. To make fiailí peet, the fiailí weed and peet are combined with mud and compacted into a mold. The mold is left to dry for several days, and the result is a brick or ball of fiailí peet. Once ignited, the mud crumbles, leaving a long-lasting flame.

Fís crystals (*fiss kris-tle*) - vision crystals. These crystals are typically a tetragonal shape of roughly two to five inches in length. When fís crystals are found in nature, they are white, but when they are used for visions, they turn a variety of colors. The more common colors are green, blue, purple, red and black. However, they can turn any color. To imprint a vision onto a fís crystals, one must concentrate on the images and sounds they want to project; the more detailed the vision, the longer one must concentrate. Regardless of length, the vision is infused with the crystal by a breath. The breath that is expelled from the user is like a colored fog, and the transmission is complete when the crystal turns a solid color other than white. The visions are expelled from the crystal once they have been broken.

Fomoire (*fo-more*) - a creature summoned from the dark realms; many realms would refer to a fomoire as a demon.

Frìth (*fri-th*) - eastern region of Sori, home to the Veirlintus.

Gaeltacht monks (*gal-tacht*) - monks that guard the history of Sori and secrets of the Faileas Herimen. The monks live in an underground cavern located under the Naofa Forest, whose location is known to elder members of the Faileas Herimen clans and to the most powerful of ascenders. However, most, if not all, of the Galenvargs and Veirlintus sect have forgotten about the monks.

Gach Bua (*gaw - bow*) - the undefeated. Gach Bua is the nickname given to Stephan of the Tammi Clan due to his impressive undefeated streak in capall cuaille tournaments.

Gáire-gáire (*are-are*) - a childlike taunt that is the Faileas Herimen equivalent to the Duine "neener-neener." Gáire-gáire is typically used in response to having something that someone else doesn't have.

Galenvarg (*gay-lin-vie*) - one of the four sects in Sori; closely associated with what most in other realms would call a werewolf.

Gan Dídean (*gun die*) - region of Cala that is home to the transient populations. Believed to be home of upwards of fifty clans.

Gangus ag siúl bás (*gang-us ah sul boss*) - a deadly herb that causes ones flesh to fall off, ones limbs to deteriorate, and gives the appearance of the living dead just prior to passing. Commonly referred to as gangus.

Gé (*glee*) - the feathers of the gé bird are used by the Leigheasan as an insulator for clothing. Gé birds live in the wild, but due to their high demand, many Leigheasan clans raise gé so that they will not become extinct.

Ghabháil (*ga-ul*) - Duine prison located in Frìth, overseen by Galenvargs and Veirlintus; its inmates serve as a source of subsistence for the two sects.

Glannigh (*gla-nee*) - a cleaning solution that Leigheasan dochtúirs used to disinfect equipment or anything else in need of sanitizing.

Gleann (*glen*) - valley.

Gnéastis (*ga-nas-tis*) - a Leigheasan word developed by women to refer to a sexist man or men.

Gofannon (*go-fan-on*) - a god of ancient societies known for his metalwork and weaponry. Gofannon is still worshiped by the Leigheasan and is the giver of the Tástáil for a Leigheasan Earcach.

Gort (*gore*) - Galenvarg and Veirlintu birthing center located in the Bennachie region.

Halvvägs Sten (*hall-vags stee-en*) - a large boulder, often call the Midway Stone, that is located in the middle of the Gleann; the distance to the north and south is equal from this point.

Hund(s) (*hound*) - a hund is a mixed breed between wolf and dog. It became a slang term used to refer to the Galenvarg due their mix of Duine and Varg.

Ifreann (*i-fran*) - one of the Sori versions of hell.

Iomlán bás (*im-lon boss*) - the annihilation of an entire clan. In ancient days of the Leigheasan sect the iomlán bás was used to deter treasonous acts. Every member of the guilty party's clan is forced to fight to the death against the Berserker Clan. However, there is no way to win their freedom. The guilty clan will fight consecutive matches until they are dead, thus eliminating their treasonous clan from poisoning the sect any further.

Ionad Ghleann (*i-nad glen*) - a fertile farmland valley.

Keltoi (*celt*) - capital city of Beinn.

Láibduille (*la-dull*) - a mixture of mud and aló (aloe) plant that is used as a compress for wounds. The mud secures any medicine to the body but will eventually fall off. The aló remains for some time after the mud falls off and serves as a healing and pain relief agent.

Lámh go lámh (*lam go lam*) - hand-to-hand combat contest of the Cluiche.

Laufeyjarson (*lu-fey-jar-son*) - the god of deception. Laufeyjarson is rumored to be the father to the Loki Clan, a clan who uses the powers of deception, both visual and auditory, to achieve their desires. In his youth, Laufeyjarson created a series of rinns (a-rines) that can make the wearer invisible.

Leigheas (*lee-us*) - one of the four sects in Sori, closely associated with what most call a witch or warlock. It applies to a single person.

Leigheas Gleann (*lee-us glen*) - eastern region in Sori, home to the Leigheasan. Leigheas Gleann is often referred to as just the "Gleann," despite there being many gleanns throughout Sori. The sects know that when a person says "Gleann," they are referring specifically to Leigheas Gleann. Other locations will be denoted by their specific name.

Leigheasan (*lee-us-an*) - referring to more than one Leigheas, a group, or the entire sect.

Liathróid (*lath-rod*) - a hollow iron ball mounted to a pusher that allows it to roll. Primarily used at capall cuaille tournaments, liathróids are fueled by fiailí peet and are pushed across the area floor to eliminate shards of wood.

Litriú Bóthar (*li-true bo-ther*) - Spell Road, road leading the way from Gleann to Balla.

Liús eite (*lus ette*) - a plant full of poisonous thorns that causes death within minutes. Found only in the Caillte Forest, the liús eite thrives with little sunlight and in colder temperatures.

Mactíre Cosán (*mac-teed-a co-san*) - road leading from Beinn to Balla. Mactíre was the name of the most vicious Varg known in Sori's history.

The beast was responsible for the deaths of thousands, and it is speculated that he killed thousands more. Duines say that Mactíre was responsible for spreading the Galenvarg disease.

Máistir searmanas (*mas-ter cer-man-as*) - master of ceremonies. Title given to the announcer of the Cluiche and any other stage events, such as plays. In most stage events, the máistir searmanas will be dressed in a multicolored outfit and wear the mask depicting the face of the messenger birds, a symbolic gesture to say the máistir searmanas is but a messenger.

Marbh Talamh Lochán (*mar tal-ma loch*) - a water reservoir that is located next to Aon Fear Talamh; commonly referred to as Dead Man's Pond due to its frequent use by inhabitants of Sori to dispose of bodies in more ancient times.

Manach cochall (*monk kall*) - a species of the aconitum flower that is commonly referred to as monkshood. It is a rare flower whose poison is scentless, and the only known amounts of it are held by the Gaeltacht monks.

Meadarloch (*meader-lock*) - village on the edge of the Naofa Forest.

Moill (*mole*) - a group of people that become addicted to the hallucinogenic flower of the donnimhe tor. It is easy to spot those who have consumed the flower due to their trance-like state in which their mouth hangs open and drool is profusely produced.

Muc (*mock*) - a type of pig that is raised by the Leigheasan.

Nantosuelta (*na-to-su-la*) - a nature goddess of ancient societies who formally grants elemental powers to the Earcach. Nantosuelta is the primary goddess still worshiped by the Leigheasan sect.

Naofa Forest (no-i-fa) - sacred forest to the Leigheasan where the Turas must be completed.

Oiliúint (*a-lute*) - step in Turas where the Earcach trains in a variety of fields with the guidance of their ascender(s).

Onóir (*o-nor*) - warrior code. The code of the Onóir is a philosophy that honors the warrior and battle. The Onóir code has many stipulations and is a way of life for those who practice it. Among its teachings is the commitment to, above all things, honor the warrior, even if he defeats you.

Oráiste Gealach (*oar-stay gay-lock*) - orange moon. Oráiste Gealach is an annual, month-long period in Sori when the night sky and moon have an orange hue. The month of the Oráiste Gealach is widely celebrated in Frìth as the month of cuimhneachán (*come-nee-can*), or remembrance. During cuimhneachán, couples celebrate their relationship, new couples are joined, those deceased are remembered, births are celebrated, and many other joyous occasions are honored. In honor of this, the Veirlintu council takes a leave and only convenes in cases of emergency. In addition, the business sector of Frìth does not take on new business and operates on a part-time basis.

Peet (*peat*) - a black powder that provides a fiery explosion.

Péine (*pi-ne*) tree - a tree whose sap is used in the making of beacha céir.

Plandaí Peninsula (*plan-da*) - area of fertile farmland located in southwestern Sori under Leigheas Gleann. The area is occupied by Duine farmers.

Rinn(s) (*a-rin(s)*) - a cape that renders one invisible. The Rinn of Laufeyjarson has the power to make one invisible with one side and is powerless on the other. This is so the wearer can select when they want to be seen and when they do not. Once the cloak pin connects the rinn, the cape then conceals one's identity; however, there are drawbacks to the rinn. Anything that touches the rinn while it's invisible will become invisible as well. For example, if a person steps on or touches the rinn, then they will become invisible. It can cause a scene due to people randomly disappearing and reappearing.

Rudianos (*ru-di-an-os*) - clan of bounty hunters. Their primary job is to find those who break inter-realm laws.

Saol fada (*soul fa-day*) - a tonic made by the monks that contains the leaves of the lotus tree, root of the crann na beatha tree, and the juice from a grape. The drink enhances healing properties and strengthens the body beyond its typical abilities.

Sciathán Tiomáint (*ski-han ti-mont*) - road leading from Frìth to Balla. Sciathán ruled the air around the same time that Mactíre roamed the land. Though not as deadly as Mactíre, Sciathán was responsible for the deaths of hundreds of Sori children. Just like Mactíre, Duine say Sciathán was responsible for spreading the Veirlintu disease.

Scoirfidh (*scor-fith*) - a meeting of peace, usually where terms for surrender or armistice are discussed.

Seoltóir eyes (*shole-tore*) - known also as seer eyes and characterized by a foggy white glaze over the eyes. Seoltóir eyes cause poor vision—usually anything past a few feet is indiscernible—but gives the ability to have visions of the future.

Seomra (*sem-ra*) - Leigheasan bank operated by the Adelsköld Clan.

Sioc Lake (*sic*) - also known as Frost Lake. Sioc Lake lies to the north of Ghabháil and is known for its cold waters year-round.

Sinsearach (*sin-zarch*) - senior. Sinsearach is used when referring to the eldest in a group of Berserkers. The Leigheasan use elder, which is a title that is earned, but the Berserkers use sinsearach to keep order amongst the ranks. Each Berserker under the sinsearach is called a sóisearach and given a number from one to nine.

Sinsear Plateau (*sin-zar*) - plateau located in the middle of Naofa Forest where the Ascension step is completed.

Shillelagh (*shil-la-le*) - walking stick; also the step in the Turas where the Earcach gains the shillelagh.

Slabhra (*sla-ra*) - one of the many mountain ranges in the region of Beinn.

Soiléir cóta (*so-ler kot*) - a clear polish that adds shine to metals. Made from muc lard and used mainly by competitors in the capall cuaille.

Sóisearach (*so-zark*) - junior Berserker under the command of a sinsearach. Sóisearachs are given a number from one to nine according to their age as their rank. One: aon (*an*), two: dó (*do*), three: trí (*tree*), four: ceathair (*kath-ar*), five: cúig (*k-og*), six: sé (*see*), seven: seacht (*set*), eight: ocht (*act*), nine: naoi (*no*). If the sinsearach falls in battle, then the sóisearach aon become the new sinsearach.

Sori (*soar-ie*) - the term for the eastern half of the realm in the ancient days. As the continent split, Sori became the name for the middle continent.

Taifeadta (*tal-fed-a*) - recorder. Taifeadta is used to refer to anyone who is a record keeper, and the term is commonly used at sign-in stations during the Cluiche.

Tástáil (*tast-ail*) - step in Turas where the Earcach completes a test.

Taran Forest (*tar-ran*) - dense forest located in eastern Sori, bordering the Aiten Díog.

Threorú (*tre-o*) - a guide. Threorús are from the Clan Athreorú and serve as guides to the Tammi Clan. They have a white aura that creates a barrier to the seeing powers of those in the Tammi Clan, which means they are the only ones who can touch or get close enough to Tammis without causing visions. Due to this, they have bound themselves in lifelong servitude to the Tammi Clan in all aspects of daily life.

Tosaithe (*toss-ie*) - someone new to a trade or craft.

Triskelion (*tri-skel-on*) - a unique form of knotwork that is characterized by three spirals connected at the center and enclosed by a circle.

Troid bás (*tred boss*) - fight to the death versus a single opponent.

Tune (*toon*) - tower.

Turas (*tor-es*) - the challenge an Earcach must complete to become a Leigheas.

Ualach (*you-lack*) - ancient term that is typically no longer used in referring to non-contributors of a society. Ualachs tend to rely on others for food, clothing, shelter, and any other need that they are unwilling to obtain through work and earnings.

Varg (*vie*) - an ancient breed of wolf that many claim to be responsible for the Galenvarg disease. Varg is commonly used by younger members of the sects to refer to a Galenvarg.

Veirlintu (*ver-lent-too*) - one of the four sects in Sori; closely associated with what most in other realms call a vampire.

About the Author

D.W. SAUR HOLDS DEGREES from Emory and Henry College, East Tennessee State University, and the University of Southern Mississippi. In addition, Saur received his teaching certification from Roanoke College and is currently a middle school social studies teacher.

Saur's first children's book, Metal Like Me, deals with bullying. *Dark Days* is Saur's fantasy debut and was written in part to give his students and other young adult readers a heroine that goes against traditional norms of young adult works. Saur is a member of the Society of Children's Book Writers and Illustrators.

CPSIA information can be obtained
at www.ICGtesting.com
Printed in the USA
FSHW010948231220
76916FS